As Pinch dangled helplessly by his fingers, the slithering below grew louder. It was as if a host had been roused and not some single thing. In the near darkness, Pinch could barely see a gleam of white, perhaps the floor, though strangely folded and misshapen. He looked again, harder, straining to see clearly, when all at once the floor heaved and shifted.

Damn, I'm looking at bones.

His fingers creaked and almost gave way, so that Pinch couldn't suppress a shriek of pain. The cry reverberated through the pit and, as if in eager concert to it, his voice was taken up by a sussurant hiss as the white gleam of the bones rippled and pulsed in a slithering crawl.

The floor was alive!

FANTASY ADVENTURE

Recommended Readings
for Realms Wanderers

THE NOBLES

FORGOTTEN REALMS
FANTASY ADVENTURE

King Pinch

The Nobles
Volume 1

David Cook

To Helen

King Pinch

The Nobles
Volume One

Cover art by Walter Velez. Interior art by Dawn Murin.

First Printing: May 1995
Printed in the United States of America
Library of Congress Catalog Card Number: 94-68135

ISBN: 0-7869-0127-6

TSR, Inc.
201 Sheridan Springs Rd.
Lake Geneva, WI 53147
U.S.A.

TSR Ltd.
120 Church End, Cherry Hinton
Cambridge CB1 3LB
United Kingdom

Prologue

In a far southern land, ten thousand people gathered in the afternoon haze, a miasma that started at noon along the shores of the Lake of Steam. From there it swelled through the streets of Ankhapur and cloaked the city in a moist cloud until sweat and air became one. No breezes fluttered the white banners on the rooftops. Not even the collective breaths of all those gathered could swirl the clotted air. Cotton plastered to flesh like a second skin, so that clothes hung limply on people's bodies. Ten thousand people stood waiting in the clothes of the dead and the lifeless.

These ten thousand—the grandfathers, fathers, and sons of Ankhapur; the grandmothers, mothers, and daughters of the same—squeezed against the sides of the narrow streets, overflowed the balconies, and squatted in jumbles on stairs that coiled out of sight.

They lined a single winding avenue, choked the streets that led to it, even crammed their boats along the quay where the avenue passed. At the edges of this mass were the kebab vendors with their sizzling meats, the wine boys who siphoned draughts from the kegs strapped to their backs, the fruit sellers pushing over-ripe wares, the gamblers who cunningly lost in order to win, and the ladies who profited from any crowd.

A traveler, caught in the edges of the thronged multitude, would at first assume he had stumbled upon a festival unknown in his far-off homeland. Perhaps the hordes waited for the devout pilgrimage of a revered saint. Maybe it was the triumphal entry of a conquering lord, or, most wonderful of all, the perambulation of a revealed god before the very eyes of his worshipers. That truly would be a story for the traveler to tell upon his return to some distant home.

As he pushed his way farther in, though, the traveler would begin to have doubts. Where were the lanterns, the bright streamers, the children's toys he was accustomed to at every festival in his home? Was this the passing of a particularly dour saint, a victory too costly for the citizens to bear, or, worse still, the march of some vengeful death god whose gaze might strike down some unfortunate? There was no cheer or eager expectation in those around him, and as he plunged farther into the crowd, he would find only ever-increasingly somber face of duteous sorrow.

Upon finally reaching the center of this dour crowd, the traveler would be greeted by masses of red bunting, great swathes of the brilliant cloth hanging listlessly from the balustrades and lampposts that magically light Ankhapur's nighttime streets. Were this the traveler's fledgling journey, he might be mystified by the colorful riot that hung over his head. His journey had brought him, perhaps, to a city of the mad—lunatics who lived out their lives as the inverse of all normal reason—melancholy in their joy, merry when others called for sorrow. Shaking his head, he would quickly resolve to leave Ankhapur, perhaps noting its dementia in the notebooks of his travels.

This would not be the conclusion of a traveler more steeped in the whirling customs of different lands. He would look at the scarlet bunting and know that the language his own culture saw in them was not the language of Ankhapur. Before him was stretched a funereal display, just as black or white might symbolize the same in his land.

If he were truly cunning, he would guess the nature of the departed. No crowds throng for the passing of a mage. The deaths of wizards are intimate and mysterious. Nor was it the passing of some once-beloved priest, for then surely the people would congregate at the clergyman's temple to hear the dirges his followers would sing. The passing of thieves and rogues no one mourned.

It could only be the death of a lord, and one great and powerful at that. Nothing less than the mortality of kings could draw the people into the humid afternoon, out to stand in the sun until the processional passed. Looking at the citizens with renewed insight, the traveler would see an old courtier in despair, his almost-realized expectations dashed. A young maiden shivers with tears, overcome by the memory of some forgotten kindness His Highness had bestowed on her. A one-eyed cripple, dismissed from the guard after his injuries in the last campaign, struggles to stand in the stiff posture of old duty. Farther up, a merchant leans out the window, his face a mask of barely disguised glee as he already counts the profits he will reap now that the oppressive lord is gone.

As the traveler studies his neighbors, the procession finally arrives. The honor guard broils under its plumes and furs as it clears the streets. Behind follow the priests of all the temples, the aged patriarchs carried in shaded sedan chairs while their acolytes swing censers and drone their prayers to the skies. Finally there comes a great gilded cart, draped in a pyramidal mound of red silk and pulled by three ranks of sacrificial oxen, the first rank the deepest black, the second a hitch of unblemished white, and the third all perfect gray. As the ox cart creaks and lumbers through the cobbled streets, all eyes strain to see the throne that sits at the top. There, dressed in the robes and furs of state, immune to their crush and heat, is their late king. Only his face shows, chalky gray and hollowed by the final touch of death.

A breath, held by ten thousand souls, is released as the cart passes each man, woman, and child of Ankhapur. The king is truly dead. The people begin to move once more, each citizen taking up again his course among the living. As the traveler passes through the crowd, a hand with a knife stealthily reaches for the strings of his purse.

Years later, when the traveler speaks of Ankhapur, he will tell of the funeral of the king of a land of rogues.

Rooftops and Boudoirs

"Crap! This wind stings like Ilmater's wounds!" a thin voice loudly groused from the darkness of night.

"Quiet, you little fool!" hissed a second, deeper voice close by the first. "You'll tip us for sure with your whining."

"Fine then. You work these knots with your fat human fingers," the other voice hissed back. His words were almost lost in a roaring gust. There was the furious snap of long cloaks lashing the air.

"Just work, damn you, before we both freeze." The words were accented by the chink of metal grating against tile.

A flash of light swept across the pair.

"Down!" hissed the deeper voice. The light briefly illuminated two people—one large, the other absurdly small—perched on a precarious cant of rippled roof tile.

The larger of the two was leaning heavily on a bar wedged in a crack between the terra-cotta shapes. The smaller one fumbled with a stout cord, knotting the end around a glazed chimney.

"Relax. Just a lamplighter," the little one said. An icy gust rocked them, swirling their cloaks into fierce snarls.

Wind was a property of the winter-stung nights in Elturel. Each night it rose up with the fading sun to sweep through the hillside streets of the city's High District. On a gentle night it was a dog's whimper, patiently waiting to be let in through every opened door and window. But there were other nights, like tonight, when it snarled like a ravaging hound. The hunter's wind, people called it then, and shuddered when they heard the noise as it bayed through the streets. Everyone knew the calls were the hounds of Mask, and no wise man went out when the unshriven dead called to him from the street.

At least not the honest ones.

Poised on the high, tiled rooftop, the two shapes—large and tiny—continued their work. A chill blast shivered over them and they unconsciously shifted on their roost until their backs were carefully turned to the numbing blasts. Never once did they break their attention from the glazed tiles beneath them.

There was another grate of metal on fired clay. "It's up. Are you ready?" hissed the larger of the two.

The snap of rope as the smaller set his last knot was the answer. "Don't drop me this time, Pinch," the thin voice cautioned, only half in mirth.

"Don't try to hold back the pelfry, Sprite-Heels. Saving the best stones for yourself's not being upright. I could've let the Hellriders take you." There was no humor in the man's voice at all, and in the darkness it was impossible to see his expression. He passed the knotted rope through the small hole in the roof tiles.

Sprite-Heels mumbled an answer without saying anything, though his tone was suitably meek. Pinch, his partner, was not a man to cross needlessly. Sprite-Heels had tried it once and got caught cold at it. He could only guess Pinch must have been in a good mood that day, for the halfling was still alive. He'd seen, even helped, Pinch kill men for less provocation. He could say that Pinch just liked him, but he knew the old rogue better than that. Pinch didn't have friends, only the members of his gang.

There was a faint slap as the cord struck the floor. "Down you go," Pinch said with playful cheer. He wrapped the cord around his waist and belayed it with his arm, ready to take the halfling's weight. Little folk like Sprite-Heels were small and short, which made them good for wriggling through tiny gaps made through pried up roof tiles, but they still weren't light. Sprite-Heels for one was fond of his ale and cheese, which lent him an innocent-seeming chubbiness. That was all well and good for working the street, but the halfling was far from the lightest cat burglar Pinch had used.

The halfling studied Pinch in the darkness and then gave a shrug, unable to fathom the man. Pinch was a "regulator," the master of his shifty and shiftless fellows. The air of studied threat about him was a mask worn too long, until Pinch knew practically no other. Indeed, pudgy little Sprite-Heels was not even sure he knew the real Pinch anymore.

"Stop dallying," the rogue hissed.

The halfling jerked into motion. Squirming his rear for balance on the tiles, he tugged off a pair of thick boots and flexed his furred feet. Barefoot was better for working the rope, but a terra-cotta roof in the winds of winter was no place to creep unshod.

Pinch thrust the rope into the halfling's calloused hands.

The halfling fingered the rope. "Why don't you go down, Pinch?" he finally asked with a brazen smile. "I'll steady you."

Pinch smiled back with a grin just as predatory. "Bad knee—never any good at climbing." They both knew the answer anyway. "Get going. We're to be gone before the Hellriders come around again."

The halfling grumbled, knowing what argument would gain him. He wriggled through the hole, snagging his cloak on the uneven edges. "Climbed up here well enough, you . . ."

The grumbles grew inarticulate and then disappeared as the halfling descended into the darkness. Pinch's arms, wrapped tight around the rope, trembled and quivered with each jerk of the line.

As he sat on the roof, back to a small chimney, every second in the wind and darkness dragged into hours in Pinch's mind. Time was the enemy. It wasn't the guards, the wards, the hexes, or the beasts rumored to roam the halls beneath them; it was time. Every minute was a minute of more risk, a chance that some ill-timed merchant next door would rise from his secret assignation and step to the window for air, or that on the street below a catchpole would look up from his rounds to stare at the moon. There were endless eyes in the dark, and the longer the job took, the more likely that someone would see.

Pinch cursed to a rat that watched him from the cornice, flipping a chip of tile toward its pit black eyes. As the rat squeaked and ran away, Pinch damned Sprite for his slowness. There was another, Therin, who was a choice target of his oaths. It was he and not Pinch who should have been on the roof; that was the way Pinch had planned it. In fact it was all that damn-fool's fault for getting caught in a nip when he shouldn't even have tried. He hadn't the skill as a cutpurse to try for a mistress o' the game's bodice strings, let alone the purse of a Hellrider sergeant.

Pinch was just pondering who was the right man to give an alibi for Therin when the line went slack through his fingers. Instantly he bobbed forward face first into the hole, catching himself before he plummeted to the marble floor thirty feet below. He strained to hear any sounds of scuffle or alarm, even the lightest tap of a soft footfall.

There was nothing and that was good. So far everything was going according to plan. Sprite-Heels was living up to his name, now padding silently through the halls of the Great Temple of Lathander, making for the great holy relic kept there.

Pinch had a plan, and a grand one at that. The relic was useless to him, but there were others who would pay dearly for it. Splinter sects and rival faiths were the most likely, but even the temple beneath him might be willing to pay to keep their honor intact.

It was by far the most ambitious thing he and his gang had tried yet, a far cry from the simple curbing and lifting they'd done in the past. Diving, like this, they'd done, but never on so grand a scale. It was one thing to house break some common fool's dwelling. Sending Sprite-Heels diving into the temple was quite another, almost as bad as cracking a wizard's abode. Temples had guards, wards, priests, and beasts—but the rewards were so much more.

The plan was simple. The dark stretch of Sweet-sweat Lane, an alley that barely divided the temple from the festhalls on the other side, was where Pinch had plotted their entry. A few nights' pleasant scouting from the high floors of the Charmed Maiden had assured Pinch that the guards along that section were particularly lax. Still, Pinch shed a few coins so that two maids, Clarrith and Yossine, were sure to do their washing up in back, to draw off any curious eyes. Sprite-Heels had shimmied to the temple roof without a snag while Pinch took the rope and followed shortly thereafter. All went well.

Once on the wall, the pair of rogues had scurried across the guard walk and plunged into a maze of gables, eaves, and chimneys until Pinch's estimate put them over the main hall. With a pry bar and a petter-cutter, they had pulled up the tile and carved through the lead beneath—and now Sprite-Heels was inside.

Which was taking all too long. Pinch didn't like it. His calculations were right, and the halfling was certain to be over the altar by now. All Sprite-Heels had to do was grab the relic and whatever else he could put his hands on quickly, and get back to the rope.

The problem was that Sprite was taking too long.

Carefully, so as not to lose his windswept seat, Pinch leaned forward to peer through the hole. At first his eyes, a little weak in the night, saw nothing, but slowly the inside divided itself into areas of profound dark and mere gloom. Straining, Pinch tried to interpret what he saw.

"Infidel!" roared a voice just as the darkness flared with light. Pinch practically flopped through the narrow hole as his gaze was filled by a corona of blinding after-lights.

"Seize the thief!" roared the voice again, echoing through the vast empty chamber of the temple's great nave.

In Pinch's blinking gaze, a small hunched blur darted across the broad marble floor. Close behind was a pack of clanking men lit by the brilliant flare of a priest's wand of light. The old rogue heaved back out of the hole, suddenly fearful he'd been seen and breathless with surprise.

The rope, previously slack, jerked and snapped as a weighty little body grabbed it and scrambled up the line. "Pinch!" wheezed Sprite-Heels through lungfuls of air. "Pinch, haul me up!"

The man seized the rope and heaved. "For the gods' piss, be silent!" he hissed through clenched teeth, too softly for anyone to hear. It was bad enough Sprite-Heels had blown the job, but he had to drag Pinch's name into it, too.

Straddling the hole, Pinch suppressed the urge to drop the blundering halfling to his well-deserved fate. Do that and there was no doubt the little knave would sing hymns for the catchpoles. So he had no choice but to pull, heedless of the strain, until he drew up great arm-lengths of rope and the halfling was hurtling toward the temple's painted ceiling.

"To the roof! Alarms! Blow the alarms!" came the muffled bellow from below.

"OWWW!" came the more immediate cry as the rope suddenly came to jarring halt. " 'inch, lay aw a liddle! Yer bregging by dose!"

A foot of line slid through the rogue's fingers and the weight on the other end bounced with a jolt. A small hand thrust through the hole and flailed until it gripped the edge. "Up—but slowly!" wailed Sprite-Heels from below.

Pinch cast his gaze over the windswept rooftop, trying to guess how long they had. "Did you get it—the pelfry?"

" 'Course I did!" came the indignant reply. The halfling's arm struggled and heaved until his curly head popped into view. "Pinch, help me out of here! They're getting archers!"

"Pass me the garbage—all of it!"

Sprite-Heels looked at Pinch's out-thrust hand. "A pox on that!" he spat out as he lunged forward and caught the rogue's wrist in his tiny grip. "You'll not drop me twice!"

Pinch didn't resist, but heaved his small companion through the hole. "I should take it, for the way you've bungled this job!" he snarled.

"Bungled! You're the one who—"

CR-RACK! A burst of splintered tile slashed across Pinch's arm. Wheeling, Pinch saw the silhouette of two guardsmen, one twirling his arm over his head.

"Slingers! Down!" The man shoved the halfling as he dropped toward the rooftop. There was a whirring buzz just over his head and then his feet slipped out from beneath him. Unbraced on the pitched slope, Pinch skidded and rattled several feet down the tile roof before he was able to arrest his slide. The darkness beyond the third-story eave loomed ominously below.

Pinch scrambled for purchase, his feet skittering across the tiles. Sprite-Heels was facing him, back pressed against the brick pile of the chimney. The only advantage gained in his fall was that the stack screened his attackers, but not seeing them hardly made them go away. Over the fits of the wind, Pinch and the halfling could hear the heavy-footed clunk of the temple sentinels as they picked their way across the angled tiles.

A throng of voices rose up from the courtyard below as the alarm leapt like an elemental spark through the temple compound. Pinch twisted around just in time for the brilliant glare of a spotter's lantern to sweep over the eaves. The wash of light swung their way, not quite on them but close enough to highlight the fear in Sprite-Heels's countenance.

The rogue's sharp whistle jerked the wavering halfling back to action. A snap of the head and a sharp gesture were all that Pinch had to do before his small partner nodded in agreement. The knowing eye and the sure hand were the language of all thieves.

As if on a spoken signal, the pair sprang into motion. They barreled around the chimney, one to each side, and straight into the faces of the two guardsmen who'd been trying to creep forward with ox-footed stealth. "Clubs!" bellowed Pinch, letting loose the time-honored battling cry of Elturel's apprentices. The astonished guardsman flailed madly with his sword, the blade slashing the air over Pinch's gray-curled head. The thief didn't stop to fence but swung his balled fist in an uppercut beneath the other's guard. Knuckles slammed into hardened jerkin right below the breastbone. The guard sucked air like a drowning man; Pinch cursed like a sailor. The sword hit the tiles with a sharp crash and skittered over the eaves like a living thing while the guard took a floundering step back. All at once, he tipped precipitously as one foot found the burglars' hole and disappeared from sight.

At the rim of his attention, Pinch saw Sprite-Heels was no less quick. As the halfling easily dodged beneath the tall guard's lunge, there was a flash of metal and a bewildered scream. Like a rag doll, the guard tumbled against the chimney, hands clutching the back of his leg below his armored coat.

Ignoring all else, Pinch scrambled up the wavering slope of tile and lunged over the ridge. Momentum skidded him halfway down and then he was up and running with short, acrobatic steps. He clambered over a gable and then swung precariously around the edge of a conic tower before he came to the dark and shadowed alley they had started from. Moving with greater care, he searched for their rope to the alley below. Just then Sprite-Heels tumbled over the ridgeline, coming from a different direction.

"Anyone following?" Pinch demanded.

Sprite-Heels grinned while he caught his breath. "Not a one . . . of the patrico's men . . . not even a rat," he gasped.

"And the pelfry?"

The halfling reached inside his vest and pulled out a crudely forged amulet embossed with a stylized half-sun symbol. Pinch snatched the booty and pulled the startled halfling to his feet.

"Right, then. To the rope."

As they neared the line, Pinch instantly knew there was trouble. A noise carried over the wind that others, less keen, might miss. It was a steady creak, the sawing to and fro of a line. He signaled Pinch to silence and crept forward over the terra-cotta terrain.

Sure enough, there was someone on the rope. It jerked from side to side as someone pulled himself up. Signaling Sprite-Heels to stand watch, Pinch carefully peered over the edge of the roof.

Halfway below was the dim shape of a climber. From the bulky shape and the oversized helmet, there was no mistaking it was one of the temple's men. In the middle of the alley was a pool of light where the climber's partner stood holding a lantern.

"Pinch, they're coming!" Sprite-Heels hissed. As if to prove his warning there was a thunderous clatter of boots across tile.

The pursuit was hard on, and their escape route was blocked. In a few more moments the climber would reach the roof, putting the two thieves between enemy swords. There was no forward and there was no back.

With barely the touch of thought, a small knife seemed to materialize in Pinch's hand. The blade flashed in the lantern light as he reached over the eaves. A yelp of alarm burst from below. With a single swipe, the razor-sharp edge severed the thin silken line. The yelp became a squeal until it ended in a solid whump of flesh and steel.

"At the back!" roared a voice from the top of the ridgepole. The vanguard of their pursuers was silhouetted against the shivering night, the wind furiously whipping their plumed helmets as they blundered forward.

Fear making their thoughts fleet, Pinch and Sprite-Heels frantically cast about for an escape, now that their rope was gone. Suddenly Pinch saw dark, moving branches in the void of the alley between the somber temple walls and the garish lanterns of the festhalls. A plan formed in his mind; he knew it was a bad plan, but it was the only choice he had.

"With me!" Pinch shouted to encourage himself. And then, even though he wasn't a strong man, the rogue scooped up the halfling around the waist. With three all-out strides and before Sprite-Heels could even squeak, Pinch leapt into the darkness, his partner tucked under one arm. With his other arm he reached out as far as he could and with his eyes closed, Pinch prayed.

"PINCH! ARE YOU—"

All at once the pair hit the top branches of the only tree in Sweetsweat Lane. Flailing for something to grip, the master thief dropped Sprite-Heels, who was squirming and howling enough already. The branches tore at Pinch's face, shredded his fine doublet, and hammered him in the ribs. Still he crashed through them, seeming to go no slower as momentum carried him in a sweeping arc toward the ground.

Pinch was almost ready to welcome the impact with the earth when his whole body, led by his neck, jerked to a stop. His fine cloak that had been billowing out behind him had snagged on a broken branch. A cheaper cloak with a clasp of lesser strength would have torn right then or its clasp would have come undone, but Pinch didn't dress in cheap clothes. Instead the cloak tried to hang him, saving the patrico of the Morninglord the job.

There was a brief second when Pinch thought his neck might snap, and then he realized he was still plunging downward—though not as fast. The one tree in Sweetsweat Lane was little more than a sapling, and under Pinch's weight the trunk bent with the springiness of a fishing pole. He felt as if he were floating, perhaps because he couldn't breathe, but there was no doubt the fall was slowing.

And then, through a shroud of pain that narrowed his vision, Pinch saw salvation. It was as if Mask, god of thieves, had reached down and parted the branches to reveal the brightly lit patio of the Charmed Maiden just below him.

Gurgling and kicking, Pinch fumbled his bung-knife from its wrist sheath and slashed at the cloth above him. The pop of threads breaking turned into a rip, and suddenly he was plunging as the branches whipped past him. With a loud crash, he bounced off a table, hurling trays of candied fruits and pitchers of warm wine into the air, and ricocheted into the warm and amply padded embrace of an enchanting lass of the Charmed Maiden. Not far away from him landed his smaller half, but with no less solid a thump.

"MAD!" Sprite-Heels howled over the shrieks of the Charmed Maiden's consorts and the outraged sputters of their clientele. "MAD, MAD, MAD! You tried to kill us! You suicidal son of a cheating apple-squire!" Sprite-Heels paid no attention to the panicked rush of the ladies or the bristling posturing of their gentlemen friends. They'd undoubtedly come out to see the commotion and were now getting more than their share.

"Stow it!" Pinch snarled as he reluctantly freed himself from the young lady's arms. "It's our necks on the leafless tree if the Hellriders take us." Though battered and hobbling, Pinch nonetheless seized the halfling by the nape of the neck and half-dragged him into the back passages of the festhall.

The pair staggered through the scented hallways, their haste increasing with each step. They passed locked doors where only soft giggles where heard, passed salons where dells awaiting the night's suitors adjusted their gowns . They hustled down the back stairs. As they neared the bottom, a chorus of shrieks and indignant cries filled the floor below. Over it all, Pinch heard the discordant clang of hand bells.

"Hellriders!" The rogue thrust his little partner back up the stairs. "Second floor—end of the hall!" he barked.

Sprite-Heels knew better than to argue. The chorus of hand bells was enough to say the watch was at the front door. The halfling could only trust the rogue's orders; gods knew the man had been here enough times.

At the top of the landing, Pinch forced his way through the sweaty couples who surged from the richly draped rooms, dodging elbows as women struggled into their gowns and the hard slap of steel as men buckled their swords to their belts. Behind them the bells and the shouts of "Hold fast!" and "Seize him!" grew stronger along with the furious pound of boots as the Hellrider patrol mounted the stairs. Forced like rats to flee rising water, the host of entertainers and clients crammed the staircase upward, so that it was mere moments before Pinch broke free into the near-empty hall. The rogue assumed his partner would follow; the halfling was able enough to care for himself. Pinch sprinted down the hall and painfully skidded around the corner.

"It's a blank wall!" wailed the voice right behind him, and indeed the words were true. The hallway ended in a solid wall, albeit one pleasingly decorated to imitate a garden seat. The small niche with a marble bench, all draped in false vines of silk and taffeta, was charming enough, but completely without a door.

"There's a way through here, Sprite. Maeve told me about it," Pinch assured. Even as he spoke, his long-fingered hands were swiftly probing the panels in search of some hidden catch or spring.

The halfling snorted. "Maeve? Our dear sweet drunken Maeve—here?"

"She was young once and not always a wizard. Now cut your whids and get to searching." From the commotion behind them, the Hellriders had reached the landing.

The halfling ignored the command. "So that's how you met her. Maeve, a—" he jibed.

"Stow it," Pinch snapped, though not out of sentimentality. He needed to concentrate and focus—and press just-so the spring-plate his fingers suddenly found.

A small panel over the garden bench swung out, opening to reveal a well of darkness. An exhalation of dust and cobwebs swept from the gap.

Pinch pulled the panel back and nodded to the halfling. "It's jiggered; in you go."

The halfling looked at it with a suspicious eye until the clomp of boots in the hall overcame his objections. With a lithe spring he was up and through the door.

Pinch wasted no time in following, surprised that he could wriggle through the small opening so quickly after all the battering he'd taken. Grabbing the inside handle, he pulled the door shut and plunged them into darkness. With one hand on Sprite-Heels's shoulder, Pinch followed as the halfling descended steps the human could not see.

They padded downward as the thumping and thunder of the 'riders behind them faded, and then snaked through passages that wove beneath the city. In places Sprite led them through water that splashed up to Pinch's ankles and smelled so bad that he was thankful not to see what he walked through.

Their escape was so hurried that neither had a light. Several times Sprite stopped and described a branch in the sewer tunnels. Each time Pinch did his best to remember the path, though his confidence grew less and less the farther they went. He was an "upright man" now, the master of his own cohort of rogues—years away from his beginnings as a sewer rat.

At last they reached a landmark Pinch knew well from his underground days, a jagged gap in the brick casing of the sewer wall. From Sprite's description,

Pinch could see it almost unchanged in his mind—the ragged curve of the opening, the broken tumble of bricks that spilled into the muck—from the day he and Algaroz broke through the wall to complete their bolt hole from the alehouse above.

"Through there," Pinch ordered with silent relief. Up till now he had only hoped that Algaroz, who now owned the Dwarf's Pot, kept the bolt hole open. Pinch knew it wasn't out of sentimentality. Algaroz had good reasons for keeping a quick escape route handy.

The dirt-floored passage ended in a planked door, tightly fitted into a wall. Designed to be hard to find from the other side, it took only a few moments of probing to release the catches and swing the hidden door slowly open. Muddy, smelly, and blinking, the two thieves stepped into the soft light of the alehouse's cellar.

*   *   *   *   *

It was several hours, almost near dawn, before a man of average height and average looks finally found his way to a table at the back of the common room. Still, he commanded attention. His clothes and manner stood him apart from all the rest. The man wore the costume of an aspiring courtier—a red velvet doublet generously trimmed in gold braid, cross-gaitered woolen hose without a tear, and a fur-lined mantle draped casually across his shoulders. The tangled curls of his graying hair were neatly brushed out and his thick mustache trimmed. Most wondrous of all, he was clean and bathed, which was far more than any other customer in the smoky ordinary. A few hours before he'd been crawling on a roof, but now gone were the dark and sludge-stained clothes from the night's escapade.

The Dwarf's Pot, or the Piss Pot as some called it, was not noted for its fine clientele. Infamy more than fame brought a man here. Most of the lot were foists and nips who swilled down cheap sack and haggled with their brokers over the day's pickings. In one shadowed corner a dwarf pushed a few pieces across the table for a pittance of coin, while at another table a wrinkled old dame, a curber by trade, showed a wig and cloak she'd hooked from a window left carelessly open. Boozing hard near the entrance was a whole tableful of counterfeit cranks, those beggars who specialized in sporting their appalling deformities and maimed limbs to the sympathetic citizens of Elturel. Here in the commons, they looked remarkably hale and whole, no doubt due to the restorative powers of the cheap ale they swilled. Mingled among the crowd were the doxies and dells finally returned from their evening's labors.

"Greetings, Pinch dearie," said the sole woman at the table Pinch joined. Though far past her prime, she still dressed like she once might have been—pretty and alluring—but years and drink had long stolen that from her. Her long brown hair was thin and graying, her skin wrinkled and blotched. It was her eyes, weak and rheumy, that revealed her fondness for drink.

"Well met to you, Maeve," Pinch answered as he pulled up a chair and joined the three already there.

Across from Maeve, Sprite-Heels sprawled on a bench like a child bored with the temple service. He thrust a hairy halfling foot into the air and waggled his oversize toes. "You took your time. Find a distraction upstairs?" the little being mocked while at the same time breaking into a yawn he could not stifle.

The fourth at the table, a big overmuscled man with farmboy good looks, snorted his ale at Sprite's tweak. He broke into a fit of coughing, the scarf around his neck slipping to reveal a thick scar underneath. "Pinch don't got no time for women. 'Sides, he's got Maeve." He snickered at his own great wit.

"Ho, that's right. He's always got me, if I'd ever let him!" Maeve added with a laugh.

Pinch let the comments slide, eying the man across from him. "Therin, my boy," he finally asked with only a little comradely warmth, "what happened? I thought the constables had you for nipping a bung."

The younger man smiled knowingly. "Seems I had good witnesses to say it wasn't me with his hand in the gent's purse. By their eyes I was here, drinking with them at that very time."

Sprite's boozy voice came from below the edge of the table. "Our farmboy's learned to hire good evidences, even if he ain't learned to nip a purse. Isha shame—always learnin' the wrong thing first."

Therin rubbed at the scarf around his neck. "I've been hanged once. I don't need to be hanged again."

"See!" came the hiccup from below. "Mos' men saves the hanging lesson for las'."

Pinch propped his head on the table and gave Therin a long, hard stare, his face coldly blank. "There's some who'd say you're just bad luck, Therin. Maybe not fit to have around. It was you supposed to be there tonight." His mouth curled in a thin smile. "But then, your bad luck seems to affect only you. It was your neck for the noose and your money for the evidences. Sprite-Heels and I did just fine, didn't we?"

"Ish true, Pinch, ish true." The halfling heaved himself up till he could look over the top of the table. He was still spotted with the muck of the sewers. Fortunately the air of the Dwarf's Pot was so thick with wood smoke, stale ale, and spiced stew that his reek was hardly noticed. Right now Sprite-Heels breath was probably deadlier than his filth. "Wha'd we get? I' didn't look like more 'an a cheap piece of jewelry."

Pinch scowled at the question and waggled a finger for silence. That was followed by a series of quick gestures that the others followed intently.

Magical . . . important . . . temple . . . wait for money. The gestures spelled it out to the others in the handtalk of thieves. From the quick finger-moves, they puzzled it out. Clearly what they'd taken was of great importance to the temple, so important that it was going to take time to sell. Pinch's sudden silence told them as much as his hands. The rogue was suddenly cautious lest someone hear. That meant people would be looking for what they had stolen, and Pinch saw no reason to openly boast of what they had done. Even Sprite-Heels, fuzzy-minded though he was, understood the need for discretion. The three turned awkwardly back to their mugs.

"What's the news of the night?" Pinch asked after a swallow of ale. They could hardly sit like silent toads all through the dawn.

Sprite collapsed back onto the bench since he had no answer. Therin shrugged and said with a grin, "There was a job at the temple. Somebody did them good." He, too, had nothing to say.

Maeve squeezed up her face as she tried to remember something the hour and the drink had stolen away from her. "There was somebody . . ." Her lips puckered as she concentrated. "That's it! There was somebody asking about you, Pinch."

The rogue's drowsy eyes were suddenly bright and alert. "Who?"

The memory coming back to her, Maeve's contorted face slowly relaxed. "A fine-dressed gent, like a count or something. Older, kind of puffy, like he didn't get out much. He was all formal and stuffy too, kind of like a magistrate or—"

"Maeve, did he have a name?" She was rambling and Pinch didn't have the patience for it.

The sorceress stopped and thought. "Cleedis . . . that was it. He was from someplace too. Cleedis of . . ."

"Cleedis," Pinch said in a voice filled with soft darkness. "Cleedis of Ankhapur."

Janol of Ankhapur

It was one of those statements that could be understood only with mouths agape, and the three did so admirably. Maeve blinked a little blearily, her slack mouth giving her the look of a stuffed fish. From out of sight, Sprite-Heels suddenly stopped hiccuping. The grumbling of a drunk as he argued the bill, the clatter of dishes carried to the back by a wench, even the slobbering snore of an insensate drunk filled the silence the three scoundrels created.

It was up to Therin, naturally, to ask the obvious. "You know this Cleetish?" he asked, wiping his sleeve at the drool of ale on his chin.

"Cleedis—and yes, I know him," was the biting answer. This was not, Pinch thought, a subject for their discussion.

" 'Swounds, but ain't that a new one. Our Pinch has

got himself a past," the big thief chortled.

By now Sprite had hauled himself up from his sprawl on the bench. Though his hair was a tangled nest of curls and his shirt was awry, the halfling's eyes were remarkably clear for one who only moments ago was half done-in by drink. Still, his words were slurred by ale. "Wha's his nature, Pinch—good or ill?" The little thief watched the senior rogue closely, ever mindful of a lie.

Pinch tented his finger by his lips, formulating an answer. All the while, he avoided the halfling's gaze, instead carefully scanning the common room under the guise of casualness. "Not good," he finally allowed. "But not necessarily bad. I haven't seen him in a score of years, so there's no good reason for him to be looking for me."

"From Ankhapur, eh?" Therin asked more ominously, now that the drift of things was clear. "Where's that?"

Pinch closed his eyes in thoughtful remembrance, seeing the city he'd left fifteen years ago. He tried to envision all the changes wrought on a place in fifteen years, see how the streets would be different, the old temples torn down, the houses spread outside the outdated walls. Still, he knew that the Ankhapur he imagined was as much a dream as the one he remembered.

"South—too far south for you to know, Therin," the rogue finally answered with a thoughtful grin. It was no secret that Therin's knowledge of the world ended about ten leagues beyond Elturel. Pinch could have claimed that Ankhapur drifted through the sky among the lights of Selûne's Tears for as much as Therin knew. Still, maybe it was the remembering that made Pinch more talkative than he had ever been. Home and family just weren't topics of conversation for those of his trade. "It's the white city, the princely city, built up right on the shores of the Lake of Steam. Some folks call it the boiled city. Take your pick."

"So who is this Cleedis, Pinch?" Maeve wheedled. "He seemed like a gent."

"An old, foolish man," Pinch answered offhandedly to end his reminiscence. Maybe there was more to be said, but the rogue offered no further explanation.

Sprite, his judgment decidedly impaired, was not going to let Pinch slip away. "So wha' do we do? We goin' to meet with him?"

The other poured a blackjack of sack and gave Sprite a jaundiced glare. "*You're* not doing anything. This fellow's looking for me, not you. We've had success tonight, and it calls for some drinking. Here's to my little diver!" the rogue raised his leather mug for the toast, and the other three quickly followed.

"Here's to Sprite," Therin and Maeve chorused.

"Aye, here's to me," the halfling burbled happily. He buried his childlike face deep into the overfull mug of wine, greedily tipping it back with two hands until the drink streamed down his chin.

Pinch took a judicious draught of his wine, while Therin and Maeve drank long and hard. Even before the others had finished, their master stepped away from the table. "I'll look for you in the usual places," Pinch advised. "Finish your drinking and keep your eyes and ears sharp. The patricos are going to be looking hard for their thieves. It won't do to have any of you scragged now."

"As you say it, Pinch," Therin murmured dourly as he set his blackjack on the greasy table. Brown Maeve nodded her receipt of Pinch's caution. Sprite was silent, already insensate and snoring on the bench.

Gathering his mantle tight, Pinch stepped over the sleeping dog by the door and walked out into the bracing dawn.

The muddy lane was flecked with clumps of long-lasting snow that clung to the patches of daytime shade. Right now it was neither light nor dark but the

point where time hovered between the two. The false
dawn that dimmed out the lower stars was fading, replaced by the true dawn. Here though, the sun's first
light struggled against the winter mists common to Elturel. How like Ankhapur, Pinch thought as he watched
the hovering frost swirl through the night alleys. The
comparison had never occurred to him before, not even
when he'd arrived fresh from the south. Travel had all
been new, wonderful, and terrifying then; there was
never time for such frivolous speculation.

The man shook his head with a snap of his curly
hair, as if to shake loose these romantic notions and
rattle them out his ears. Such thoughts were all fa-
tigue, and he could not allow himself that luxury of
rest. First there was Cleedis.

The Five-League Lodge was far from Pinch's normal
haunts. It perched halfway up the slope of Elturel's
High Road, halfway between the base world of the common man and the uppermost crest of nobility. In Elturel, a man's address said much for his status.
Chaperons in their salons counted how many streets a
prospective suitor was from the top of the hill. Rag-
pickers always claimed their gleanings were gathered
from the very summit of Elturel, an artless lie their
hopeful customers accepted anyway.

For Pinch, all that mattered was that the best pickings were found in the streets that looked down on the
city. Of course, the higher streets had the most watchmen and wizards, too. It was here that the city's leaders
lived in aeries at the top of the great High Hill, the temples of those gods currently in favor clustered around
them. Farther down, those merchants who aspired beyond their class vied for the choicest—hence highest—
streets left to choose from. The Five-League Lodge had
done well, holding practically the last address before
the realms of the privileged crowded out all others.

By the time Pinch reached the block of the inn, the

morning vendors were already straining their carts through the streets. Eelmongers and bread carts competed for attention, along with the impoverished prestidigitators who went from door to door offering their skills. "A quick spell to clean your house, a word to sweeten your wine? Or perhaps, madam, you're looking for something to make your husband a little more amorous. I can do these things for you, madam. It'll only take a few coins . . . and he'll never know what happened."

Pinch knew these old tricks well. Tomorrow the house would be dirty again; in a few days, the husband would be as doltish as ever. The wizard wouldn't care. Some probably wouldn't even remember, the grinding scramble of the day drowned away by cheap wine in taprooms like the Dwarf's Piss Pot. That was the way things were—everybody out to make their coin.

It was the hypocrites who pretended to live above it who irritated Pinch. He'd dealt with constables, trusties, watchmen, even executioners, buying them with a few gold or silver coins, and yet they still pretended to be pure and unimpeachable. That was a joke; nobody was beyond gold's reach. Rogues knew the lies and self-deceptions men used, and made their living trading on those weaknesses. Perhaps that was why Pinch stayed in the bottom town, unlike other upright men who pretended to the ranks of the gentry. Down among the common folk, at least a man knew his business and wasn't ashamed of it.

Pinch abandoned his ruminations at the door to the Five-League Lodge, a sprawling compound of timber and stone. He stepped through the door and into the common room, this one a good deal cleaner than the place he had just left. The hall was empty save for a single charwoman cleaning the floor. Her dress hung in greasy tatters, far out of keeping with the fine appointments of the room.

"Girl, come here," Pinch commanded as he took a chair. After a start of surprise, the woman hesitantly shuffled over. As she drew near, Pinch laid a silver coin on the table and idly pushed it about with one finger. "Do you have a guest named Cleedis?"

The charwoman's gaze was fixated on the promise of the coin. "The one that looks like an empty money sack? Aye."

Another coin, matched by a scowl, was laid on the table. "That's the one. Where?"

"Up the stairs to the best chambers in the house."

With a deft tap he scooted the silver toward her and she snatched it up before it had even stopped moving. Coin in pocket, she hurried to disappear before the chance of blame arose.

Pinch was up the stairs before the innkeeper might stop him, since no doubt like all innkeepers, the man truly believed he was the lord of his domain. At the top of the stairs, it was hardly difficult to find Cleedis's room; the one entrance with double doors had to be it. The doors were a rich wood unseen in these parts and probably shaped by elves, judging from the elaborate carved panels, not that Pinch was much of an appraiser of the forest folks' handiwork. He did, however, note the keyhole of thick dwarven iron. Locks were something more in his line, and this one looked formidable. Worse still, it was probably enchanted. The last thing he needed was for the lock to shout out an alarm.

A good thief was always prepared, and Pinch prided himself on being a good thief. The slim rod of dull bronze he pulled from his pouch didn't look like much, but getting it had cost two others their lives and Pinch very nearly his. Not that his killing them bothered him; if there'd been an honest beak on the bench, both would've been hanged long ago. Death was their reward for plotting against him.

The old rogue knelt by the door and gently touched

the rod to the metal lock, so carefully as not to make a single clink or tap. At the barest contact, the rod melted before the dwarven metal, dripped down its own shaft before it coagulated into a thick mass. Pinch shook it briefly, as if scattering the excess metal. When it was done, what had been a plain rod was a perfect duplicate of the lock's true key, form and shape stolen from the memory of the dwarven metal itself.

Still, Pinch held his breath as he slipped the forged key over the tumblers. There was always the chance of another safety, especially with dwarf work. The dumpy smiths were always vying to outdo each other in one form or another, building in this new intricacy or that. Fortunately, this lock did not look particularly new.

The tumblers clicked and rotated, the bolt slid back, and nothing screeched in alarm. Still Pinch waited to be sure. When no innkeeper roused from his morning kitchen came puffing up the stairs with guardsmen in tow, Pinch pushed the door open until he could just slide his body through into the gloom beyond. Once inside, he checked the lock's other side. Dwarves had a fiendish fondness for little traps like one-sided locks and other infernal tricks.

Once satisfied that the Five-League Lodge was not at the forefront of lock design, the old rogue softly pressed the door shut and looked about the room. The front salon alone was larger than any private room Pinch had seen in Elturel. The entire common room of the old, dark-stained Piss Pot could easily have fit in here. Worse still for Pinch, everything was of the finest quality—the brocades, the statuary, the plate. It was a cruel thing to have to suppress his natural acquisitive instincts. He restrained himself, not from any sense of morality but because he had business that he did not want to jeopardize. Besides, the rogue knew he wasn't equipped to do the job right. Pilfer a little now, and the owner would surely tighten his wonderfully lax

precautions. Instead, Pinch made a note of the place, its
best treasures, and its weaknesses. Any man who
guarded his treasures so ill just might be fool enough
to turn over the lot to a quick-witted coney-catcher like
himself, Pinch guessed.

But the rogue shook his head ruefully, knowing his
thoughts were getting away from the matter at hand.
With all the stealth he could muster, Pinch slipped to
the bedchamber door and gently pushed the gilded
panel open. It swung on silent hinges, which suited the
thief well. A dying glimmer in the fireplace lit the
gloom in the far corner, casting its rays over the dark
hump in the center of the bed.

With a supple twist, Pinch slid his wrist knife into
the palm of his hand. He had no intention of killing
Cleedis, but there was no point in letting the man know
that. In three quick strides he would be at the bed.

Halfway through his second step, a light flared from
the corner opposite the lamp.

"All night I've waited," groused a figure in the light,
filling a high-backed chair like a lump of fallen dough.
"I expected you earlier."

"Cleedis!" Pinch gasped, though his teeth were
clenched. Instinct seized the thief. He whirled on the
balls of his feet, blade already coming up—

"None of that!" the other barked sharply. He shifted
slightly and a flash of steel glinted from his lap. "I know
you too well, coz. It was me that taught you the sword."

Pinch rocked back with wary slowness. " 'Coz,' indeed, Chamberlain Cleedis. What brings you so far
from Ankhapur? Fall out of Manferic's favor?"

The swordsman rose from his seat, his overweight
and flaccid body filling with the stern strength of piety.
"Your guardian, King Manferic III, is dead."

It was clear the old courtier was playing the news for
shock, and Pinch was not having any of it. With his best
studied coolness, he laid his knife on the nightstand

and settled onto the bed, disinterestedly pulling the coverlet back. Underneath, a breastplate and clothes made up the lumpy outline. "So?" the rogue drawled. "He turned his back on me years ago."

"The kingdom needs you."

That got to Pinch. He couldn't help but stare at Cleedis in surprise. He looked at the courtier closely, comparing what he saw to the man he once knew. The hair, once black and rich, was receding and almost pure white. The weather-beaten campaigner's skin was now cracked and loose, his eyes sad pits without humor. The soldier's muscles were now flaccid and tired. In Cleedis, Pinch saw the fate of the warrior turned statesman, the toll that years of compromise and patience would extract from the flesh.

Pinch stared until he realized he was staring, then he gave an embarrassed snort of disgust as if to claim his shock was only an act. "I'm not such a gull, Cleedis. There are my dear cousins; what about the princelings four?"

Cleedis thrust the sword into the carpet and hobbled a step forward using the weapon like a cane. "Bors is an idiot—can barely hold his drool in at a temple service," the king's chamberlain growled. "The other three hate each other with a passion. Each claims sole right to the Cup and Knife. Vargo started it, figuring he could muscle the other two out of the race. With only one claimant, the priests would nullify the test and pronounce him the true heir."

The tale was beginning to amuse Pinch, in as much as it was all his adopted family deserved. He lay back on the pillows, although one hand was always near the knife. "Throdus and Marac didn't agree? By Beshaba, dissension in the house."

"There'll be civil war!"

"So when they're all gone, you want me, the forgotten ward, to come to Ankhapur's rescue and carry on the family name? How generous, Cleedis."

Cleedis stabbed at the floor in anger. "I'll not put a thief like you on the throne!"

Pinch sprang to the edge of the bed. "Ho! Little king-maker Cleedis now! My, what you've become. So what is it you want of me then?"

The courtier stalked back to his chair. "Just a job. A quick and quiet solution to our problem."

"Why me? You could get any queer-bird to lay them down with a cudgel, just for freedom from the gaol—or have you lost all your influence with Manferic's death?" The aged courtier's glare told Pinch all he needed to know. "Aye, now there's a turn of Tymora's wheel. You used to inspire fear in them, and now you probably don't even have the coin for a black spell from a Thavian outcast. That's why you've come to me." The rogue let loose a gloating chuckle and settled back onto the silken pillows.

"It's not that way," was Cleedis's terse reply. "First, it's not the princes we're after. If anything odd should happen to your cousins, there'll be war for sure. In the second part, you can dance on the twisted hemp before I'd come looking for you. I'm here at Manferic's bidding."

"Oh, dear guardian; so like Manferic. He plots even after his death." It was time to be off the bed and to the door. "Go back to his grave, Cleedis, and tell him I'm not coming. I like things just as they are here."

"Heard there was trouble in town last night," the elder drawled like a snake uncoiling. Pinch knew he was hearing trouble, but he kept his stride steady. He wasn't going to play the chamberlain's game.

"You are a fool, Janol—or Pinch, should I call you? Here I am in Elturel, where nobody's even heard of Manferic or Ankhapur, and you don't even wonder how I found you."

That stopped Pinch with his hand at the door.

The seat creaked and then the floor groaned with a heavy thunk-clunk as Cleedis hobbled over, sword as cane. "The priests of Ankhapur," the courtier wheezed out, "have gotten quite good at tracking you. Shall I tell you where you were last night?"

Pinch stared blindly at the woodwork in front of him. "I was drinking." He could hear his own words locking into the cool monotone of a lie and cursed himself for getting caught.

"Maybe you were. It doesn't matter," the courtier allowed with the smooth, cold smile of a basilisk. "Guilty or innocent, it doesn't matter to me or the constables—what are they called?—Hellriders of this town. Just a word is all it takes."

Pinch turned a half step toward his tormentor.

"Not a bit of it, Janol," the old man said as he weakly swung his sword to guard. "You can't imagine me trekking to Elturel alone. I die and you're surely doomed."

"Bastard fool, you've got no proof and I've got evidences who'll swear for me."

Sword still up, Cleedis blew on his free hand to warm his finger joints. "Of course you do, and that's all good for the constables, but are a high priest's bodyguards less impetuous here than in Ankhapur? The news through the entire city is that they lost a pretty piece of property, a piece of some high holy man's jewelry they'd been safeguarding."

Resigned, Pinch leaned back against the door. If he couldn't bluff the old man, he would at least pump the chamberlain for what he could. "You know a lot for being new here."

"Don't assume I came in yesterday. I learned a lot in Manferic's service that's served me better than the sword. So, are you coming or will you wait for some temple brave to cut you down? They will find you, trust me."

There was no choice. Pinch needed to stall.

"I've got others who need consulting—"

"Let them hang on their own."

"And things to get together. This evening—we'll meet again."

The old chamberlain considered the offer, the fierce energy that had sustained him all night draining away. "Where?"

"Here," was the quick answer. Pinch wasn't about to reveal any of his hideouts, either the boozing kens where he spent his days or the stalling kens where he passed his goods to the brokers.

Cleedis nodded acceptance. "Don't turn me, cousin. I found you once; I'll find you again."

And I'll be ready for you next time, Pinch thought to himself. At the door, he gave a quick bow, part old habit and part mockery, before leaving the apartment and slipping through the dawn-drowsy halls of the inn.

* * * * *

The rogue was wary as he made his way back through the early morning streets. By now his head was thick with the sluggish residue of stale ale, sleep deprivation, and overexcited nerves. He had to thread his way through the sunrise press of greengrocers, tinkers, and kitchen maids on their morning rounds. A butcher's apprentice splashed by, hurrying through the muddy streets and balancing a fresh side of mutton on his shoulder while a pack of gnome striplings chased him, trying to nick bits of meat off the carcass's dangling shank. Here and there Pinch saw a fellow knave—Dowzabell, the prison trusty; Dun Teddar, who did a counterfeit of mad singing; and Ironbellow, a dwarf who limped because one foot was a bronze peg. He begged coins, claiming he'd lost his foot as a Hellrider fighting the Zhentarim, but Pinch knew in truth that a surgeon had taken it last winter after Ironbellow had passed out from drink and got a case of frostbite and gangrene.

It wasn't the unpredictable palliards or the murderous wild rogues that made Pinch wary, though. Like him, the ragged tramps and overdressed cutthroats were from the night world, the land of darkness and shadow. Now, as the sun rose, they, like himself, felt their powers wane.

It was the ones who knew no hour that worried Pinch—the Hellriders who patrolled the city. It was the rogue's greatest failing that he was too well known to the catchpole and his constables. No doubt they'd be looking for him after last night.

And the Hellriders weren't all either. The patrico's guard would want a hand in this also, to redeem the damaged honor of their jobs at the temple. With daylight, they'd be out in force.

Finally, there was Cleedis. Given whom the old man had served all these years, it was certain the swordmaster was not to be underestimated. Hellriders, even temple guards, Pinch could predict. He could not say the same for Cleedis.

It's all my own vain fault, a biting voice gnawed within him. It was hardly fair to call this his chiding conscience, for while always at his shoulder, the sharp words didn't care about the causes of things. Pinch's inner voice saw the flaws in plans that might have been perfect. The trouble was, it almost always spoke in the rogue's ear when it was too late to do much anyway. The voice seemed to relish the power of hindsight that Pinch denied himself.

So Pinch moved warily. He slipped down alleys with names like Kennel Lane and Mucker's Mews, where the half-timbered houses leaned so close over the street that their roof peaks almost touched. He chose ways that kept him on the edges of the day markets and far from Elturel's High Hill. Traveling thus, skirting this and flanking that, it was not until well into the morning that Pinch returned to the Dwarf's Pot.

As the old rogue pushed open the alehouse's creaky door, Therin unexpectedly stepped out from the shadows. "Piss in Ilmater's wounds—where've you been, Pinch?" The thug's voice was torn between relief and stress, and it was mirrored in the long knife clutched in his hand even as his body sagged back against the wall. Pinch knew by the knife it was serious business, not just because Therin had a knife out, but because it was a skene, a long, thin dirk. It was a blade favored by Therin's honor-obsessed people, the Gurs—Selûne's children, the people of the highway. The skene was a sure sign of deadly intent.

"Pizzle it yourself. What's the play here?" Without waiting for an answer, Pinch slipped to the side where he could get his back against the wall and face his foes directly. Even though Therin wasn't threatening anymore, a man would be a fool to think all was well. With his hold-back dagger already in hand, Pinch scanned the common room for more danger.

It was empty, which even at this hour was not right. There was always at least one drunk or well-paid doxy toasting the day—but today there was nothing. Save for Therin, there weren't even any of Pinch's gang. "Hellriders, did they—"

Therin didn't need the rest of the question. "It was the patriarch's catchpoles. Came in here like apprentices to a cry of 'Clubs.' Set to bust up the place looking for you and the little fellow." He stooped and slid the long knife back into its boot sheath.

"Damn Cleedis and his spies! Sprite-Heels—where is he?"

"Up here" was the muffled answer. Pinch looked up in time to see a small stream of dust fall from the roof beams, and then Sprite was dangling by his awkward little arms.

Therin nodded up with a grin but made no move to help. "Slipped out of sight and got himself up there." He purposely raised his voice for Sprite to hear. "Can't imagine how a runt like him managed it, though."

"I heard that!" the halfling shrieked.

They both ignored him. "And Maeve?"

"Right here, my dear Pinch," cooed a voice at Pinch's ear. The old rogue could feel her warm, ale-scented breath on his cheek, but she was nowhere to be seen.

"Got meself invisible as soon as trouble come through the door. Just in case." Vanishing was Brown Maeve's first reaction to most danger.

"Well, make yourself whole, woman." Pinch addressed the air where he thought she stood. "And you up there, get yourself down. We're leaving town." He strode through the near-deserted hall toward the upstairs.

"Leaving?" There was a loud thud as Sprite dropped to the floor. Halflings, it seemed, did not land like cats. "None too soon, I think."

A bottle on the Piss Pot's bar suddenly upended and burbled a healthy swig. "Oy, Maeve—you'll be paying for that!" snapped Algaroz as he came through the door from the back kitchens.

Caught with the snappings, the frumpy sorceress flickered into existence. "It's a going-away drink," she chided. "Old Pinch wants us to leave town."

"And none too soon, if the officers keep ruining my trade—"

"Leave, just cause we had a little trouble with the constables? Things were looking good here. I say we stay." Therin marked his objections by leaning significantly against the front door. With his big muscles and rope-scarred neck, he made an imposing obstacle.

"Fine for you to say when they haven't made you, moon-man!" Sprite snapped.

Therin reddened at the name "moon-man." It was an

old insult for his kind, one that reminded him of the
suspicion he'd always faced as a Gur.

From the stairs, Pinch cut it off before the pair went
to their blades. "Settle it later!" Pinch shouted from the
stairs. "Listen, you bastards. It's not because the catchpoles showed, but that they showed unnatural fast—
and they knew whom they were looking for. Don't that
strike you as queer, either of you?" He spat toward the
spittoon, getting the flavor of treachery out of his
mouth. "It was Cleedis's doing. He's got a job he wants
me to do, and he's tipped the temple to make me do it."

"So we're running then?" Therin asked archly.

Damn the man's pride, Pinch thought to himself. "Of
course we are. And if we're lucky, Cleedis will follow—
and then, Therin, I'll let you take care of him."

He didn't like it. The game he thought he knew was
getting out of control. First Cleedis's manipulations,
and now he had to satisfy Therin's honor. Pinch didn't
like any of it. "Satisfied?" he snarled when Therin
didn't reply quickly.

"I'll go," Therin replied with a face like the losing dog
in a challenge.

"Good then. You've all got a little time to get your
things. It'll be a trip to the country until things settle
down in the city." The man didn't wait see if anyone
questioned his orders but went up to gather his own
few clothes.

* * * * *

An hour later he was making his way through the
midday streets, accompanied by a puffing Maeve and a
scowling Therin. Darting in and out among them, like a
planet orbiting its greater sun, was a small, heavily
cloaked figure. It was only when the cold winter brushed
up the edge of the creature's hem that a man could even
notice a pair of curly-haired feet underneath.

"Take the Waterside Road; the guards ain't so choosy there," suggested Therin, their Gur. In their shiftless lives, the Gurs were masters for knowing the little ways in and out of the city. They were a group always ready to pack and leave on a moment's notice. Pinch idly speculated that Therin's newly tasted stability had made him reluctant to leave.

They followed his advice and hurried past the public docks and the fishmonger's market, where rats challenged cats for the choicest fish entrails. Just before the city gatehouse, they broke from the main avenue and wove through the side lanes until they reached a smaller, almost forlorn gate. Two indolent guards protected the old gate and all within its walls. Pinch recognized it as the Old Trade Gate, named before commerce dictated building something more.

Sure enough, the guards were lax here. In fact, the only thing that animated the bored pair was the size of the bribe they'd get from the group. After being driven down to only four gold each—business was slow for them—the two watchmen stepped aside and let the party through unquestioned.

Outside the walls, the road threaded through a jumble of shacks that had once been thriving inns when the trade route had passed this way. Now, with the merchants using the New Road, only a few struggling hostels survived here. Nonetheless, the group did not slow its pace. This close to Elturel was still too close. Pinch wanted them farther away.

At last they reached the breakwater of the city's expansion, a largish creek that separated city from countryside. The sluggish water was spanned by a claptrap wooden bridge that looked unsteady and probably was. Across the way, a horse grazed while its rider lounged in the midday sun of winter. As best they could tell, he sported no livery of the temple or the distinctive black-and-red armor of the Hellriders. Satisfied that all was clear, Pinch led them across.

It's too easy, chided the rogue's inner voice. Cleedis won't give up, and then what will I do?

Pinch had been avoiding the question because he didn't have an answer. Well, we can fend for ourselves, he firmly decided, without interference from any others.

In this, Pinch was wrong.

They had barely set foot on the other bank when the true nature of the rider was revealed. It was Cleedis, and before Pinch could react, the old warrior had gotten unsteadily to his feet.

"What kept you so long, Janol?" the foreigner casually asked. Before anyone could answer, a ring of bodyguards, all pointing crossbows, stepped from the gloomy bushes. "I expected you much sooner."

"Cleedis, you borsholder," Pinch snarled.

Sprite elbowed the old rogue's knee. "Don't provoke him. He may want you, but there weren't a thing said about the rest of us." Pinch's three companions froze with indecision, uncertain if Cleedis's invitation was extended to them or if they were unnecessary in the foreign chamberlain's eyes.

"Aye, play it out Pinch," Therin warned.

To the relief of the others, their leader slowly nodded—whether to them or Cleedis, it didn't matter. "It seems, Cleedis," the thief said in his most politic tone, "that maybe we should travel with you. Elturel was getting stale."

The old swordsman looked at Pinch's three companions and then at the determination in the rogue's eyes. The chamberlain's face was a mask as he calculated how his charge's compatriots changed the rules of the game. Finally, he turned and hobbled away. "Well and good. Daros, bring horses for them all. The rest of you, watch them close. We've found whom we came for; it's home for Ankhapur."

Travelers' Tales

"Dammit, Pinch, you owe us some words!" Therin hissed softly so that the trooper riding next to him wouldn't hear. Although it was midafternoon, it was the first chance any of them had to speak to Pinch. The small column—for Cleedis commanded his men like an army—had been forced to a halt by a poorly planked stream. As their escorts plodded across the narrow bridge, Therin seized the opportunity to maneuver close to Pinch while they waited. "Who are they and why'd you let us get taken?"

Pinch bristled at his underling's questions. He didn't see that Therin or the others needed to know about his past, and certainly not on their demands. His life was his own, to share as he chose and pizzle take the rest of them. Even his horse felt that anger and started to bolt, only to have the thief savagely rein it in.

"If you'd stayed in Elturel, you'd be dead by sunset."
The master rogue couldn't hold back the snarl that drove
his words. "Do you think the constables were just lucky?
Are you that dense? They were tipped. They got sent—"

"That wa'rnt no reason to leave," the younger man
countered hotly, his whispers becoming dangerously
loud. "We've beat the catchpoles before. Piss and fire,
you even cheated me off the gallows tree! We could've
slipped the lot and hid out in another ken. Those constables ain't got the wit of us. For Mask's eyes, their
idea of searching was just to bust up a few things and
say it was good! There was no cause to go abroad."

"Think on it, Therin. Ain't they got the wit of us? Then
how'd they find you—by twirling Tymora's wheel? It was
that Cleedis found me over how many leagues distant
and it was him that tipped the authorities. Do you think
a few hide-holes and lasts would stop his priests from
spying us out?" Pinch had had enough of the Gur's dis-
puting and nudged his horse into the line, but not before
giving one parting shot. "Besides, I'm curious. There may
be a profit in going with Cleedis after all."

That left the awkwardly perched gypsy musing in
his saddle, just as Pinch knew it would.

Beyond the stream and well on their way, it was time
for Pinch to ask the questions. With a cheerful nod to
his armed chaperons, the rogue trotted his horse up to
where Cleedis rode.

In the saddle, the old chamberlain was a transformed
man. His horse was a spirited gray stallion with a mane
streaked charcoal black. Its eyes were clear and its bite
hard on the bit. Even to Pinch, who was no judge of
prancers, it was clear that this beast was the best breed of
the southern lands. Under the reins of a weaker man, the
horse would have ridden the rider, but under Cleedis there
was none of that. Here on the roads, in the open air, and
fitted in his commander's armor, the chamberlain was
once again the cavalry captain Pinch had known as a lad.

Pinch reined in alongside and launched in without preamble. "Cleedis, you've got me now. What's the job and what's the booty?"

The chamberlain pulled his open-faced helmet back to hear better. "Job? Wait and see."

"Not good enough, coz," the rogue said as he brushed a fly from his face. "I need time to plan and think. And I'll not be killing." At least not by intention, Pinch added to himself.

"You're tired and not thinking clearly, Janol. I already said there would be no need for killing—not if you do your part well. As for more, you'll have to wait."

A little part of the mystery became clear. "You don't know, do you? You were just sent to bring me back. Who sent you—Vargo, Throdus, or Marac?" Pinch watched carefully as each name was mentioned, hoping for a telltale on Cleedis's part. There was no such luck. The chamberlain maintained a statesmanlike demeanor. "You must wait, Janol. You were, and still are, impatient. It will be your undoing someday. When we reach Ankhapur, what you need to know will be revealed."

But no more than that, Pinch heard in what was not said.

He did not press the issue. The gleaning of information was an art, and there was time between here and Ankhapur.

* * * * *

The rest of the day passed no worse than it had begun. By late day, the burden of the last two days' plots, schemes, escapes, and yet more plots came crushing down on Pinch and his companions. Their energies were sapped. While the guards jounced along uncomfortably in their saddles, Pinch and company slept. The old rogue was skilled enough to sleep in the saddle, but for the other three riding was an untested talent.

Therin, mounted on an impossibly small pony, would nod off until one of his cramped legs slipped from the stirrup and scraped the ground. Just when it seemed he might ride like this for miles, until all the leather was shredded from the tip of his boot, his toe would catch on a rock with a solid thwack and rouse him from slumber. Maeve and Sprite-Heels, the halfling squeezed into the saddle in front of the sorceress, lolled precariously and in unison from side to side until one or the other woke with the panic of a headlong plunge.

So it went until they stopped. The four gingerly massaged their sore parts while the troopers made camp, cooked, and saw to the needs of the travelers. By then, Pinch's companions were too tired to talk, too wary of their escorts to ask questions of the leader.

The fires were near embers and guards had taken their posts at the edge of the hostile darkness when Cleedis produced a bottle from his saddlebags. "When I was a young officer out on campaign," he began in the rambling way of a man who has a moral he feels he must share, "we used to spend all day hunting down orc bands from the Great Invasion. We'd ride for miles, getting hot and full of dust. Sometimes we'd find a band of stragglers and ride them down. It was great work."

Clawlike fingers pulled the cork free, and he drank a long draught of the yellowish wine. Breathing hard to savor the alcohol's burn, he held the bottle to Therin across the fire.

"After a day of butchering, we'd gather around the fire like this and drink." The old man looked at the suspicious eyes across from him. He pushed the bottle again toward Therin until the big man took it. "Drink up, boy," the worn-out campaigner urged before continuing his ambling tale. "Men need to share their liquor with their companions, because there's no telling who you might need at your back. Back then, a man could get himself surrounded by a throng of orc swine at any time, and then it would be too late to discover he had no friends. Drink and a tale, that's what kept us together. Doesn't that make sense, Janol?" Cleedis's eyes turned on the master rogue. The brown in them was burned black and hard by years of concessions and expediencies.

"A man can drink for lots of reasons, and most stories are lies," Pinch commented acidly.

"They say bad hearts sour good wine. Is it a good wine, Master Therin?"

The young man held the jug out in front of him considering an answer. "Tolerable, I wager."

"Tolerable, indeed," the chamberlain sighed, taking the bottle back. He set the bottle to his weather-cracked lips and gulped and gulped, and gulped at it some more until the yellow stains of wine trickled from the corners of his mouth and clung in sweet drops in the coarse beard on his chin. At last he pulled the bottle free with a choking gasp. The old man shoved the bottle into Sprite's hands and began without preamble.

"There's a lad I knew, must have been fifteen, twenty, years ago. He was a boy of a high family. His father was a noted captain in the king's guard and his mother a lady-in-waiting to the queen. She was pregnant when the captain was killed in the wars against the trolls. The lady wailed for the priests to beg their gods, but there was no bringing the captain back. She being a lady, though, the king and queen saw to her needs all the time she was with child. It was double tragedy that she died bearing her male child."

"Wasn't there a priest who could bring her back, what with the baby?" Brown Maeve asked. Her veined face was swelling with a whimper of tears, for the sorceress could never resist a sad tale. "Where was her kin?"

"She didn't have any," Cleedis answered after a long swig on the bottle he pried from Sprite's hands. "That's why she stayed at court. There wasn't any family to pray for her. It wasn't her wish to be raised; she hoped to join her husband. The king and queen pledged to raise the boy as their ward."

Maeve gave out a little sob.

Across the fire, Pinch glared at Cleedis in stony silence, eyes glinting amid the rising sparks.

Cleedis continued. "Without mother or father, in some other place he would've been one of those little beggars you kick away on the street. That's how it would have been, you know, except that didn't happen to him.

"He got lucky, more luck than he ever deserved—"

Pinch spat

Cleedis persevered. "He was favored. He didn't have family, but he was taken in by nobility, a king no less. They dressed him, fed him, and educated him in the best ways. And you know how he repaid them?"

Pinch spat, ferociously this time, and the gobbet hissed and cracked in the flames. Springing up, he broke from the circle of firelight, making angry strides past the startled guard whose sword half-cleared its sheath.

The old chamberlain motioned the man back to give the rogue his peace. Pinch trembled at the edge of the firelight, hovering at the rim of the winter blackness.

"He repaid them," Cleedis slowly dogged on, pulling back the attention of the rogue's friends, "he repaid them by stealing all he could and fleeing the city. Now, what do you think of that?"

Man, woman, and halfling exchanged uncomfortable glances, their thoughts clearly centered on their tall master. He continued to scorn the warmth of the group.

"Did he make a good profit?" Sprite asked nervously, but the joke fell flat.

"Why stop the tale there, Cleedis?" murmured the upright man's voice from the darkness. "There's so many little embellishments you've left out. Like how the king thought his queen was barren and wanted a son for his throne. How he raised the boy with care and the best of all things—until one day his wife *was* fruitful and bore him a son, and then three more over the years. That was three more than he needed and certainly better than an orphan boy."

The man brought his anger back to the fire and leaned close to share it with the others. Perhaps the old man didn't like his story shanghaied, or perhaps he could feel the pain in the other's voice. Whatever the reason, his joint-swollen fingers knotted painfully about his sword.

"Or how he drove his queen to death once she'd whelped heirs for him. And then one day the dear old man woke up and decided he didn't need the boy he'd taken in, the one who wasn't his seed. All his life, the boy had lived in luxury, expecting and waiting, only to be pushed out by a group of mewling brats. How about that, Cleedis?"

The rogue turned to the other three—short, plump, and broad—sitting like rigid stones in dumb silence.

Smoothly a smile expanded on the rogue's face, oil spreading across the storm of his emotion. The coiled tiger's spring eased from his frame, and with a cheerful bow he scooped up the wine jug. "Good story, eh? One's as true as another, and they're both as true as a vagabond's tale."

The three still sat nervous and quiet, vassals unable to fathom their master's mad caperings.

Pinch threw back the jug and drained a long swallow, quenching the wine-dark thirst deep inside him. He then flung the uncorked jug toward his gang. "Drink and sleep, that's what you need!" he thundered.

As they scrambled to catch the jug and stay wide of his moods, Pinch quickly settled close to his old fencing master till his wine-breath whisper tickled the old man's ear. "You need me or you'd not come this far. No more tales—"

"You're forgetting the priests, boy," the other growled, never once breaking his stare into the darkness.

"No more tales or you'll not wake up some morning. Do you think your guards can keep us away?"

Cleedis blinked. "If I'm dead, there's no profit for you. That's all you want, isn't it?" The old man quickly shifted the terms.

A contented sigh swelled in the rogue. "I'm sure you've got enemies in Ankhapur. Wouldn't they pay to see your head packed in a pickle pot?"

He didn't wait for an answer, but left the old man chewing his words. "To bed!" he thundered once more as he herded his accomplices to the small ring of tents that was their traveling home. With cheerful wariness, they swarmed to heed him.

In the fading firelight, Cleedis watched as his former student never once turned his back on his supposed friends. The old swordsman smiled—a cold, dark smile like the dead winter night around him.

* * * * *

For the next three days, there were no more tales; not even any talk. It didn't take years of familiarity to read Pinch's mood. Even the coarsest soldiers knew there was a sour gloom hanging around the man. He spoke only when necessary and then barely more than a grunt. He ate quietly and drank without sharing. Most ominous of all was that he abided every inconvenience—the trails reduced to slicks of mud and slush, the streams of thin-crusted ice, even the stinging blows of sleet—with an impassive stare into the wilderness beyond. To his friends, it seemed the memory of Ankhapur roused in him a furious anger, like some furious scorpion retreating into its lair. If that were the case, nobody wanted to jab him lest they get stung.

Sprite-Heels, who watched his old companion as closely as the rest, formed a different opinion, one that he kept to himself. The halfling knew Pinch better than anybody and sometimes he held the conceit that he understood Pinch better than Pinch himself. Sprite was

sure he could read the machinations in the old rogue's
eyes, could divide them into patterns and stages. First
the thief studied a guard, never one close to him, but
one who was detached and unaware of the rogue's
scrutiny. Sprite knew Pinch was finding the weaknesses, the passions, and the follies that the long ride
betrayed in each man: Who gambled and lost poorly;
who drank when he thought the captain wasn't looking;
who shirked his duties; who betrayed others. All these
things became Pinch's catalog of the levers by which he
could move the men, elves, and dwarves of their escort.

After six days, the party came to a way-house on the
southern road. It wasn't more than a rickety handful of
a house and outbuildings enclosed in a palisade of
sticks, but it offered protection from the icy sleet that
had pelted them all day. The riders were frozen through
to their bones. Even Cleedis, who by his station was
better equipped than any of them, was chilled to his
marrow. The horses were caked with mud and their
hooves skittered across the sleet-slicked ground. It had
been a painful lurching day in the saddle for everyone.
The prospect of an inn, even a barn, right there in front
of them, was a thousand times better than another
night sleeping on half-frozen mud and pine branches.

A boy splashed through the melting snow, shouting
out their arrival, so that by the time the Ankhapurans
reached the gate, a band of grooms and farmhands
faced them on the other side. The inn's staff was armed
with a smattering of spears, scythes, and flails, the
weapons of a ragtag militia. The signboard over the
closed gate creaked in the wind, announcing that this
was "The House of Pity."

"Where you be bound?" shouted one of the lot as he
struggled his way to the front.

"We are Lord Cleedis of Ankhapur and his escort,"
shouted back the captain of the guard, the one Pinch
knew was a brute to his men. "Who are you?"

"The landlord's cook," replied the cadaverously thin man who stepped to the front. He wore a greasy apron and carried a heavy cleaver, the uniform and tools of his trade.

"So much for the food," Therin whispered to Sprite.

"Well, open the gate, lackey, and give us a room for the night. My lord is not accustomed to waiting in the mud." The captain was flushed with impatience to be out of the foul weather.

With slow deliberation, the cook peered first into the woods on one side and then on the other, searching the shadows and the darkness for something. Finally he turned back to the captain. "Can you pay?"

"Can we pay?" the officer sputtered. "Pay depends on service, lout!"

Now the cook slowly, and again very deliberately, looked over the riders, counting out the number on his fingers. When he'd counted both hands, his face furrowed in concentration until at last he nudged the man next to him with over-broad secrecy. Heated whispers flew until at last the second fellow held up his own hand and the cook continued to count. The captain barely suppressed his rage at this dawdling.

"Twelve!" Pinch yelled out when the count was clearly above three hands.

The cook and groom paused, looked at their hands, looked up, looked back at their hands, and then very slowly and deliberately began the count again.

The captain twisted in his seat to glower at Pinch, and for the first time in nearly a week the rogue beamed a wickedly cheerful smile and stoically endured the icy discomfort.

Behind Pinch a chorus of snickers and snorts struggled not to break into a round of guffaws.

When the pair's count reached three hands, every eye of the cold and wet escort turned on Pinch. The rogue only nodded and smiled.

"Three!" chimed Sprite's high-pitched voice.

The count began again.

The guards edged in closer, this time watching all four vagabonds.

At two hands, Maeve could stand the ludicrousness no longer, and a hysterical cackle burst from her lips. It pealed down the wooded lane.

The count began again.

The captain wheeled his horse back through the mud. "If they say anything—" he paused in midsnarl, realizing he could not carry out a threat against his master's guests. "Well," he finally continued with teeth chattering, "don't let them!"

Now the guards, sensing a pattern, paid particular mind to Therin. The big Gur smiled back at their fixed scowls and pointedly kept his mouth closed. The count passed one hand and he did nothing. Maeve, Sprite, and Pinch waited to see what he would do.

Two hands.

Therin didn't say a word.

Three hands.

The big man beamed in calm silence.

Seventeen . . .

Eighteen . . .

Nineteen . . .

Therin stretched his arms in a broad yawn. The guards reacted with the singing steel of drawn swords. The rude militia splashed back from the palisade fearful of a fight.

The count began again.

Pinch, Sprite, Maeve, and Therin all looked at each other and smiled.

* * * * *

It was moonset before all the horses had their fetlocks washed, their coats curried, and their mangers filled with moldy hay. The soldiers plodded back into

the commons. Pinch and his crew came up last; in this,
like all things, the last of everything.

In a night the color of simmered wine, the sway-
backed inn breathed vaporous smoke from every crack
in its wooden skin. As the men slouch-shouldered their
way through the door, Therin drew off the last pair with
the tempting rattle of dice. If the guardsmen expected a
fair game, they didn't stand a chance; the Gur was a
sharper with the barred bones. A quiet corner in the
barn and a few hours of work would leave them poorer
but probably no wiser.

The chairs inside had all been claimed, the benches
overfilled with troopers. The small commons had little
space for a squadron of troopers, but the innkeeper still
managed to squeeze a few more customers into the
space. Unimaginably, one more table was found for the
three scoundrels. It barely fit at a corner in the back,
which was all to Pinch's liking.

"Sour beer's all that's left," the landlord said, more as
defense than apology. The spare man sloshed a kettle of
brew onto the table, a stump-footed little creature of
tin. Cold scraps and stale bread were the only choices
left for dinner.

As they ate, the senior rogue let his eyes wander lest he
notice the poor pickings before him. Since he was bored
with the study of guardsmen, whose lives offered no imag-
ination, Pinch concentrated on the non-Ankhapurans in
the hall, a whole two tables' worth. It was clear from their
seating—one table near the door, the other by the fire—
that the two groups traveled apart. Those by the door
Pinch had seen when he first arrived. The other party
could only have arrived while he was stabling his mount.

There was a worth in studying the other guests,
after all. If any were wealthy, there was always profit to
be had in visiting their rooms before the dawn.

The two men seated near the door were garbed in
hard-used traveling clothes, the type favored by old

hands at the caravan trade—long riding cloaks water-proofed with sheep fat, warm doublets colored with the dried salts of sweat, and thick-sided boots stuccoed with yellow mud. Practical clothes for practical men with no obvious vanities that would mark them as good coneys to be snared.

The men themselves were as hard as their clothes. The first, who always kept an eye to the door, Pinch dubbed the Ox. He was huge, with a belly that rolled out beneath his doublet and quivered with any shift of his frame. The trembling flesh ill-concealed the massive muscles of the man, though. Every time he reached for the capon that sat on the table between the two men, his swollen biceps threatened to burst the stitching of his doublet's seams. Though his face was clean shaven, it was nearly obscured by a wild mass of hair that hung in snarls and tangles.

The other man Pinch quickly dubbed the Lance—the Ox and the Lance, they were. The Lance was no more slender than Therin, though his shaved head made him look thinner. What truly distinguished him was that every move was a sharp strike using the minimum of effort for the maximum of gain. The Lance didn't tear at the capon, he dissected the choice meats from it with complacent ease.

It wasn't their dress or their frames that raised a caution in the rogue, though. There was a way about them that only those in the trade, for good or ill, would recognize. The way one always watched the door while the other discretely scanned the room; the way neither let both hands be filled at once; the way they held themselves on their chairs.

"Maeve, Sprite," Pinch whispered as he casually tore at a chunk of bread, "those two, what do you make of them? Hellriders?"

The halfling feigned a stretch as he leaned back to get a better look at them. "In disguise and come this far? Not likely."

Maeve set down her drink. "Hellriders is mean ones, Pinch, but I ain't never heard of them coming after someone on the road."

"Maybe not." The rogue stroked the rim of his mug. "Can you read them, Maeve?"

"Here? With all these people?"

Her leader nodded.

The wizard rolled her eyes in exasperation. "It ain't wise to use powers when you might get caught."

"Maeve, you know you won't. You're too good," Pinch flattered.

The woman harrumphed but was already digging out the material she needed. Pinch and Sprite pulled their chairs close to screen her from the others. The mystic words were a chanted whisper, the gestures minute tracings in the air. An onlooker would have thought her no more than a person distracted by her own inner dreams.

Without really looking at them, Maeve turned her unblinking gaze on the two men. This was riskiest part of the process, Pinch knew. A stranger staring at you the way Maeve did was always cause for a fight. When at last she blinked, Pinch was just as happy no one had noticed.

"You've got them dead on, Pinch. They're in the trade and none too happy tonight." Maeve smiled as she turned back to her dinner. "Got their nerves up, what with a room full of our handsome escorts. Don't know what they make of us, but they've set their eyes to the other company here. Ain't no more but some terrible thoughts I won't say in public."

Sprite sniggered. "Wouldn't have been on you now, would they? Or was you just hoping?"

Brown Maeve swiveled away from the halfling with a snap of her greasy, unwashed hair.

"Heel your dog, Sprite-Heels," Pinch rumbled. "You're none too sweet scented yourself.

"Maeve, pay this ingrate no mind. Those that count know your quality." Pinch put a soothing hand on Maeve's shoulder. "Now, dear Maeve, can you read me the other table?"

Her face a sulky pout, Maeve let her blank gaze wash for a moment toward Pinch, only to be warned off by the fierceness of his glare, shadowed by the curve of his tender smile.

"The other table, Maeve," he directed.

The witch-woman sighed and lolled her gaze where he nodded.

Meanwhile the old rogue studied their target. It was a small table by the fire, where sat a lone traveler, unusual enough in a countryside where few traveled alone. That wasn't the least of it, either, for the traveler was a woman—not unheard of, but just that much more distinguishing. The inn was in the land between lands, an area just beyond the reach of anyone who could claim it, and thus had been laid claim to by highwaymen and beasts of ill renown. The lone traveler who stumbled into this void was prey for any stronger ravager.

Ergo, Pinch reasoned, this lone woman was not weak, but possibly foolish.

"She's saying her words over dinner," Maeve puzzled out.

"Invoking what church? And what's her business?"

The sorceress stared owl-like before giving up with a sigh. "No good, that is, Master Pinch. She's got a most fixed mind. What only I got was an image of her roast chick and the thanks to some faceless power. Kept seeing it as a glowing orb, she did."

"Sound like any you know, Sprite?"

The little halfling's grasp of odd facts was a surprising source of answers. If he knew, it wouldn't be the first time he'd remembered some chestnut of useless lore to their mutual benefit.

This time Sprite-Heels shrugged. "Could be any

number of trifling sun gods, let alone the big ones like Mask or the Faceless Ones."

Pinch leaned forward and looked at the woman with false disinterest. "What about that temple we did?" he asked softly.

"Not from what Maeve said. Scared, Pinch? She's probably just some wandering nun, set herself to doing good deeds on the road."

The human rapped his mug against the table in irritation. "She's more than that."

"He's right, you nasty little Sprite," Brown Maeve crowed. "She's tougher than some gentry mort. Got that from her, for certain."

"What more can you do, Maeve?"

Pinch was answered with a resigned slump. "No more, love. Spell's all spent."

Sprite, trying to restore himself to the pair's good graces, offered, "I could pinch her, see what we'd learn."

Her clothes were commonplace, sturdy, dusty, and dull, the mark of one with much sense but little coin. Pinch shook his head. "I'll not be your snap for the strike, halfling. Not worth getting caught. Have you forgot the rules? Never lay your coin on a lean horse or—"

"—your knife to an empty bung," Sprite finished. "I know the old rules. I just though it would help."

"Ain't you two just the pair. Worried you're being hunted and worried you'll get caught when here we are out where there ain't nobody and nothing! Not that we ain't got enough worries, what with your Lord Cleedis and all his soldiers, or do you two need to go searching for more?" Maeve snapped her words at them and then punctuated her tirade with a stiff drink. "One night in a decent place to sleep and all you pair do is peer at every stranger and guess which one's going to gut you. I'm telling you—you, Sprite-Heels, and you Master Pinch— to just quit peering under the bed sheets and drink!"

Both men, human and halfling, stared at her in surprise, thrown from their horses by her outburst. They looked at her; they looked at each other. There was nothing they could do but take up their mugs and drink until there was no more.

They drank until Therin reappeared with a purse full of extra coin and tales of how he cogged the dice to assure his wins. They drank some more to Therin's good luck, as if the Lady had any chance of swaying the Gur's dice. They drank until Sprite slid beneath the table and the innkeeper closed them down. Just in case, they took an extra skin upstairs, carrying it with more care than they carried Sprite-Heels, who had all the un-conscious dignity of a sack of potatoes.

When the guards roused them before the too-early dawn, the four lurched down the stairs, their heads thick as mustard. They paled at the offering of bread smeared with bacon grease, and hurried themselves outside to gulp the farm-fresh air. It did little good ex-cept remind them of how miserable they felt. Trembly weak, they fitted the bits and saddled their mounts and unwillingly seated themselves for the day's ride. Even through all this, even though his eyes never quite fo-cused and his head wouldn't stop throbbing, Pinch no-ticed last night's guests—Ox, Lance, and woman—were gone already. He wondered if each had gone a different route. The woman didn't matter, since she was not likely to see them again.

When all was ready, the troop, twenty-strong, plod-ded down the yellow-mud lane, lurching on their fresh mounts, until they overwhelmed the little track. Flanked by old tress that played father to stands of lush brambles, the group set out on the day's ride. Whether it was by word from the commander or just wicked luck, the trail was jolting and steep, rising and falling over gullies and streambeds. Every bounce re-minded Pinch of just how miserable he felt.

"Don't you wonder where that priestess went?" Sprite

asked with a cheerfulness that matched his name. Of the four, somehow the halfling was the only one unfazed by hangover; it was probably something to do with the runt's liver, most likely that it was a pure sponge. "Which way do you think, Pinch?" he pressed, though he knew full well the others could scarcely focus.

Pinch tried his fiercest glower which, right now, looked more like a pained squint. "What am I—a woodsman? Who knows in this muddy waste? Now shut up before I box you!" The rising tone of his own voice made the rogue flinch.

Snickering, Sprite-Heels whipped the pony he and Maeve shared safely out of the man's reach.

The ride continued, cold, wet, dull, and aching, through the morning and well into the afternoon. At one point, where the trail ran along a cut arched over with leafless elms and dead-gray vines, something coughed beastlike and the winter-dead branches rustled. The troop had to stop while a group of unfortunate soldiers slowly flanked the cut and beat the brush. Nothing came of it, but it delayed them an hour during which no one dared relax.

Perhaps it was that false alarm that caused them to almost blunder into a fight. The captain had given over command to a sergeant while he rode with Lord Cleedis to curry favor. The sergeant, in turn, was too busy with his flunkies to notice that the outriders were no longer so far out and the whole troop had closed into one small bunch. It was a bad way to travel, where one fireball could wipe them all out.

Thus it was that there was no one on point to shout " 'Ware!" when the soldiers slogged around the bend and straight into the midst of a battle. Right where the trail shored the bank of a half-frozen river, a ring of eight mud-splashed men—and then in a flash only seven—awkwardly stalked a single adversary. Armed with bills, hooks, and flails, the seven lunged with the stoop-shouldered awkwardness of peasants. Only one fought with any grace, so much that it took Pinch no time to recognize the Lance. Finding the swordsman, Pinch easily found the Ox.

The troopers were on top of the men before either side even knew it, the lead horseman splitting the ragged battle line from behind. The distance was to the footmen's advantage. A wild shriek tore from the lips of the nearest, and before the rider could throw down his useless lance, the billman swung his great poleaxe at the man. The blade scored the horse's neck, the beast reared and kicked, and ungoverned confusion erupted in the ranks. The closeness of the lane prevented any maneuver. The first man was thrown from his horse, and the panicked beast wheeled to gallop back down the lane. Almost immediately it crashed into the front rank of the troop, too close to part. Two more men and a horse foundered while a bloodthirsty war cry rattled the forest's dead leaves. The peasant bandits, for their dress of motley proclaimed them as such, sprang upon the fallen outrider, broad blades glinting wintry in the sun.

With their great polearms held over their shoulders like battering logs, two footmen rushed the broken line, casting more confusion ahead of them. The sergeant screamed orders, the captain screamed, Cleedis screamed, the dying men and horses screamed all at once and all at cross purposes. The twenty horsemen were already down by almost a quarter and showed no signs of turning the tide. Panic was in their ranks as the front crashed into the back, desperate to escape the hordes of murdering berserkers just behind them.

Equally desperate, Pinch tried to ride his own horse free of the mass, beating it toward the woods when a howling, mud-smeared bandit crashed out of the thicket dead ahead of him. With a shrill whinny, the mount reared. As the rogue flew off backward, he heard the popping crack when hoof smote his attacker's skull.

The churned mud cushioned Pinch's landing so that he kept his breath, but the man barely had time to slither out of the path of a galloping trooper. Struggling up, Pinch was immediately knocked flat by the charging flank of another horse.

"HUAAAA!" shrieked a man as he leapt forward to straddle the fallen rogue while whirling a poleaxe over his head.

I'm saved! I'm dead! Pinch couldn't tell which until the axe tore out the belly of a passing rider. While the bandit yanked to wrench his weapon free, the rogue drew the handle of his mucky dagger and without hesitation drove it upward into the soft gap at the belly of the man's ill-fitting brigandine armor. The man, all wide eyes and bearded slack jaw spitting blood, squealed in horror until the weight of the still-hooked rider pulled him over.

That was enough for Pinch. Dagger clenched in a clawlike hand, he scrambled blindly through the blood and slime for safety, dodging the flailing hooves of dying horses, stepping on soft things that he really didn't want to know about. He wasn't a soldier accustomed to battle and wasn't ready to become one, but each time one of the dirty highpads lunged in front of him the thief lashed out. He struck with all the wicked expertise of his knife-fighting, his anger and fury growing with each blow. "Cyric take you, you poxy bastard! Let 'em play hob with your skull in Hades!" He lashed invective as wickedly as he did his knife.

At the height of his rage, Pinch crashed onto the river and through the thin ice. The swift-moving water shocked up to his thighs, burning out of him the madness but not the killing passion. The blindness that had animated him was gone, and he could see the whole battle once again. The soldiers, finally rallied from their initial panic, were attacking in a dressed line, prancing their horses over the fallen bodies. Now it was the bandits' turn to panic, their previous discipline a fraud unmasked by the conflict of desire to loot and fear of death. Within moments the lot would break and run.

A squeal up the bank pulled Pinch's attention to the cause of this fracas. The lone traveler, who he knew was the priestess without having to see it, lay sprawled on the shingles of shore ice, her shoulder pricked by the blade the Lance held to her. Behind her the Ox lumbered up with a great, jagged 'berg in full press over his head, ready to deliver the *coup de grace*.

If he had been less passioned or there had been more time for thought, Pinch surely would have acted differently, considering his own self-interest before all. Instead, against all his sense, he reacted. With a snap, his long dirk flew from his hand and buried itself in the throat of the Ox. Croaking from his shattered windpipe, the fat-swaddled giant jerked up and back until the weight of the ice block he still carried over his head bore the man backward. With two staggered steps he cracked through the frozen riverbank and toppled into the fast-flowing water. The flow churned as it sucked the floundering man away.

The Lance goggled in surprise, which was the more his mistake. Though pricked, the traveler was not pinned. As the Lance hung in indecision between the woman and the menacingly slow advance of Pinch, the choice was taken from him. The mace in her hand lashed out, breaking across his knee. The leg popped out at an unnatural angle and, deprived of his underpinning, the Lance keeled to the side. She struck again, driving the iron into his padded gut hard enough to change his trajectory. The Lance hit the icy stones with an awful crack, jerked, and then didn't move again.

Cold, sweaty, and panting, Pinch stumbled across the ice to the woman's side. With a dripping boot, he gave the Lance a shove; the body rolled almost completely over before it twisted, the head along with it.

"May Kelimvore grant him swift justice," the woman intoned as she slowly got to her feet. A trickle of blood ran down her arm, another swath coated her face.

"More concern than he deserved," Pinch snarled. Remembering where they were, he looked about for more attackers but the battle was all but won. The bandits had broken and foolishly fled, and now they were the helpless prey of the faster riders. Here, in the land between lands laid claim to by bandits such as these, Cleedis's men showed no mercy. They were the law and they had friends to avenge.

"I'm Lissa of the Morninglord's Temple in Elturel. I think it would be right to say you saved my life."

At the mention of her temple, Pinch felt the rise of paranoia in his craw. There could be only one reason why a priestess of Lathander would be this far south, on this particular trail. She must surely be looking for the thieves who desecrated her temple. "A pleasure, surely, to meet you under better circumstance." Pinch paused to take a steadying breath and consider just what to say next. Certainly "Pinch" was not a good name to use at a moment like this. There was every chance she was familiar with the criminal element of Elturel. Finally, he put on his most valiant smile and, while leading her back to the trail, said what he never thought he would freely tell anyone. "I'm—Janol, ward of the late King Manferic of Ankhapur."

"Indeed!" The priestess was impressed.

"Why do you travel such dangerous land alone?" Pinch pressed the question while her thoughts were still unsettled.

"I'm searching for a thief, a scoundrel who robbed our temple," she confided.

Pinch smiled inwardly to himself. She'd revealed more than she should have and enough to give him her game. "What base villainy! On this road, bound for Ankhapur?" They stopped at a fallen log and Pinch began to examine her wounds.

The priestess winced as her rescuer prodded her shoulder, feeling the pain of his touch even through the armor she wore. Seeing the effect, Pinch poked her a little harder as she spoke, just to keep her unsteady.

"There was word the thief might flee south and sell his treasures there. Our proctor sent us, one to each road. I drew Ankhapur."

Pinch turned his attention to her scalp. A graze ran across the hairline, hardly serious but bleeding heavily like wounds to the head would. "You suspect us?" Pinch gave the words just a tinge of offended nobility.

"Certainly not, lord," Lissa hurriedly assured while the rogue wrapped a muddy cloth around her forehead.

As he dressed her wounds, Pinch considered just killing her and having done with it. Her dead body here would be no more than another, but with her suspicions lulled, it seemed a waste. Better to keep her around and uninformed, in case she proved useful someday.

Choosing an appropriately bold shyness, Pinch said, "This thief, if he is in Ankhapur, may be hard to find. If you should need some help, you must let me know. A king's ward does have some influence, after all."

Lissa flushed a little at the imagined generosity of the offer. "Again, thank you, my lord."

"This is nothing, priestess. But one last word of advice. Tell no one what you have told me." Pinch whispered the words in soft conspiracy as the riders slowly returned. "Indeed, you should not have told me. This is best as our secret, lest your quarry grow scared."

The priestess scooped a little handful of water from a muddy footprint and tried to wash the blood from her face. "Of course you're right. I've been foolish. Thank you, Lord Janol."

"Just Janol. I'm only the king's ward, not one of his blood. Now, I've a friend named Maeve. Let's see if she can properly tend to you."

A Shortcut

Cleedis did not welcome the news of an additional traveling companion.

"The woman is no concern of mine," he huffed, after pointing out that eight of his men were dead because of meeting her. The miserable performance of his troopers had stung the old warrior's pride, and he had already given the captain a blistering rating over the shabby performance of the company. All failure lay upon the officer, in Cleedis's mind—failure to drill them properly, failure to stem the rout, failure to issue clear orders, failure to grasp the basics of tactics, even a failure of will. Cleedis ignored his own contribution to the debacle and ignored the indignant captain's fuming efforts to point it out.

Given the losses, Cleedis was at least wise enough to lay no blame on the men. The captain was beside himself with rage and at one point came to the brink of offering

up his commission that he had paid so dearly for, an offer
Cleedis would no doubt have taken on the spot.

Pinch was for the woman, and his firmness was aided
by the cool moral strength that comes after the rush of
battle. While the two argued, Lissa knelt beside a
trooper who'd taken an axe blow just above the knee. His
tentmates were certain the leg could not be saved and
were fretting over whether to finish the amputation with
a clean blow or bind him and hope that shock and gangrene didn't set in before they reached civilization.

The priestess ended the debate with sharp orders to
hold the man down, orders given in the tone a soldier
was conditioned to obey.

They pressed him flat in the bloody mud, two men
holding his shoulders while a third sat on his kicking
legs and ignored his screams. While the patient writhed
in their grasp, Lissa laid her hands on his gaping
wound, closed her eyes, and prayed. Within moments
the gash was gone and the trembling pain passed from
the man. His screams gave way to murmurs as he
lapsed into blissful sleep.

After that, there was no question that Lissa would
ride with the company.

The priestess healed all she could while the soldiers
buried their dead, for whom there was no help. Pinch
warned off Sprite from rifling their pockets by pointing
out that the troopers would surely spit the little halfling if
they caught him at it. "And I'll let them," the upright man
added. "Get your booty from those two high lawyers."

"Waste of time—after all *they* was robbing her," the
halfling groused while looting Ox and Lance. The slim
pickings he got—a ring, two wallets, and a necklace—
were commandeered by the troop sergeant.

"Pensions for the dead men's wives, you thieving ter-
rier," said the windburned sergeant, as shallow a lie as
any the halfling could have put up.

After fumbling and grousing about certain overzealous hypocrites, Sprite gave up his booty. Still, when the halfling rejoined Pinch, Therin, and Maeve, his face was a bubble of unsuppressed glee. "What gulls! I could dine off them for weeks," he chortled. With a quick nod to his hand, the little rogue flashed a fistful of cut stones and worn coins. "Didn't think I'd let him have it all, did you?"

"Then we'll divvy up tonight," Pinch stated, as coolly matter-of-fact as if he'd just done the job. "Square splits for all." The other two, sorceress and bravo, nodded their agreement.

Sprite-Heels scowled but nodded too. He had better sense than to cross his partners so openly. "Tonight then," he muttered before scurrying away.

"Maeve—"

"I'll keep an eye on him," the witch assured before Pinch could finish his words. Slip-slopping through the mire, she was already falling in behind the halfling, her voice wheezing from the effort of talking while she rushed after. "Sprite, hold slow for me, dearie . . ."

Pinch watched the pair weave through the scattered packs of men, Sprite poking what he shouldn't at every chance. They played the roles they had played in many a throng, that of mother and child, old Corruption's family.

Then the cold-shock settled onto Pinch. The wet, the chill, and the grime stroked his bones with their ferocious touch and drew their cruel pale to his skin. Two troopers, one a pock-faced veteran who had spent his years raising malingering to a substantial art, the other a bull with a broad, flat nose smashed in a tavern brawl, had stoked up a fire for drinks, as troopers will do given any short stop. Pinch took Therin by the arm and led him toward the growing blaze.

"Pinch, what about her?" Therin whispered with a quick tilt of the brow toward the only woman at the circle—Lissa the priestess, already favored with a seat in the troopers' midst.

"We don't panic," the regulator whispered back,

cheek to cheek.

Therin turned himself away, conspicuously trying to avoid her notice. "I saw her sign when she was working spells! She's one of the temple—"

"Stay that!" Pinch hissed. He pulled the man back around and pushed him forward.

The big rogue stumbled a little step forward and stopped. "But what's she doing here?" Therin's whisper was filling with panic.

"She's looking for a thief." The dig of an elbow got Therin moving again so that his terrified stare was not so obvious.

"Damned gods, she's made us!" he blurted. "You go first, Pinch."

"Stow it and get going, you fool. She's not made me, you, or anybody. The temple's sent out patricos to watch every road out of Elturel. She's fishing and, by damn, I'm setting her to the wrong catch."

"Uncle said, 'Never rob a temple.' Too many people get too interested. Get myself hanged all again, I will—"

"I told you to stow it, so clamp your flapping lips and play a dumb show." Pinch hissed one last time as he pulled Therin toward the camp circle. The old rogue couldn't stand such whining. Their lives were their lives, not given to them, not chosen for them. Therin had chosen to be a high lawyer and a rogue, and right now that meant taking the dues in full.

I won't snivel so, Pinch scornfully reminded himself, *not while there are other choices to be made.*

"Now let's get warmed up before we freeze." There was no bother to wait for an answer. The rogue sent Therin stumbling into the bunch with a firm shove from behind.

The cold shivers of the group, the tight banter of near death, and the swallowed scent of blood were an effective disguise for the pair. Nobody sat comfortably around the fire, so there was nothing to note when Therin sat himself opposite the priestess and tried to stare at her without staring from across the flames.

Cleedis didn't waste time with orders to bury the
highwaymen. His men heaved the bodies into the
brush, far from the stream, where their decay wouldn't
pollute the water. The burials of their own, dug down
into the muddy half-frozen soil, were ceremonies of brutal custom—the wrapping of the body, the sergeant's
words, the file-by of those who lived—all done by pas-
sionless drill.

The work done, Cleedis came by the fire and stood in
the sputtering warmth from the too-wet wood. His fur-
lined robes were hitched up above the muck so that he
was nothing more than a grotesque mushroom, a stem
of two feeble legs that tottered under the bulging top of
thick winter robes. "Put it out. We're leaving."

Cloaking their irritation behind dutiful yes-sirs, the
two guards set to packing their kits. Therin, proudly
clinging to the image that he was uncommandable, tore
his gaze from the priestess. "Now? You've already
wasted your light. You won't get a mile before dark."

"We're leaving. There may be more bandits about,
but you can stay if you want," Cleedis offered, his hands
spread in willingness.

"You best come with us, miss," said one of the two
troopers, who'd been goldbricking till now. The pock-
faced veteran touched his eye in a sign to ward off evil.
"There's unblessed dead here and evil they was, to be
sure. Ain't wise to sleep near 'em, what with them so
recent killed. Sure to know they'll come for live folks in
the night. 'Course, you being a priestess and all, this
ain't no puzzle to you."

"Tyr's truth to all that," murmured his flat-nosed
companion.

"Quit stalling, you two!" boomed the sergeant's baritone from across the glade. "Lord Cleedis wants us on
the trail now, so get your arses in your saddles, if it
would not be too much effort, gentlemen!"

With a flick of his thumb, Therin went off to get their horses.

"Get to work," bossed the pock-faced fellow when his companion gawked dully. The veteran reinforced the words with a kick of mud in the other's direction. While the flat-nosed fellow juggled the still-scorching pots into his haversack, the veteran snapped off his own rude gesture as soon as the sergeant's back was turned.

"Prig-faced jackass."

"Lost his sense of the trooper's life, has he?" Pinch's question hung with the air of casual conversation.

The veteran's wary weather eye, sensing the gray front coming, fixed on the rogue. "He's well enough, and a damn stretch better than you, magpie."

The words slid off Pinch's well-oiled conscience. "Least I don't make others dance to my jig."

"That may be and that may not. Your friends don't ride too far from you." Therin slogged back through the slush, leading two horses by their jingling reins.

"Only fools split their strength in the camp of the enemy." With a middle-aged man's grunt, Pinch got one foot into the stirrup and swung himself into the saddle. A snap of the reins moved him away from the fire.

"What was that all about?" the younger thief puzzled as he trotted up beside.

"Salt in the wounds and oil on the water, my aide-de-camp." The old fox grinned. "Never miss a chance to rile them up and make them think you're on their side. Right now he's testy, but maybe by Ankhapur that horse soldier won't snap back so hard."

Therin saw the message. "Friends in the right places, eh?"

"Friends in all places, boy," the master corrected as the troop fell into line. With a wink and a nod to his lieutenant, Pinch reined up his horse alongside the priestess Lissa.

"Greetings, Lord Janol." Her eyes, previously open,

were now wary.

"And to you, milady." Pinch bowed in his saddle. Years of tutoring in courtly manners had not all been a waste.

"Thank you again for saving my life." Although she could not be but grateful, her words lacked conviction. They were the pleasant hedge of small talk behind which she could hide her true convictions.

"What else could I do?"

"I could have been a criminal and they the innocents." The mask of suspicion was beginning to slip from her eyes.

Pinch smiled and shifted in his saddle, trying to find comfort for his sore legs. "I'm a quick judge of character."

Perhaps he answered too glibly, for the words stung. The hint of Lissa's smile, almost visible in the torch-flicker shadows, collapsed. "I'm learning to be one," the priestess announced.

"I've noticed, Lord Janol, that they do not treat you with the respect due a peer," Lissa continued. Pinch had let slip the advantage in their volley and the woman was quick to seize on it.

"Prisoners seldom are so treated."

The priestess's eyes narrowed. Without shame she asked, "A prisoner . . . for the crime of—"

"Inconvenience."

Pinch had to continue before his unwitting pursuer could form deductions of her own. "Too much popularity, and too little of it with the right group of people. Leaving Ankhapur was expedient, just as coming back now seems . . . prudent."

The rogue was lying extemporaneously, an unfair advantage he had over her.

* * * * *

It went as Therin had said.

In less than a mile the sun, bleeding orange, was all but screened out by the winter-barren trees. Dusk held sway briefly in the sky before vanishing into the reach of night. Winter owls and wild dogs paced them through the darkness, chasing down the mice and rabbits that bolted from the clattering horse hooves. Other things marked their passing too, with grunts of humanlike bestiality that were passed down the line of march. Torchlight brightly reflected creatures with eyes too many or too few. The clatter of steel sent them scurrying away.

It was only after hours of night riding that Lord Cleedis signaled a halt. The troopers hurled themselves to the cold, wet ground until the sergeant came by and pressed them to their duties with the hard application of his boot. With much grumbling and reluctance, the tents were pitched, double guards posted, and cold meals prepared. Pinch, Therin, and the others avoided all details and collapsed in their tents as soon as they were pitched.

For three more days the squadron rode, Cleedis holding the riders to a steady pace. Three more men were lost to a catoblepas, a beast so vile its mere look could kill. It had ranged out of the great swamp to the south in search of food. That battle had been sharp and dangerous, and seeing as there was no profit in it, Pinch and his gang had kept well back from the beast's horrifying visage.

The old rogue was concerned, though he kept his counsel to himself. Ankhapur was months away, across a great stretch of wilderness where beasts far worse than the catoblepas were far more common. They'd barely ridden the smallest portion of that distance and already eleven out of the twenty troopers had been lost. The odds seemed strong to Pinch that he and the others would be stranded well out in the wasteland without the protection of men and weapons. Could it be that Cleedis, empty without Manferic to serve, was embarked on a mad effort to lead Pinch to his doom? It wasn't impossible. In his years, the rogue had certainly heard of stranger passions—the wizard who built a magical prison just to tor-

ment his unfaithful wife or the war captain who led his
entire company into Raurin, the Dust Desert, to do
battle with the sand. Word was, in the stews of Elturel,
the soldier destroyed his company just to avenge an insult. It was madness like this, beyond all norm, that
Pinch worried about. Cleedis was old and had never had
the wit of a great wizard or statesman.

And then Cleedis called the march to a halt, stopping
his dwindling command at the edge of the woods, where
the trees abruptly gave way to a brown, dry meadow of
winter-burned grass. Even though there was still a good
half day's light, a commodity precious in the shortness of
the days, the sergeant bellowed out the camping drill
command. The sergeant played the role of martinet ex-
tremely well, abiding no goldbricking from his men.
Pinch and his companion were thankful for the cold effi-
ciency of the squadron, since it spared them any labor.

"Pitch your tents, boys. I want a detail of five men to
gather firewood—remember, two men on guard at all
times. Troopers Hervis, Klind—get your bows. Bag
some fresh meat for the whole camp."

The rogues couldn't help notice the reaction of the
troopers to this announcement, more than just delight
at the reprieve from stale rations. Never before had the
sergeant sent out a hunting detail.

The three men stomped in the mud, hugger-mugger,
while Maeve stayed in her saddle. "New business, this
is." Sprite Heels punctuated his observation by spitting
into a lump of melting snow.

"Aye." There was nothing much to say about it. Pinch
spied Cleedis nearby, struggling to read something from
an unruly scroll of parchment. The sheet would curl
every time he let go of the bottom to trace out a line.

Catching the page, Pinch pulled it tight. "Why camp
now, good lord?" the rogue asked bitingly. Looking over
the top, he noted the scroll was a scrawled grid of suns,
moons, stars, and seasons.

"What day is this?" Cleedis grumbled as he battled the ever-curling sheet.

Pinch felt annoyed at being ignored so clumsily. It wasn't that he hadn't been ignored before. His stock-in-trade was to pass unseen under the eyes of those who had good cause to watch for the likes of him. But it was his choice now to be seen and heard. He, the master regulator of Elturel, was important, and it wasn't even a lord chamberlain's place to forget it. Pinch hadn't come looking for Cleedis; Cleedis had come this far just for him, so the old man had no right pretending he didn't matter.

With less than good grace, the rogue pulled aside the scroll with a brusqueness certain to get his escort's attention and repeated, "Why are we camping? Ankhapur is months away, and I for one don't want to dally out here as your invited guest."

The chamberlain did something with his face, and his beard swelled to the proportions of an irate porcupine. "We're stopped because it's not the right day and we'll stay stopped until it is. You're so clever, Master Pinch, that I thought you'd have the sense to see I didn't waste my days trekking through this uncivilized land. It would have taken the whole bodyguard of Ankhapur to make the distance and months more than I've got. We're waiting for an appointment to be kept. By my calendar, tomorrow is the first of Nightal. On that particular day, at a particular hour, certain wizards in Ankhapur, still loyal to Lord Manferic's memory, will gather and cast a spell. When they do, on this spot at that time will be our way back home—without hiking or riding that whole distance.

"Now who's so clever?" Cleedis trumpeted as he bundled the scroll and thrust it under his arm.

I am, Pinch thought to himself as the man stormed away. You need me in Ankhapur more urgently than it seemed, enough to make the wizards send a whole troop across the continent to find me. Pinch didn't say a thing but shrugged like a man outsmarted and went away.

Lissa had joined their little knot by the time Pinch returned. In the days since their first meeting, he had carefully cultivated his relationship with her. Her awe at his
position as Lord Janol hadn't hurt, and he carefully
played on it. She was, to his mind, usefully naive, apparently unable to impute base thievery to anyone of rank.
Thus, his careful suggestions that Cleedis was suspect
were met with amazed acceptance. She behaved as if the
veil had been lifted from her eyes, yet all the time Pinch
was obscuring her target even more.

It had taken a little more art to explain away his
gang to her satisfaction. They hardly met the image of
suitable servants. Pinch could hardly present himself
as wise and trustworthy if he employed such a crew of
ingrates, unthrifts, and rinse pitchers as Therin, Sprite,
and Maeve. Maeve would get drunk and confide something completely beyond the pale of any household
cook. Therin, though a good lieutenant, was too proud
to play the role without bristling. And Sprite-Heels—
well, he might play along for a while, but only if he
could ruin it with some disastrous prank.

Instead Pinch took a tack not too far from the truth.
He was, the rogue explained, the once-wastrel ward now
destined to be redeemed and reformed. Still, Pinch
claimed, he could not surrender old companions without
remorse, no matter how vile and fallen they had become.
These few companions had stayed steadfast friends
through his darkest days. For him to abandon them now,
simply because he had regained the proper sense of his
true class, was the height of callousness. He owed them
and so was bringing them home where he might bestow
on them small pensions for the rest of their years.

As tales went, it had just enough pathos and honor
in it to appeal to the young priestess. Pinch was just,
the meek were raised, and the proper order of the world
had been restored. Still, the rogue couldn't resist

adding a fillip: Cleedis was the villain, albeit not a
grand one. The old campaigner was the shadow of
Pinch's enemies, those who might not want him in
Ankhapur alive. The lean shark didn't press the idea,
even allowing as how he might be mistaken, but let the
suggestion float through his tale.

The woman listened with a disdainfully worldly finger to her nose, dismissing most of what her traveling
companion said. She was not so naive, contrary to what
the youthful brightness of her face proclaimed. When
she snorted at his claims or poked at her cheek with her
tongue, the senior rogue pretended not to notice any
more than a suitor would his paramour's sour moods.
Pinch didn't expect her to believe the whole story, indeed she didn't need to believe any of it. She needed to
doubt her suspicions, whether it was because she was
naive or just entertained.

All that didn't matter anymore. She'd have to find
her own way to Ankhapur now. Cleedis's arrangements
were at least going to remove one gnawing worry.

"We've stopped." It was a cool observation, not profound but as if she held Pinch somehow responsible.

"The venerable's given orders to camp. I think he in-
tends a rendezvous."

"Ah?" It was one of her favorite expressions.

"Arranged with the court wizards of Ankhapur, I'd
guess."

"Ah." Without more comment, Lissa strode through
the mud, intent on catching up with Cleedis. Pinch was
about to follow when his attention was snagged by the
raised squeal of an enraged halfling.

"Put me down! It's not my fault you lost!"

The halfling was dangling by his arms at eye level with
a swarthy trooper, so close he could have licked the man's
grubby nose. "Let's see yer dice," slurred Sprite's captor.

Pinch sloshed casually through the mud, picking his
way through the sudden clot of onlookers. He took his time,

curious to see if Sprite just might lick the man's nose.

"It's not my doing you lost the hazard. How could I say I'd throw a bale of deuces? It's just bad luck and you're not taking it well!" the hanging thief protested.

"Pigsy luck, indeed. When it's 'Let's play for drinks,' he throws a whole set and never makes a point—"

"There, you see, just luck!" the halfling kicked and squawked.

"But nows it's 'Lets play for coin' and he can't lose. Play for my coin maybe. I'll be wishing . . . you'll be wishing you was wishing you was playing somewhere-body else." The drunken trooper tried to unmangle his meaning while he groped for the purse at Sprite's waist. "Lemme see them dice and then maybe I'll gut you—"

Darkness slid forward and dealt the man a sharp rap across his fumbling fingers.

"Maybe you want to gut me, too."

The trooper looked at the bright-bladed dirk that hovered just over his hand, slithering to and fro in Pinch's shifting grasp. It was a snake, violently coiled and tempting the other to foolishness.

"Set him down and go, before I tell Cleedis you were boozing on duty."

Fear-drunk eyes darted to his fellows for support, but he had gone invisible before their gaze. Suddenly, the soldier knew where he stood: alone, wet, and dirty in the beech wood. Something unholy hacked out an asthmatic howl just across the stream, a howl that almost shaped hungry words of welcome.

Slowly the man set the halfling down.

A pointed flick of the dirk sent the man scurrying, and without him the crowd drifted away to jeer his cowardice. Already the stinging puns and cruel poesy were forming in their minds.

"YOU," Pinch intoned while snagging Sprite before he disappeared, "give me the dice."

Sprite fumbled in his shirt and produced the pair.

Pinch didn't even ask if they were loaded. There was only one answer.

"Get to the tent."

"What's this, Pinch? Since when would you be knocking in fear from these king's men?"

The rogue answered the challenge by shoving the runt forward. "It's time for a little talk," he whispered through clenched teeth.

The tone was enough to get Sprite doing what he was told. The two squeezed into the small tent where Therin and Maeve were chatting, squatted on the ground.

"Listen well." Pinch thrust Sprite onto a pile of blankets in between the other two. Ducking sideways to avoid the ridgepole, he continued without preamble. "We'll be in Ankhapur soon, a few days at the latest. When we get there, things are going to change. Cleedis came north to get me, and just me. I don't know why he's allowed the rest of you along, but I'd guess he means to use you to keep me in his shackles." The old rogue smirked darkly. "Though you're a damn sorry lot of hostages.

" 'Course, he might not be such a fool as to think you've got any sway over me. We all know what happens when somebody gets caught. He's on his own."

Therin rubbed at the scar around his neck and noted bemusedly, "You snatched me from the gallows once."

Pinch didn't like being reminded of that now, or the others might think his motives then were sentimental. "I didn't get you off the gallows. I let you hang and then I brought you back to life. And I did it for other motives. From here on, this is different. Ankhapur's not Elturel."

"Ohhh?" Maeve cooed. "They're both cities. What makes this one so special?

"Besides being your home," Sprite chimed in.

Pinch looked at Maeve's thick-veined cheeks and the knobby little carrot that was her nose. He could not describe the true Ankhapur to her, the one that filled him with despised love.

"Ankhapur the White." The words came reverently
and then, "Piss on it. Bloody Ankhapur, it's lesser known.
City of Knives, too. Ankhapur's fair; it's got whitewashed
walls that gleam in the sun, but it's all hollow and rotten
inside. The Families"—Pinch stressed it so that there
was nobody listening who didn't hear the salt in his
words—"control everything they want, including lives.
You'll never find a more cunning master of the confidence games than a man from Ankhapur. Who do you
think trained me to run a gang like you? Elturel?"

Therin flopped back on his rick, clearly unimpressed.
"So it's got competition. We've taken down worse."

Pinch snorted. "You're not competition—none of you
are. What kind of competition are you for a king who kept
a personal assassin on the payroll? Or his sons who
taught playmates how strike down their enemies? This
isn't just doing the black art on a weak lock or ripping the
cove from a temple roof." Pinch slipped the Morninglord's
amulet from his shirt and plopped it on the damp ground
between them. "They're playing for stakes that make this
look small—title and crown of all Ankhapur.

"We're just a bunch of petty thieves. They're princes,
dukes, and barons of the land. First Prince Bors, Second
Prince Vargo, followed by Princes Throdus and Marac—
there's a murderous lot. Bors is too much of an idiot to be
any danger, but don't worry. Our dear Lord Chamberlain
out there, the duke of Senestra, has gone begging for a
fool to protect his own interests. Oh, and there's more.
Tomas, Duke of the Port, is Manferic's brother, and Lady
Graln was his sister-in-law. She's got whelps, princelings
of the Second Order, for whom she'd kill to see crowned.
Finally, there's the Hierarch Juricale. They call him the
Red Priest, he's got enough blood on him. He and his sect
hold the Knife and the Cup, so you can imagine no one
gets crowned without his say." With slender fingers,
Pinch counted out the titles until there were no fingers
left. "Every one of them's a scorpion in the sheets. Com-

pared to them, we're lewds."

"They sent Cleedis up here for you," Sprite mused, as his foot gently slid toward the bauble at his feet.

"Royal Ward Janol, Pinch to you," the regulator mocked. A light kick with his boot kept the halfling's furred foot at bay. "It's not as though the royal ward has any chance or claim. Cleedis wants me for some reason, but it's just as like there'll be a mittimus for your arrest as soon as we strike Ankhapur. From here on, abroad or in the city, cut your words goodly and keep your eyes open like quick intelligencers or somebody'll cut your weasand-pipe for certain." That said, Pinch scooped up the amulet and turned to leave.

"And you, Pinch dear?" Maeve asked.

The rogue considered the truth, considered a lie, and then spoke. "I'll stand by you all and cross-lay old Cleedis's plans any way I can." He smiled a little, the way he chose when no one was to know his true thoughts. The afternoon shadows, creeping through the door, gave all the warmth to his thin reassurance.

Outside, after ten steps, he met Lissa as though she'd been lurking around waiting for this casual rendezvous. The woman had finally shed her saintly armor, and the effect was a transformation. Pinch had become so used to the rumpscuttle mien of a warrior woman that he was taken aback by her change to more demure clothes. Her silvery vestments, though long and shamefast, were still more flattering than battered steel made to cover every weak point of her sex. Her arms were half-bare to the cool air, and her slender, fair neck uncased from its sheath of gorgetted steel. Hair, brown and curly, tousled itself playfully in the breeze. Without all that metal, she stepped lighter and with more grace than did the clank and jingle of her armored self. The transformation from amazon to gentry maid was startlingly complete.

"Greetings, Lord Janol," Lissa hailed, catching the rogue

not at his best. "How fare you and your companions? Lord Cleedis says we shall be upon Ankhapur on the morrow."

"We?"

With a knowing, impish smile, Lissa brushed a loose wisp back into the tumble of her hair. "Certainly. Like yourself, Lord Cleedis is a gentleman. He's offered me passage to Ankhapur rather than leave me in this wilderness."

Either she now suspects me and favors Cleedis or the chamberlain is playing the game, using her and her temple as a threat over me. If that's the case, does she know her part, or can I still direct her? Taking up his mantle as the lordly Janol, Pinch smiled and bowed while making his cold calculations.

"As well the chamberlain should. And if he had not, I would have insisted upon it."

"Well, I'm glad you would because I'm still counting on you to help me find a thief." Her voice dropped to a whisper of winter wind through the beeches.

"If your thief is here."

Lissa nodded. "They are—I've had dreams."

"Dreams?"

"The voice of our lord. He speaks to us in our dreams. It's our way."

She could be naive, misled, inspired, or right; Pinch withheld judgment. He couldn't think of any good reason why a god shouldn't talk to his priests in their dreams, but why not just burn your words in a rock or, for that matter, limn the offender in holy fire? Had she seen him in her dreams? If not, then what was her god revealing? At least so far, that seemed to be nothing.

Gods always took roundabout ways to the straightest of things, and he for one felt they did so for his personal benefit, although perhaps not in the case of Fortune's master. Pinch did feel that the Mistress of Luck was a little too indirect in his own case—so much that he, only acting from a sense of just deserving, did what he could to speed the turn of her wheel along. So if the gods wanted to be indirect with him to the point where he helped move them along, it was apt that her god was equally oblique.

In this simplified theology, it was clear to Pinch's mind that Lissa was being tested. Succeed at the test and she would find the thief. Fail—and well, who knows?

He pulled at his ear to show doubt. "I could never place so much stock in dreams. What if you have a nightmare?"

The seminary student got the better of the priestess. "It's my duty to interpret the meaning in what I have received. If I can't, then I need to dedicate myself even more."

"Well spoken," he applauded, while settling onto a punky log, fallen several years back and now riddled with insects and mold.

She reddened at the compliment.

"So you don't really see the thief in your dreams, only some sort of symbol?"

"The words of our god transcend simple images. He speaks a different language from us. In our dreams, we filter though the things we know and find parallels for his voice." Lissa's hands flew as she talked, sometimes cupping the words only to spill them in a burst of excitement.

Pinch let her go on to explain how to tell true dreams from false visions, the five precepts of action, and more than Pinch needed to know. Still it was a good diversion from the hectic preparations for home, and before the rogue had completely succumbed to boredom, dusk wafted in from the east and it was time to retire.

The night passed quickly, dreamless for Pinch. As for the others, none would say. What kinds of dreams were left to an outcast Gur, a drink-sodden sorceress, and an unrepentant halfling?

Dawn scratched at the canvas, scarring the tan haze

with morning shadows. Pinch stepped out of the sweat
of tent air. It was a clammy dawn of stale wood smoke
and horse manure, but over it all was the incongruous
thick scent of geraniums and jasmine. The jarring
sweetness clung in the throat and choked more than
the stench of ordure. In the cold of coming winter, it
could only be that the wizards were here, borne in on a
wind of flowers of their own making.

Stumbling out of his tent, the rogue wandered
through a queue of clay-colored troopers, pilgrims
awaiting their turn at the shrine. Each man led his
horse, fully packed and carefully groomed. They jostled
and talked, smoked pipeweed or whittled, and every
few minutes plodded ahead a few more steps.

At the head of the column was a small cluster of
strangers, as uncomfortable as choirboys milling outside
the church. As each man of the column came abreast,
one of the strangers stepped from their shivering mass,
thin robes clutched about him, and gestured over the
line. A greenish flash bubbled out from his fingertips and
swallowed trooper, spellcaster, and more. When the
bright air cleared, wizard and soldier were gone.

"The time is best for you and your companions to
take their place in the line," Cleedis noted as he ambled
over to where Pinch stood. There was no haste or desperate urgency in the man's way; those who weren't
ready could be left behind.

A swift yank on the tent pole roused the rest. As they
stumbled out, Lord Cleedis, playing host and master
and accompanied by Lissa, led Pinch to the front of his
troop. The rogue's mates fell into line, grumbling and
slouching, unruly children mocking their parents. At
the front a pudgy, boy-faced wizard who couldn't be
much older than twenty and hadn't gotten himself
killed yet—more than a little feat for an ambitious
mage—bowed to the Lord Chamberlain. With apologies, the wizard arranged them just so, positioning the

five of them to some invisible diagram. Cleedis's impatience and Sprite's impish refusal to cooperate made the young mage all the more nervous until, by the time he was to say the words and make the passes, Pinch worried whether they would have their essences scattered across a thousand miles. Pinch always worried though; suspicion is what kept rogues like him alive.

Then, before the last words had gotten through the boy-mage's lips, the air around them went green, lightly at first like a fading hangover on a too-long day. It got brighter, swallowing the blue out of the sky, the cold from Pinch's boots, even the creaking of saddlery from the line of men behind him. In flickering moments, the evenness of the green overwhelmed everything, eventually even the green of the color itself. The world became a perfect color and Pinch could not see it.

The world returned with a nauseating rush. The green vanished, flooded out by other colors: blue sky, curling gray clouds, the brown-mottled turf of freshly turned fields, the fleshy green of still-leaved trees, and the glittering silver of a nearby sea. The ground lurched beneath him, practically toppling him from the unexpected jolt. Lissa clutched at his sleeve and he seized the belt of someone else. A heave of nausea washed over him and then passed.

Blinking in the sudden new light, Cleedis tapped Pinch and pointed toward the sea. Sited on the shore, between the water and the close nest of hills, were the tarnished gypsum-white walls of Ankhapur. A fog had rolled back from the thrusting wharves. Atop the hills, the morning bells of the temples had started to sound. And filling the top of the very highest hill were the colonnaded buildings of the royal palace, millipedes clinging to the rich garden slopes.

Cleedis turned and beamed a drillmaster's smile as he waved his hand up-slope. "Welcome back to Ankhapur, Janol."

Dinner in Ankhapur

Their arrival was well outside the walls of Ankhapur, in the shadow of the Villa of the Palantic Road that crowned the top of Palas Hill, one of six hills surrounding Ankhapur. They appeared at the edge of a grove, as if they had ridden through the woods and emerged to survey the vineyard-filled valley that lay between them and the city. Thus it was that their descent through the fields, while hailed by the peasants with the appropriate concern and homage, raised no questions of wonder or gossip.

Furthermore, they all looked gray, muddy, and spent, even Lord Cleedis himself. Pinch's foreign elegance was all but indistinguishable from the old-fashioned tabard Cleedis favored. Brown Maeve, Sprite-Heels, and Therin the Gur—no one could identify them as any more than merchants or servants among the entourage.

Only the wizards in their white clean shifts stood out from the ordinary, and that too was quite ordinary. No wizard was like the rest of the world, so it was only natural for them to be easily marked. At least that was the reasoning of those who watched the column pass.

In the two hours it took for the column to wend down the hairpin lanes and cross the bridge over the bog-banked Thornwash, a score of petty details returned to Pinch from the life he had fled fifteen years ago. The chill of snow and ice, that in fifteen years in Elturel he had never grown accustomed to, was gone, replaced by the faded green of Ankhapur's winter. The rhythmic lines of grapes were bare vines stretched over frames, the roads were rocky sloughs of clammy mud. To Pinch, the warm sun breathed the promise of spring, fresh grasses, and new growth. After fifteen years' absence, the sun of life was returned to him.

The warmth filled Pinch with a confidence bordering almost on joy, unwarranted by everything he knew, but that was unimportant. He was home, as much as he hated it, with all its memories and pitfalls. He was no longer Pinch, master of thieves, living his derring-do life in the slums and back alleys. By the time he rode through the gates, the ragtag scoundrel was nearly gone. In his place rode a man identical in dress, one who had invisibly traded places during the two-hour ride.

It was Janol, royal ward of the late King Manferic I, or at least some part of him that Pinch had not forgotten, who sat straight in his saddle, giving a supercilious nod to the liveried watchmen who stood at their parade best as the Lord Chamberlain and company rode underneath the whitewashed stone arch of the Thornwash gate.

There was one thing that was no different for Pinch or Janol, no matter his position. As either, the rogue felt power. These guards feared and respected men higher than them: the chamberlain, Janol, even the palace's

elite bodyguard. It was the same awe and terror Pinch
commanded from the thieves and constables of Elturel.
There was in the common folk, he was certain, an in-
nate sense of their betters. Even his gang understood it,
though none of them might ever admit it.

To the hoarse cries of the sergeant, bellowing their
procession over the squalls of the fruit sellers and the
enticements of the fest queens, the company rode as directly toward the palace as the interwoven streets of
Ankhapur allowed.

This morning, Ankhapur was alive early with the
hurly-burly of market day. Pushcarts rocked like over-
loaded ferries in the sea of heads, their decks loaded
with the glinting round flesh of fall squashes. Tides of
serving-cooks and housemaids rippled from one stand
to the next all down the shores of the streets. Chains of
fishmongers heaved dripping baskets from the boats
along the river, their still-twitching contents disappear-
ing into the eager crowd. Children stole fruits and leapt
over the smoky fires of the kaff-brewers, who sat cross-
legged on their mats, pounding bark to steep in brass
pots. The scent of that strongly bitter beverage made
Pinch yearn for its rich sourness mixed with honey, a
drink he'd not had in his fifteen years of self-exile.

Sated with musing, since too much reflection made a
man weak and hesitant to act, Pinch leaned in his
saddle toward Therin so that he did not need to shout.
"Welcome to home."

The Gur shifted nervously in his own saddle while
trying to negotiate his skittish horse through the
throng. "Your home, maybe. It's just another ken to me.
Although," he added with a smile and wave to the
crowd, "one filled with opportunity. Look at all the
coneys and marks out there."

"Mind your hands with caution, boy. Take some time
to walk the field before you bowl the pins. Besides our
game's up there, not in these stews."

Therin's eyes followed where Pinch pointed, to the clean, scrubbed walls that cut the commoners from their masters, the king's palace at the top of the hill.

"Piss and Ilmater's blood!" the enforcer breathed. "Sprite, Maeve—he's serious. He means to have us all in!"

"Gods' wounds, I ain't ever forced a ken like that in all my time," the halfling swore, half-hidden on Therin's other side. "Think of all the plate and treasures sure to be inside."

Because Pinch couldn't, Therin took the pleasure of fiercely berating the little scoundrel with a mindful thump to his shoulder. "Think of the headsman's axe too, you lusker, and let that sink on your wicked heart. Remember our warning of last night."

Sprite did his best to look wounded, but it was to naught on his companions. Further debate on the topic was broken by the need to negotiate an island of wagons that split the flow.

Pinch looked about the rest of the way, marveling at the similarity of the differences he saw. On that corner he remembered a saddler's shop; the building was the same but now it housed an ordinary from which wafted the smell of richly roasted meat. The great square where he used to practice riding was now adorned with an equestrian statue of his late guardian.

The sculptor had been good at capturing old Manferic's likeness, the flaring beard and the leonine mane of the king's regal head. He had molded into the face a sinister and scowling visage that well conveyed the king's savage love of intrigue, though Pinch felt the sculptor had been too kind by a half. In his saddle, the bronze king held the Knife and Cup, Ankhapur's symbols of royal power, as if he still owned them even in death. The Cup was raised in one hand for a bitter toast, while with his other the statue-sovereign thrust the Knife at those who stared up from his feet.

"Stand open for the Lord Chamberlain Cleedis,

Regent of the Assumption!" the captain demanded as
the column drew up at the gate.

There was a scurry of movement on the palace's
ornamental battlement, and then a herald stepped between the merlons and replied over the clank and rattle
from behind the doors. "Welcome is the return of our
sovereign lord and joyous are we at his safety. The
princes four wait upon his pleasure and would fain
wish to greet him."

Cleedis, whom Pinch now rode beside, smiled his acceptance of this formality, but from the corner of his
mouth he added an aside that only his guest could hear.
"Three of those princes would fain see me dead. That's
what they were truly hoping."

"Perhaps it could be arranged."

The warhorse-turned-statesman barely raised an
eyebrow at that. "Not well advised."

A white dog ran before the gate. Pinch noted it,
though it was completely unimportant. The incongruity
of it caught his eye, the mongrel's unmarred coat
against the scrubby gray of faded whitewash. "You've
got me here without a hold. Do you think I care enough
about those three you dragged along with me to toe
your line? Kill them if you want. I can always find
more." The footpad scratched at a dried patch of dirt on
his cheek.

Cleedis glanced back at the trio, squabbling among
themselves. "What do I care about them? I have you."

"If you kill me, your outing's been a waste."

"Still think I'm an old fool, don't you, Janol?" With a
grin the chamberlain prodded Pinch with his sheathed
sword. "You're as replaceable as they are. Let's just say
I had some hope of bringing you back into the fold. Besides, you're more convenient, seeing as you know the
ground of the battlefield."

While he spoke, the brass embossed gates cracked
with a faint burst of sparkling motes as the magical

wards placed on them were released. The doors swung
into a shadowed arch lined by royal bodyguards,
resplendent in wine-and-yellow livery.

Just as the horses were about to move, Cleedis's bare
blade slapped across Pinch's reins. "One more thing,
Master Janol." And then the chamberlain ordered his
aide, "Bring the priestess here."

In short order she trotted her stallion to their side.
Cleedis slid the blade away and pretended not to have a
thing more to say to Pinch, even though the rogue knew
every word was for his own benefit. The old man's
crabbed body shriveled even more as he gave a perfunctory nod from the saddle.

"Greetings, Worthy. Here is where we must part
anon, you to your superiors and I to affairs of state. I
wish you to understand that I, Lord Chamberlain, know
you seek a thief and extend my hand in any way I might
to give you success. Should I learn any morsel that
would aid your duty, it will be faithfully brought to you."

"Your lordship is most generous," Lissa murmured as
she bowed stiffly in her rigid armor.

The old noble made slight acceptance of her obei-
sance and continued. "Let our contact not be all duty,
though. In these days, I have been charmed by your
company. You must consider yourself a guest in my
household. I will arrange an apartment for you in the
palace. Accept, milady. The approval of your superiors
is already assured."

Lissa blushed, a freckled shade against her curled
hair. "I'm . . . I'm honored, Lord Chamberlain, but
surely one of my masters here would be of better standing. I've no knowledge of courtly things."

"Precisely my goal—a refreshing bit of air. Besides,
your superiors are crushing bores. Now, forward men!"
With a cavalryman's bellow, he set the whole column in
motion, leaving the flustered priestess behind.

As they passed under the gate, the Lord Chamber-

lain spoke, as if things were of no consequence. "Priests
lead such limited, suppressed lives. All those passions
and thoughts, penned up in such rigorous souls. If their
passions were given free reign, can you imagine the
types of punishments priests could devise for apostates
and blasphemers? Fascinating possibilities. I think I'll
keep the worthy Lissa close at hand."

The chamberlain said nothing more as the entourage
passed through the outer palace, exchanged escorts,
passed gates, crossed courtyards, and finally entered
the cream-white compound of the inner palace. By this
time, Maeve and the others were agoggle. They had
passed servants in better finery than most of the
freemen they knew. In their world, they had seen only
glimpses of this life through keyholes, by scrambling
through windows, and in the tumbled mass of their
booty. Pinch wondered just how well they would be able
to restrain their larcenous souls.

At last they entered a small, private courtyard
turned off from the main processional route, a guest
wing attached to the main household. Pinch remembered this section of the compound as particularly se-
cure, bastioned by a bluff to the rear and deep enough
into the palace grounds to make unnoticed departures
nearly impossible. Short of the dungeons, it would have
been his choice for housing a crew such as his, although
Cleedis was wrong to think this would contain them.
Pinch and his gang had escaped from lock-ups more determined than this in their years spent looting Elturel.

A resounding chorus of yelps and howls greeted their
arrival, and disabused the regulator of any hope that
Cleedis had underestimated them. While they handed
off their mounts to the waiting grooms, a chaos of sul-
furous fire and smoke boiled from dark kennels on the
east wall. At first it seemed a wild pack of hounds
charged, until one saw the beasts' chops drooling embers and each yelp a belch of flame. The hounds were

things of hellish fire, coal-black coats seared with eyes and breaths of flame. The horses kicked and reared with fearsome fright, dragging the boy-grooms with them.

"Gods' pizzle on the heads of the ungrateful!" blurted Therin in an old Gur curse. With a slick hiss his sword cleared the scabbard. "Pinch, strike right. I'll take the center. Maeve, your spells at ready." It was for moments like this that Pinch kept the Gur around, ceding battle command to him.

Just as the four set themselves for the slaughter—theirs or the beasts', they could not be sure—chains clanked as a trainer single-handedly dragged the lunging beasts backward across the smooth flagstones, coiling the iron leashes around his arm. Lumbering from the shadows of the wall, he was a brute, not quite a giant yet greater than a man. He was bare skinned save for a steel codpiece, scabrous fur and warts stretched over grotesquely knotted muscles. Everything about him was disproportionate. His ears and nose—a broad, corded thing—dominated his head, overpowering the weak eyes buried in ridges of bone. His arms were greater than his legs, which were mighty, and his forearms greater than the rest of his arms. Even while straining with the hellhounds, the ogre swaggered with the dim confidence of muscle.

"Surrabak hold them, small chief." It was a voice burned by bad firewine and cheap pipeweed and stretched harsher by three days of carousing, but it was his natural voice.

"Rightly done. Take them back to their kennel." Cleedis boldly stepped forward, holding a hand out to stay Pinch and the others. "Stay your hand," he said *sotto voce*. "He can be unpredictable."

Although he wondered how much of that was for theatrical benefit, Pinch made a quick gesture to the others, the silent hand language of their brotherhood. With slow, wary care the weapons were put away.

"Surrabak do. Hear small chief come back. Bring Surrabak orders from great chief?" The hellhounds were now within reach of the ogre's cudgel, and he unhesitatingly laid into them until their snarls became yelps of pain.

"The great chief is honored to have a killer like Surrabak. He says you must always obey . . . little chief." The last words bit against Cleedis's pride. Nonetheless, he pointed to the four foreigners and continued, "Little chief—me, Cleedis—tells you to guard these little ones. Do not let anyone come here unless they show my sign. Do you remember the sign?"

With the hellhounds in a tense pack at his feet, the ogre scowled, flaring his lumpy nose as he tried to remember. Tusks curved out from under his thick lips. His dim eyes sank farther in as he pondered hard.

"Surrabak know little chief's sign."

Cleedis gave a sigh of exasperated relief. "Good. Guard them well, or big chief will become angry and punish you."

"Surrabak guard. No one get in." With that, the ogre barked to the pack and slouched back to the kennels, half-dragging the iron leashes still wrapped around his arm.

"Little chief, big chief . . . That thing doesn't know Manferic's dead, does it?"

Cleedis ignored Pinch's question and stopped at the entrance to the wing, a small cluster of rooms once the queen's summer rooms. "The servants will show you to your quarters." As Sprite and the others stepped to go inside, the royal bodyguards stopped them. "Not you three. There are other rooms in the west hall for you." As if to reassure them, the chamberlain nodded across the way to another colonnaded building.

"We should be with him," Sprite snapped. "We're his friends and it's up to us to stay together."

"Objections, Pinch?"

For a moment nobody said anything as Pinch looked to his companions. The Gur had his hand to sword, ready for the word if it were given. Maeve looked to Pinch for protection, while Sprite glared back with cold defiance. The Lord Chamberlain let a devil's smile seize his lips and turn up the corners.

"Well?"

"Take them. They're not a damn to me."

The bodyguards sidled forward, eager for the fight. If the wind had blown a leaf a different direction across the courtyard, there might have been battle, but it didn't and there wasn't. The three stood frozen as their regulator turned his back on them and went inside.

"We're not done with you, Pinch, you bastard!" Therin bellowed as the door slammed shut.

Inside, Pinch paused, waving off the valet who hustled forward. He strained his ears for the sounds of trouble, fearful there would be a fight. It was part of the playact to turn his back on them, but as he pressed himself against the wall, the rogue was assailed by doubts. Was he playacting? He might need them; that was as much as he understood friendship. The thought of risking his life to save them simply because they were his gang . . . They know the game, he reasoned to himself. They'll know the playacting from the real. And if they don't . . .

Pinch didn't know what he would do.

Finally, when it was clear nothing would happen, Pinch followed the servant to his rooms. A bath had been drawn and clothes already laid out: a fine, black set of hose with burgundy and white doublet and pantaloons of the best cut.

It wasn't until he was washed, shaved, trimmed, and dressed that a runner arrived from Lord Cleedis with orders to attend in the west hall. The timing was no accident, Pinch knew. No doubt the servants assigned him reported directly to Cleedis's ear. The rogue had no

illusions about the degree of freedom and trust the
Lord Chamberlain was allowing him.

Sauntering through the halls, the rogue took his
time. No doubt everyone expected his appearance with
whatever eager maliciousness they possessed. Certainly his dear, dear cousins were hardly reformed;
kindness, love, and generosity were not survival skills
in Manferic's court. The rogue guessed that things were
only worse now; while he was alive, the fear of Manferic
had always been a great restraint.

So Pinch ambled through the halls, refreshing his
memory for the layout of the palace, appraising old
treasures he once ignored, and admiring and appraising pieces new to him. It was almost fun, looking at his
old life through the eyes of another. Portraits of the
royal line, with their arrogance and superiority, were of
less interest for him now than the frames that held
them. Vases he rated by what a broker would pay, fur-
niture by the amount of gilt upon it. Always there was
the question of how to get it out of Ankhapur, where to
find the right broker.

The tip-tap of feet across the age-polished marble
broke Pinch's reverie. "Master Janol, the court awaits
you in the dining hall," said the prim-faced Master of
the Table, a post identified by his uniform.

Let them simmer in their pots. Without changing his
comfortable pace, Pinch nodded that he would be coming. He was not about to be dictated to by a petty court
functionary—or by those who sent him. He would arrive late because he chose to.

Then the stone corridors echoed with a crackling
chuckle as Pinch laughed at his own conceit. There was
no choice for him. He would be late because they all expected him to be late. Anything else and the royal ward
Janol would not be the prodigal scoundrel they all envi-
sioned—rebellious, unrepentant, and unsubtle. Let
them imagine him how they wanted; he'd play the

part—for now.

By the time he pushed open the ridiculously tall doors and strode into the magically lit dining hall, the diners had dispensed with acceptable gossip and were now trapped listening to the Lord Chamberlain describe his journey. The old chamberlain looked up as the doors creaked open and, barely breaking his tale, nodded for Pinch to come to the center of the great curved table and present himself to the royal heirs.

The old rogue, a man of steady balance on a rooftop, icy nerve in a knife fight, and sure wit to puzzle out a magical ward, felt the thick, slow-motion dread of stage fright. It was a decade and more since he'd last been in such company, and suddenly he was worried about forgetting all the subtle niceties and nuances of courtly etiquette. It's not that he minded insulting some portentous ass, it's just that doing so accidentally took all the fun out of it.

Consequently, to hide the feeling of self-conscious care, Pinch studied those at the table as hard as they studied him. Passing the outer wing, the rogue gave only cursory interest to faces that confronted him, concentrating on guessing rank and position by their dress and badges. These were the minor lords of the court, those who wanted to be players in the intrigues but were only being used by the masters. For the most part these factotums and their ornaments were dull as cattle, unaware of who he was and content with their petty positions and their ordained superiority over the common masses. They worried over who sat next to whom, dripped grease into their ruffed collars, and catted about whose looks had been enhanced tonight by some illusionist's hand.

Still, here and there, a pair of bold eyes met Pinch's or a snide comment was whispered to a neighbor as he passed. Pinch took special note of these: the forthright showed some hopes of cunning or fire, the gossips were

clued enough to have heard already who he was. Both
might be valuable or dangerous in times to come.

Past these room-stuffers, invited mostly to fill the
table, was the second tier, and now Pinch's interest became keen. Here the rogue noted faces and made brief
nods to ladies and lords he remembered. Every lord and
lady sitting here was a prince's ally. Pinch recognized
the proud Earl of Arunrock, commander of the navy, by
the out-of-fashion goatee he still kept trimmed to a
point. Farther along, the rogue almost gave a start to
see the merchant Zefferellin, who used to broker loot
from an inn near the market. Judging from his robes of
severe opulence, business must have been good enough
to buy respectability. Next there was a lady he didn't
know but definitely wanted to. She had a refined elegance that suggested she could break the spirit of the
purest man. Finally, there was the Hierarch Juricale, a
woodcutter-sized man whose black eyes glowered at
people over his long bent nose and spreading white
beard. He was a man whose word could inspire the
faithful to kill for his cause. Even at the table he sat
aloof, apart from all the others as if he alone were
above all this. It was a lie, Pinch knew. There was no
man more directly involved in the court's intrigues
than the Red Priest.

These were the hands that held the knives of the
princes and the Lord Chamberlain. There was nothing to
distinguish them in dress from the pawns of the lower
tier—who believed that clothes determined rank through
the strange alchemy of fashion—but this inner tier knew
where the true power lay. They had chosen their sides.
Which wing, which side, how close to the center of table,
all these were clues waiting to be deciphered.

At last the regulator reached the center, where he
turned to the table and casually bowed. Along the opposite
side of the curving main table sat the princes four, their
backs safely to stone walls. Interspersed between them

were the rest of the family: Duke Tomas and Lady Graln. At the very center, in the king's normal seat, sat Cleedis, Lord Chamberlain and Regent of the Assumption.

Pinch waited to be recognized, but now it was their turn to make him wait. Cleedis continued with his story.

Unlike the others, Bors the idiot prince, was the only one who seemed to show interest. He was still an idiot, that was clear. Flabby faced and jaundiced, he dumbly mouthed Cleedis's words, barely understanding most of it. His napkin, tied under his chin, was awash in soup spill and crumbs, and it seemed to take most of the First Prince's effort to get his spoon to his lips. Every once in a while, he would giggle softly about something that amused only him.

Next to Bors, and looking none to happy for the seat, was Duke Tomas. Had he been two seats over, Pinch would have mistaken the duke for Manferic, his late brother, even though the duke was gleamingly bald where the late king had had a full head of hair.

"Dear coz, the years have made you forget your manners." The jab brought Pinch back to the front and center, and he bowed quickly before even looking to see who had stung him. It didn't matter; even after fifteen years it was impossible not to recognize the voice, a baritone of biting silk ripe with arrogance.

"Quite true, Prince Vargo. Otherwise I would have remembered your impatience, too."

Across the table glowered a muscular man, Vargo, second son of Manferic. He was several years Pinch's younger, although his face was hard and sharpened to a point by his impeccably trimmed Vandyke. His casually tossed blond hair offset the red of his beard, and he easily could have been a dashing cavalier if it weren't for the unsatiated savagery that twisted even his brightest smile.

"I present myself, Lord Chamberlain," Pinch-now-Janol continued before his adversary could recover

from the rogue's *bon mot*. "I am Master Janol, royal
ward of the late King Manferic."

A susurration of muted surprise trickled from the
outer wings, as those guests previously clueless of
Pinch's identity grasped the import of his arrival.

"I . . . beseech . . . your permission to join you at table
as was the courtesy my late guardian extended to me."
This part of the ritualistic greeting came hardest for
the regulator. It was galling to go through the show of
asking the favor after the old man had forced him here
in the first place. Hiding a grimace, the prodigal
courtier bowed once again, this time with more flam-
boyance. The fear that threatened to paralyze him was
fading as the familiarity with the air around him grew.

Lord Cleedis raised a glass of amber wine as if this
were the first time he had seen Pinch in years. The gold
elixir sparkled in the light from the mullioned windows
that lined the base of the dome above.

It was all a conceit. Everyone at the table knew the
old man had gone to fetch the errant ward, though the
thief couldn't imagine why the chamberlain had risked
absence from the court for so long. Gods knew what the
princes had done—or might have done—in the regent's
absence.

"Truly we are pleased to see our long-absent cousin.
I, who was your guardian's servant, will not dishonor
his name by sending you from this hall. Prepare a place
for Master Janol where he can sit with honor."

In an instant the servants silently swooped on the
diners, producing a chair, linens, goblet, and trencher.
It had all been prearranged, of course, so there was no
need for direction as they uprooted the foremost noble
of the second tier and laid a place for the rogue. This
displacement triggered a chain reaction of shifting and
squeezing as each noble vainly refused to relinquish his
position in the chain of importance. At the very end of
the semicircular table, the lowest courtier of the lot

found himself dangling off the end, trencher perched on his knees.

Pinch squeezed himself into place between Prince Marac and a glistening courtier simmering at the insult of being supplanted by a mendicant relative. The man sipped his wine through clenched teeth and eyed Pinch in way that was reminiscent of the lizards he used catch. Pinch considered being friendly, but the man was a reptile and hardly worth the effort. Instead the rogue ignored him, because it made Pinch's presence all the more stinging and that made Pinch happy.

"Prince Marac . . ." The rogue's cup raised in a genial toast.

Marac, youngest of Manferic's sons and the one Pinch liked the best of the slippery lot—because the youth had been easy to intimidate—eyed Pinch the way one neighbor eyes the other when his best hound has disappeared. He tried to look for the evidence of a bloody knife while trying not to seem like he was looking.

Marac was no longer the ten-year-old youth that Pinch remembered. That one had been replaced by a poor imitation of Prince Vargo. His face was fuller and rounder than sharp-cheeked Vargo, and his beard had the thin, brushed softness of youth, but already the eyes were hidden barbs. His straw-blond hair was longer than his brother's and straight where the other's was tangled. With all these differences, there was still a foundation that was Manferic's bloodline. Perhaps the two weren't Manferic progeny, but unfinished duplicates the wizard-king had fashioned in some long-forgotten laboratory, and their lives from childhood to death were one vast experiment. It would be so like the way he raised me, just to see what he could build, Pinch thought.

Prince Marac acknowledged the toast, and the glow of his face melted into a lipless smile. "Your unexpected return is a pleasure, cousin Janol."

That was all lies, from front to end.

The prince sipped at his scented wine while the servants dished out the next course, a sweetly stewed, steaming joint of some meat beyond the rogue's ken.

"An excellent cut, isn't it, Your Highness?" suggested the lizard-eyed noble at Pinch's other hand. The man was determined not to be left out of the conversation.

"Quite good hunting on your part, Lord Chalruch."

As if the words were a signal, the table that had been so quiet while Pinch sat himself roiled into gossip and banter once more.

"Thank you, milord. I bagged him in a perfect—"

"So cousin, how fares it you've come back here? How long has it been?"

"I've been abroad on fifteen years, Prince Marac."

"Not long enough," Vargo suggested from the other side of the pearly Lady Graln.

She laid a hand on his. "Vargo, you're being unkind."

"And what possessed you to return now?"

"—shot at a range of a good hundred rods—" the bore continued to a young lady on the left, who being reduced to helplessness by the seating struggled to feign interest.

"Indeed, what?" spoke a new voice from the other side of the Lord Chamberlain. Pinch had to lean out to get a clear look at his interrogator. It was Throdus, the sharpest thinker of the princes. In looks he was coal to his brothers' bonfires: dark hair, smoke-filled eyes, lean, and pale—as unlike Manferic as the other two were like him. Only the icy rigor of his manner showed the true family line.

"I brought him back," Cleedis intervened while chewing on a piece of bread. "It was your father's request, one of his last. He wanted his ward reunited with the rest of the family. Toward the end, he greatly regretted certain events of the past. It was for his memory that I tracked down and brought back Master Janol."

"Father's mind went soft," Vargo stage-whispered to

Lady Graln.

"And now Cleedis's, too. It must be contagious," added Marac.

"—clean through the slug's heart." The bore prattled on, apparently determined to slay his trapped audience as surely as he had the beast. Tired of the man's determination to plow blindly onward, Pinch deliberately jerked away from Marac with staged indignation.

"They wrong you, Cleedis!" At the same time, the rogue banged his elbow against the bore's arm just as the other was about to sip his wine. The yellow liquid splashed all over the man, soaking his white silken doublet an off-color stain.

"Sir, you've bumped me!" he blurted out, seizing Pinch by the arm.

Pinch gave the lord a cursory scan. "A terrible accident, indeed," he said with a fraudulent sympathy. "If I were you, I'd go change or people will think I didn't have time to go out back and pluck a rose."

"Pluck a . . . ?" The indignant bore stopped when he followed Pinch's gaze to the honey-hued stain that spread over his hose. His face reddened. "Perhaps that's sound," he said as he slid away, holding his napkin strategically in place. "But you'll hear from me again, sir, and soon I promise!" With that dreadful parting threat, the man hurried away.

"I'm sure I will, though any time is bound to be too soon."

A sigh of relief rose from those who'd been audience to the man's court.

"I must say cousin Janol has at least livened conversation at the table," the Lady Graln smirked from her seat. "These dinners were threatening to poison us with dullness." She held up her goblet to be filled from the fresh bottle the servant was pouring down the line.

"Better poisoned words than poisoned wine," Pinch suggested. He raised a fresh glass in toast. Everyone automatically lifted their glasses, only to hold them just at their lips, suddenly alarmed by the rogue's hint. Each watched for someone else to take the first sip.

"Come, drink!" urged Pinch once again raising his glass high, cheerfully stinging the group like a sandfly. "Drink to . . . oh, the memory of King Manferic! A toast to the late King Manferic!" he offered loudly so that no one could ignore it.

"To Manferic!" echoed the room. Glasses tipped back as the lesser tiers drained away their cups, while at the main table, indecision still paralyzed the lords. Refusing the toast meant a loss of face, drinking required trust. For a long moment, nobody did either.

Finally, disgusted or courageous, Vargo gulped down his portion. As he thumped his goblet down on the table, there was a long swallow from the others as they followed suit. It was only when they had all set their goblets down that they noticed Pinch had not touched his.

The rogue smirked a know-everything smile. "No taste for the bub, I guess."

"We were wondering why Father had you here," said Throdus from down the line, "and now we know. You are dear Father's last cruel jest. This way he can mock us even from beyond the grave."

"Enough of this!" Marac blurted with all the grace of a master-of-drill. "Cleedis, when do we hold the ceremony of the Knife and Cup? Things have gone long enough without a true king."

"Hear, hear!" chimed in Throdus. "You've been stalling four months now, first saying one thing and then another. I say we have the Hierarch declare the date today."

"There should not be haste," Vargo countered, sounding uncharacteristically statesmanlike.

The Second Prince was stalling, Pinch realized, until he could get other plans realized. That was important knowledge, since it meant the Second Prince was a man to be watched.

"Prince Vargo speaks wisely," defended Cleedis. "Rushing the ceremony will bring evil luck to the whole kingdom. The Hierarch has chosen the date—the first day of the Money Festival. He says that is the best day to guarantee profit and prosperity for the new reign.

More time was not a bad idea by Pinch either, since he wasn't even sure of his own part here. Cleedis had dropped enough hints for the rogue to know his job involved those instruments of the succession. Whatever he was to do, after the ceremony would be too late. Thus it was the rogue weighed in, "Fools spend a copper and hurry themselves to the gaol, while sages spend an ingot and buy the judges."

"What's that supposed to mean?" sneered Marac.

In his years abroad, Pinch had faced witnesses in a score of trials and, as was the obvious testament of his being here, had yet to feel the noose. "Patience for fools."

At that, Marac abandoned the table with a snarl. "If that's the decision, then I see no cause to remain here!"

"Nor I," calmly added Throdus. He stepped away from the table. To Vargo he added, "You have a plan and I will find it out."

The creaking thump of the great doors marked the pair's departure. After they were gone, Vargo, too, took his leave. As he left, he laid a hand on Pinch's shoulder and whispered a word in his ear.

"I don't know what your game is, dear coz, whether you're sided with Cleedis or another, or whether you're just a fool to come back here. But remember this: Cross me and you'll cross no one else in Ankhapur."

With that, the cruel huntsman left, leaving Pinch to enjoy the rest of his meal.

The Prodigal Received

When dinner finished, Pinch joined the flow of family to the private salons, the inner sanctums of his youth. At the door to the grand study, Marac suddenly stepped in Pinch's path, one finger poised like a dagger at the regulator's chest. "You are not welcome," he announced, loud enough for everyone to hear him. "You're not one of the family. Things change."

With the grace of an eel that slithers through the conger's nets, Pinch curled his lips in a smile of polite understanding and bowed to his hosts. Vargo clapped his hand on the youngest prince's shoulder and loudly said, falsely thinking it would pain Pinch all the more, "Come, brother, leave him till the morrow. There's wine to be drunk!"

As the salon door closed behind him, Pinch padded through the dark and heartless halls to his own room.

The lane had been paced, the pins set, he thought to himself. Now it was time to see how the bowl would play.

Returned to his room, the master thief settled into the carved wooden chair that was scorched dry by the heat from the fireplace. He sat immobile, gazing at the flames with the same fascination a drunk might share.

Behind the visage, though, his mind raced. Preparation, Pinch knew, warded bad luck. First there was escape, if he needed it. His apartment was large and spacious, with a public salon separate from the bedchamber. However, the two rooms were cunningly less than generous about windows. These were all small portholes set high in the wall, hardly suitable for a rat to scurry though. That left the door, discreetly locked by a guardsman after Pinch had entered. Could they believe he hadn't heard the slow grind of the heavy tumblers?

Pinch had every confidence he could work the black art on the door, even if he was a little rusty. Then in the hallway, where would he go? After fifteen years, there were changes and additions made that no longer appeared on his mental map of the palace. He replayed every step he could recall in his head, getting the sense of distance and direction sound in his memory until he was confident he could slip through the halls to the outside world.

Outside were the ogre and his hellhounds, an entirely different type of problem. Pinch couldn't see a solution there immediately. He set it aside for later study when he could get a clearer view of the ground.

Beyond the ogre, only the palace gate was certain. The here-to-there could be fraught with perils or tediously easy. It was impossible to say who might challenge him or let him pass.

The palace gate was a certainty, though. There would be a curfew after which the doors would be

locked. Here his youth as the royal ward stood him in
good stead. One of his patent rebellions had been to slip
into the city against Manferic's wishes and get himself
back well after the curfew horn had blown. Back then
there were other ways over the palace walls, and the
rogue trusted that they still existed. Some gates remained unsealed even at the latest hours to accommo-
date those visiting their mistresses or back from a
night of mingling with the lewd folk.

Finally, silver and gold were always a solution. Unless there had been some catastrophic change in the
barracks rooms, it was always possible to find a guardsman willing to turn a blind eye for the right price. Of
course, he'd need to find himself some cash, but for a
good thief that was hardly a problem.

So much for escape, should he need it. The next
question concerned his companions and what should be
done about them. Pinch mulled over his options, sinking deeper into the stillness before the fire.

Did he need them? If not, there was no need to worry
about them. Certainly he was their upright man, but he
felt no compulsion of mere loyalty to save them.

Pinch once again decided to choose in favor of prudence. He still did not know what task Cleedis intended
for him; until he did know, there was the possibility the
trio might be needed. Pinch hardly felt he could rely on
old friendships in Ankhapur; he'd already been reminded how fifteen years could change a man. Grudges
lasted longer than loyalty. Without more time, Sprite,
Therin, and Maeve were the only rogues he knew well
enough to rely on.

Having judged and deemed worthy, the regulator
needed to communicate with his gang before they felt
abandoned and reordered their brotherhood. They were
no more loyal than his lingering presence. All he knew
was the wing they were in. Tomorrow he would make
sure to see them.

All these things Pinch did in his head, never once setting his thoughts to paper, never once stirring from the chair. This was more than just his usual nature. His staying in these two rooms, he was sure, was no haphazard choice. Cleedis had wizards at his side, powerful ones as evidenced by their leap across the vast distances this morning. Those selfsame wizards could be watching him this instant. He had put Maeve to it often enough in their efforts to scout out a new case before they broke during the night. He also knew from Maeve that it took a little knowing the place to make the spell work. There was no doubt Cleedis had put at least some of his spell-men to the task of knowing these rooms inside and out.

Even his own thoughts weren't safe, Pinch knew. Those wizards could pry through his mind, dredging up his plans if he wasn't careful. Again, Maeve and hard experience had taught him some tricks for resisting, but they weren't sure by any means. The best of all things was not to plan, but to act by pure instinct. Instinct was something that couldn't be measured, plumbed, or dissected by the arcane powers.

"Well," he announced to no one, "let the committers make something of this." And then Pinch settled in and let his mind be filled thoughts as impure, vile, horrific, and vivid as he could imagine.

And Pinch could imagine very, very well.

* * * * *

The next morning, Pinch took his breakfast in his room, reveling in the luxury Cleedis was willing to bestow. Even a master regulator didn't live in princely comfort. That had been a hard adjustment when he'd first fled Manferic's court. It had been a long time since he'd had sweet porridge laced with fatty smoked meat and dried fruits. It was a childhood comfort, a memory of dawns spent hiding in the kitchen, nicking bowlfuls from the pot when the cooks weren't looking.

Reverie ended with a knock at the door. Before Pinch could rise or say "Enter," the door swung open and Throdus sauntered into the salon as if the whole world were his privilege. The dark prince radiated a jaunty cheer. Without so much as a comment, he plopped into the chair opposite Pinch.

The rogue glanced up and then buried himself in slurping spoonfuls of porridge as if Throdus weren't there.

Throdus watched this until a wry smile curled his lips.

"Good cousin, I regret my brothers' behavior last night. It was a crude display." The prince stopped to examine some speck on the back of his hand.

"No doubt you would have done better," Pinch suggested between swallows, never once looking up.

"Of course. Marac did that just for our benefit."

"I know."

Throdus looked up from his digitary studies. "One might question his motive."

"Not me. He's just become more like his brother."

"Vargo? Those two were always close."

"Afraid they're plotting against you?"

"They're always plotting against me. And I plot against them. Remember, Janol, it's a game we've played since childhood."

"I haven't forgotten."

The prince went back to looking at his hands.

"I do find it interesting that you've chosen to come back now."

Ah, so that's where my lord is casting his net. Let's play the game and string him along, Pinch decided.

"My other choices were less pleasant."

"Ah, the wastrel's life—your exploits are known here."

Pinch was surprised and not surprised. His adopted cousins certainly had the resources to learn about his past, but it surprised him that they bothered. He would have thought their own intrigues kept them busy enough.

"Father always had a curiosity about your fate." The prince brushed back his black hair and watched his adversary's reaction. "Since he was curious, we had to be curious."

"Always afraid that someone else was working the cheat."

"Information is power." The words were sharp.

"So you know my life. What will you do, give me up to the constables?"

"I just want to know why you're here."

Now it was Pinch's turn to be amused. "Just that? Why I've come to pay my respects, my dear guardian dead and all. After that I'll make myself master of the trugging houses in the city. Maybe I'll even do a little brokering, not that you'd have anyone else's goods to sell."

"Cheap lies only irritate me. You hated Manferic more than all the rest of us."

"I had my cause. Try growing up like the household dog."

"He was hard on us all, but we didn't run away."

"You? You were all too afraid—afraid of him, afraid you'd lose your chance when he died."

Suddenly the shadows fell across the prince's sunny facade. "I, at least, have the right to be king. You, however, have no such claims. You're just an orphaned waif raised above his level by my father for the gods know what purpose, and then you come back here thinking you can be like one of the blood. The only reason for you to come back here is to beg for scraps. Is that it?" The prince ended the question with a sneer.

Pinch didn't answer, glowering at Throdus while he continued his breakfast.

"I didn't think so," the prince said, dismissing the possibility with a wave of his hand. "The real question is, who are you working for? Marac? That would make sense for his little show. Publicly disavow you, privately deal."

Pinch stopped in midladle and blew on his porridge. "I told him it was too obvious."

"Now you're too obvious. So it wasn't Marac. Someone brought you here for a job and I want to know."

This was getting tedious, and Throdus's temper was getting up.

"As you well knew before coming here, it wasn't Marac who took me abroad."

Throdus laughed. "You're suggesting Cleedis? He's a trained monkey. He just wears the hat of regent and dances when somebody else plays the music. You've seen it; he can't even keep Vargo from unseating Bors at the head of the table."

Pinch remembered the arrangement, unremarkable at the time, but now of greater importance: Bors drooling at the end of the family row while Vargo sat in the first son's seat at the regent's left hand. It had never been that way at Manferic's table. The old man had kept his gods-cursed firstborn in the place of honor even after his deficiencies were clear to all.

"Why should I tell you anything? I'm no intelligencer for the constabulary."

Abruptly the prince was no longer humorous, the indulgent mask peeling from his flesh to reveal the corded muscles of a snarl as he sprang to his feet. "Because you're nothing but a rakehelled orphan who lives by our indulgence! Because I want to know who you're working for and you'll tell me."

"A pox on that!" Pinch swore, shoving the bowl away. "I'll not be your intelligencer, not when you come here threatening like some piss-prophet."

"Then I'll have your heart and roast it for the dogs!"

Throdus's hand went to the jeweled dagger at his side. It wasn't hanging there just for show. The blade was brilliantly polished and glittered in the morning light.

The rogue grinned as he kicked the chair back and sprang to his feet. He drew his slim-bladed skene, with its leather-wrapped handle and well-oiled blade, and let the point trace imaginary circles in the air before the prince's chest. "And I say you're a pizzle-headed ass for thinking you can best me with your little cutter. What do you know about knife fights? Have you every jumped a man in a dark lane and pulled your blade across his weasand-pipe? Fought with a blade in one hand and a bottle in the other?" Pinch started a slow pace around the table, one that forced Throdus back from the center of the room.

"One time a captain of the guard wanted to dock me. He was a fine gentleman and thought I was too. Thought I'd fight fair. I burned his hair off before I left him hamstrung. Scarred him for life—even the priests couldn't do anything about it.

"Do you think being a prince will protect you?" Pinch whispered softly as he picked up a heavy jug with his free hand.

Throdus's rage had started to go pale, and suddenly he acted in desperate panic. With a snap of his arm, he flung his dagger.

Pinch reacted almost as fast and just managed to swing the jug into the blade's path. The hard clay shattered in his hand, sending shards skittering across the floor like mice, but the knife went tumbling away. The rogue threw the useless jug handle back and Throdus bobbed beneath it.

Pinch lunged but not so hard as to be sure of a hit. Throdus escaped harm, though his waistcoat died in the attack. Pinch's dirk pierced the fabric and stuck into the wall. As Throdus yanked frantically to pull the fabric loose, Pinch slammed his free arm against the man's chest. The air blew out of Throdus like a puffball squeezed too hard. While still skewered to the wall like a gutted rabbit, he sagged against the rogue unable to do anything but helplessly twitch as he choked for air.

Bronzewood cracked as the dirk wrenched free of the wall and came free of the punctured clothes. Pinch slithered in close, his knee poised below Throdus's gut as an extra insurance of good behavior. The rogue let the knife blade tickle the prince's torso as he deftly sliced away the doublet's strings, tracing just the thinnest line of blood down the man's hairy chest. Gently, almost tenderly, he brought his lips close to the noble ear, till he could smell the perfumes in Throdus's oiled hair and guess the flavor of breakfast the man had eaten that morning.

"What should I do with you?" the regulator whispered ever so softly, as if the prince within his clutches weren't even there. "If I killed you, who would complain? Vargo? Marac? Cleedis? Maybe that's why I'm here . . ."

It was to Throdus's credit that he did not cry out, but that may have been only because he couldn't. His gasping had broken into shivers the man could not restrain, so strong that he couldn't even work his lips to form words. His eyes welled up with water as he stared at the knife, unable to shift his gaze from it.

"What should I do?" Pinch whispered again. "Perhaps they'll reward—"

A rich reverberation rebounded through the apartment, the musical tolling of a bell. The sound stood out by its otherworldliness, but Pinch ignored it. It was just some errant matins bell of yet another sect, echoing up from the common city below.

"STOP."

It was the bell, now formed into a single word. It was a phantom of his thoughts, not real noise, the rogue realized now. It's my conscience, he thought almost breaking into laughter. I didn't think I had one.

"DO NOT KILL HIM."

It wasn't his conscience. It was a voice, more powerfully deep than was humanly possible and somewhere behind him. Pinch flung the quivering Throdus aside and spun to face his challenger—

There was no one there. The room was empty and silent save for the prince who crawled, mewling, toward the door. Pinch whirled here and there, jabbing the air in case his threat were invisible, but there was nothing.

Throdus had reached the door and was struggling to his feet. It's him; he's doing this. I can't let him go, Pinch thought, his own mind racing on the verge of panic. "Tell your wizards to stop or I'll kill you!" he shouted.

"NO, HE IS NOTHING. LET HIM GO."

The voice was behind him, Pinch was sure. In a single move, he spun and threw his dagger at the source. The skene twirled across the room and stuck fast into the wall, quivering. Nothing was there.

Behind him, the door creaked and then slammed as the prince bolted for safety. By the time Pinch could turn, Throdus was gone.

Frustrated, the rogue whirled back to face the empty room. "Damn you! Who are you?"

"LATER . . ." The deep tones faded away, leaving behind only a hollowness of muffled sound.

Pinch tore through the rooms, overturning chaises, throwing aside coverlets, flinging the armoire doors wide. There was nothing, nowhere. No hidden visitors, sorcerous imps, or mischievous gremlins. He was alone.

At last the rogue collapsed in the center of the frenzy, in the nest of bed sheets and clothes that littered the floor. What had happened? Who had happened? And what would happen next?

For once, the thief couldn't say.

Visiting

"Stand aside, damn you! He attacked Prince Throdus!"

There was the leathery scrape of a tussle outside, over a handful of shouted voices. Not a one did Pinch recognize, but they were full of youth and vigor and he could well guess that they were rakes of Throdus's circle intent on currying favor with their patron.

By the time the courtiers bulled their way past the guard outside the door and smashed through the lock, Pinch had shucked his linen nightshirt, pulled on trousers and boots, and was standing ready for them. In each hand casually held behind his back he held a dagger by the blade, ready for the toss. Another was in his boot top.

These blades were not his first line of defense, though. Pinch had no illusions that a few puny tossed daggers would stop this group. Princes surrounded themselves with hardier worthies than that. At best he could remind them he had a potent sting.

Of course, they had to find him first. Invisibility, or a thief's version of it, was his strongest protection. While they were fumbling outside, the rogue slid into the shadowed folds of his bed canopy, between the wall and the monolithic headboard. There he shifted his shoulder so that the lines of gloom fell across it just so, tilted his head into the darkness, and pressed his legs close to the headboard until they looked like part of the carved bronzewood. There he waited very, very still. There was, after all, still the great risk that he had missed some telltale and they would discover it in a nonce. That's what the knives were for. Fools who relied on only one chance were short-lived fools.

All in one packet, three bravos cracked through the lock and crashed into the salon, a swirl of silken capes and flashing blades. The group, with their curled hair and puffy half-slashed sleeves, made a romantic trio as they whirled and thrust bloody holes into the air.

Pinch almost gave himself away, so utter was his contempt for what he saw. They practically stumbled and fell over each other in their eagerness to be the first to make the strike, the first to avenge the tainted honor of their lord. Their capes, colorful in courtly dance, snared each other, one's silk foiling the stroke of another.

"Stand clear there!"

"Step aside yourself, Faranoch."

"He's mine. You fall back."

"I yield to no man my lesser."

"Lesser?"

"Stop flailing that ham slicer. You've cut my sleeve!"

"A mortal blow, Treeve."

"Hah! I have him!"

"Hah indeed, Kurkulatain. You've killed a pillow."

"A fierce battle Prince Throdus fought," said the pudgiest as he looked about more closely, tired of blindly lunging. He prodded the spilled contents of the armoire at the entrance to the bedroom.

"Indeed," commented another, a painfully handsome fop who was just as relieved that there was no prey to be found. "They must have battled from one room to the other." As proof he swept his sword across the tangle of hurled goods Pinch had created in his search for the possessor of the strange voice.

"A skilled swordsman to have kept Throdus at bay so long," the third courtier nervously added. He was a thin stick topped by droopy ringlets.

The other two looked at the evidence for this new judgment. "Quite formidable . . ."

"And he forced Throdus to retreat."

As they spoke, the trio slowly bunched together, back to back to back. They eyed corners, flowing arras, even snarled lumps of linen with a newfound fear.

"Maybe he's dead."

"No blood though."

"He might have run away."

"True . . ." The six-legged knot blindly edged toward the door.

"Might have."

"He could have bribed the guard," the stick man brilliantly deduced.

Pinch stifled a laugh, and the urge to come roaring out of his shadow and send the lot scurrying back around Throdus's legs like yipping little pups.

"Of course. He knew someone would be coming!"

"Like us."

"We should sound the alarm," the fat one dutifully suggested.

"And let the guards hunt him!" The handsome one seized upon the idea.

"It would be the right thing," agreed the stick-pole man.

The clot backed to the door and jammed, none of the trio willing to break rank to let the others through. As they hovered there, unwilling to go forward, unable to go back, a shadow fell on them from behind.

"WHAT'S GOING ON HERE?" thundered Cleedis in his best military voice. The trio-as-one sundered itself in terror and blindly darted through the doorway as the old commander shouldered through them, batting his way clear with his cane.

As soon as he was inside, the white-haired chamberlain closed the door and planted the cane in front of him, leaning heavily on it as though it were a tent pole.

"You can come out now," he said like a man trying to coax a beast from a thicket, addressing the air that filled the light and dark between them. "I know you've popped yourself into some corner waiting for an unguarded moment to strike. Well, if you mean to do that to me, I'm not going to give you the satisfaction. If you want to fight me, Janol, you'll have to come and get me."

"I'd never fight you, Lord Cleedis," Pinch flattered as he stepped into view.

The old man squinted his weak eyes to be sure of what he was seeing. "Lies and pissing-poor ones at that. I'd kill you given half a reason, Janol, and I suspect you'd do it for even less."

"Killing always has a reason. If I do any less, I'm a beast." The rogue tucked the daggers in his belt and spread his arms to prove that he was unarmed. White arms spanned from his hairy dark chest, a heart eaten by shadow.

"Philosophy from a scoundrel. There is no end of wonders in the world."

"There are. I came back here."

"And dammit, what happened? I hear you brawled with Throdus."

Pinch didn't deny a word of it. He scoured the chaos of clothing for a clean doublet. "He's a jackanapes ass. Let's say he was checking the prancer's teeth when it bit him."

"And then?"

"And then nothing," came the muffled answer as the regulator pulled on an undershirt. Pinch wasn't about to mention the strange voice, not until he'd had a chance to learn more. These walls for one—he wanted to check them much more carefully.

"What did he ask?" Seeing that he was being ignored, the chamberlain lumbered to a chair and settled down.

The rogue turned his attention to the washstand. "Just as much as it pleased me to inform him."

"And what did you inform?"

"Everything, the lay of it all." The regulator ambled back into the salon, drying one ear with a towel. "Which is to say, nothing. The minstrel can't play the tune without an instrument.

"I've been thinking that now is the time to inform me, Lord High Chamberlain."

Half-dressed, Pinch stood over the seated chamberlain and let one hand stray to the daggers in his belt.

It was a tribute to the old man's years of soldiering that he looked his adversary square and firm and never once flinched. The implied threat didn't faze him; either the chamberlain had made peace with death long ago or he was canny enough to know the rogue's bluff.

"Not yet. Soon."

Sensing the determination of the rock against the rain, the rogue relented. "Anon it is, but if you don't give good words on it soon, I'll have a grievance with you, Lord Cleedis." He stepped back, a signal that the threat was naught. "Just remember, a grievance is good enough reason for killing."

The old man scowled with irritation, not exactly the reaction Pinch expected from such a promise. "Morality gets in the way. Better to just kill and be done with it. Don't think—a proper soldier knows that. You would have learned that if you'd stayed."

"Just as long as I killed in Manferic's name?"

Cleedis shrugged off the question as no matter. "It's a warrior's duty." The cane clawed the floor as the old man got to his feet, stooped back bent under the load of bloody decades of duty. "Killing's just another task."

"Then I choose to kill for my own name." The rogue frowned darkly at the figure he saw in the salon's mirror.

The chamberlain possessed a voice he seldom used anymore, a voice illsuited to the sycophantic parasitism of court and embassy halls. It was a voice he'd learned long ago on the back of a horse, when every choice confronted death, a voice that made wiser men jump into the fire he chose. He used it now, but it was something that had long ago shriveled unused, no better than a rusted watch-spring on an ancient clock

"Stow your rubbish. A true killer makes no idle threats." The sense was there in what he gargled but the conviction was gone. "You'll wait your time with patience, and when the time's right you'll learn your job."

"I didn't come here to be your lap-boy," Pinch spat venomously.

"And it wasn't my idea to fetch you."

In his brain, the regulator seized on the statement. It was the first proof he'd been given that another mind stood behind the chamberlain's. His impulsive side, normally given to boozing and women, wanted to blurt out the question. Who had given the word? In moments like this, though, Pinch's cool heartlessness took hold. Calculating the reactions, he said nothing. The information would come to him, slowly and with time.

He made no show of noticing the old man's slip.

The door hinges creaked. "By this afternoon, I think."

And then he was alone.

A short while later, a shadow of wine-red velvet and white lace slipped past the bored guard beyond the door.

The salt-and-pepper-haired ghost padded through carpeted hallways, just slipping into dark doorways as stewards and ladies hurried by. They were blinded from the stranger's presence by their duties. Guards protected doorways, ignoring the arched halls behind them.

Pinch stayed to the darkest hallways, stuffed with their out-of-fashion trophy heads, past the servant quarters, along long avenues of interconnected halls. From the open windows that looked out over the courtyard where a squad of trainees drilled came the whiff of roasted sulfur and animal dung.

Trainees, he thought as he caught glimpses of the recruits bungling their drill. By rights, only the elite served here, but these amateurs bore the crest of Prince Vargo. These men were hasty recruits brought in as fodder to strengthen one princeling's hand. So it's come to this, each prince dredging the city for his own personal guard.

In the western wing, the search ended at a trio of guarded doors. That amused Pinch—the hopeless thought that his underlings would be challenged by a stand of overtrained watchmen. In this he was sure Cleedis or whoever was just naive; believing that only he was the threat, they underestimated the others.

It did not take long for Pinch to find a way to slip in unnoticed, and if he could get in, they could get out.

"He's fobbed you with a bale of barred cater-treys," the regulator chuckled as he sauntered off the balcony and interrupted Therin and Sprite's friendly dice game.

The game stopped in midthrow as the two twitched alert, their faces openly showing their native suspicion.

"Well, well. Doesn't need us for a damn, does he? Now look who walks in."

The halfling, perhaps with a better sense of caution, kept his mouth shut.

"You should know how things stand, Therin."

"Perhaps I do—Master Pinch. Or is it Lord Janol here?"

Pinch sidled away from the open window, just in case someone was watching. "As your prefer. Tell me, should I call you a fool?"

"Watch your prattling!" The dagger that suddenly appeared the man's hand reinforced his warning.

The regulator remained unruffled. "You really think I'd given you up, after I'd saved you from hanging in El-turel? It's a game, Gur, like those dice you hold. If they think you're worthless to me, then they'll not kill you to make me mind. Put your skene away and use your head."

The halfling gave a gentle restraining tug on the bladesman's sleeve. "Whether he's telling the truth or lying, he's right, Therin. Maybe we don't mean anything to him and maybe we do—but if they think we're a hold over him then we're all dead as a surety."

The master rogue nodded agreement to the halfling's words. "The game's to get them to think what you want them to think, not to play fair." He pointed to the dice in Therin's palm. "I'll wager you a groat you can't roll a five or a nine with Sprite's dice."

"I would never, not to my friends!" Sprite protested in his tinny voice.

The Gur eased back from his coil, slid his knife away and eyed the dice casually. "That might be," he drawled with particular serenity to make his point, "or maybe I've crossed him with a bale of contraries." He reached into his blouse and produced a pair of identical-looking dice. "That's how the game is played."

"Unfair! You've been figging me!" squealed the half-ling. He scrambled to gather up the winnings before anyone might stop him. Therin moved almost as quick, and there was a flurry of reaching and grabbing as the coins and notes in the pot vanished from the floor.

"Well played, high lawyer!" The release of anxiety welled up inside the regulator and translated itself into spurt of laugher.

When they were finished, Pinch settled into the softest chair in the room. Compared to his, this small bedroom was spartan; compared to the previous rooms of the lot, it was luxurious. The rascals had been given a set of three connected chambers, which gave them more space than they really needed.

"How fare you three?" the rogue asked.

"Well enough . . ." Therin was too busy counting his loot to be bothered.

"Can't say much for the rooms, but they made a fine breakfast."

Pinch wasn't sure if the halfling was being sarcastic or true to his nature. Whenever there was loot, Sprite-Heels was always squandering his on homey comforts and food, pretending to live the burghermeister's life. He'd talk about going home, describing a place of rich fields, rolling hills, and barrow homes where he could work an honest life and everyone was 'Uncle' or 'Grandmother' or 'Brother.' Contrary to this, a few times when he was truly drunk, the Hairfoot revealed another choice for his upbringing: an orphan's life in cold, wattled shacks along Elturel's muddy riverbank. Pinch could only wonder which, if either, was real.

"Where's Maeve?"

The Gur nodded toward the closed door on the left wall. There were three doors, one on each wall, and the smallish balcony behind Pinch. The door to the right was open, hinting at a room like this one. The door on the wall opposite was larger, probably locked, and a guard stood on the other side. That left the third door where Maeve was, in a room identical to this one. But not perfectly identical; from the outside only the center room had a balcony.

"She sweet-talked a guard for a couple of bottles of bub last night and she wasn't in a sharing mood. Sleeping it off, she is." Sprite pocketed his crooked dice and brushed his clothes clean.

"Damn Lliira's curse. Roust her."

The other two exchanged a wicked grin. "As you say!"

In a few moments, a splash followed by a shriek of sputtering outrage echoed from the other room. This was followed by man and halfling tumbling through the door.

"By troth, she's in a foul humor!" Therin's words were punctuated by a sizzle of sparks, green and red, that arced over his head followed by a billow of bitter smoke, a pyrotechnic display of her anger.

Pinch planted himself on the balcony and waited for Maeve's handiwork to clear.

Maeve emerged with eyes of red sorrow, her body sagging in the knot of nightclothes, wet with water dripping from her stringy hair. Spotting Therin, she fumbled into her sleeves looking for some particularly nasty scrap of bat wing or packet of powdered bone.

"Good morn, Maeve," Pinch interrupted as he stepped from the balcony.

Without missing a beat, the wizardess bowed slightly to the thief. "Greetings to you, Master Pinch. You sent these wags to soak me?

"I sent them to wake you. You were drunk."

The witch drew herself up. "Hung over. Not drunk."

"Drunk—and when I need you sober. Fail me again, and I'll cut you off." With that the rogue turned to other business, turning away from her in disdain for her temper and her spells. "What have you learned?" he asked of the other two.

"Damned little. It's only been a day."

"We aren't going to have many days here," the regulator snapped back. "Do you think this is a pleasure trip? How about escape—the ogre and the hounds?"

As he expected, the pair had done more than they allowed. "The hounds are kenneled in the southeast corner," Sprite began. "I don't know where the ogre sleeps."

"Close by his pack would be the best guess," the Gur added.

"After that, there's three gates to the city. Counted those when we came in."

"What about getting out of here?"

"They keeps us locked in all the time, 'cept for meals and necessaries." The halfling scratched his furred foot. "Well, there's the balcony where you got in. The other two rooms got windows we can climb down."

"You maybe, you little imp, not me," Maeve sniped.

"You'll do as you must, dear. What about secret passages—Sprite? Therin?"

"None we found, Pinch."

The older man nodded. "I'm thinking there's one in mine."

"What do we do now, Pinch?"

The regulator laid a soothing hand on Maeve's damp shoulder. "Watch, wait. Whatever they want, it'll happen soon. I want the lot of you to get the lay of Ankhapur. Get yourselves into the city proper. Talk and listen. Nip something if you want, just don't get caught. Cleedis means you to be hostages, so you'd best be careful."

"Well, that means he won't scrag us," Therin said with morbid cheer.

Pinch looked to the other man with a cocked eyebrow of disbelief. "Just don't put him to the test. You've more enemies than Cleedis out there."

"Your cousins?"

The rogue tapped his temple. The man was right on.

"Why? Now's time we deserve to know."

Looking at their hard faces now that the question had come up, Pinch shrugged.

"They're Manferic's spawn. It's in their blood, I think. There's not a measure of kindness granted by them that doesn't pass unwaged. Their hate's like a snake, cold and slithery."

"So why do they hate you?" Sprite pressed.

"I ran away; they couldn't."

"This king of yours must have been the dark one's own kin." Maeve sniffed a bit, sounding positively touched. She'd always been like that, the softest touch for a story. "What'd he do to you, Pinch?"

Pinch glared at the intrusion. His past wasn't any of their business. But now he'd started down the path and, like the genie from the bottle, opening it was a lot easier than pushing all the vapor back in.

It was an impossibility to try telling them, though. There was no way to adequately explain Manferic's cold, manipulative heart. On the surface, he'd been raised with kindness and generosity, far more than was warranted to an orphaned boy—even if his father had been a knight and his mother a lady. He had no memory of them. Cleedis said his father had died on campaign, carried off by a swamp troll; his mother had died in childbirth. Manferic himself had taken the foundling in and raised him as one of his own.

When he was little Jan, as he was known then, he never wondered, never questioned. In his eyes, the king was kind and good, his "brothers" mean. He quickly learned their meanness stemmed from arrogance and jealousy. He was the intruder at their hearth, a thief of privilege duly belonging to them.

It was only later that he learned a harsher lesson: that kindness and love were only masks for cold self-interest. That was the day he learned the true reason that the old king had raised him with such care.

"He was . . . evil." It was what he meant, but Pinch couldn't say it with the conviction the word needed. Good, evil were no longer for him the sharp lines of separation they once were.

"Enough wasted time. There's more I want you to do. The three princes are likely to make trouble. An ear to the wind should give good warning of any moves." The rogue turned to his lieutenant. "There's three idiot courtiers in Throdus's camp—Treeve, Kurkulatain, and

Faranoch. Make a conveyance to know them, Therin; they may be ripe informers."

"Sprite, find us a hole in the city." Pinch tapped his temple. "My memories are past use. After fifteen years, things change."

Finally he turned to the hung-over sorceress, who winced at every sound, and in his gentlest voice said, "Now, dear, I want you to dress your finest and make friends here in the court. Use your spells. Find out what these fine people are really thinking. I may need to know were everybody stands."

"Me? Out there with them? They's a bit above my rank, Pinch. I won't know how to behave like a proper gentry mort."

The rogue touched her reassuringly. "There now, you'll do fine. A little touch of makeup and some new clothes and you'll be sitting right beside them at their tables. You always were a quick doxy."

There were no more orders to be said. Each of his journeymen nodded off on their part. The roles were not new to them; each had the eye and skill for the part Pinch gave them. With no questions, Pinch went out onto the balcony again. Just before slipping over the rail, he added one last caveat. "Therin, mind your sword. There'll be no blood in the house. Sprite, mind where you filch, too. They draw and quarter thieves here without waiting for the start of term-time. And Maeve," he added lastly, "keep yourself sober. Drink despoils a lady."

And then, like a morning mist, the rogue melted through the rail and away.

Iron-Biter

"Well indeed, Iron-Biter, see who comes upon us."

The voice rang clearly through the hallways as Pinch made his way back to his apartment. It resounded from the smooth surfaces, as cold as the gleaming marble was even in the generous sun.

Pinch's first reaction was that the subject was someone else, and he could still divert his track down another hallway before he was made. There was no need to hide, no one had restricted his movements, but it was the natural urge of a man who has spent his life in hiding.

There was no place to escape. The click of boots on stone told him his captors were already there, coming upon him.

True enough, there ahead was Prince Vargo and a stocky dwarf. Vargo was every bit the lord of the manor, casually dressed in green hunting breeches, shirt, and riding cloak that was anything but casual. The material was brushed to a dazzling sheen so that if the day's light had managed to angle through the narrow windows and strike him he would have burned with the fire of a roman candle, flooding everything with reflected green.

The dwarf was a barrel overturned and given legs. His chest was broader than he was tall and carved to Herculean proportions, and his little arms could barely touch fingers in the center. The traditional dwarven beard and braids formed a golden-hued knot for a head. Here was a dwarf who probably cracked his dinner bones with his fingers just to suck out the marrow.

They formed an improbable couple, the lean and the tall, the short and the blocky.

Pinch hadn't noticed them because they'd been hidden behind a statue.

"Well, little Jan," Vargo hailed with unexpected good cheer, "it is a surprise to meet you here. Quite surprising, don't you think, Iron-Biter?"

The dwarf looked over Pinch, starting at his toes then moving upward, assessing every bone for its likely resistance to his marrow-popping fingers.

"An unexpected occurrence," the dwarf said after finishing his scan of Pinch's curled head, more interested in the cranium beneath the scalp.

"Iron-Biter, Master Janol. Janol, Iron-Biter. Iron-Biter's my right hand, useful in all manner of things. A master of useful trades. Janol is the late king's ward, Iron-Biter. I'm sure you've heard me speak of him."

The dwarf made a sharp, precise bow to Pinch. He moved far more gracefully than his squat little body should have allowed. "It is a pleasure. I seldom meet worthy adversaries."

"Indeed," was all Pinch could manage. Two lines into a conversation and already he was being challenged.

"Iron-Biter's just a little overanxious," Vargo purred. "We heard about your meeting with Throdus."

"Oh."

"Throdus is an idiot. He should not have wasted time talking to you."

"No?"

"If it had been me, I would have gutted you on the spot."

That got Pinch's bristle up. "If you could have."

Vargo examined the ceiling for a moment. Iron-Biter did nothing but glare at Pinch. Finally the prince said, "You remember our fencing instructor? The one you could never beat?

"Yes . . ."

"A month after you left, the fool irritated me. I ran him through at our next lesson. I still remember the look on his face when he realized it was no longer a lesson."

"It's been fifteen years, Vargo. Thing change."

"I've only gotten better," the prince replied with complete confidence. "Haven't I, Iron-Biter?"

The dwarf, who to that point had never taken his eyes from Pinch, spared the briefest glance toward his lord. "Certainly, Prince Vargo."

"I think, Jan, that you are not worth bloodying my hands. Iron-Biter, show him why I drag you around."

The dwarf barely acknowledged the insult. There was in him the devotion of a killer mastiff, the beast eagerly awaiting its master's command. A grim smile crossed his lips as now he got to perform. Gesturing to the statuary that filled the niches of the hall, he asked the rogue, "Do you like art?"

"Only for its resale value."

"Ah, a true connoisseur. So, which one has the most worth?"

Pinch smiled because he knew where this game was going. He would choose one and then there would be a crude demonstration of Iron-Biter's might, all to supposedly impress and terrify him. The Hellriders of Elturel had often used this clumsy ploy. It did have one good effect, though; it showed which enemy you should eliminate first.

"That one, I think." He deliberately chose one of lesser value—a large marble hydra, its seven heads carved into elaborate coils. The work was solid but unimaginative in pose and pedestrian in its craftsmanship.

The dwarf *tsked*. "A poor eye. Perhaps you're not the challenge I thought." Instead he turned to a small piece carved from a block of jade the size of a melon, a delicately winged sprite perched on the blossom of a fat-petalled flower.

The dwarf muttered softly while he gently stroked the statue. Slowly, under his gentle caress, the stone twitched. With a snapping creak the little wings fluttered, the head swiveled, the flower petals drooped. All at once, the clouded green sprite took flight, its wings clicking frantically to keep its slender stone body in the air.

It soared upward in the great arched hall. Darting into a gleam from the transom windows, the translucent stone shattered the ray of light into emerald-hued brands that blazed the walls, statues, even the trio that stood watching below.

It was beautiful, and the secret of its beauty was both in its grace and in the power that had created it. This Iron-Biter was no mere thug, as Pinch had first presumed. There were few who could bring movement to cold substance; it was a feat given only to priests of power.

"Enough," Vargo sighed in utter boredom.

The dwarf-priest plucked the stone flower from its stand. Holding it out, he gently chirped, drawing the jade sprite down. It hovered uncertainly before finally allowing itself to be coaxed onto the crystal leaf. With his thick hand, Iron-Biter stroked its back and the sprite responded with a clattering purr.

"Iron-Biter, I have other things to do," Vargo snapped with impatience.

The dwarf nodded and in midstroke squeezed the stone fairy between his palms. The stone wings crackled, the slender arms shattered. Shards and dust fell through his fingers. The hall filled with the shriek of it all, though Pinch wasn't sure if it was just grinding stone or if the animate little sprite had found its voice in the last moments of death.

The pair left without further word, leaving only a pile of jade rubble for the servants to clean.

When Pinch returned to his apartment, he was displeased to see two new guards posted outside his door. Unlike the fellow he'd left behind, these two looked alert and attentive.

They were polite and gracious, stepping aside so that he could enter. The corporal of the pair bowed and said, "Lord Cleedis is concerned for your safety, Master Janol. Thus he asks that we stand ready to protect you from dangerous visitors."

Pinch poked his tongue into his cheek. "And whom might those be."

The corporal was unfazed. "Within these walls, it could be anyone. Our orders are to let no one in without our lord's approval."

"And if I want to leave."

There was an answer for that too. "Lord Cleedis feels it would be best if you did not risk your safety beyond these chambers. We are instructed to see that you remain safe and unharmed."

"In other words, I'm a prisoner."

The corporal frowned. "If that would make Master Janol more comfortable—yes."

"My comforts are not Lord Cleedis's concern," the

rogue snapped as he closed the door.

So this was it; the ring was closing in. Cleedis wanted him, but only on the old man's terms. Is he truly afraid for my safety, or is he afraid I'll make alliances with the others? It didn't matter really. Whatever Cleedis's motives, the regulator refused to be bound by them, but to do that he needed a way out.

The prospect from his windows was dim. The portholes were no larger than before and, even if he could wriggle through one, climbing was not his strong suit. He'd only managed to reach Therin's balcony because the way had been ridiculously easy.

If he wanted an escape, he had to find another way, and he was convinced there must be one. It was a combination of several things that made him certain. First there was the voice. Whoever had uttered those words had seen what was happening. It could have been done by magic, but he didn't think so. There was a hollowness in the echo that suggested someone there and close to the scene.

There was also the reality of family history. Pinch knew Ankhapur's past, the intrigues, assassinations, and plots that defined the character of the city. He could not accept the idea that the queen who'd built these rooms would leave herself trapped by only one door. There had to be another way out.

Methodically, the rogue started an inspection of every inch of the fine wood paneling on the walls, even so far as to stand on a chair for extra height. He ran his fingers down every tongue and groove of the walls, poked and turned every baroque ornament, pulled wainscoting, and kicked baseboards. Given his thoroughness, it was hardly surprising when a section of the wall, just inside the bedroom door, responded with the faint click of a hidden spring. A small piece of the woodwork slid away to reveal a small handle.

This was it then, what he had been looking for.

With a swollen wax candle to light the way, Pinch pushed against the door. The wooden wall budged a fraction of an inch and then stuck. Clearly, this old passage was long forgotten and never used anymore. Pinch shoved harder, cursing Mask, god of deceptions, with each straining breath. The panel yielded an inch with each shove, the old wood grinding across a hidden stone threshold.

Dead air and the odor of cobwebs breathed through the gap, exhaling the soft dust of centuries. With one more shove, the doorway popped open, swirling a fog of powder from the floor. Inside was a stygian passage, all the more gloomy for the feeble glimmer of the candle. Without the taper, the way would have been merely dark, but in its light the walls quivered away into blackness.

Fastidiously slicing the cobwebs away, Pinch rounded a corner and almost tripped down a flight of steps. "No soul's been here recent," he muttered to himself. The gray blanket on the floor was undisturbed. It was all the more a puzzle. Pinch was sure in his heart that someone had spied from this passage, but there was no trail of anything or anyone. The descending stairs ruled out the possibility of another path that led to a different section of his rooms.

Pinch pressed on. A passage like this led somewhere, and he wanted to know just where that was. One end was grounded in his apartments. The other could be— well, anywhere.

The staircase was long and kinked around several times until the rogue was completely separated from the surface world. He could no longer say this was north and that south, or that he had progressed any sure number of rods in a given direction. Was he under the courtyard or the west wing, or perhaps neither. Dwarves, he was told, could innately tell you these things at the snap of a finger, and he'd heard a few of the grim little potbellies cite with fondness that they were once this-and-such leagues beneath the surface as if it were the most natural understanding of things. He didn't like it. Plunging into the depths was too much like being sealed in one's crypt. It was a stifling feeling that he choked down even as he pressed forward. He needed the moon and the open night over him.

Somewhere underground, probably at the depths where bodies were interred in catacombs, the stairs splashed into a narrow hallway. Left and right, the choices were twofold. As Pinch leaned forward to look, a wind racing through guttered his lone flame and splashed hot wax on his hand. The thief pulled back at this reminder of how tenuous was his connection to the daylit world.

Over the hiss of the wind, or commingled with it, the regulator heard a clear note that rose and fell in jerky beats. Was it another voice snatched up by the wind and carried to his ears, or just the handiwork of nature in the air's headlong rush? It was beyond Pinch to say. The cry, if it could be called such, had the sad quality of a lamentation, the type sung at wakes by drunken kin almost in time and harmony.

As he paused to listen, the rogue spotted a new element. All down the length of the passage, from left to east, west to right, were tracks. Not just rat trails or the squirms of snakes, but real footprints.

They were human, or at least as much as Pinch could tell, and there were at least two sets, but beyond that he couldn't say. The rogue was no huntsman. The overlapping jumble of tracks before him was beyond his ability to decipher.

Shielding his candle, Pinch guessed on a direction and followed the trail. Who did each track belong to? The princes? Cleedis? Or someone else? One set seemed too small and dainty for prince or chamberlain, the other quite possible. Still, Pinch ruled out the princes.

He couldn't imagine any of them traipsing through cob-webbed corridors, not when they had flunkies to do the job. Cleedis, he knew, would do his own dirty work. Perhaps the old man had been spying on him.

A flickering light immediately ahead ended all speculation. It had emerged without a preceding glimmer, perhaps the shutter raised on a lantern. Pinch immediately hid his light, tucking the candle into a sleeve. The flame scorched his arm. There was nothing to do but bite back the pain and endure in silence. Without a stick of Kossuth's sulfur, there was no way to relight the candle should he need it later.

The distant light darted back around its corner, frighted by his own gleams. The rogue lightfooted after, determined not to lose this other interloper. He moved with quick puffing steps, years of stealth aided by a thick carpet of dust.

He peered around the corner, candle still cloaked and dagger ready, barely in time to see the rays disappear around another bend. The rogue's breath thrilled at the challenge of the chase.

His prey was as quick as he was stealthy, darting through the labyrinth of passages. Pinch guessed they were in some old catacombs beneath the palace. Left, right, right, left—he struggled to remember the turns. It would do no good if he could not get back.

As he rounded one more turn, the floor vanished, replaced by empty space. Unable to recover, he plunged forward, hit a step, lurched, and then the candle slipped from his hand. As the rogue frantically batted at the flame in his sleeve, he lost all hope of balance and tumbled into the darkness.

The fall was mercifully short, but not short enough. Pinch managed to crack what seemed like every bone against the jagged stone steps. His hose snagged ripping edges, his hands tore along the rasping walls. And then it ended with a hard crash as the man spilled onto a floor of cold, greasy stone.

Slowly and with a great deal of pain he could easily have lived without, Pinch tottered back to his feet, supporting himself on a wall he could not see. It was black, without even the little twinkling lights they say a man gets from a sound whack to the head. His head throbbed enough, but no whirling colors appeared.

What if I've knocked myself blind? The thought triggered panic.

A gleam of light dispelled that fear. Whomever he pursued was still up ahead. They had certainly heard his fall, there was no more point in secrecy.

"Whose light? You've lured me this far. Show yourself and let's have done with it." Pinch tried bravado since surprise was out.

There was no response. The light wavered and then began to fade.

"Damn you," the rogue muttered to no one but himself. "You're not slipping me." His only choices were to follow or grope his way back, and he couldn't remember the turns to his room. The fall had knocked the order loose and they drifted around, right-left, left-right, he didn't know for sure. There really was no choice but to hobble forward.

The lantern bearer continued their game and moved away just as Pinch reached the corner. The rogue broke into an off-stepped run.

Around the next corner, it happened again. Even in the instant his foot stepped into the void, Pinch cursed himself for blindly running into the trap. He lurched forward and this time he could sense there was no jagged stairs, only emptiness and death below.

The light knew it too and hurtled back into sight. It wasn't a lantern bearer but a glowing diffusion of the air that throbbed eagerly in time with the man's waves of pain and despair.

Pinch hung on the rim of the precipice forever, one

second of time subdivided by his senses into eternity.
The feeding light, the bottomless hole, the crumbling
stone of the walls, the ever-steady plunge forward—so
this is how I die. The thought came coolly to him.

In that infinite moment, Fate intervened—or something at least. It could have been blind chance, cosmic
design, or the whim of some god Pinch had inadver-
tently forgotten to blaspheme. Two things occurred almost simultaneously, and were the rogue to examine
them later, he would not be able to say what they both
were. Out of his torn doublet swung the amulet he'd
stolen from the Morninglord's temple. As it hung free,
the artifact flared with the brilliant hues of dawn washing out all sight with a roseate haze. The luring light
dwindled against it as if in pain.

Ironic that I should die in a blaze of glory.

As the thought formed, something seized him. A
strong hand or maybe a claw clenched around his arm
and heaved him back.

And then the moment ended. The flare subsided, his
plunge stopped, and he stood blinking in the darkness
on the edge of nonexistence. A hand took his and pulled
him away, and the rogue stumbled after, too stupefied
to resist.

When his wits recovered, all was completely black. A
hand, slender and feminine, led him through the darkness, around several corners, and up a flight of stairs.
His guide moved with confidence through the ebon
world.

"Who are you?" Pinch demanded as he stumbled in
tow.

There was no answer.

Pinch tried to pull up, but the hand tugged him in-
sistently forward.

"Trust."

The words were the whisper of dried husks, papery
brittle and filled with the music of tears. It was a voice

Pinch had never heard, but still it seemed to wrap him in comfort.

"Trust me, little one."

The hand pulled forward again.

Perhaps because his senses were dulled by all that had passed, the rogue let himself be led on.

Right, left, left, and more they went until at last they stopped. The invisible guide placed Pinch's hand to the wall and whispered, "Up." His foot blindly touched the bottom of a step.

"Up to safety. Go." The guide gently pushed him forward and yet wanted to hold him back.

"Who are you?" The question finally formulated itself for him.

"A . . . friend. Go." The voice struggled against a choking sob and then the hands left him.

He was alone in the darkness once more. Faintly through the air drifted the sound of weeping.

Pinch climbed, carefully groping out each step lest there were any more traps. No lights came to torment him, lead him astray, and the way climbed and twisted until he was sure he was back on the stairs to his room.

Along the way, the regulator fingered the amulet and wondered. What have I gotten into? Murderous dwarves, strange passages, mysterious saviors—it was all much more than he had bargained for. Did Cleedis know the mysteries that filled this palace? Would he even tell me if he did?

The stairs came to a platform and wall and Pinch felt out a handle. Pulling firmly, he dragged the stiff panel ajar, flooding his eyes with the blinding candle-light of his room.

Beyond the Grave

"Open the door, Janol. It's time."

From the other room came the relentless thump of a staff pounded against the door.

"This is your last chance before I have them break it down." The muffled voice belonged to Cleedis, and he did not sound pleased.

Pinch hurried to the apartment door, but instead of opening it, he pulled a heavy chair over and wedged it under the door handle. If they went so far as to break the door, it would take them time and, looking in a mirror, he needed time.

First he pulled the wall shut. There was a chance that no one had magically scried his discovery of the passage, so there was no point in advertising it.

"Open it."

Pinch worked quickly. Off came the torn and dusty clothes, replaced by a sleeping robe. Shoving the clothes out of sight, he brushed the cobwebs out of his curly gray hair and splashed cold water over his face. His raw hand stung, and clearing away the dirt only made the bruises and scratches on his face more vivid.

The door lock rasped and the guard's key ratcheted in the lock. When they went to open the door, though, the chair slid for a few inches before wedging itself firmly into place.

"Damfnit, Janol, do I have to break this door down?"

The door rattled on its hinges, and the chair creaked as someone bounced off the other side. Pinch could see an apoplectic Cleedis ordering his men to throw themselves at the barrier until it was shattered.

Pinch let them hit it a few more times so he could get a sense of their timing. The last thing he wanted to do was open up to face a flying wedge of guardsmen.

"Let your hounds off, Cleedis. I'm coming."

Saying that, the regulator waited just to be sure. When no more thuds resounded through his suite, he unwedged the chair and sat in it.

"It's open, Lord Chamberlain."

A furious squall entered the room, beet red and thundering. The old soldier showed more fury and emotion than Pinch had seen in him since their first meeting. "And what was the purpose of that little game?"

"Privacy. I was sleeping."

The hard sergeant in Cleedis growled disapproval. "It's midday."

Pinch shrugged.

"What happened to you?" the nobleman demanded, noticing Pinch's battered face.

The rogue refrained from a smile, though the chamberlain had given him the opening for the tale he'd planned. "I had more visitors—Prince Vargo's thugs. That's another reason for the chair."

"Vargo's? Will it stand to the proof?"

"Does the prince make gifts of his livery?"

"My men were outside." Cleedis's voice was full of wishful loyalty.

"Indeed." Though it hurt, Pinch raised an eyebrow in skepticism.

To that the old man could only stomp about the room, rapping the floor with frustration. Now Pinch allowed himself a smile, unable to restrain the malicious joy of his own handiwork any longer. There was no way to confirm his story, nor would any denial be trusted. Cleedis had no choice but to doubt his own men. There was even a chance the old soldier might set his men on Vargo's. In any case, it was a weakness in the strength of his hosts and captors. Any weakness of theirs might give him an edge.

"Get dressed," Cleedis ordered in his gruff sergeant's voice. "We're to meet your employer."

"Finally." As he rose to get dressed, Pinch kept his words sparse and light, although inside he was seething with curiosity and eagerness. At last there was a real chance of getting some answers.

He came back quickly, dressed and clean, and limping only slightly from his fall. Cleedis hadn't expected such haste, but Pinch brushed that away as the desire to get on with his duties, though in truth he'd been partially dressed beneath his robe.

As they left the room, Cleedis dismissed the guards on the pretense they should rest their aching shoulders. Only the chamberlain's personal bodyguard was to accompany them on this trip.

Hooded and cloaked more for secrecy than warmth, the small party rode from the postern gate of the palace toward the far side of Ankhapur. At first Pinch couldn't figure where they were headed, but after they'd crossed several avenues and not turned off, he knew. They were making for the grave field.

The common practice to get from place to place in

bowl-shaped Ankhapur was to climb or descend to the avenue desired and then make a circuit around the center.
The chamberlain had done neither. In leaving he wove
through the interconnecting streets, first taking this
boulevard then that avenue. The route was in part to reveal any unwanted followers, but after crossing the Street
of Shames the only place left to go was the grave field.

No city likes its burial grounds, festering sores of
evil. Too many things buried came back for such places
to be safe. In a few cases, the dead came back of their
own volition seeking revenge or just flesh. More often
than not, the dead were disturbed by others—wizards
and priests who saw the graves and crypts as raw material for their dark arts. The dead don't like to be disturbed and generally make ill company for the living.

Thus, different cities adopt different strategies for
dealing with the problem. Some bury their dead outside
the city, others behind strong walls. In a few, cremation
is the rule. Ankhapur used to dump its dead far out to
sea, until the Year of the Watery Dead. In that year,
Ankhapur's ancestors returned: a host of sea zombies
and things less wholesome that clambered over the
docks seeking revenge on the city that had cast them
away. The assault lasted more than a year, new waves
of terror striking every night, before the undead host
was finally overcome.

Aside from the death and destruction, the greatest
consequence was that the citizens would no longer con-
sign their kin to the waters. Burial and veneration of
the dead suddenly became the way of things.

Unfortunately the city had grown without a burial
ground and had no proper place for one. The farmlands
around were all fiefs of the nobility, and no one could be
persuaded to surrender lands for the dead. The only solution was to raze a section of the ghetto that lay just
within the walls and crowd the crypts into there. To en-
sure the safety of the citizens, all the temples of Ankha-

pur, or at least those that could be trusted, were levied
with the task of providing priests to guard the perimeter.

This was where they were headed—the Street of
Crypts. As a youth, even though he'd been reckless and
wild, Pinch had prudently avoided this district. All that
he knew about it he knew by rumor, and the rumors
were not pleasant.

The perimeter of the district was marked by a low
wall, hardly enough to keep anyone out or anything in.
At regular intervals along its length were small stone
watchtowers. In each was a priest, probably bored or
asleep, whose duty was to be ready with his spells and
his faith lest the dead wander from their tombs.

The group waited at a small arch while the priests
there set aside their books and prayers and undid the
iron gate. The rusted hinges squealed for oil as they
pushed the grill open. Pinch barely gave them a notice
until he saw a tousle-haired woman among them: Lissa
of the Morninglord. He considered greeting her, asking
her how the search had gone, perhaps even giving her
clues that he suspected someone, but there was no privacy and no time. Instead, he merely let his hood slip
back so she could see his face, gave her a wink, and set
his finger to his lips. She practically jumped with a
start and gave it all away, but that wouldn't have mattered much. Pinch just wanted her to feel a conspirator,
to draw her farther into his web.

He and Cleedis left their horses and their bodyguard
just inside the gate, and the commander gave word for
the men to see to the animals and get themselves a
drink. "What are you fearing?" the aged hero chided.
"It's day. We'll be safe enough."

The old ghetto district hadn't been very large, and
death was a popular pastime in Ankhapur—someone
else's death preferred to one's own. The dead were
crammed into the space so tight that the lanes between
the crypts were barely big enough for a team of pall-

bearers to wind their way through. There was no grid
or path through the grave markers. The route had all
the organization of spaces between a tumble of child's
blocks. The way went straight, branched, and shunted
constantly. In an effort to squeeze more space for the
honored dead, crypts stood upon crypts. A staircase
would suddenly wind up to another lane that ran along
the roof of a mausoleum, passing the sealed niches of
yet more bodies.

The ornamentation on each building was just as haphazard, dictated by the fashion of the decade and what
the family could afford. In one dark corner a fountain
perpetually splashed up bubbles of a tune loved by someone in the last century, now more a tribute to some wizard's art. From the cracks around a crypt door blazed
rays of endless sunlight from within, as good an assurance against vampires and wights as any Pinch had
seen. A foul-faced carven gargoyle fixed over another
door howled aloud the sins of all who were buried within.
Pinch stopped to listen a bit, rather impressed by the
litany of villainies, until Cleedis testily urged him on.

They had plunged a considerable way in when the
narrow path yawned into an improbable courtyard, not
large but jarringly empty nonetheless. Nothing should
be open here, so this space was the ultimate in conspic-
uous arrogance.

On one side was the royal tomb, of course. No other
family could command such real estate in this cramped
necropolis. The mausoleum itself was a fixture of restrained style, trumpeting its tastefulness in contradic-
tion to its garish neighbors. The other crypts around
the square, noble families all, sported hideous mon-
sters, garish polychrome colors, and overwrought iron
ivy. They were a mishmash of styles over the centuries.
If Pinch were of the mind to, he could have read the
tastes of Ankhapur as they passed over the years.

Cleedis sat himself on a bench some kin had thought-

fully provided just in case their dearly departed wanted
to rise and catch a little sun. The old man, stooped and
wrinkled, looked a part of the landscape. He fiddled
with his sword, as was his wont when he was compelled
to do nothing but wait. Waiting ill suited him; he was
once a man of action and the habit of patience had long
ago been marched out of him.

"Lo, here. You've escorted me this far to sit?"

"Bide your time, thief."

Pinch sighed and leaned himself against a wall.
Knowing they were to wait, he could do a masterful job
of it. Half his career was waiting with one eye to the
mark and the other ever watchful for the constables. He
fished two bales of dice from his pocket and practiced
his foists, throwing first one set and then changing it by
a quick sleight.

Some time went by in this manner, until the old man
nodded into a doze on the sun-warmed bench. Just as
Pinch was considering nipping the chamberlain's purse
and rings, the door to the royal crypt creaked open.

"Janol, it has been a long time."

The blood ran in icy droplets down the length of
Pinch's spine.

"No kind greeting?"

It was the voice that froze him, a bass growl where
each word was sharply enunciated. He hadn't heard
that voice in fifteen years. It was different, a little thinner and breathy, but there was no mistaking.

He didn't expect to ever hear it again, either.

"Manferic?"

A dry chuckle echoed from inside the tomb. " 'Your
Highness, King Manferic,' my ungrateful ward."

"You're . . . dead. Or you're supposed to be."

There was a long pause. "What if I am? Death is only
another challenge."

Pinch swallowed hard. For maybe the second time in
his life, at least since he was old enough to appreciate his

feelings, Pinch was scared. Deep, hard squeezing-in-the-gut scared. It was like a cold snake coiling around his throat, squeezing on his lungs till his breath came hard.

"Come here." The dark shape moved closer to the open doorway, always taking care to skirt the shafts of light.

Pinch shook his head fiercely against that suggestion. He was not about to step into the dark with that thing. The living Manferic had been enough to drive him away; an undead one, if Manferic was truly dead, could only be worse.

"State your business with me," the rogue croaked out, doing his best to sound bold.

"I've watched your progress, son." Manferic had always called his ward "son." Pinch was never sure if it was mockery or done just to irritate Manferic's true sons. It certainly wasn't love. The king hadn't an ounce in him then, and there was certainly none left now. "You did me proud."

"I wasn't trying to. What do you want?" The rogue kept fear at bay through his bluster.

The shadow sighed within. "And I hoped this would be a warm and touching reunion. I need a thief."

"Why me? There's ten score of them in Ankhapur, and more than a few are a match for me." Pinch bumped into something solid behind him. He jumped, but it was only a pillar.

"I need someone discreet and with no connections here in Ankhapur. You."

Pinch assumed this was a lie. In life, Manferic had never been this direct.

"You are to steal the Cup and the Knife."

The Cup and Knife! Ankhapur's symbols of royal prerogative and the two holiest artifacts in the city. It was only through them that one of the four princes would be able to claim Manferic's throne. Now Pinch was beginning to understand why Cleedis had been stalling the ceremony. Cleedis and Manferic, or more likely Manferic and Cleedis, were plotting something.

"It won't stop them from choosing a new king. They'll get their king with or without the test."

The voice chuckled again, and Pinch imagined hearing the echoes of heartless mirth.

"They will never know. You're going to switch them with another set. Another Cup and Knife. I have them here. Cleedis arranged for them to be made. Come and get them."

Pinch was immovable. "Bring them out."

The dark crypt echoed with a rasping hiss. "That would be difficult. At a future time."

"Set them in the light, then."

A charcoal gray bundle slid just barely into the light that poured through the ajar door. No hand or foot came into view.

"And after I've made the exchange?"

The voice from the crypt answered. "Give everything to Cleedis. He will know what to do."

"I work for myself. What's my booty?"

"Your life, your freedom."

Pinch snorted. "Small threats. What about coins?"

The voice chuckled again. "Cleedis will see that you are rewarded.

"The work must be done quickly. Old doddering Cleedis there can't stall my eager sons much longer. The Cup and the Knife must be traded before the ceremony—and no one must suspect. Understand this clearly."

"Your points are clear," Pinch snidely answered. He stepped over to Cleedis and sharply kicked the old man. The chamberlain woke quick and alert, a legacy of years of military service. The rogue nodded to the package and lied, "You're to carry it. I'm not trusted."

The chamberlain glared with resentment at being ordered so, but nonetheless waddled over and fetched the bundle from the doorway. It was heavier than it appeared, and he hefted it with a grunt.

The crypt door creaked shut. "Betray me and die. Fail me and suffer," promised the sepulchral voice from inside.

Pinch seized the bag from Cleedis's grasp and furiously undid the strings. Carefully reaching in he pulled forth the larger of two items he felt. It was a large goblet sharply chiseled from a piece of perfect black quartz. The rim was lipped with a band of gold studded with faceted rubies. At the very bottom of the smoothly polished bowl was the largest white pearl Pinch had ever seen. It was real, too, not fake. His eye was practiced enough to tell the real goods from cheap glimmers.

Blood quickening, Pinch produced the other item from the bag, a silver knife cast as a single piece. It had no rivets, no wrappings, no stones, no gold. The handle was molded into a fluid form whorled and knuckled to the grip of a hand. Perhaps the caster had cooled the molten ore in his hand, molding it the way a child squeezes clay. The blade was ground to a razored line that promised to slice skin, sinew, even bone with the smoothest of grace. The craftsmanship lavished on the copy was perhaps the equal of the original.

Hands trembled as he held the small fortune in hand, and the sheer thought of the magnificence before him overwhelmed the utter fear that had shaken him moments before. Dead king or no, thing in the crypt or what, even these terrors could not drive away the avarice the rogue felt on examining these earthly glories.

The chamberlain testily seized the treasures and stuffed them back into their bag. "I'll keep them. Out of sight. And remember my lord's words," he added with more than a little distrust of his accomplice's passions.

That reminder brought Pinch back to the reality of his situation, and as Cleedis hurried from the courtyard, the rogue's initial fear turned to calculation. He took stock of everything that had happened. He'd heard a voice, saw a door move, but never saw the departed king. There was always the possibility that what he'd imagined was true, but there were other alternatives.

First—and this thought came to him as they passed a golden-flowered tree perpetually in bloom, the remembrance of a lord for his deceased mistress—old Manferic might be secretly alive. Pinch could only rule that as very unlikely. There was the elaborate business of staging his own death and sitting in immobile state at his own funeral. A statue would never have fooled the discreet inspections of every enemy who suspected such a trick. Then there was the question of giving up power. It was a sure guess that Manferic would never trust anyone else to front him when the odds were so great. Cleedis might be loyal, but once he was named regent no one could ever say just how loyal. No, Pinch was certain the king was dead.

Dead didn't mean gone, though, as the protections around this necropolis assured. The old tyrant had been a sorcerer of considerable skill, and his arcane arts had done much to insure his steadfast grip on Ankhapur. If that really had been Manferic hidden from view, then perhaps the late king had found the path to never-ending unlife, the soulless void between the flush of blood and the feast of worms. The thought frightened Pinch. In life, Manferic had been a master of cruelties; the wrenching transition of nonlife would certainly heighten the most degenerate passions in his festering mind.

Another fear entered his thoughts as the rogue surveyed the passing crypts with their heavy doors, great locks, and carved wards. By the perverse pleasure of the gods, in death those once living gained more power. If Manferic was a thing of the darkness, his might could be beyond contending. Sorcery and death were a potent combination, a forge to fashion truly devastating power.

There was a third possibility, far more likely than that, however. Pinch hadn't seen Manferic. He'd heard a voice, a disembodied one. It didn't take too much art to conjure up a charlatan who could do a fine impression, especially given Pinch's absence of fifteen years. The whole thing could just be a dumb show, staged by Cleedis.

To what end? What purpose had the old man in concocting such an elaborate plot. Why travel to Elturel just to collect a rebellious ward and then go to such lengths to convince him his late guardian still lived? Where was the gain for Lord Cleedis, Chamberlain of the Royal Household and Regent of the . . .

A possibility struck him and Pinch stopped, letting the nobleman laboriously march onward through the narrow lanes. Cleedis was regent only so long as no prince was crowned. No prince could be crowned without the Cup and Knife—

No, that made no sense. If that were the case, why the elaborate substitution? Hurrying to catch up before his host became suspicious of his lagging, Pinch set his mind to work out the snares. It was a puzzle as twisted and double-dealing as his own nature. If no prince were crowned, Cleedis could rule forever—but that would never happen, because the three princes would surely unite against him and force the selection of one of them. That's why he couldn't steal the symbols outright.

That's when Pinch remembered there was a fourth prince, Bors, the one everyone discounted. Bors was an idiot—he couldn't rule. If he were the chosen king of Ankhapur there would have to be . . . a regent. Royal law did not allow a queen to rule while her husband lived, so no lady was likely to marry Bors on the hope that the idiot-king would die, no matter how conveniently. The gods had a way of foiling plans like those.

That left Cleedis. Somehow Pinch was sure he was planning to get Bors crowned and then continue his regency. Looking at the old man doddering ahead of him, Pinch realized that the chamberlain's thinning white hair concealed more cunning and deviousness than anyone suspected. All those years of loyal dullness were a deep mask for the man's true ambition.

As for his part in it, Pinch guessed he was the foil. If the theft was discovered, he, master rogue and unrepentant ward, would get the blame. The upright man had always understood that; it was his lot in life, both here and in Elturel. It was also his lot in life to see that such a fate didn't happen, either by not failing or by crossing those who hoped to snare him.

Why switch the regalia and why the charade with Manferic, Pinch didn't know. Before their purposes were revealed, he needed to find out.

They were somewhere near the fountain that sang when the chamberlain called a rest. Bracing on his cane against the palsied shiver in his legs, the ancient settled onto a cool stone bench. Behind the drooping lids, bright eyes studied the younger man.

"That was Manferic?" Pinch curtly challenged

The senior nodded.

"He's just chosen to lurk out here?"

"It has been planned for many years," was the dry response.

"And you're still his lackey?"

The lined faced tightened. "I am a loyal soldier. I will not serve those worthless sons of his, schemers who fear an honest battle."

"And you're not?"

"I have never been afraid to challenge my enemies. I was a great duelist! I've just gotten . . . old."

"The voice said I'd be paid."

"I heard my lord. I wasn't as asleep as you thought."

"What sum?"

"Ten thousand bicentas and passage to where you desire."

Ten thousand bicentas was no small sum; a bicenta was the equal of an Elturel groat. He'd risked his life for far less.

"One hundred thousand."

Cleedis sputtered in contempt. "Twenty."

"I can make that by farcing your suite."

"I can give you over to the Dawn Priests."

It was the rogue's turn to scowl.

"Seventy."

"Thirty."

"Sixty."

"Forty."

"Fifty even, then."

Cleedis's smile was that of a diplomat who hears the other side propose his terms for him. "Fifty it will be—but only when the job's done."

"Transportable, but not script," Pinch added. He didn't want to be hampered by a wagonload of coins, and he didn't trust any note of credit the chamberlain might draw up. It wasn't one hundred thousand, but it was a fair take for a single job. Of course, he doubted Cleedis had any intention of paying it. Pinch would just have to convince him otherwise.

The chamberlain cast a glance to the westering sun. Already shadows filled the alleys between the crypts. "Time to march on," the chamberlain ordered as if the rogue were a squadron of knights. He assumed the order was being followed and hurried ahead with renewed vigor.

The musical fountain was closer to the necropolis gate than Pinch remembered, since it took them only a few more twists and turns before they saw the cones of the clerical watchtowers over the rooftops. Shortly after, the small gatehouse came into view. The priests huddled at the iron grill, any arrival providing something to break their boredom. The chamberlain's bodyguard and their horses were not in sight, presumably warmly waiting at a neighborhood tavern. A few beggars were clustered outside the gate, probably drawing their trade from the masons and hired mourners who worked inside the dead city's walls.

Pinch cast a look behind, entertaining the thought that he might spot Cleedis's accomplice, the voice of Manferic, scurrying along behind. As far as he knew, this was the only exit.

"Ho there! Stand aside Lord Cleedis! Our argument is not with you."

Pinch spun around and came face-to-face with three swordsmen stepping from the shadows. He recognized them from this morning: Throdus's three clowns. Now each stood poised with a naked rapier, and they didn't look so clownlike.

"Knights of Ankhapur," Cleedis blustered, "stand aside yourselves. I order you as regent of all the realm!" The aged warrior-lord tremblingly swept his cane as if it would clear his path.

The flaxen-haired leader of the three, the one Pinch remembered as Treeve, batted the cane aside with a quick swipe of his sword. "Prince Throdus is our lord, not you. We will not fight you, old man, but do not prevent us from ridding the city of this cancer."

"I'll hang you for this!"

"We're protected by Prince Throdus. You'll do no such thing."

The regent sputtered. "Mutiny! If you were in my command, I'd have you all flayed!"

"Kurkulatain, keep him out of the way."

The slightest of the three grinned and flicked his sword tip under the chamberlain's chin, only to have the old man bat it away. The swordsman's smile went cross as he tried to find a way to subdue the irascible lord.

Keep them preoccupied, Cleedis, Pinch silently urged. He already had one hand on his sword and just needed a moment of diversion to act. So far, Cleedis held them in indecision, but they were still too watchful for the rogue to strike.

"GUARDS!" Cleedis bellowed!

The three bravos sprang toward the lord in surprise,

desperate to shut him up.

It was just the distraction Pinch needed. Ignoring the one whose blade was on Cleedis, Pinch struck at the other two. With a single sweep he produced a dagger in his off hand and struck, driving the blade like a nail into the sword hand of the third attacker, Faranoch.

The man shrieked as the blade plunged through tendons, scraped off bone, and thrust out through his palm. The rapier clattered from his grasp. Pinch gave the skene a vicious twist and let go, leaving the bravo to gape at the bloody memento the rogue left behind.

The leader, realizing he'd cornered the sheep while the wolf still prowled, flailed around in a desperate attempt to correct his error. Pinch was unarmed; there'd been no chance to draw his sword. He stepped aside from the courtier's frantic lunge, but instead of using the man's recovery to draw his own sword, Pinch seized the other's wrist and stepped forward, bringing his foot up in a sweeping kick between the man's legs. Pinch connected just below the waist, and the ringleader shrieked falsetto as all the air inside him blew out in one massive gust. Treeve writhed on the ground while Pinch's first target stumbled back onto a bench where he sat clutching his transfixed hand.

"Hold where you are!" shrilled the last ambusher as he held Cleedis by the throat, sword point pressed into the sagging folds beneath the man's chin. "Make a move and I'll kill him!"

Pinch stepped away from his whimpering victim, shrugged, and finally drew his sword. "So what? Kill him."

The little man swallowed in terror.

"You expect me to fight fair. You expect me to care." The regulator walked forward, leveling his sword at the man. "I don't care if you kill him. I just want to kill you."

"Janol . . ." Cleedis gurgled.

"Shut up, old fool. Do you think I'll risk my life for

you? You haven't earned it."

From the distance came the rattling clank of the gate being opened. Voices carried over the silent rooftops.

The man wanted to see who else was coming but was too terrified to take his eyes from his nemesis. Unintimidated, Pinch continued to close. At last the man's nerve broke, and he flung his hostage forward while bolting into the mazed warrens of the necropolis.

Pinch dodged to the side as the chamberlain gasped and stumbled to freedom. For a moment he thought about chasing the man but easily decided against it. Instead, he turned his attention to the fellow on the ground. Remarkably, perhaps driven by fear, the man had regained his sword with every intention of using it, once he caught his breath.

Pinch didn't wait for that. With a quick thrust he brought an end to this comedy. The body fell hard on the muddy lane.

The last survivor threw up his blood-covered hands to surrender, and the hue and cry of the arriving bodyguard forestalled the need for any action on Pinch's part.

"Seize him!" Cleedis commanded as his bodyguards sprinted to the scene. The armored men fell upon the courtier and savagely pinioned him on the ground. The man's expression was a wrenched mass of pain and terror.

"My lord chamberlain, what shall we do with him?" queried the captain of the bodyguard. A coarse-shaven man adept at killing and following orders, he looked over the rogue's handiwork with no small amount of approval.

"Keep the priests away," the chamberlain ordered. The captain nodded and ran off.

Cleedis walked over and placed the tip of his cane on the man's bloodied hand. "What's your name, fool?"

Perhaps he was too dazed to understand; perhaps he was too stubborn, but the man didn't answer.

Cleedis leaned forward. The prisoner screamed.

When the screaming stopped, Cleedis tried again.

"Sir Kurkulatain," was the burbled answer. Sweat and tears shined the man's face. "Vassal of Prince Throdus."

"Did the prince send you?"

"No, my lord!"

"Too easy." Cleedis leaned on his cane again. "Who sent you? Tell me and things will be easier."

The man could barely whisper. "Treeve. Word was Throdus offered us titles."

"This is the result of ambition," Cleedis admonished Pinch who'd been patiently sitting on the bloodstained bench until the questioning was done.

"It's the result of ill planning."

"Whatever," Cleedis shrugged. He turned to the captain of the guard, who'd returned from his mission. "This man"—Cleedis pointed at the prisoner—"is a traitor who has attacked the rightful regent of Ankhapur. Execute him."

"Shall there be a trial, my lord chamberlain?"

The chamberlain looked to Pinch with a cold vulture's eye. "I see no need for a trial. Do you?"

The rogue shook his head and got to his feet. "No, none at all."

"Rejoin us, en route to the palace," the chamberlain ordered, and the two took their leave. "I doubt there'll be any more attacks today."

"Lord Cleedis, have mercy!" shrieked the prisoner. His screams rang through the silent company he was about to join, until his echoes were one with the choir of silent ghosts pleading for their own justice.

Thief Hunting

The pair passed through the gate, leaving the captain and his men to clean up the untidy details. The priests, drawn by the screams, thronged on the other side but their entrance was blocked by a pair of soldiers who stood casually in the way. No one was going to antagonize a man who wore the golden serpent of the royal household.

Unless, of course, they weren't from Ankhapur.

There was a tussle in the midst of the holy men as Lissa struggled to break through the line. She was held back by another, Pinch could see, a pumpkin-bellied servant of Gond. She fought with the conviction of moral purity, but the pragmatism of girth was on his side. She was stuck fast.

It was interesting to watch the reaction of the rest of the small band, so seldom did such a diverse collection of faiths cluster together. The loyal servant of Gond, the pragmatic Wonderbringer, was saying "Such is the result of treachery," as he held Lissa off. Torm's man, the defender of justice, all but drowned him out by shouting—no, demanding—to know the proof of the assassin's crimes. The Oghmaites and the Deneirians quietly observed; watching and noting was what their lords demanded of them. The priests of the god of song seized upon the moment to begin a golden-toned dirge. In the back, the armored priest of Tempus watched with dour approval, satisfied that victory and defeat had been properly rewarded.

Pinch could imagine the clergy of the darker gods—the fallen Cyric, the grinding Talos, and the cold Loviatar—smiling to themselves in the corners where shadows became walls. Unwelcome among the necropolis guardians, nonetheless they were still there. The hidden temples of Ankhapur were always close at hand.

Cleedis gave the priests the backhand of his attention. The bodyguard formed an aisle, their swords a blued-steel fence. Given the determined disregard the chamberlain showed, the priests let their curiosity and outrage quickly fade. They made a great show of falling back into their daily habits. How fitting of man's noblest sentiments, the thief sarcastically noted. Only Lissa remained undaunted.

"Lord Cleedis, I take your leave," the regulator said. "I've some contriving to do, now that the job's clear."

Deep beneath the regal finery, the paunchy wrinkles, and the white-frosted pate, Cleedis still had the soul of a barracks-room trooper. He saw how Lissa had caught Pinch's eye and got it completely wrong. He leaned over to whisper, "She's not the kind to have you, or any man, you poxy rascal. I'll hazard my finest firewine you can't charm her."

Pinch met the suggestion with a jump of one eyebrow. It could have been an acceptance of the challenge or it might have been a gambler's tic, the sort that betrays a man's astonishment before he's even sensed it fully.

"I'll be happy to drink good wine," the rogue drawled encouragingly. He didn't correct the lord; indeed, he wanted the old man to go on dreaming of Pinch's peccadilloes. It would keep his mind from the thief's real motives.

"And what will you pledge?"

Pinch shrugged. "What little I wear is barely more than I came with, but perhaps a purse or two of your choosing."

"Fair on. My wine against your fingers."

Pinch raised his hand and waved the aforementioned fingers in farewell. "I'll make my own way back."

When the troop rounded the corner, he sought out Lissa. The man found her gathering her holy scrip. Pinch gave a weather eye to the sky. The long shadows had pushed out from the narrow lanes and were thickening in the broad lane to the gate.

"Going somewhere?" Pinch nodded toward the gate.

"What you did in there, executing—"

"I didn't execute anyone."

"You walked away while they killed one," she protested.

"What was I supposed to do? Interfere with the direct orders of the royal chamberlain?"

Lissa pressed her fingers to her eyes, confused. "You could have argued against it—"

"Asked for leniency? Those men came to kill me."

Lissa's eyes locked with his. There was the jagged hardness of rock in her glare, something Pinch hadn't expected from a priestess of the Morninglord.

"You're a bastard, you know that?"

"Dyed through and through," Pinch answered gleefully. The priestess opened her mouth to say something, but Pinch did not stop and rocketed through a litany of infamy. "I'm also a fiend, rakehell, wastrel, and ne'er-do-well as well as a shirker, cock-lorel, swigman, swadler,

and wild rogue, but not a palliard or a counterfeit crank."
He stopped to gasp in a huge breath. "My clothes are too
good for that," He explained as an aside before launching
in again with a hurried, earnest whisper favored by theatrical conspirators. "If I were you, I'd count my rings
and silver and lock up my treasures when that Janol's
around. I'd change the locks to the wine cellar and cast
new wards on the royal treasury. I'd even make sure all
the ladies-in-waiting were ugly and well out of sight."

The rogue tapped his nose with a wink and a grin,
like a child's favorite old uncle. " 'Struth. I haven't seen
one since I got here."

Lissa had stopped her packing, quite taken aback by
Pinch's sardonic good spirits. "You're teasing me. No
one's that bad."

"That bad? What about Core the Cuckolder or Fine-
Cloth Durram? Now, they were that bad, I assure you. I
once heard how Durram drank the best of a lord's wine
cellar in one night and then came back for the goblets
on the next!" Pinch kept the banter flowing while casually steering her away from the necropolis gate. He
didn't want the priestess brooding on what had just
happened. He needed her to like him, if not trust him.

"Let me escort you to safer streets," he said casually, offering her his arm. His gaze swept over the mud-spattered
street. Save for the boulevard they were on, the neighborhood was a tangle of narrow, crooked stews and warrens of
ill intent. The little garretted town houses rammed up
against each other piecemeal, in places so furiously trying
to steal the sunlight from their neighbors that no light
reached the streets and alleys at their base. Throughout
this tangle, the gardens of the festhalls provided touches
of color, tenderness, and sweet fragrance that the cheap
stews disdained, but only for a price. They were streets
full of the unsavory, the unstable, and the immorally ambitious. They were the streets of Pinch's youth.

"Why, I could be that bad, I'm sure," he continued. "No

doubt every father and mother in town would live in fear of seeing my pepper-haired pate come knocking at their door, because, you see, they'd know I had no morals, few scruples, and far too many dark habits to be safe around their daughters. Nay, if I were a proper priestess like you, I'd not spend time with that Janol, or your superiors would think you're no more than a bawdy basket."

He grinned the cat's grin and gave her a sweeping bow to cap his whole speech.

Lissa reddened and tried to wear a scowling smile but only succeeded in twisting up her face and betraying every one of her emotions: suspicion, belief, skepticism, and amusement. "Enough already. You're telling me tales."

"Of course, nothing but." Pinch made sure that his answer was too eager, like a man in the trial box denying a truth—which he was, of course.

She looked at him in just the way he hoped she would.

People who are too innocent become eventually distrusted, tripped up by some trivial character flaw; the obviously guilty never gain trust to start with. The best course was to be neither and both—believably unbelievable. Done right, the priestess would vacillate between suspicion and trust until guilt made her blind to his faults.

"How goes your hunt?" he asked, sliding the conversation into a topic she could not resist.

Now it was her turn to be evasive. "Slow progress."

Pinch nodded. "That poorly, eh?" He could see in her eyes he'd cut to the quick of her lie.

She kept her counsel on that matter, instead focusing on the cobblestones of the street.

"Well, perhaps I have news."

"You do?"

"I cannot be sure—you remember I warned you of Cleedis?"

She nodded.

"Things have happened that make me wonder."

"Things?"

"It's hard to say. What are the powers of this thing you seek?"

"Powers? It has no powers."

Pinch shook his head. "Never try dissembling with an Ankhapurian. They—we're masters of the art. I learned how to spot a lie a long time ago, a lesson from my royal cousins.

"Your temple has hunted this thing enough for me to know it has special powers. It's not just sentiment that makes them search so hard; otherwise they would have given up long ago."

"It's a relic of the great Dawnbreaker. Isn't that enough?"

Pinch searched through his royal tutor's lessons for what he might know about a Dawnbreaker. There was nothing.

"Depends. Who or what is the Dawnbreaker?"

Lissa slid naturally into the role of patient missionary. With so many gods, so many martyrs, every priest became accustomed to explaining the myths and icons of his faith.

"The Dawnbreaker was a great prophet who served the Morninglord."

"Of course." They were all great prophets—or profits. Temples without prophets or seers tended to be poor, miserly things. This Pinch knew from experience.

"He was. He predicted the Wintry Summer and the razing of the Unshadowed Palace of the Night Queen."

"Never heard of it."

"It's very ancient history. The gospel is that when the Dawnbreaker died, the Morninglord burned away the impurity of his flesh and commanded an amulet be made from the bones of his skull."

Pinch arched an eyebrow at this.

"So this bauble is really a skull? Is that what I'm looking for? 'Struth why my examinations have failed. I was looking for a mere trinket, not some old prophet's pate!"

"No, it's only a piece of his bone bound inside an amulet of rare metals."

Pinch nodded and pursed his lips as though he were imagining the relic, though that was hardly necessary since he wore the thing beneath his shirt. He hesitantly asked, as if shy at intruding into the secrets of her sect, "It wouldn't have any special powers, would it? Things that might reveal its presence?"

"Why do you ask?"

"Well—and this may sound folly—curiosities have plagued me at the palace. Voices, witchlights, and the like. That wasn't . . .?"

Lissa cocked her head, letting her curly hair spill from the edge of her hood. "The scriptures do say the Upholder of Light called on its might against the Sun-Devourer."

"Upholder of Light?"

"The Dawnbreaker. It is another sign of our respect for the great prophet."

"Upholder, Dawnbreaker—what does it mean he 'called on its might'? What did it do?" Pinch leaned against the stuccoed wall of the first building across from the necropolis gate. It was a smoke-blackened ordinary with a very grim signboard overhead: The Shroud. Nonetheless, it sounded festive enough inside. Their conversation had steered her well away from her assigned post.

"The scriptures are very vague on all that. They just refer to some great power without really describing much. Not everyone could use it either; only the faithful are described as being able to use it."

" 'Tis not me, for certain, to gain from such a thing," Pinch lied. "I never knew about the Morninglord until I came to Elturel."

The truth was that Pinch's gain would have been all

in coin. He'd spent weeks casing the Elturel temple, working out its wards, guard schedules, and even just where to make the break in the roof. The plan had been to filch the amulet and then pass it off to Therin. The Gur was to carry it west in the next caravan until he found a good broker on the Sword Coast to take it off his hands.

Cleedis had ruined all that.

Now the rogue felt like he was stuck with the thing. True, there were more than enough brokers in Ankhapur who would pay for an artifact of mysterious power, but Pinch knew his chances of getting good coin were very slim. The hue and cry embodied in Lissa's presence made matters all the worse. Every broker in the city would know where the object came from and probably who had stolen it. That knowledge could be a powerful threat to Pinch's freedom. The rogue had no ambition to discover the pleasantries of Ankhapur's prisons.

"So many questions. Maybe you've heard news?" The quick tones of Lissa's curiosity intruded on Pinch's reverie. She spoke with allegro phrasing in tones and shades that carried more meaning than her words. Pinch could imagine her in the ranks of the temple choir, a place that better suited her than the slop-strewn stews that surrounded them now.

"Maybe." The rogue kept his answer short. Talk killed thieves.

"I think the Dawnbreaker's amulet is here, in Ankhapur."

"How can you be sure?" Pinch really wanted to know her reasons, but he had to take care not to sound too intrigued. If she suspected someone, he had to include the possibility she suspected him.

"The patriarchs in Elturel have divined that the amulet is not within that city. They've sent word."

Pinch scratched at his stubbly beard. He'd not had time for grooming since some moment yesterday. "That hardly places the proof here."

Lissa lowered her voice as a drunk ambled out of the Shroud, a hairy brute whose naked chest barely fit beneath the scarred leather apron he wore as a shirt. The man strutted past them, arrogantly challenging these well-dressed strangers who ventured onto his turf.

"The amulet is in Ankhapur. Believe me on this."

"An informer? Someone's given you word, or tried to sell it. You think I have it? Or another?"

The musical pleasantry of her voice suddenly disappeared. "If it were one of your friends, would you reveal them?"

"Sprite, Maeve, Therin—you think it's one of them?"

"I meant hypothetically. Someone brought it from Elturel. I can feel it."

"You think I consort with this thief." Pinch straightened himself in indignation.

"I've said too much already. It is here, though, and I will find it." Her tone was unabashed by his accusation.

Pinch assumed an air of almost theatrical injury. "I've known rogues and thieves most of my life, priestess, but do not mistake me for one. I like their company. They drink better and they're more honest than the snakes of the court. Just because a man's company is not to your taste, don't impute on his friends. Yes, Sprite is an imp and Maeve drinks a bit, but they're good people. As for me, I'm only seeking to recover what you've lost. If you're not pleased with this, then I shall cease."

Perhaps he just pressed too hard, perhaps she was just wary, or perhaps he had always been the target of her suspicion. Whatever the reasoning, if there was any reasoning to it at all, the priestess suddenly withdrew even as she rejected his offer. She pulled her things about her with the urge to go, although the rogue noted his words at least caused her to keep one hand at her dagger.

"I meant no affront, Master Janol, but I will find this thief, no matter who he—or she—is." With that the priestess broke away as if afraid that Pinch could somehow charm her to think otherwise.

Pinch let her go, watching her carefully pick her path around the turgid puddles of slops. There was no breaking the frost of cold courtesy that had settled on her.

Pinch looked up to the Shroud, with its wooden drapery creaking from the signboard overhead. There was work to be done, and a drink was as good enough a place as any to start. Alcohol keened his plotter's mind, perversely laying bare the twisted paths of a multitude of schemes. Besides, he was thirsty.

* * * * *

Pinch sat at a dark table in a dark corner the way he always preferred. From the dawn light until now, he reviewed the day's events. Too much was happening that he didn't control: strange voices, stranger hands in the dark, Manferic returned, and Lissa retreating. Everything about it was the design of fates beyond his control, and that Pinch could not abide. For fifteen years he had fought to be the master of his own life, and now in the span of a few days, everything was conspiring to take that apart.

One by one the drinks came, and as part of the ritual his mind followed in its cunning, Pinch dedicated each mug to a threat to future well-being.

"Here's to Manferic," the rogue toasted to no one in particular on his first blackjack of heady wine. "Were the bastard's memory truly dead." It was a toast to more than just bitter memories. The undead king was the first and foremost problem. There was little doubt what Pinch's reward would be when his job was done. King Manferic had always been brutally efficient at removing useless pawns. The rogue drained the mug in one long gulp, slapped it on the table, and sat brooding as he stared at the chisel work of a previous customer. Several times he waved off the landlord while plots played themselves out in his mind.

At last he called for a second blackjack, and when it came he raised it high. "To Cleedis." Again he repeated the ritual of drink and brood. What was the chamberlain's part, and just whom did he serve? Dead Manferic used him, but the late king trusted no one, that Pinch was certain. But old Cleedis wasn't a fool, though he played the role for others. As a general he'd had a cunning mind for traps and lures. The rogue was running the gantlet for these two without knowing even where it would end.

With these two, Manferic and Cleedis, at least the threat was clear. They wanted him to do the job and then they wanted him dead. The rogue was clear on that. Already he was threading plots within their plots, plans to keep himself alive. It was life as normal in Ankhapur.

With his third mug, Pinch contemplated the coldest challenge of all. He raised his blackjack to Lissa and her quest. She was close, too close. The rogue was sure she'd gotten her suspicions from Cleedis or maybe one of the princes, though Pinch doubted they were that well-informed or clever. It was a way for Cleedis to keep him under good behavior, to control his life.

He could kill her and have done with it, like he'd once considered on the road, but the thought didn't appeal to him. He was getting sentimental, fond of her easy gullibility. There had to be a use for her alive.

The only other choice, though, was to give her a thief. It couldn't be just any thief. It had be someone she suspected. Which one could he do without, Pinch wondered: Maeve, Therin, or Sprite? If it came to it, which one could he give up?

Pinch ordered another drink and brooded even more.

Low Cunning

The great, swollen, and single eye of the Morninglord was not yet gazing upon Ankhapur when Pinch sidled out of the mist and back into the marbled confines of the palace. The thick, warm steam, fresh from the sea, cast him up in its wash, the great cloud that blanketed the commons of Ankhapur breaking into its froth just at the hard stones of the palace gate.

Pinch sauntered under the portcullis, raised for the cooks and spitboys off to market, passing the guards with the confidence that he belonged there. It had been years since the feeling of arrogant privilege truly belonged to him. He had never forgotten it and carried it with him through all his dealings with petty thugs, constable's watch, prison turnkeys, and festhall girls. He always held that knowledge of his own superiority as the key to his rise and dominance in Elturel. Having the sense of it, though, wasn't the same as the confirmation of one's entitlement that came in moments like this.

At other times and places, fools had tried to convince him that respect was the mark of a true leader—foolish old men who believed they were the masters of great criminal clans, but in truth little men with little understanding. Pinch knew from his years under Manferic's sharp tutelage that respect meant nothing but useless words and bad advice. Fear is what made men and beasts obey—utter and base fear. Manferic had been an artist in instilling fear. The common people feared the terrors that awaited dissidents and rivals who vanished in the night. The nobility dreaded the moment Manferic might strip a title or confiscate lands. The princes feared the moment their father might turn on them and bloodily solve the question of succession. None of them knew the scope of the chasm that was his soul, and none of them dared find out.

Fear is what made the guards stand to, not admiration.

Pinch made his way through the long interconnected halls of the palace. His fine clothes, the vanity of his days, were sagged with loose wrinkles that come with constant wear and the dull edge of morning sobriety.

The wrinkles were reflected in his face, a leathery map of his nighttime indulgences, with sad, pouchy bags under his eyes and feeble folds around his neck. Pinch was battling time, as all living things do. Even the endless elves slowly succumb to the Great Master's advances. Death could be beaten, cheated, and postponed, and the gods were frail by comparison. Even they felt the yoke of years settling over them. Time was the enemy Pinch could not outwit, the treasure locked beyond his bony fingers.

Right now exhaustion was weakness. Pinch felt want of sleep in his bones, but there was no time for the luxury of rich sheets. Plans were already in motion, some of his own doing and more that were not. Plots needed counterplots, and those needed their own counters. Looking forward, there was no end to the webs that filled the future, not here or even if he left Ankhapur.

So Pinch slipped through the halls, down colonnaded corridors that threatened to devour him with their hungry boredom, past galleries that whispered with the ancestors of a past not his. A blind man would have heard only the random wet slap of leather polishing a marble that was green veined and solid like cave-ripened cheese.

It was at the entrance to the Great Hall, as he was being swallowed farther and farther into the deceitful stagnation of the palace, that Pinch spied Iron-Biter, the grotesque. Before purposeful thought could will it, Pinch had already sidled out of view, angling himself where he could watch but not be watched.

Once there, he observed. What he hoped to see, he did not know, but this dwarf was an adversary. Vargo's displays had foolishly revealed the misshapen courtier's strengths; now Pinch hoped to see weaknesses. A direct confrontation with Vargo's enforcer was unwinnable without an Achilles' heel to exploit. "Thieves' courage" some called it. Pinch didn't give a damn.

Sheltered by a window shuttered with pierced rosewood, Pinch watched as the dwarf prowled the grand chamber. Apelike Iron-Biter appeared to move with no purpose, paying mind first to a candelabrum, then to the cracks between the marble blocks in the walls, with all the intention and interest of his kind. Dwarven fascination for stone was beyond Pinch's understanding. A block of marble was a block of marble. You couldn't sell it, and even carved well it hardly had enough value to make it worth stealing. Dwarves would go on about how well veined and smoothly solid a single stone was—for days if one let them.

Still, if there were collectors willing to pay for a block of stone, Pinch would steal it. It was all a case of what the brokers wanted.

Approaching footsteps clacked through the sterile halls. Pinch coiled around the pillar and watched as a servant tottered into the hall. The old servitor's arms were draped with fabric—costumes of succulent silk that spilled out of his arms in hues of minted gold, their buttons like fat nobles worn smooth between a usurer's greasy fingers. Explosions of lace flared in pleats of ethereal smoke, banded roots of brocaded ribbon bound everything into one mass, and perched on top of it, like a vessel on a wave-tossed sea, was a pair of masks, grotesques of the finest manufacture.

Masks?

Iron-Biter raised the first one with all the critical judgment of proud torturer examining his craft. It was a face of sharp-stretched leather, a cow's flayed skin stretched to fiendish form. The honey-gold leather glistened under a sheen of wax buffed to shellac hardness. It was a face of deception, a gleaming smile of diabolic cheerfulness.

Apt for the owner, Pinch felt, but why masks?

The scrape of a door signaled more arrivals. Iron-Biter waved the servant away as Prince Vargo entered the hall, dressed in the careless elegance of his morning gowns. The royal heir stretched with feline abandon, ignored his dwarf henchman, and went to the table where he idly poured a goblet of ruby wine and poked at the silks and leathers cascading over the back of the chair. The dwarf stood patiently silent, his little hands barely touching across the vast plain of his chest. The soaring darkness of the hall heightened the little man's grotesque proportions, making him a fat, bright-shelled beetle over which some human giant would tower.

With an arch sniff at his wine, Vargo flipped the mask he'd been examining back onto the table. "Not very original . . . best you could do, Iron-Biter?"

Echoes bedeviled Pinch's ears, taunting him with words he could almost hear.

"I chose them to show restraint, milord," the dwarf
rumbled like a kettledrum. ". . . appear modest during
the ceremony. It will not do for the chosen . . . decked
out like a harlequin."

Vargo glanced over his shoulder at Iron-Biter, deign-
ing to give the man the least of his attention. "I . . . calling for the ritual in the . . . masque . . . undignified
enough. You . . . advising . . . a fool of me?" With a gentle brush at his mustache, Vargo sipped at his wine.

Behind the pillar, it was hopeless for Pinch to hear
their conversation clearly, and he dearly needed to.
They were plotting, and plots discovered were what
would give the rogue the edge. He needed to be closer.
Carefully he scanned the ground between himself
them. On the opposite side of the hall and much closer
to his quarry was another line of pillars, a good spot to
lurk and pry. The morning sun and the flickering stubs
of the night candles cast a weave of half-shadows across
the floor between here and there, not quite darkness
and not quite day. A quick, quiet shift and he would be
in position to hear all.

With the care of a carnival tightrope walker, Pinch
sidled away from the shelter of the pillar. Iron-Biter
seemed absorbed in the presence of his lord, and Vargo
viewed the world with bored indifference, but Pinch knew
the latter, at least, was a lie. His elder cousin was the
hawk who never quite looked on the world with closed
eyes.

With one eye to the floor and the other always on his
adversaries, Pinch drifted across the gap to the other
side. Years of practice made the move look effortless, indeed casual. He took care never to move fast enough to
catch attention, stepped softly so that the kiss of
leather to stone would not give him away. Nonetheless,
his blood raced at the thrill of risk. There was little
question that if Pinch was discovered, Vargo would find
some excuse to let his sadistic underling play.

Precaution and skill carried the rogue to the blind safety of the other colonnade. Once there, he quickly flitted from pillar to pillar until he was so close he could have reached out and poured a sample of Vargo's wine.

During the time it took to reach his new position, Pinch had been focused on silence, not words. The conversation had gone on without him. Vargo was asking something, a question in response to Iron-Biter's plottings.

"And what makes you certain I will be king?"

The huge dwarf bent his knees in the best imitation of a bow that he could manage. "Are you not the most worthy ruler of Ankhapur, milord?" The flattery was oily and insincere, though it did not presume on Vargo's talents. The lie was couched in the vagaries of the choosing, for even a priest could not attest to the will of the higher powers and the creaking wheel of fortune.

"Besides, milord," Iron-Biter continued, fully knowing the weakness of that explanation, "there will be no other choice. The test be damned. You will seize the throne as is your right. Throdus is a coward. Before the masque, he will have heard one hundred reasons not to challenge you."

Vargo nodded agreement but held out a finger in caution. "True enough, though it must not be too obvious. The lords who support him have considerable backing."

"It shall be discreet, milord."

"And Marac? He has more spirit. My youngest brother will not be bullied so easily."

Iron-Biter shrugged, his massive shoulders grinding like a builder's cranes. "Perhaps you are a better judge of him than I." The words held a cocksure arrogance, not quite openly challenging the lord. "His power is weak, his support thin among the nobles and the army. Most of the guests at the masque will be your vassals. Challenging you at the festival will be impossible, complete folly. If you act forcefully and proclaim yourself king by right of possession alone, Marac will not dare challenge you."

"What about Bors—and Cleedis? The troops are more loyal to him than anyone."

From where he was hiding, Pinch could barely see Iron-Biter grin. "Bors is an idiot. Even the gods wouldn't choose him. Let him take the Cup if you want—but only after the other two have declined. When Bors fails, it will only confirm that you were meant to be king.

"As for Cleedis—well, he is only the chamberlain. If he protests, I will kill him for you. After all, he will be a traitor to the state, won't he?"

Pinch couldn't see him, but he heard Vargo chuckle. There was a clink as another glass of wine was poured. "The Feast of Wealth." Vargo's thin hand came into view, holding a glass

The dwarf accepted the drink. "To your coronation, Your Highness."

Pinch smoothed himself against the cold, polished column as the two left the hall. He understood so much more now. The masks made sense and so did Manferic's haste. The Carnival of Wealth was coming, that time of year when the city erupted into riotous gaiety. He'd been away too long, forgotten the days, the dates, and the order of things. Every year the city celebrated its greatest resource and its greatest benefactor—gold—in a three-day celebration of greed and cunning. There would be drinking in the taverns, feasts sold in the markets, dances and celebrations, and all culminating in the Great Masque held at the royal court itself.

And this year, it would be the scene of a royal coup. Pinch had to admire the plotting, the sheer boldness of the crime. In all his years as a rogue, he'd stolen just about anything that had come across his bow, but never had even he imagined a robbery as bold as this. Vargo proposed to steal an entire kingdom, to rob his brothers of even the chance at their heritage. Oh, Pinch dearly wished that he could someday plot such a crime.

The festival had to be soon. Feeling chagrined to have forgotten it at all, now memory rushed in. He remembered it was always on the new moon. That part was clear, for the fat purses he found on those dark nights had always meant good takings for him, a youth learning the cutpurse's trade. After fifteen years, though, he'd lost track of the dates and must have assumed the festival had already passed. It could surely be no more than a week or less away.

That did not leave much time for plans or action. There were too many players in this game for Pinch's taste, and too many unexplained things. What was the voice he'd heard in the tunnels? Who had saved him from death? Was Manferic truly something undead, or was this a trick on Cleedis's part? Did Manferic or Cleedis or both suspect Vargo's plans? What was their reason for switching the regalia anyway? Should he betray them to Vargo? Or should he betray Vargo to them?

And how did he stay alive and on top, when all was said and done?

Pinch puzzled away at these as he resumed his mission through the morning-chilled halls.

* * * * *

Therin's strong hand seized Pinch's doublet just as the thief came even with the bottom rail of the balcony.

"Up you are, then!" the Gur grunted as his fingers dug into Pinch's shoulder and, with a strained heave, he hauled the regulator half onto the platform.

Pinch was hardly surprised that Therin was there and waiting. Climbing was never the regulator's strong suit, and he'd made enough noise to sound like a bull elephant to a thief's trained ears. Sure enough, Therin, Sprite, and even Maeve—looking clearer-headed than usual—were there to greet him.

With a certain lack of dignity, Pinch kicked his legs
over the rail and flopped to the wooden floor of the balcony. Easy climb or no, the effort, combined with a full
day and night of no sleep, was exhausting.

"Gods, dearie! You've been hitting the blackjacks a
bit, haven't you?" Maeve exclaimed. The regulator was
a sight, at least by his own standards—rumpled
clothes, bleary eyes, and a full day's crust of grime. He
hardly looked their leader, the one who kept himself ur-
banely polished and clean.

"Found himself a woman, too, I'll wager," Sprite
added with merciless glee. It wasn't often he got to
pluck such fun at his senior.

Pinch struggled against the urge to yawn and lost.
"Found more than you know, furry foot," he finally shot
back as he made a grab for the halfling's curly toes.
Sprite skipped out of reach, giving Pinch enough space
to heave to his feet and stumble inside. Yesterday's, last
night's, and today's adventures fell on him as he collapsed into the largest chair he could find.

Arms flopped over the rests, he looked at the three
sideways as they filed in and stood semicircle around
him: Sprite amused, Maeve curious, and Therin with
the clear gaze of suspicion. Someday, Pinch thought to
himself, someday that Gur is going to get it in his head
to challenge me.

"We've work to do." Sprawled in the chair, the regulator hardly looked serious, but his companions knew to
judge by the tone of his words, not simple appearances.
"How have you come on finding a bolt hole?"

"Slipping the ring here's no problem, Pinch," Therin
bragged. "Like you said, the door's always watched but
the balcony's easy. We can avoid those cursed hellhounds by climbing up instead of down and taking out
over the roof. Once we get up there, it's an easy scramble to the wall. Then we just watch the guards and go
over the side."

"What about you, Maeve? Can you keep up with these two monkeys?" Pinch knew the wizardess wasn't trained in acrobatics like the other two.

"We'll help her along," Therin assured, before she could say a word.

The woman glared at the big, cocky Gur and added, "I've got spells, too. Don't you go worrying about me."

"Well laid, then." Pinch cut their bickering short. "Use it tonight. Go to the ordinary across from the lower end of the fish market. It's run by an old man named Sarveto. He'll have rooms for you."

"What's the job, or are you just running us off, Pinch?" Therin posed suspiciously.

"Work." Pinch glared at his lieutenant. Ever since starting this journey, the man had been insolent. After this, Pinch decided, Therin may have to go. Without taking his gaze from Therin, the regulator continued.

"Sprite, you've an eye for the stones. Find me an artificer of cunning hands, one who's hungry or likes the women too much. Just as long as he does good work and keeps himself quiet."

"Aye, Pinch. What'll his commission be?

"I want a copy of the Cup and the Knife. He'll know what I mean." The man leaned back and rubbed his eyes. "Therin, you and Maeve case the temple of the Red Priests. Mark their guards, whether the catchpoles are near at hand, and what the hour is of their walks. Maeve, use your charms to get yourself through their doors. Make friends with their servants. Note the hasps on their doors and what spells they lay about. Oh, and pay particular mind to their gossip. We're looking for this Cup and the Knife."

Therin smirked, perhaps wondering if Pinch had finally gone mad. "A cup and knife? Any old one or one that's particular?"

Pinch was suddenly alert and forward in his chair. "Not a cup and knife, *the* Cup and Knife."

"And what makes this set of trinkets so special?"

"They're the royal symbols of Ankhapur. Without them, a body can't be king or queen."

"So you're going to steal them and become king of Ankhapur!" Sprite blurted in a dazzlingly ambitious leap of conclusions.

"Hah! Me, king?" Pinch actually broke into laughter at that one. "Can you imagine me sitting on some throne. I've as much chance of becoming king as you, Sprite, have of becoming the lord high master of the Zhentarim."

"I think I'd make a fine Zhent. Don't you, Therin?"

With a grin the Gur twirled up a dagger. "Good Zhents are dead Zhents, Sprite. Want I should scrag you?"

The halfling comically ducked behind a bronzewood chest. "Well taken. I'll not be a Zhentarim and Pinch'll not be king of Ankhapur. "

"But I don't understand," Maeve said with a quizzical whine that cut through their play. "If you had this cup and knife, why couldn't you be king?"

The regulator, playing the role of wise teacher of the lore, settled back into his chair. "It's because of what the Cup and Knife do. You see, a long time ago—oh, back whatever ages of man it takes to forget such things—"

"Yesterday, for Maeve," Sprite-Heels sniped. Therin guffawed. With a mouselike shriek, Maeve kicked a footstool the halfling's way.

"However long it was, there was a falling out of the royal household. The first king of Ankhapur was dead. Apparently, the old king had been fond of his bedchamber though, 'cause he left behind more than a score of sons and grandsons, at least as many as what people knew about."

"One of the rewards of royalty," smirked the Gur as he settled into the chair across from his senior. Sprite turned up the stool and plopped onto it while Maeve leaned over Therin's shoulder. It was beginning to look like a long tale and one that might merit their attention.

Pinch yawned as the morning sun warmed the chair. "Of course, every one of those sons and grandsons considered himself the only fit successor to the old king. The rest were fools, idiots, and just plain enemies who didn't deserve the throne. It was a terrible time for the city."

"Assassins stalking the halls and all that?" Sprite asked eagerly. To his mind, this was shaping to be a fine story. "Lots of slaughter and only one survives?"

Pinch shook his head. "If it were only that, it would hardly be a crisis at all. The gentlefolk of Ankhapur are long used to solving a problem with a quick and fortunate death. No, this was worse for them—"

"I'd think losing my head would be about the worst you could get," Maeve whispered to Therin. She stroked the hangman's scar that peeked from under the scarf at his neck. "You'd know about that, wouldn't you, moon-man?"

The Gur bristled at the slur but said nothing. He wanted to hear the rest of the story.

"Worse for them—civil war. It would have torn the city apart. There were factions in factions ready to fight for their man."

Therin brushed Maeve away from the back of his chair. "So what's it got to do with this cup and knife?"

"Patience with my tale," Pinch advised as he held up one hand to restrain his lieutenant's impetuousness. "It turns out this story has a wise man, a priest—like there always is in these things. He said the choice should be up to the gods; let them pick the royal heir who was most fit to lead the city. He pointed out they could all slaughter each other for no gain but a smoking ruin of a city, or they could take their chances with the gods. How he got them all to agree, I don't know, but he did.

"So as the story goes, this priest and his servants go off praying and doing whatever it is they do, and after some time they return with the answer. And that answer is the Cup and the Knife."

"I don't see it," Sprite protested.

"Whenever there's a new king to be chosen and there's more than one contender, it's the Cup and the Knife that decide. Each heir takes the Knife, pricks his wrist, drips a bit of blood into the Cup, and mixes it with wine. Then he drinks the stuff straight down. If he's the one chosen by the gods, he'll be wrapped up in a ball of holy light, or something such. I never saw it done for real."

"So then, that's what's going to happen here soon, eh Pinch?" Maeve asked.

"And without this Cup and Knife, none of the princes can be crowned?" Therin added.

"So if someone were to steal them, they could name their price?" Sprite chimed in, scuttling to Pinch's feet. "We're going to steal them, aren't we? And then we'll ask for a ransom and clean out the royal treasury! It's genius, Pinch. Why, they'll know our crime from here to Waterdeep!"

He'd told them too much already, the regulator decided, and there was no need to tell them any more—not about Manferic, the switch, or what their fates were likely to be when the job was done. They were with him now, and there was no point in giving them unnecessary details, especially ones that might make them question his plans.

"Yes, we're going to steal them and sell them back. Something like that."

"Temple robbing again." Given their last try, the halfling sounded almost cheerful at the prospect. He gave a nod to Maeve, who seemed in almost as good a cheer.

"It'll be the death of us yet," Therin gloomily countered as he pulled the scarf up to cover the rope scar on his neck.

Ikrit

After he gave them their missions, arranged to meet, and slipped away; after he'd padded through the halls avoiding everyone and bluffed his way past the guards at his door, Pinch collapsed into bed. Bleak exhaustion flowed into him. He knew he should be drawing his plans, setting his traps like a master rogue, but his mind could not get his body to obey. His eyelids insisted on folding shut, his brow on sinking deep into the eiderdown pillows.

I'm getting old, he thought. The nights of carousing, dashing from rooftops to beds to taverns, the nights sitting in the cold alleys, they're sapping the youth from my marrow. I have to be smarter now, work from my web and pull the lines like the spider that senses its prey. I have to think.

A pox on all that, he decided. I'm old. I'm going to sleep.

As he slept, Pinch dreamed, and he remembered those dreams—a thing unwarranted for him.

A shadow shape stalked him. First it was Manferic who, weeping by his own tomb, tried to draw Pinch into his mourning. The dead king's face was hooded, but the fabric of it shifted ever so slightly with the mewling wriggling of something alive. "Help me, son," clacked the dry jaws.

A panic clenched Pinch's dream-self. Then the shadow became Cleedis in a Hellrider's colors, hangman's noose in hand. Pinch could feel, if he truly felt in a dream, the cut of the hemp on his neck, burning the flesh to leave a scar like that around Therin's neck. Cleedis became Iron-Biter and Vargo, two creatures so alike, height to height the same. His dream attached great importance to the fusing of that pair. The one-who-was-two converged on him with the gleaming blade of the Knife held high and the Cup eager to receive his blood. His legs struggled to run, but his toes only brushed the ground. The noose cut into his neck, lifting him higher and higher. He soared above the reach of the Knife, above the scrape of the ground, up to the gallows height. His menacer changed again, and there was Therin laughing on the ground below, past the view of his own dangling feet. The lieutenant wore Pinch's clothes and was counting out the silver of his purse. Somewhere a magistrate's voice read the roll of his crimes and the punishments he had earned. Darkness closed till he hung in a single point. The roll was almost at its end, the creak of the executioner's lever eagerly waiting to finish the litany.

A woman's voice, cracked with age but holding a gentleness uncommon to Pinch's ears, carried through this darkness. "Janol," was all it said, over and over, unearthly hollow and never growing closer. It wasn't Maeve, the only woman Pinch had ever felt close to, although his dream-self half-expected it. It was a cry of anguished

poignancy, yet one that offered safety in the darkness.
Pinch strained against the noose, the logic of his dream
creating ground beneath his dangling feet. The noose cut
tighter, cold blood ran into his collar, but the cries grew no
nearer. The rope creaked and a black-gloved hand came
into view, ready to pull the trapdoor lever.

The hand pulled the lever. There was a rattling
thunk. The rope swished. Pinch was falling.

"Janol."

The rogue jerked forward, hands clawing to pull
loose the rope around his neck. It actually took moments, during which he ripped at his collar, before
Pinch realized the noose was not there. He was sitting
up in a mess of bed linens, still dressed in his day
clothes, and gulping air like a fish. His mouth was dry
and his jaw rigid with fright.

"Janol."

The regulator whirled about. He heard the voice. He
was certain it was here somewhere and not just in his
dream. It came from somewhere, anywhere in the
room—but there was no one. He froze and waited ex-
pectantly for it to repeat.

Nothing happened; no cry came.

It had been only the residue of his dream, his nightmare. Sliding out of bed, he rubbed his temples until
the echoes and the fog fled away.

Nightmares and dreams. Pinch didn't like either.
There were priests who said dreams were the work of
the gods, omens to be studied for their insight into the
future. Perhaps because of this, Pinch had made a point
of banishing dreams. He slept, he woke, and he never
remembered what the gods might have foretold for him.

This nightmare was all the more galling because it
would not go away. If it was a message from the gods,
then his future was grim indeed.

Still, there was no point in brooding over what he
couldn't control.

The small light though the windows, such as they were, suggested the best of an honest man's day was gone. It was time then for him to get to work. The regulator shrugged out of his tired clothes and into a doublet and hose of dark crepe that the servants had provided. He disdained the fine lace and silver buckles—too visible in shadows—and chose instead his worn hanger and well-used sword. Working clothes for a working man, he mocked as he admired himself in the mirror.

Ready, he cracked open the door to the hall slightly, although there was no reason for such caution. It was just old habit. Cleedis would have his guards outside, but there was no reason to conceal his goings from them.

The view outside reminded him that old habits existed for reasons. Cleedis's guards were there all right, their backs to him in an indifferent slouch, but beyond them were two more men equally bored, but wearing the livery of Prince Vargo.

"Damn!" the regulator breathed as he closed the door. Vargo's men complicated everything. They'd report to the prince and he'd be followed. If Vargo learned what he was up to, it would scotch all the plans. It was not likely the prince would allow Pinch to make off with the Cup and Knife.

In a few moments, Pinch reviewed his options. He could do nothing. He could hope that Cleedis came and provided a rescue or that the guards grew weary and slept. These were unpalatable and unlikely. He could try to create a distraction, but that would seem too obvious.

Still, there was another way out of the suite, though Pinch was loath to use it. His first and only experience in the tunnels had not been uplifting. He could only assume the tunnels went somewhere, but he had no idea how to find that somewhere. Then, there were things down there, including Manferic. He had little doubt the tunnels reached the necropolis because he was certain the late king had been spying on him before.

Thieves and fools were never far apart, though, so now was as good a time as any to learn his way through the underground maze. This time, though, he was fore-warned and had every intention of being forearmed.

By the time he opened the door, he carried an oil lamp and a piece of charcoal in one hand and his sword in the other. His pockets were stuffed with candles, and a glowing coal was carefully hung in a little pot from his side. The ember heated the clay until it threatened to scorch his hip, but Pinch was not going to be without some way of rekindling his light.

The dust still lay in a thick gloom on the floor and, although Pinch was no tracker, he could see footprints other than his own in the churn. "Manferic," he muttered, interpreting the marks as best he could. This was a confirmation of his suspicions—and also a guide out. He'd follow the trail back until it certainly led to some escape to the surface. He'd just have to hope Man-feric didn't have a direct path to the necropolis.

The plan stood him well at the bottom of the stairs. His own trail, which he could recognize by comparing to his prints now, went left, the other went right. He fol-lowed the latter.

The underground was a honeycomb of more passages than he imagined. The trail passed first one branch, then another, and finally so many that he gave up count. At any point of doubt, he marked the wall with a streak of chalk, showing that "I came this way or took this turn." He didn't intend to come back by the tun-nels, since he cared not who saw him coming into the palace, but prudence was a virtue, and he with so few virtues needed all the ones he could garner.

He'd traveled so for twenty minutes without a guess where he was under the palace—if he was under the

palace at all—when the plan went awry. The trail did
something it wasn't supposed to do—it split. There
were two sets of tracks where he'd been following only
one. One was a thin trail in the dust, and it threatened
to melt into uniform gray around the next double-
backed corner. The other trail was solid and profound,
clearing a route of constant traffic.

He tried to interpret the thick marks in the powder.
The lesser trail was probably no more than the scuttles
of rats; if he followed it, he'd end up in the palace
kitchens.

The larger trail was more a puzzle. It smeared across
the ground the way a wench mopped a table, in ragged
swipes that blotted out what had come before. Here and
there were traces of a boot or a shoe, showing some
human progress. Tattered drapes of old cobwebs confirmed the passage. What slope-footed thing had sham-
bled through the hall?

Pinch chose the latter route. Of course it was the
worse choice. It was like a verser's play in a game of
sant, where the obvious card was always the wrong
card. Looking at it, though, there really wasn't any
other choice. He was a thief and a confidence man, not
some wild woodsman. The signs he could read were the
marks of greed, gullibility, and the law. If he lost the
trail—and the one looked damned slight—he'd be
forced to come back here anyway.

It was with a profoundly greater sense of caution,
though, that Pinch advanced. If there was something
ahead, he was in no hurry to meet it unprepared.

The dry dust of the broken webs tickled his nose. The
air was a dark sweetness of rotted spider strands and
forgotten time. No breeze except for the unknown
strangers rustled through the stygian corridor. There
were no clicking insects in the darkness and none of the
sinister squeaks of rats that he was accustomed to as a
prowler. He'd crept down secret ways before, but the si-

lence of this one was unsettling.

Remembering the pits and falls of his previous visit, the rogue felt the floor carefully with each step, reassuring himself that the stone was solid beneath his feet. At the same time, he strained his ears, wondering if he'd hear the same inexplicable lamentations he'd heard before.

He went a long way in this fashion, creeping and listening, and perhaps the strain of the effort dulled his keenness. He almost missed a sound that, had he been more alert, would have saved him from harm.

As it was, it was only just too late. He heard a snorting grunt and before he could assess it, anticipate its source, and shift the knowledge to his favor, it was too late.

A form, thick and furred, sprang from an as yet unexamined niche just at the edge of Pinch's probings. The creature stood like a man, half again as tall as the smallish rogue. It lunged forward in a burst of fury, its fur gleaming dirty white in the flickering light. Pinch jabbed at it with his long dirk, but the thing smashed his hand against the wall with a casual backhand blow. The biting stone shredded the skin over his knuckles and ground at the tendons until Pinch, unwilled, screamed at the fire that jabbed through his fingers.

With its prey's only guard dispensed, the man-thing lunged forward. Its head, a bearlike face twisted into a brutal snarl, was squashed between its shoulders to make a rounded lump above oversized shoulders. Before Pinch could dodge, the thing flung its limbs around him, pinioning one arm to his side. Rip went the back of his fine doublet as thick claws cut through it like paper. The nails pierced his back, burning between the muscled knots of his shoulder blades. The creature drove them in hard, pressing him close into its greasy chest. It smelled of sheep fat, grubs, night soil, and salt, and he could taste the same crushed up against his lips.

The skewed perceptions, the over-pure sensation of it, vainly tried to fill his mind and drive down the sear of pain as it worked its claws deeper into his flesh.

He distinctly heard the ragged course of his breath, the helpless scrape of his feet against the flagstones, and the creak of his ribs. He tried to twist himself free, but this was a futile play at resistance. The beast had struck too quickly and was too strong for him to resist.

Still, in the writhing, he managed to get a little leverage with his dagger hand. He couldn't jab the blade in, the way it should be, but was able to make a clumsy slash along its side. There was little hope of seriously wounding the creature. All the rogue wanted was a deep gash, one that would hit nerves and spill blood, distract the thing and give him a measure of satisfied revenge.

The knife cut as if through thick leather, and Pinch was rewarded with a furious squeal. Seizing the chance, he kicked out and twisted to break himself free. The hope was a cheat, like trying to win against a cole who's cut the dice to his advantage.

The squeal transformed into a snarl and, in one effortless sweep, the beast raked its claws out of Pinch's back to sink into his shoulders. Heaving up, the creature cleared the thief's feet from the floor and slammed him against the stone wall so hard his head cracked on the rock.

The world, a gloom already, darkened to a single tunnel. Somehow Pinch kept his dagger, though he could do little more than wave it around in weak blindness.

The creature slammed him against the wall again, its yellow fangs bared in brutal joy. And again. A fourth, a fifth, and more times until Pinch lost all count. With each crash a little more of the volition drained from his muscles until he flopped like a helpless doll in the monster's grasp. The world was all blackness, save for the tiniest point of the real world—

the candle he'd dropped, still guttering on the ground.

The bashing stopped. Pinch could barely loll his head up. The rogue still hovered over the ground in the beast's bloody grasp.

"Whot your naim?" The basso words rumbled through the hall.

I'm hallucinating, the thief was certain. He forced his pain-dazzled eyes to focus. The creature was watching him, its flattened head cocked owl-like as it waited.

"Name!" the beast bellowed in badly slurred trade tongue. It rattled him a little more just for emphasis.

Pinch understood.

"P—Janol," he croaked. He almost used the name of his old, Elturel life, but a spark held him back. He was in Ankhapur, and here he was Janol. Gods knew who or what this beast might report to.

"Ja-nol?" the creature snarled, trying to wrap its fangs around the shape of the word.

Pinch nodded.

All of a sudden he dropped to the floor, the creature's cushing grasp released. It was so unexpected that Pinch, normally of catlike footing, tumbled into an angular pile of clothes, blood, and pain.

"You—Janol?" it asked a third time, with less ferocity than before. It could have been almost apologetic in its tone, if it reasoned at all like normal beings. The rogue doubted that, given its behavior so far.

"I'm Janol . . . royal ward of Ankhapur." Between each word was a wince and the struggling determination to get back to his feet. "Kill me . . . and the royal guard will . . . scour this place with fire and sword." It took a lot of effort for Pinch to stand and say all that, although it wasn't hard to give the lie a little conviction.

The beast stood and said nothing, its face puckered up in concentration. This finally gave Pinch a chance to study it clearly. It was bowlegged, broad, and re-

minded Pinch of Iron-Biter in that, except for the fact
that where he could look down on the dwarf, this thing
was a full head taller than him. He'd seen such beasts
before, though during the brute's battering that recog-
nition was not uppermost in his mind. There was cold
solace in knowing just what was killing you.

Now that it wasn't trying to smash his skull against
the wall, there was some chance and gain in that recog-
nition. Naming the thing, though, added more to the
mystery than solving the problem.

It was a quaggoth, an albino beast of the far underground realms. They were virtually unknown on the
surface. The only reason Pinch knew of them was his
youth here in Ankhapur. Manferic had raised a few, like
slavish dogs, as his special lackeys. They were hunters
and jailers, one of old Manferic's "special" punishments.

"You not Janol. Janol boy." Amazement that the
thing knew him once was increased by urgency as the
thing reached down to continue its beating.

"I've grown," he blurted hastily.

He tried to duck beneath the sweeping arms, but the
monster was quicker than its speech. With the thief in
its grip, the quaggoth slowly and deliberately squeezed.
The wind crushed out of him in a last series of choking
words. "I . . . am . . . Janol," he gasped in vain.

The beast snarled and crushed harder. Pinch heard a
crack from within his chest and the sharp burn of a broken rib, but there was no air left in him to scream. The
dim tunnel of light was quickly becoming even more
dim.

"Ikrit—stop!"

The pressure ceased. The pain did not.

"Is he Janol?" It was a woman's voice, quavering and
weak but unmistakably female.

"He say, lady."

"And you?"

"Me, lady, say he not Janol."

"Put him down."

Pinch tumbled to the floor. This time he made no move to get to his feet. He gasped for air like a landed fish, and each heave brought a new lance of pain that drove out all the wind he had regained.

"You want look, lady?" From his hands and knees, Pinch looked up to see the beast addressing something or someone in the darkness.

". . . Yes." There was a pained hesitancy in the framing of her simple answer.

The beast stooped to seize Pinch and present him like a prisoner before the dock. The rogue tried to crawl away, but all he did was trigger a paroxysm of choking that ended with a mouthful of coughed-up blood.

"No—wait." Her words shook, as though they were a dam to her fears and uncertainties. "You say he's not Janol?"

"No, lady. Not Janol."

There was a drawing of breath from the darkness, a drawing of resolve. "Let me see him."

The quaggoth bowed slightly to the darkness and stepped aside. Pinch, suspecting that his life might hang on this display, wiped the blood from his chin and lips and struggled to stand upright. He peered into the gloom of the tunnel, but even with his thief-trained eyes, he could not make out the slightest shadow of his examiner.

At last a sigh, pained and disappointed, floated from the darkness. "It's too long. Who can tell? . . . Let him go, Ikrit. Take him out."

"Who are—" Pinch's question was forestalled by a spasm from his chest, the broken bone protesting even the rise and fall of words. There were so many questions inside him, all strangled by the lancing pain inside.

"Who am I?" The echo was a confused musing of his words. "I'm . . . one who loved unwisely."

Riddles! Every answer led to more riddles. If he
hadn't felt so lousy, Pinch would have cursed the voice
in the darkness. He forced himself to frame one last
question.

"What am I—" he paused to force back the pain, "—
Janol, to you?" The effort left him collapsed against the
wall.

Footsteps crept closer from the darkness. The quaggoth took a protective step to intercede between Pinch
and its charge. There was covert tenderness in its
move, uncharacteristic for its race. "Janol is—" Suddenly the whispers halted in a gagging retch, like a
drunken man. When it stopped, the woman tried again.
"Janol is . . . hope," she said weakly, although it was certain those were not the words she wished to use.

Pinch gave up. He hadn't the strength to ask any
more questions, and the lady, be she human, sprite, or
spook, was not going to answer him straightly. The pain
exhausted him so that all there was left was to let himself sink into aching stillness.

"Ikrit, take him out."

"He attack lady," the quaggoth argued as its duty.

The weakness faded from the woman's voice as if
filled with kind strength, the will of a mother imposed
on her child. "Take him out—gently."

"Yes, lady," the big white creature rumbled obedi-
ently, even though it was clearly not happy with the
command.

Pinch moaned as it picked him up. The lances were so
constant now that their pain became almost bearable.
The cracked bone had settled, not in the best place, but
was at least no longer trying to reshape his muscle tis-
sue. The quaggoth strode in great jolting strides, and
with every lurch the rogue thought for sure he would
pass out. They moved quickly through the total darkness, the quaggoth easily picking the way with eyes
adapted to the dark. Even if he still had his full wits

about him, the rogue could not have studied the way.

At last the beast stopped and lowered the rogue, weak and sweating, to the ground. "Go there," it growled. In the pitch blackness, Pinch had no hint of where "there" was. Perhaps sensing this, a great clawed hand shoved him roughly forward, and he would have fallen if his body had not collided with a stone wall. "There—the bright world. Your world." No more was said as the thump and clack of clawed feet signaled the beast's departure.

Not ready to die in the darkness, Pinch forced himself to reason. The beast claimed this was the way out, therefore there had to be a door. With his trained touch, the rogue probed the stone searching for a knob, handle, crack, or catch. Patience rewarded him, and with only slight pressure, which was fortunate, he pushed a section of the wall aside.

It was the very last of twilight outside, the embered glow of the sun as it pulled the last of its arc below the horizon. The lamplighters were out, wizard-apprentices who practiced their cantrips activating the street lamps. Faint as it was, the wilting dusk blinded Pinch after his sojourn in darkness. Everything was orange-red and it hurt his eyes.

Blinking, he stumbled into the street, unable to clearly see where he'd emerged. It was good fortune that traffic was light at this hour and he was not trampled by some rag-picker's nag that chafed to be home in its stable. As the glare finally faded, the buildings resolved themselves into shapes and places. Here was a tavern, there a gated wall, and farther along it a cramped tower.

It was from these clues that Pinch realized he was standing outside the necropolis. The necropolis meant priests and priests meant healing. A plan already forming in his mind, Pinch stumbled toward the barred gate.

When the priests saw a bloody and bruised wretch staggering toward them, they reacted just as Pinch expected. Most held back, but a few, guided by the decency of their faith, hurried forward to aid this miserable soul. As hoped, among them was Lissa, and toward her Pinch steered his faltering steps.

As she caught up to him, Pinch collapsed dramatically in her arms. It wasn't that hard, considering his state. Real wounds added far more realism than what he could have done by pig's liver, horse blood, and a few spells.

"Lissa, help me," he murmured. "Take me to the temple of the Red Priests."

"I will take you to the Morninglord," she insisted, intent on repaying him with the works of her own faith.

"No," he insisted, "only the Red Priests. It is their charge to minister to the royal clan. Take me to another and you insult their god."

Lissa didn't like it; it was against her inclinations, but she could not argue against custom. She called for a cart and horse, and Pinch knew she would take him.

Soon, as he lay on the straw and watched the rooftops go by, Pinch smiled a soft smile to himself, one that showed the satisfaction that broke through his pain. He'd be healed in the halls of the Red Priests, and he'd case those same halls for the job he intended to pull. Sometimes his plans realized themselves in the oddest of ways.

Scouting

Healing hurt more than the whip that laid the wound, or so it seemed to Pinch as he lay on the cold marble platform that was the Red Temple's "miracle seat." The priests greeted his arrival with more duty than charity and proceeded to exact their fare from his body. There was no kindness as they reset his rib and pressed their spells into him to knit it together. Into his cuts they rubbed burning salves that boiled away any infection, then dried the ragged gashes and pulled the torn skin back together, all in a process designed to extract every fillip of pain they could from him.

As if the pain were not enough, the priests simply weren't content to let him suffer in silence. They chanted, intoned, and sermonized as they went about their task. Each laying on of hands was accompanied by exhortations to surrender himself to the workings of their god, to acknowledge the majesty of their temple over all others, and to disavow his allegiances to other gods. The Red Priests were not of the belief that all gods had their place or that man was naturally polytheistic. For them, the Red Lord was supreme and there was no need to consider the balances of others. It was little wonder why the princes preferred self-reliance to the aid of the temple.

It was long hours and well into darkness before the priests were done. At last Pinch was allowed to rise, naked and shivering, off the icy stone. For all the pain, the priests had been thorough. Drawing his fingertips over his back, Pinch felt no scars—better handiwork than the priest who'd left his knee a web of whitish lines.

"When you are dressed, you may leave," urged the senior brother, who stood at the head of a phalanx of brothers, though no sisters, Pinch noted with disappointment

The elder was a dark-skinned man whose triangular face was pinched by constant sadness. He nodded, a curt little tilt that could only be mastered by those who'd been in command too long. Another brother produced a rough-stitched robe of itchy red wool, normally allotted acolytes to teach them patience through poverty and discomfort. "Your own clothes were beyond repair, and suspect by their filth. They were burned. We give you these so that you do not go naked into the world."

"Thanks, most beatific one," Pinch drawled, though he hardly felt grateful for their mean furnishings. His doublet had cost three hundred golden lions and the hose had come all the way from Waterdeep. Itchy red wool was hardly providing him in the style he was due. "Fortunate for my soul, perhaps, but I don't think I can depart so soon."

The brother's sad face grew even more dour. "Pray, why not?"

With a show of exhausted effort, Pinch struggled

into the robe. "This day's been an effort, patrico. Give me time to rest before sending me on my way."

The elder yielded with sour grace. "Indeed, it is sometimes the case. Your strength should return to you within the hour. I will return to give blessings on your way then." The elder priest bowed slightly and left, sweeping his entourage out with him.

There was a deadline inherent in that hour, but Pinch didn't care. If he offended any of the Red Robes, it was only as they deserved. It was an old animosity carried over from his youth, when he sat in a palace chair at a palace desk and wrote the lessons of a droning temple tutor.

Although he was certain to be watched, Pinch made no effort to skulk about or slip away. Instead he ambled from the healing chapel and into a massive hall, the festival floor. The squat pillars of the temple fixed the high of the sky so large it almost took his breath away. The Red Priests clearly did not consider modesty a necessary virtue.

Sure as he'd sworn, Pinch had himself an escort, a lesser pater who lingered over the holy fonts with too little purpose and too much attention. The rogue noted the man with only the barest of glances. Years of spotting peelers and sheriff's men made this shaved-head plebe painfully obvious. Pinch wandered out of the hall with seeming aimlessness, half-feigning the weakness he felt.

The thief strolled through the soaring nave fixed with a mask of contemplative awe, the face of the impressed sinner confronted by the majesty of greater power. Inside, though, his thief's mind ran a cunning round of scheme and counter-scheme. How many windows were there? Where did the doors lead? What would be the round of the night guards? Here was a pillar to stand behind, there was a window whose casement was rotten. He made note of the shadows and what lamps and torches were likely to be lit in the long hours after the last benedictus was said.

All this was good, but the one thing it lacked was telling Pinch just where the Knife and Cup lay. The rogue tried strolling toward the main altar, keeping a veiled eye on his watchdog priest. There was no effort, no alarm to stop him, and from that Pinch guessed the regalia were not in the great nave. He was hardly surprised; stealing the Cup and Knife could hardly be that easy.

Pinch expanded his wanderings, passing through the nave's antechambers and out to the cloistered walk that ringed a damp garden, verdant with spell-ripened growth. The trees leafed fuller than the winter should have allowed, the shrubs curled thicker, and flowers blossomed in brighter hues than true nature.

At the very center of the garden square was a tower of dark stone, a somber spire that thrust above the roofs and walls of the rest of the temple grounds till it rivaled even the great dome of the main hall. No doors marked its base, and at its very top was a single window, a tall, narrow slit that was clearly big enough for a robed priest. A faint glow shifted and weaved from inside the stone chamber.

There was no need to search any farther. This, the rogue knew, was his target. There could be no other.

It was with a sudden-found burst of fitness and strength that Pinch greeted the elder patrico when he returned. The man scowled even more than he had before, suspicious of his patient's good cheer. Nonetheless, he was not going to interfere with Pinch's leaving. He was more than content to cast one he saw as a viper out of his house.

So, the temple doors closed with a certain finality behind Pinch and he was standing at the end of the Avenue of Heroes, clad only in an itchy red robe and cheap sandals. With his hair and his bruises, he looked like a wretch given charity by the friars inside. Passing tradesmen made studious effort to avoid his gaze in hopes that they could forestall the inevitable harangue for coins that was sure to come. In this Pinch surprised them, keeping his needs and his counsel to himself.

The rogue was not forlorn and abandoned though. He'd barely taken three steps through the gelatinous mud that passed for a street when someone cried out his name. Old habit spun him around quick with a hand already on his dagger, which the Red Priests had at least not thrown away, by the time he recognized the speaker. It was Lissa, sitting at a tea vendor's stall in the shade of a pale-branched willow.

"Master Janol, you are recovered?"

The rogue light-stepped through the muck and joined her.

"Well enough, for which I must thank you." The answer was as sincere as Pinch understood the term. "Perhaps I may even owe you my life."

The priestess dismissed the suggestion. "If not I, it would have been another there," she demurred in reference to her part in getting him to the temple.

"My thanks, nonetheless."

"What befell you?"

Pinch had already anticipated the need for a good story to explain the attack, and so answered without hesitation.

"Thieves. A cowardly lot waylaid me with clubs at an alley mouth. It was clear they planned to beat me to death and then rob me."

"Did they?"

"Beat me to death?" Pinch asked in jovial amazement. "Clearly not."

"No—rob you?"

"They got something from me they'll remember," he boasted on his lie. "A few sharp cuts with my blade put them off their prey."

Lissa nodded as if with great relief, but then she drew up hard as she pushed something across the table. "It is most fortunate they did not get this . . ."

On the table was the amulet of the Dawnbreaker, the same he'd stolen from the temple at Elturel.

If she could have opened his heart, the priestess would have seen a churning tide of panic and rage. The sudden fear of discovery, the self-rage to have clumsily forgotten such a detail in the first place, and the panicky rush to create a plausible reply all would have played open on the face of a normal man with a normal life. Pinch, though, was no common man who carried bricks here and there. He was a regulator, and regulators survived by their wits. Inwardly he boiled, but outwardly all Lissa saw was a flooding collapse of relief.

"Praise your god!" he extemporized. "It's safe. I would have a bet a noble those Red Priests had stolen it. Where did you find it?"

"Where you were carrying it," was her icy reply.

"Precisely. I was worried I'd dropped it in the mud," the rogue continued, thinking fast. "Priestess Lissa, although it is not as I intended, let me present you with your temple's treasure." The only hope of coming out of this, Pinch figured, was to claim credit for what he never intended.

"You—what!"

"I was bringing it to you."

"I surely cannot believe this."

Now was the time for Pinch to assume the air of roguish effrontery. "I told you I had means."

"How did you get it back?"

Pinch let knowing smile play across his lips. "I have had some experience with thieves and their like. I understand them. It just takes the right threats."

"A few threats and they give it up?" It was clear the woman wanted to scoff.

Pinch pressed the amulet back into her hand. "Threats backed by sword and coin. There was a cost in getting it back—five thousand nobles. Will your temple honor my debt?" Pinch knew better than to look too pure and noble and so let his devious heart weave a profitable deceit.

Lissa was unprepared for the demand. "I . . . I am certain they will. By my word they will," she added with more confidence as she weighed the artifact in her hand.

"I will prepare a receipt for you to present to your superiors," Pinch added as an extra fillip of persuasiveness.

"Your injuries. Did you . . ."

"Fight for the amulet—no, I'm no hero." Later, when the rogue told this story around the table, this would be the place where he would pause and spread his hands with the confidence that he had caught his mark. "This was, I think, an attempt to get it back."

Lissa hastily slid the artifact out of sight. "You think they'll try again?"

"Almost certainly. If I were a thief, I would. I fear it puts you in danger."

"I can care for myself."

"They'll be looking for you."

"I'll take it to the temple."

"The Morninglord's temple here in Ankhapur is small and poorly funded. These thieves already stole it once from a better-equipped temple. They'd be certain to try here."

"Not if you turned them over to the authorities."

"I can't." Pinch was lying in this. If he ever had to, he'd turn Sprite and the others over without a qualm.

"Can't?"

"I'm not sure who they are and even if I knew, I wouldn't. Understand—my success is based in part on discretion. Lose that and no one will trust me."

The priestess was shocked. "This is a business for you!"

Pinch sipped at the brew the tea vender set in front

of him. "It is a service. Sometimes there are rewards and sometimes not. We can't all live supported by the donations of others, lady."

She felt the venom in that sting. "It's not a pure business—"

"And I am no priest, even if I am decked out in these red robes," Pinch interrupted. "You live to see the perfect world rise over the horizon like the sun of your Morninglord, and I laud you for that, Lissa. I must live to survive. Besides, isn't recovering what is stolen a virtue? Maids come to priests to find rings they have lost; I just do the same without spells."

The priestess pointedly looked at the sky, unwilling to admit the soundness of his argument. Pinch sipped his tea and gave her time, but never changed his gaze of expectant answer. He had her on the hook and was not about to let her wriggle away.

"There is virtue even in the cloud that hides the sun," she finally murmured. It was a quote from something, probably some scripture of her church. It was her admission to accept his point, her faith overruling her good instincts.

Priests always made the best prey, Pinch thought to himself. Others were unpredictable, but priests had their codes, for good or ill, giving a sharper lever to tip them one way or the other.

"What will you do with the amulet?" he asked, abruptly changing the conversation. "It's not safe either with you or your temple."

"I can find some place to hide it."

Pinch shook his head in disagreement, as if he were considering the point to himself and she were not across the small table from him.

"What?"

"What was taken can be found. It's a saying among their kind."

"You have a better plan?" she challenged as Pinch

hoped she would.

"Yes, but there's no purpose in naming it." Like the hunter in the blind, he was baiting the trap to lure the prey near.

"What do you mean?"

"There is a way you could keep it safe, but you'll not do it, so I won't say it."

"You are so certain!" she fumed. "How can you be so sure about me?"

"Then you will give me the amulet?"

"What?"

"See! 'Tis as I said. There's no point in pursuing it."

"What do you mean, give you the amulet?"

"Nothing. It was a foolish idea. Hide your treasure and let it go."

"Tell me."

"It's pointless. It requires trust."

"How does your having the amulet protect it?"

"First, because they'll assume you have it, not I. We've met; what other point was there but to return your treasure? Therefore, they'll look to you as the person who must be robbed.

"Second, they know my sting and fear it. Why do you think they gave it back in the first place? For five thousand gold nobles? Hardly. This treasure's worth far more, if they could sell it to some rival priest or wizard." Pinch paused and took a sip of tea. "They're afraid of my connections and my position. As the late king's royal ward, I could have anyone arrested and executed on my word alone. They will not cross me like they would you."

Lissa studied her hands. "I don't—"

"As I said—trust," Pinch countered with disappointment. "You injure me, which is why I would not bring this up. First, you think me a thief and wound me for it. Second, you suspect me as a liar. Another wound. Third, you think that I would refuse to give it back. Any more of these cuts and I'll take a worse beating from you than those scoundrels did to me."

Lissa tried to sip her tea, but its bitterness felt like her soul and brought no comfort. "Perhaps . . . I have been uncharitable in my judgments. I . . . believe you are right. Take the amulet and guard it for me."

"No." Now was time to set the hook.

"You won't?"

"I won't do it just to make you feel better."

"Then do so because you're right," she urged, pressing the amulet into his hand. "Hold it for me until I return to Elturel in a fortnight's passing—because I will trust you."

Pinch contemplated the amulet, feigning some doubt about the matter, before quickly slipping it away. "For a fortnight, then." He raised his mug as a bond of their word and smiled his first genuine smile since their meeting. A fortnight it would be, barely enough time to find a buyer and arrange for the artifact to disappear conveniently one more time. It was almost a shame to swindle one so pretty and trusting.

She matched his toast, blind to the intent of his good cheer. Hardly had the mugs clinked but Pinch was on his feet and ready to go. "You must give me leave, Priestess Lissa, but this robe suits me poorly. I must find a tailor with a quick hand. I have no desire to return to the palace dressed as I am." It was best to be gone quickly before she had the chance to reconsider her choice, and certainly his clothes offered the best excuse.

Their parting done, Pinch hurried down the street, into the city, and far away from the palace gates. There was still one more appointment to keep before he could begin the work Cleedis had commissioned of him.

Pinch found his company several hours later, after he'd got himself new dress. No locks were broken or heads cracked, but the Red Priests would be hard pressed to explain why one of their order was seen fleeing a laundry with a gentleman's wash.

The three had settled into the ordinary where Pinch had sent them. On the outside, it was a squalid place, just up the alley from the fishmongers' gathering place. To the south were the rat-infested docks, while the blocks just up the hill were notorious stews where man, woman, or thing could find most tawdry pleasures they sought. Here, in the gloomy zone between the two, the air reeked of seawater, fish guts, and cheap scented oils. The packed clay of the alley was slimy with fish cleaner's leavings and made musical by the chittering of rats and the belches of the resident drunks. In a way, Pinch had chosen the place for its ambiance; given the air and the locale, no honest man was likely to intrude on them.

Inside, the shop was little better. A smoky fire, sputtered by grease dripping from a questionable carcass that turned on the spit, overheated the cramped main room. This was little more than a trio of tables, scored and stained by knife fights and ale, and some rickety benches pressed up against the wall. The patrons, dock rats too hard up to visit even the meanest festhalls farther up and drunken sailors stopping in for one last toast on their way down from those same halls, eyed Pinch hungrily as he came through the canvas door. The rogue passed through their company without a word and made for the rooms upstairs.

Therin, Sprite, and Maeve were huddled at the lone table in the room Pinch had let. The rogue was pleased to see they'd exercised discipline and waited for his arrival instead of setting out on an ill-advised drinking spree. Of course, the jugs on the table showed they hadn't spent their entire time in sober contemplation.

"Run out of lamp oil while you were dressing, did you, Pinch?" smirked Therin when the master rogue found his friends. The regulator said not a word, but pulled up a chair and set himself at their table, back to a corner as was his custom. He was dressed ill matched and ill fitting, in tattered hose and a doublet that hung loose on his chest and short on the sleeves. About the only thing right about it were the somber dark colors, well suited to Pinch's needs for the night.

"Maybe he got caught catting and grabbed her husband's clothes instead of his own," Sprite snickered.

"Pinch, you wouldn't!" Maeve added in mock horror.

"Have your wit all well and good, but have you done as you were commanded?" Pinch glowered as he tried to pour the last slops out of the jug they'd already drained.

"Aye, three for all of us." Therin looked to the other two and they nodded agreement.

"I've found us an artificer who's gambled too poorly to meet his notes. He'll work quick with no questions for the right fee. I even filched us his fee." Sprite plopped a bag of coins on the table.

"Keep your profit," Pinch granted with uncharacteristic generosity, knowing full well the halfling had probably nipped twice what he was showing. "The copies?"

"Two sets of each," Sprite answered with a mischievous twinkle. "Thought maybe we could take the second set and sell it to some coney once the word gets 'round."

"How good's his work?"

"Faith, Pinch, he claims he's the best, but I ain't seen this blackjack and skene to compare."

Pinch accepted that. It was a pointless question anyway, since there was no more time.

"The layout? I've seen the inside. What more can you give me?"

Therin reached into his heavy buff coat and produced a greasy sheet of parchment that he carefully unfolded and spread over the table, avoiding the pools of drink.

"I—and Maeve," the Gur added in return for the wizardess's sharp kick under the table, "Maeve and me have compassed the whole of the place on this sheet. See this here"—he jabbed at a scratch mark on the sheet—"be the main gate, and that little mark there is their postern. Guard walks are here and go around in this fashion." The finger drew out the path on the sheet. "This cup and knife is kept in the tower—"

"I know, I saw it. Catchpoles?"

"The watch don't patrol the area heavy, according to the locals. They leave it to the priests to mind the peace."

"Good. What about spells and locks, Maeve?"

"Well, Pinch, love, I couldn't get a good read on the spells." Maeve looked down, sheepish that she hadn't been able to fulfill her role. "Those priests are awful leery. Felt like the standard set of wards on the doors and windows, but I'd wager the walls ain't guarded that way. Probably rely on watchmen for that."

"Beasts?"

"No scent, no track," Therin said.

"Well, thank Mask for that." Pinch leaned back and considered the map before speaking again. "Looks like it'll be a climbing job," he finally decided with disgust. Any hope of an easier way was dashed by the map laid out before him. "Sprite, it'll be you and me. We'll need rope and dark clothes."

The halfling spit a wad of something onto the floor and nodded.

"Therin, Maeve—get yourselves back to the palace. Get word to Cleedis that I need his package tonight. He'll find us across the square from the temple. Understood?"

"Aye, Pinch."

"Well then, summon up the landlord and get us more drink," Pinch ordered with grim cheer. "We're out to do some breaking tonight."

Night Work

The nightly steam was curling into the square from the streets and arcades. It was a thin mist but full of the flavor of fish grease and onions, bad cheese and night slops. Pinch didn't mind the stink where he sat, nestled in a dark corner. Sprite squatted at his feet, playing with his dagger in the dust. The watch had come by twice already, calling the hours past midnight. Beyond the constables, men to be studiously avoided, the square was barely alive with the dregs of the night trade—drunken sailors vainly searching for the docks, noodle vendors closing up their carts, festhall ladies returning from assignations, and rakes prowling the ways for a fight. Pinch amused himself by picking out the foins and cutpurses among the dwindling revelers. They were easy enough to spot for a man who knew how to look: men who traveled in groups and pretended not to know each other, who circled around their mark like vultures in the sky.

Pinch watched his brothers as they watched their prey, always observant but never looking. He watched them with an idle professional interest, hoping to see a strike or a swindle new to him. Of particular interest was a trio of cardsharps who set up their game on the temple steps. It was a poor choice of place, with no privacy or distracting drink, which only meant this lot was a scrounging crew. The setter lured a coney in, the verser dealt him the cards, and the barnacle, the third, egged their mark on. Even from a distance, Pinch could see the verser was an amateur. He fumbled a chopped card so badly that only the quick thinking of the barnacle kept their coney from getting suspicious. It was clear that, at least on the basis of professional interest, there was nothing to be learned from these three.

Perhaps if Pinch had not been so absorbed by the antics of the card players, he might have noticed another soul hovering at the edge of the square—but perhaps not. There was little to note, just the bend of a low-hanging branch and the way a cur kept itself far from a certain spot as it prowled the plaza. It was not that Pinch was supposed to know that invisible eyes lay upon him.

Cleedis came skulking though the darkest part of the alley as had been arranged by messenger. Pinch winced, purely from professional concern, as the old warrior stumbled over the hidden snares of the alley. Prudently the rogue had arranged their meeting beyond the range of the temple guards' hearing or suspicion. The rogue nodded to his companion and the halfling obligingly melted from sight.

No greeting was said between them, the old man's impulse to talk shushed by Pinch's admonishing finger. Cleedis handed over a bag of lusterless black and Pinch wasted no time in unwrapping the cord. Inside were the false treasures passed on by the late Manferic.

Pinch nodded in satisfaction and then steered Cleedis farther into the darkness of the alley.

"Now, tell Manferic to keep his pet jailers away from me," he hissed into the old man's warty ear, "or there'll be no job tonight or ever."

The chamberlain squinched up his face in indignation. "Don't you make threats to me, you bastard knave! The Morninglord's priests would still like to roast you—or have you forgotten?"

Pinch answered with a smile in his voice. "I forget nothing. It's just that I think now they are more likely to suspect you than me. Be sure of your threats, old man."

"I—I don't understand," Cleedis weakly stammered, unbalanced by this rapid upheaval of roles. He was supposed to be the threatener, the blackmailer, not Pinch. "What pet?" It was a weak stall, but all the flustered courtier could assemble.

"In the tunnels," Pinch snarled.

"You've been beneath the palace?"

"I met Ikrit there. He tried to flail the husk off me."

"Ikrit—" Cleedis choked, holding back a gasp, "—lives?"

Pinch stepped closer, pinning the old man along the alley wall. He could sense the advantage slipping his way. "And some lady. Why do they hunt me?"

"Lady? There was a lady? . . . I don't know," the nobleman floundered.

"You are a poor deceiver, Cleedis."

"Perhaps it was a prisoner from long ago. You know Manferic—people who angered him tended to disappear."

"But you know about Ikrit." The rogue wasn't about to let his catch slip from the hook.

"It was just that . . . that was so long ago. I was surprised to hear the creature was still alive."

"And the woman? She took great interest in me."

"I don't know. Can you describe her?"

"No. Who is she?"

Cleedis found his backbone and became defiant. "I can't tell you. There were so many. It could have been a scullery maid who broke a prized dish, for all I know. There were times when whole staffs disappeared because Manferic was convinced they'd tried to poison him."

"Hmmph. I just thought he had them executed."

"He did at first. Later, death was not enough for him. He let the quaggoths hunt prisoners in those tunnels while he watched through a scrying ball."

That matched Pinch's images of his guardian. "So you're saying this woman was part of one of his hunts?"

The old man nodded with a suggestive leer. "I would guess she had charms or maybe spells to please Ikrit."

Pinch thought on this. It had the ring of those tales like Duric the Fool—too implausible to be real—but there was a chance it was true the way Duric's tales were sometimes real under a different name.

"When I get back, old man, we will talk more." It was not threat or promise, but the cold assurance that this matter was not done. Before the other could challenge his claim, Pinch took the bag and abandoned the chamberlain to the wet darkness.

"What was that all on?" Sprite probed as Pinch rejoined him and they slipped along the shadows of the square. "Ladies and tunnels and what."

"Have you ever heard that big ears get clipped?" Pinch snapped, thus ending the line of conversation before it ever was started.

Resolutely quiet, the pair plotted their course around the open fringes of the plaza. Pinch was pleased to note the cardplayers were gone. He didn't want to deal with them, especially if they got it into their heads to interfere. Honor among thieves was a joke, for there was no better target to rob than a thief himself.

By the map Therin had made, there was a corner of the temple wall that jutted across an old alley and then pulled itself back in line, like the bastion of a fortress. No doubt it had been configured at such odd angles to nestle against some other building now long gone. Pinch could remember nothing from his youth that might have forced them to build so. At just that point, the wall came close enough for a perilous leap from rooftop to guard walk and while not safe, it was their best chance. Climbing the temple wall would take too long and risk too many chances to be seen by the guards, especially with Pinch's weak knee. With a single jump, they could clear the span and be out of sight before the watchmen made their rounds.

Getting to the rooftop proved easy. The old tenement was a jumble of sills, cornices, eaves, and railings that gave the pair easy purchase. Sprite, the more nimble of the two, led, pointing out the grips and holds to Pinch as he followed.

After what seemed the time required to scale a torturous mountain face, the roof was reached. On their bellies they slithered to the top of the ridgepole, until they could peer over the edge of the wall walk just across the way. It was a gap of ten feet, maybe a little more. Pinch figured he could do it, especially since the roof sloped down and would give his run some extra momentum. Sprite, though, with his short legs would never be able to clear the distance.

Carefully Pinch unrolled the parchment he'd brought for this need. "Stand up, but stay out of sight," he said in a curt whisper while he fought to stretch the sheet flat. Intricate whorls of writing glowed faintly in the dark, filling the entire page. "Hold still while I read the spell."

"What's it do, Pinch? Make me fly?" Sprite had positioned himself behind a crumbling chimney.

"It'll make your runty self jump good. Now let me read."

Sprite peered into the gap between the two buildings. The ground was barely there in the darkness.

"What if it don't work?"

"Then there'll be a nice explosion and we can both blame Maeve. She taught me how to read this." Pinch mumbled over the complicated phrasings on the scroll, taking care not to say them outright until he was ready. Finally, he held up the sheet and read it aloud, looking up every few words to make sure Sprite was still in front of him. It was just reading, it should be easy, the rogue kept telling himself, but somehow saying the words was more torturous than he expected. About halfway through, it took conscious effort to shape the phrases. They wanted to escape him. When he reached a syllable he couldn't remember, Pinch tried not to show his panic and guessed, hoping he'd made the right choice. Finally, with a faint damp of perspiration on his brow, Pinch uttered the final words.

The rooftop did not shake with a fiery blast but the lettering faded from the sheet, leaving only a blank page of brittle parchment.

"See, it worked," Pinch boasted. Maeve also said it was possible nothing might happen, but there was no point worrying the little halfling with that.

"I don't feel different," Sprite answered with sullen suspicion. "Maybe if I jump a little bit—"

"Don't try it. You only get one chance." Pinch nodded toward the top of the guard wall. "Just a light step over there."

"I'm not—"

Pinch didn't wait for the rest of the protest but, seeing the walk was clear, heaved to his feet and sprinted down the shingled roof. His footing was poor on the mossy shakes, but the rogue let momentum carry him past all hazards. At the very edge of the eave, he sprang forward, out across the gap. He crossed the distance with ease and tumbled onto the stone walkway, risking more in tumbling off the back of the wall than he did leaping the gap. He lay flat on his belly until he was the sure the clatter of his arrival had raised no alarms.

At last he peered over the crenellations to find
Sprite, certain he'd have to urge the halfling to make
the leap. Just as he was scanning the rooftop, trying to
spot the halfling, the little thief gave him a light poke
in the side.

"Bless Maeve, it worked," Sprite panted, his face
flushed with the thrill of it. "I ain't never jumped so far
in all my born days!"

Pinch shushed his partner and motioned for them to
move out. Now they were in the enemy camp. Caution,
silence, and speed were their goals.

The pair hurried in leaps and starts, from the
shadow of this arch to the curve of that wall, with the
sure confidence of memory. Therin's map was good,
even sketching out the passages closed to outsiders.
Pinch wondered what priest had profited from Therin's
research. It would have been fitting to reclaim that payment tonight, too.

The thieves moved through the dreary temple
grounds, never once raising a suspicion. The complacent guards, convinced their fellows on the impregnable
walls had done their job, made no effort to watch for intruders. Indeed their eyes only looked for superiors who
might surprise them slacking at the job. It was a simple
matter to elude the notice of these buffoons.

Pinch praised the Red Priests for their diligence as he
pushed open the well-oiled gates to the inner cloister. No
squeak revealed their entrance. After making certain no
priests were muttering their devotionals in some dark
corner, Pinch led the way to the tower rising in the center
of the dark, silent garden. They knelt in the bushes near
the base and looked up at the smooth stone column. Just
below the minareted top, the polished surface was
pierced by the glow from the tower's only opening. Pinch
waited for a long time, watching for shadows or some
other sign that the rooftop room was occupied. Finally
satisfied there were none, the rogue whispered to his

compatriot, "Keep watch for trouble. I'm going up."

The other looked at the smooth wall and shook his little head. "You know you can't climb for a tinker's damn, Pinch. I should go."

The look Sprite got made it clear who would climb and who would stay. It wasn't a matter of climbing—it was a matter of trust and there was only one person Pinch trusted getting these treasures. Without a word, Sprite withdrew his suggestion and set himself to watch for intruders on their plans.

From his pouch, the regulator produced another scroll, the second Maeve had prepared. Again forcing the nonsensical syllables over his tongue, barely had Pinch finished the scroll before he started to rise into the air like a cork released at the bottom of a barrel. Ten, twenty, thirty feet he rose, just a hand's reach from the wall. When he was just beneath the level of the window, he willed himself to a stop.

Pinch hung there, breathless and trembling, drifting in the air like a cottonwood fluff. The buoyancy of levitation was a ticklish sensation that threatened to unnerve his senses and disorient him for what was to come. It was more than magic, though. Pinch panted with fear, the fear of floating over nothing against the fear of threats unknown that lay beyond the windowsill. It was beyond explanation, but these were the moments he lived for, the rush of blood as he hovered in the balance of life, or maybe death. Though it lay beyond explanation, every thief knew it, lived for it, and savored that moment more than the money, the gems, and the magic that was gained. "Gods rescue us from dull lives" was an old toast of many a black-hearted gang.

A whistle from below forced Pinch into action. Spite, barely visible in the weeds, worked a sign with his hands that foretold of trouble. Guards were coming, no doubt. With a breath, Pinch seized the sill and effortlessly swung himself over.

The tower chamber was small, no larger than a fest-hall crib and decorated as dramatically. It was lit by a golden fire that burned steadily from the heart of a crystal stone hung from the ceiling in an iron cage. It was a stone that would burn as brightly through all eternity until the gods grew tired of looking on it. For all its enduring power, it was hardly special, just a cheap parlor trick of holy power. The walls were hung with arras heavy enough to stifle all breezes. Each was stitched with the exploits of kings and queens, the past rulers of Ankhapur, their glories now as faded as the rugs on these walls.

At the far wall was the treasure Pinch sought, a golden cup and a glittering knife in a case of rosewood and gold. The case sat on a small shelf, unlocked, unsealed, and unprotected from thieves like himself. And Pinch didn't believe a bit of it. The Red Priests of Ankhapur were not such great fools. They knew their treasures would draw burglars like candles draw moths. Clearly, the only reason the royal regalia were before him now was that they had to be much harder to take than it looked. Pinch wondered just how many had tried before him and failed.

It was a question to be approached with caution. From his perch in the window, Pinch studied the room. There was much not to like. The coverings on the walls hid too much, the floor was too clean—it was just too *easy*. A lack-a-wit could figure out things were not what they seemed here. It wasn't a case of whether there were traps, but just what traps the priests had stitched up for him.

As he perched in that window, pressed against the sill so that he was nothing more than a black shadow on the wall, Pinch cursed Maeve for her drunkenness. Maybe Therin was right, that the woman's drinking was out-balancing the usefulness of her skills. If she'd been more of a wizard I wouldn't be sitting here, afraid to touch the floor. I'd have me a scroll or a ring or something to find the mantraps and show me the way. As it is, she's too drunk to properly prepare what I need most the time.

Pinch allowed himself the luxury of this frustration for a few moments and then put it away. When he was down, not hanging in some clergy's window, he would take it up with her. A little cold water and drying out would do her some good, but now there was work and it was time it was done.

From his boot, Pinch slid a slender packet of tools wrapped in soft, oily leather that smelled faintly of dried fish and cologne. He undid the strings and laid out a small collection of rods, marbles, blades, probes, and saws. Working tools for a working man. He took the rod and pulled on it till it grew longer and longer, to the length of a spear. It was rigid, light, and didn't slip in his grasp. It had cost him three particular rubies that the old dwarven smith had demanded, the stealing of which turned into more of a job than the thief had expected. Right now, it was worth it.

With the wand he brushed the hangings. The first three barely stirred at his caress. The fourth quivered at his touch like a thing prodded in its dreams. Pinch poked it again, a little more firmly. The heavy cloth suddenly snapped and writhed like a thing alive, trying to envelop the slender rod.

Well enough, Pinch thought. Stay clear of that wall.

So the path led to the right, away from the living curtain. That meant the next trap would come there, where he was being herded to go.

Careful testing revealed nothing else obvious behind the walls, so Pinch focused next on the floor. The floor beneath the sill sounded solid enough when rapped, so he tentatively set one foot on the floor. When nothing gave way, he eased down into nervous crouch. He rolled a marble from his kit into the center of the tower room. Only after it came to a stop did he move again and then he never took his eyes from it as he sidled around the

perimeter of the room. If the marble moved it was a
sign that something in the floor had shifted: a pivot, a
trapdoor, or some sinister deadfall. He spread his arms
and legs spiderlike as he moved, a painful way to get
about and one that his tired, restitched muscles could
barely stand, but it was the most prudent way. Should
something shift, the spread of his weight gave him the
best chance of recovering.

It was poised like this that Pinch discovered the next
trap. With his gaze still locked on the marble, he slid a
foot closer to his goal. All at once, the floor disappeared
beneath his toes. There was no telltale creak, no rattle
and swish of the trapdoor to give him warning. There
was just suddenly nothing up to his knee and beyond.

Even expecting some trap, the drop caught the rogue
off guard. His weight had been overbalanced to that side,
and before he could correct it he slid until the weight of
what dangled over the edge pulled the rest of him along.
A frantic look over his shoulder presented a strange
sight, his body being swallowed by the unbroken smooth-
ness of the floor. Illusion! he realized in panic, the thrice-
damned floor was an illusion. Gods knew how many
floors he might plunge through or what lay below.

Desperately Pinch scrabbled at the floor, but the
vein-creased stone was polished to a perfect and ungen-
erous beauty. His fingers squeaked greasily over the
sheen. All at once the cold stone popped away from his
chin and, like a sailor drowning in a shipwreck, his
head dropped into the ocean of magic. The world of
light and substance disappeared into a swirl of irra-
tional color, the blend of mottled stone, and then gloom.

In the last instant, Pinch's fingers closed on the only
thing there was to seize, the sharp edge of the stone
rim. With the instinct of years of practice, he set his fingers the way a mountain climber clings to the smallest
ledge of rock. The strain on his arms was tremendous;
his fingertips almost gave way at the jerk of his sudden

stop. His prize tool pouch tumbled from his waistband, spilling the marbles, rods, and steel into the darkness that swallowed everything beneath him. Through the panic and the strain, he listened for them to hit bottom, to at least give him some clue in their departing plunge.

They dropped forever and then finally hit something with a soft, crunching plop. As Pinch dangled helplessly, he could only think that the noise was not one he would have expected. If there had been the clank of steel on stone or even the splash of water, that would have made sense, but a sound like that of an insect crushed under a boot was just beyond understanding.

And then deep below, he heard the sound of the floor slithering.

Just what was beneath him? It wasn't good, whatever it was. Futilely Pinch tried to pull himself back up to the floor, but his grip was too poor and his muscles too spent from the rigors he had already endured. The priests had healed him, but the healing left him still weak. Perhaps it had all been intentional on their part, and they had foreseen what the night would bring him.

Pinch fought to drive the panic out of his mind. Concentrate on what was known and drive out speculation. Think and act, think and act—he recited the litany in his mind, driving out the burn in his arms, the bone-cracking pain in his fingertips, the fear of what waited below him.

His eyes were adjusting to the darkness, which was not complete. From the underside, the illusion was like a thick filter of smoke. Against it he could make out the lip of the real floor. It curved a semicircle against the back side of the small chamber, except for a small landing at the very wall that most certainly had to be in front of the shelf. The gap formed a moat, the last line of defense around the royal regalia.

The slithering below grew louder, though not closer. It was as if a host had been roused and not some single thing. In the near darkness, Pinch could barely see a

gleam of white, perhaps the floor, though strangely folded
and misshapen. He looked again, harder, straining to see
clearly, when all at once the floor heaved and shifted.

Gods damn, I'm looking at bones.

His fingers creaked and almost gave way, so that Pinch
couldn't suppress a shriek of pain. The cry reverberated
through the pit and, as if in eager concert to it, his voice
was taken up by a sussurant hiss as the white gleam of
the bones rippled and pulsed in a slithering crawl.

The floor was alive with maggots, thick fleshy things
that coated the shattered arches of bone like pustulant
skin and mounded themselves in squirming heaps
against the walls. The skeletons beneath him were the
bones of those who'd tried before, scoured clean by a
slow death in the nest below. How long could a man live
among them? How excruciating would the pain be as
they burrowed into his flesh? Better to die in the fall.

Fear dragged from inside Pinch the last reserve of his
strength. With his fingers slipping, he kicked his legs up
madly. His toes flailed for the ledge, scraping it once as
his fingers started to pull free. Desperately he tried
again. One foot hooked over the edge and he pressed his
weight on it. The leather sole slid, then held, but his
strength was fading fast. Frantically, the rogue levered
one elbow over the edge and kicked his other foot up until
he could raise his head above the sea of phantasm and
see the real world again. Half-supported on his forearm,
Pinch risked letting go with one hand. Almost immediately he started to slip backward, so with a desperate
lunge he slapped his hand down as far onto the stone as
he could. His cramped fingers burned, his palm stung,
but his crude grip held for the least of instants. In that
second he wrenched himself up and over, seizing on the
momentum of his lunge to carry him to safety. Barely he
twisted his hips over the edge and onto solid ground.

Pinch lay drained on the cool stone floor, unable
and unwilling to try any more. All he wanted to do

was collapse and rest, to come back another night and try again. Sweat soaked his doublet, and beads of it matted down his curly gray hair. His shoulders were shaking and his fingers were knotted like claws, clumsy and useless to his trade.

Nonetheless, Pinch knew he wouldn't quit. As he lay panting on the marble, he felt alive with the thrill of it all. It was the joy of risk, the game that he'd outwitted again. This, surely, was what a thief lived for. If he left tonight, he knew he'd just come back tomorrow to risk it all again.

Sprite was waiting, he reminded himself as he struggled to his feet. There was no more time to waste here.

Barely collected or steady on his feet, the rogue gauged the distance to the ledge. The priests had designed their trap well. The moat, he guessed, was just large enough for a man to cross in a single giant stride, like clearing a puddle at the side of the street. The landing gave enough space for him to stand discreetly but well, from what he remembered from below. It was just a matter of knowing where to step and where to avoid, and he'd had that lesson already.

Taking up the bag Cleedis had brought, Pinch sized up the possibilities and then finally, with only a small twinge of misgiving, boldly stepped out over the emptiness.

The next thing he knew, he stood on the landing, the box of rosewood and gold right before him.

The Cup and the Knife were dazzling as merited their role, but even the box was extraordinary. The gold work was the finest of dwarven hammered wire, the rosewood perfectly treated and polished. Pinch dearly wished he could take the box too, as personal profit, but that was not in the plan. The switch had to be unnoticed, which meant that the case had to stay.

Still, for all his covetousness, Pinch was not about to snatch the items up and run. The greater the treasure, the more fiercely it is protected. Instead he carefully

studied every aspect of how the treasures were
displayed. He attended to the velvet they were nestled
in, the case, its locks, even the shelf and the wall around
it. These efforts gave the welcome reward of slightly
longer life when he stopped to trace out a thread no
thicker than a spiderline that ran from the dagger to the
edge of the lock. The line for a trigger, he knew without
a doubt. He didn't know what it triggered, but that
hardly mattered for it could only be ill to his well-being.

It was delicate work, cutting the thread without dis-
charging whatever it was connected to, but Pinch worked
as a master. He had no desire to be roasted, frozen, elec-
trified, paralyzed, or just killed outright. When the line
was finally loose, he checked the whole over again before
he was satisfied. Priests were almost as bad as mages for
trapping their possessions. The counting rooms of
moneylenders were almost never this difficult. The
whole thing probably had more to do with the arrogance
of the clergy than the actual value of what they protected. Priests figured that whatever was important to
them was naturally important to the rest of the world.

Still expecting the worst, Pinch lifted the relics from
their shelf. When nothing happened, his hand began to
shake, an unconscious tremor of profound relief.

Now was the time to hurry; the dangerous part was
done. From the bag at his waist came the replicas. Like
the perfect form and its shadow, the one outshone the
other. The confidence that this crude replica would fool
anyone waned when sun was held to the stars. It would
have been better if there had been more time to find a
master artificer. The only solution, of course, was to
hide the sun so that only the stars remained. Indeed,
confidence rose as he wrapped the originals so that the
copies glittered in their own right.

The quick work slowed as he set the fakes in place
and worked at reattaching the thread. Pinch doubted
his place in the pantheon of thieves would be assured if

he were blasted trying to *reset* a trap. More than likely Mask would deny him the comforting rest of shadows for such bungling.

It was a point of theology that blessedly remained unanswered. The thread was reattached and the job done. His work accomplished, the rogue's hands trembled again as the tension drained away.

With a light, almost joyous step, Pinch spanned the concealed gap, taking a mind to keep well away from the suspicious hanging Maeve's scroll had detected. Regretting the loss of his fine tools, Pinch gathered up what little gear remained, unbound a slender rope from his waist, and prepared to leave. He'd slide to the ground, feed back the rope and be gone without a trace of having ever been there to start with.

The sharp nip of a dagger point into the small of his back killed Pinch's jaunty mood.

"Please give me cause to thrust this home, Master Janol," whispered a voice at his back. It was a deep voice, familiar and cold, luxurious with the ripeness of cruelty. It was a voice filled with the resonance of a massive chest and strong lungs.

"Iron-Biter . . ."

"Chancel Master Iron-Biter of the Red Priests, Janol—or should I call you Pinch like your friend did before I stuck him?" The dagger pricked sharper into his skin in response to the contraction in Pinch's muscles at hearing the news. "Hold steady, thief. This is a dagger of venom at your back. All it takes is one prick, and then do you know what will happen?"

"I thought priests were above poisoning."

"The temple does what it must. Now give up the Cup and Knife. Just remember, one trick and you're dead. The venom on this blade is particularly nasty. It'll be a long, painful death for you."

Pinch very carefully nodded his understanding. Iron-Biter's expertly applied pressure kept the blade a hairsbreadth from piercing the skin. He reached into the pouch and very carefully removed the Knife. He offered this behind him, handle first. The rogue was not about to do anything to aggravate the dwarf.

"Perhaps we can come to an understanding . . ."

The dwarf hissed like angry steam. "Unlike some, I am loyal to my temple—"

"And to Prince Vargo. That's who you're doing this for, isn't it. You just didn't happen to be wandering through the garden in the dark."

The dwarf plucked the dagger from Pinch's grasp. "The prince is the rightful ruler of Ankhapur. We won't let Cleedis's little games change that."

"We—or just you? What has Vargo promised you?"

"The Cup. Give me the Cup!"

"Why? You'll kill me if I do."

"I'll kill you if you don't give it to me. If you do, I'll let you live."

"Why?"

"It would be better if no one asked questions about your disappearance."

"And what if I talk?"

There was a sharp laugh behind him. "I know what you are now, Pinch. Suppose the entire city knew."

The regulator paled. Exposure—it was the most fearsome threat any rogue could ever face. To be named and branded a thief was as good as death and worse still. Brokers would avoid him, marks grow wary in his presence. Old partners would frame him for their jobs, and the constables would pressure him to spill what he knew. He'd seen it happen before, even used the knowledge against his rivals. He'd reveled in how they had squirmed helplessly on the hook. It led them to penury, drink, and even suicide—and it could do the same to him.

There was no choice in it, Pinch grimly knew. With hateful reluctance he passed over the Cup. It was snatched from his fingers.

"Turn around," the dwarf ordered.

As Pinch did, he understood now how a dwarf of no skill and monumental size had managed the catch. It was not right to say he came face-to-face with his captor, for where the dwarf should have been was nothing, just empty air. The only signs of any presence were the Cup and Knife half-visible in the folds of an invisible cloak.

"God's cursed spells!" Pinch hated the way they upset his plans.

The air chuckled. "With them I can move quieter and more unseen than you'll ever hope to, scoundrel. Now, to the wall." A poke with the dagger indicated the direction Pinch was supposed to move—toward the trapped arras.

"You said you wouldn't kill me."

"I need to make sure you won't trouble me while I put things right. Move."

Pinch took a hesitant step and, when nothing happened, the dagger urged him forward again. The thief's mind was racing with desperate plots. Could he fight an invisible foe? What there any chance he could lure the dwarf into the trap instead of himself, or even get the little priest to take one step too close to the maggot-infested pit below?

With one more step, it all became futile speculation. Barely had he moved forward under the poisonous blade's urging than the arras that had hung so thick and limp on the wall suddenly writhed with inanimate life. The tassels at the top, draped over the iron hanging rod, released like little hands and lunged forward in an eager embrace. The thick cloth wound tightly around him, hugging him in its grip like the wrappings of a corpse. The speed and the strength of it spun Pinch to the floor and left him gasping and choking as the rug tried to crush the cage of bones around his heart.

Pinch fought it as best he could, writhing like a worm to brace against the pressure and steal enough air to prevent suffocation. At the same time he had to be mindful of the floor, lest he wriggle himself over the concealed lip and into the fetid pit below. Iron-Biter's dark laugh showed the dwarf's sympathy for his struggles.

At the limit of Pinch's attention, the air shimmered and a swirl of form emerged from nothing, like a curtain parting in space to reveal another world. From the play of folds and fabric, it was clear the dwarf's invisibility came from a magical cloak that he now neatly folded and stowed away. Ignoring Pinch's mortal struggle, the priest carefully spanned the gap to the shelf, barely able to cross with his short legs. There he made a few passes over Pinch's fakes and then casually replaced them with the goods the rogue had handed over. The dwarf studied the frauds for a moment and then casually tossed them through the insubstantial floor.

By the time Iron-Biter leapt back to Pinch's side of the concealed pit, the rogue could feel his ribs creak, crushed to the limit of their bearing. "I . . . die," he struggled to say with the last air in his lungs, "there will be . . . questions."

Iron-Biter looked down, his beard bristling as his lips curled in a broad smile. "You are a fool, Janol, Pinch, or whomever. No one at this court cares about you. Your disappearance will ease their worries. You were never missed and never wanted here."

With that, the dwarf seized the edge of the arras and spun Pinch to the edge of the pit. "Let the worms have you!" and with a single, twisted syllable, the rug suddenly released its hold and Pinch rolled through the floor and into the darkness.

Morninglord's Blessing

Released from the carpet's brocade embrace, Pinch
fell into the fetid darkness. In the absence of light and
form, only his heartbeat set the length of his fall. In the
two beats it took to hit bottom, Pinch's thoughts were a
dichotomy of the disquieting certainty of absolute death
and the black pleasure of malevolent joy. Doom ac-
quired a dark humor.

I'm going to die as maggot food. Not the best of epi-
taphs—but at least nobody will know.

Pinch smashed into the squirming mass, writhing in
eager expectation of his arrival as if the blind, pulpy
white worms could sense his coming. It was like landing in a bed of eggs, although eggs don't wriggle and
scrape underfoot. They were a deeper churning sea of
corruption than expected, and Pinch's body crashed
into them like a rock hurled into the waves, splattering

the maggots against the tower walls

Nonetheless, there was solid rock below, and though his plunge was slowed by the greasy, hungry mash, Pinch cracked the bottom with a brutal blow. Ribs aching, wind gone, bleeding from his scalp, the rogue lay dazed in the center of an ichor-stained crater of grublike life.

Almost immediately the living walls of that crater began to flow inward, the vermin tumbling over each other in a churning, squeaking wave. Collectively they hungered for him. They flowed over Pinch's legs, flooded through the rips and tears of his doublet, poured into his eyes and ears, and wriggled into his mouth and nose. They crawled over his tongue with their sweet, wet bodies. Pinch could not hold back his desperate spasms for air, but each breath ended in a choking gurgle as the fat maggots plopped down his throat. Things crawled under his hose, rippled beneath the cloth of his doublet, and burrowed into his hair. And all the time the little rasping mouths gnawed and scraped, a thousand stings until his skin was awash with slime and blood.

The morbid detachment of his fall was strangled out of the rogue by the doom that was upon him. His death was real and here, choking in lungfuls of mindless larvae, eaten slowly and helplessly alive in this bed of maggots. Frantic, without thought, without plan, Pinch thrashed madly, puking his guts as he weakly fought to gain his feet. The weight of the vermin crushed him, the smooth stone floor was slick with their pulped bodies, so that all he could do was flail like a drowning man. Kill them, smash them, pulp them—it was all he could think of to do; a completely hopeless effort against the countless numbers that filled the pit.

Like a madman Pinch slipped and smashed all about the floor, scattering the bones of his unfortunate predecessors, tripping over their now-worthless weapons. He raged and choked and spit, but none of it made a bit of difference. The maggots kept crawling, greedily lapping up the oozy stew of skin, ichor, blood and sweat that coated Pinch's skin.

In desperation, the man ripped at his clothes, determined to eliminate the hiding places of his tormentors. His boots were full of a squishy mass, his hose drooping with pockets of larva. Without a concern for the cost or the tailoring, he rent it all to shreds: the parti-colored stockings from Waterdeep, the Chessentian black silk doublet. He was determined to have it all off, even in patches and shreds. It was the only thought his panic-gripped mind could fixate on.

It was in the process of that tearing and rending that Pinch's fingers closed on something hard and metal next to his chest. The man didn't consider what it was or why it chose now to come to his grasp, but seized on it as a weapon, something to crush the hateful maggots with. Fingers clenched about the object and swung it over his head to strike with more force than was ever necessary.

Just as he was about to hammer home, a sun exploded in his grasp. Coruscating light flared from between his fingers and probed throughout the pit. Where it touched the maggot-thick floor, the ground bubbled and sizzled in a seething roast of putrid flesh. The maggots shrieked with the hissing pop of their fat bodies as their guts boiled away. Cloying smoke, the scent of burned fat and boiled vinegar, filled the tower and roiled out the pit-hole like a chimney. It was wet and thick, half steam, half ash, and it clung to Pinch but he was too amazed to notice.

The rogue was frozen, too incredulous to move. His hand burned like he'd pulled a coal from the fire, but even that could not break his paralysis. At best he twisted his gaze up, trying to see what was happening to his hand, but the light burned until his eyes ached and his forearm vanished into the brilliance. It was as if he had thrust his hand into the sun like a protean god playing with the heavens.

What is happening to me?

There were no answers. The blaze continued until Pinch's eyes could no longer stand it. The pain racked his hand. Gradually the sizzling squeaks of the maggots faded and the roils of smoke began to fade away. And then the light was gone.

Pinch dropped the thing like a hot stone; it had scorched his hand like one. It hit the ground with a metallic clank. Pinch looked at his hand and there, crusted in the burned flesh of his palm, was the brand of a half-sun. The edges were charred black and the impression oozed no blood, the flesh seared shut by the heat. Gingerly, Pinch tried to flex his hand, only to be stopped by a wave of pain.

Around him the smoke was clearing and as it went, the man's eyes, watering almost shut, also slowly cleared. In the dim light, he could see the room clearly for the first time. The maggots were gone, save for a feeble few that wiggled in the heaps of powdery ash that covered the floor. The bones of other thieves were still there, scoured whiter than they had ever been. Their weapons gleamed in the dim light from above, spotlessly free of rust, like a knight's armor after his squire has finished with it. The walls were pinkish white and marked with fountains of soot.

Numbly Pinch brushed away the larva that still clung to the shreds of his clothes or had wormed their way into his curly hair. He sweated blood and slime, his clothes were in tatters or burned to ash, and his hand throbbed with pain, but Pinch could only marvel that he was still alive.

He spotted the thing he'd held, lying in the ash at his feet. It was the half-sun disk of the Morninglord, the artifact he'd stolen in Elturel. He was afraid to touch it.

Wisps of smoke seemed to rise up from the amulet, but at last he hesitantly lifted it by its broken thong. Close up it looked unchanged, the same chunk of inert jewelry it had always been. When he compared it to his hand, he could see immediately that the brand and the design were the same.

What had happened? This was the amulet of the Dawnbreaker or something like that, Lissa had claimed. Somehow, he must have triggered its power or done something that brought it to life. Try as he could, though, he couldn't figure what. Fear overrode all his memories of the moment when it had happened.

"Pinch!" Sprite's thin voice echoed from above. Pinch looked up to see a little curly head peering through the floor.

"Sprite?"

"Gods, you're alive!" they blurted in unison.

"What happened, Pinch?"

"Sprite, get me a rope."

"First I gets jumped by a dwarf and then when I come up here I nearly choke in the smoke coming out of the floor, and that's how I knew you was down there."

"Sprite-Heels, shut up and drop me a rope!"

"Oh . . . right. Right away." The head disappeared to do his bidding.

While he waited for the rope, Pinch probed through the ash, mindful of the goods others had left behind. There was little of account, a few daggers with promise and some loose coins, but Pinch wasn't really searching for them anyway. At last he came across the things he really wanted—the false Cup and Knife that Iron-Biter had casually discarded. He also found his gleaming set of custom tools, though the black cloth wrapping was nothing more than a few burned scraps. By the time these things were carefully bundled up, the rope dangled within his grasp.

Getting back up with only one good hand was no

easy task, not made any better by the fact that Sprite was hardly a match to hoist him. When at last he finally thrust his head through the shimmering field of false marble and rolled himself over the lip, the man collapsed on his back and panted for breath.

"Iron-Biter said you were dead. Pricked you with that skene of his."

Sprite turned from the window where he'd been keeping watch and pulled open his cloak. Half his shirt was a great red stain, and at its center was a crude bandage the halfling had applied.

"Iron-Biter, eh? That's dwarves for you, thinking with their weapons and not their heads. See—if it were you he would have been right, but I'm not your kind. You'd think even a stupid dwarf would know a halfling's got a strength against poisoning just like them.

"He jumped me in the bushes and poked me with that blade of his. That venom was caustic, but it didn't kill me. Knocked me flat for a time, it did, so he must've figured he killed me. What I don't see is how such a cousin could get on me unadvised."

"Magic," Pinch croaked. His throat was raw from smoke and dry for lack of drink. "The bastard's got more magic than any proper dwarf I know. Snared me the same way."

Sprite nodded. "What happened down there? Was he down there?"

The regulator struggled to his feet. "He's bolted. Back to Vargo, I'd think. We're best off before more priests come. There's more to say later."

"What about that?" Sprite nodded toward the shelf where the artifacts rested.

"Let them rest," Pinch said with a smile. "Pater Iron-Biter wasn't quite as clever as he thought."

Working together, the two thieves managed to lower themselves out of the tower, not an easy task for two walking wounded. Sprite-Heels had made light of his wounds, but by the sheen of sweat that rose with every effort, Pinch could tell fighting the poison had taken more from him than the halfling let on. There wasn't much to be done for it but press on, though. By the time they'd crossed the last wall and reached the safety of the heavy shadows in the alleys outside, the two could barely stand on solid legs. Given that they were staggering anyway, Pinch paid a coin at a tavern window and bought them each a skin of good wine. His tattered and dirty state hardly raised an eyebrow with the wench who served him. In the hours before dawn her establishment had all manner of customers, and Pinch was just another filthy beggar up on his luck.

Fortified, refreshed, and rewarded, the two went lurching through the streets. "What now, Pinch?" Sprite asked after a long medicinal pull at the jug. "I could use a touch of comfort for me side."

"Healing," Pinch grunted, pulling the jug from the halfling's hands. Sweet wine trickled through his beard as he gulped down their improvised painkiller. His hand throbbed mightily, so much that he could barely flex it. "Got to get this fixed 'fore it ruins my trade.

"Can't go back to the Red Priests," the rogue muttered to himself, pondering their problem with excessive effort. A night's worth of black work and the beatings he'd taken made the alcohol doubly potent. "Don't want no one knowing of this . . ."

"What about Lissa? She's still around, ain't she, Pinch? It's a wager you could persuade her into helping us—especially if you got me there to cross-lay the tale."

The suggestion made Pinch grin. " 'Struth, she stands mostly favorable with us—and I've got just the tale for her. Come on, Sprite. We're off to the house of the Morninglord."

Half-lurching, the two walking wounded wound through the alleys to the temple of the Morninglord. Being mindful of their previous company and made worrisome by drink, the pair watched their trail closely for any sign that might reveal an invisible shadow. Only when no alley cats hissed unexpectedly, no splashes appeared in empty puddles, and no gates opened of their own accord did the two set course for the temple.

The Morninglord's shrine was a pizzling affair compared to the grand glories of the house they'd just left. As was the custom of the Dawn Priests, the temple was at the easternmost end of the easternmost street in the city. It was one building with a single tall tower, both featureless from the west. The eastern side of the building was no doubt lavishly decorated for the dawn god to see, marked by stained glass windows that opened onto glorious altars. This was all well and good for the faithful but did little to create an impressive public facade, and the temple languished as a consequence.

It was an elf who answered the door, dressed in the garish yellow, orange, and pink robes of the order, although the colors were faded and his sunburst tiara a bit shabby. Though it was near enough dawn for worshipers to come to service, the sallow-faced elf viewed their arrival with a start of surprise, as though visitors here were as unexpected as rain in the desert. He murmured expressions of greeting profusely as he showed them in, and for a race noted for its haughtiness, he managed to bow and scrape most ambitiously. It was a sign of how hard up the temple was if this elf was willing to fawn for donations from a pair as raggedy as them. The regulator put up with it as long as was necessary to send for Lissa.

When the priestess appeared, it was in the full robes of her order, and Pinch was frankly shocked at the transformation. The robes imbued her with a radiant femininity that had been hidden beneath her plain working dress. It was clear he'd been too quick to dismiss her before. The orange, the pink, the golden ribbons, and the sun-sparkled headdress that had looked tawdry on the elf shone on her like cloth of gold. Her hair escaped the edges of her headdress, and her face beamed with fresh-scrubbed brightness.

"Greetings, Lissa," he began with an unfeigned awkwardness, so suddenly taken aback by her beauty, "I—we—have come for you help—"

"You look terrible, Master Janol! What happened?"

Lissa's compassion was just as Pinch had hoped, and his nervousness faded as she gave him the opportunity to spin his tale. "Thieves—we were set upon by thugs looking for the amulet. Sprite's been stabbed." The halfling picked up his cue and gave an appropriate groan at this point.

"But you—your clothes—" She stopped, noticing the putrid smell about him for the first time. "And . . . your appearance."

"A bath and clothes will set me right. I seem to be going through my wardrobe of late." Pinch tried to make light of his own state. Now that he was here, it did not seem such a good idea to reveal the brand that the amulet had given him.

Discretion failed him though, for Sprite blurted, "And his hand—he hurt his hand too, miss."

Pinch gave Sprite one of those glares, and the halfling could only look drunkenly sheepish as Lissa firmly examined the regulator's burned hand.

"What did this?" she demanded. By her tone, it was clear she already knew the answer. "You've been marked, haven't you?"

"Marked?"

Her soft compassion was replaced by earnest concern. "The amulet—you were holding it?"

Pinch nodded to buy a little time to create an embellishment to his story. "When the thieves jumped us, I sought to protect it. I was sure they meant to steal it, so I held it in my hand."

"And?"

"I don't know. It flared in a brilliant burst of light—"

"Killed them outright it did!" The halfling blurted out the fabrication to corroborate his leader's tale. Unfortunately, at that same moment, Pinch finished with "—and scared them away."

"Killed them or scared them?" Lissa asked suspiciously. It was clear there was more to this than she was being told.

"Scared them," Sprite hastily corrected.

"Both," Pinch expanded, though once again tripped up by his companion. The regulator gave Sprite another look to shut up. "Some were . . . killed and the others ran away."

Lissa gave the rogue a hard look. She doesn't believe me, Pinch thought. A better story was needed. "I—"

"Where is the amulet?" She poked at his burned hand and Pinch bit back a wince.

"I have it."

"Give it to me." She held out her hand without even looking up from her inspection.

"There's no cause for worry. I have protected it."

"I have unjustly put you at risk. Please, give me the amulet.'

Argument was hopeless, especially here in the center of Lissa's stronghold. Reluctantly Pinch produced the bauble and handed it over to the priestess. Sprite sucked his teeth in unvoiced disappointment.

"Will you see to Sprite now?" the rogue asked pointedly. It was his nature; he couldn't help but set a price for all things.

Lissa took the amulet and hung it around her neck. "Brother Leafcrown will tend to him." She nodded to the elf who waited patiently behind her.

"Ooh, an elf!" Sprite said in mockery of the stereotype of elf-fascinated halflings. The jibe was not lost on the brother, whose expression of benign beneficence soured at the comment.

"As for your hand," Lissa continued as Sprite was led away, "I can heal the pain, but the scar will remain. You have been marked by Lathander."

"What! I'm going to have this brand for the rest of my life—like some common thief," blurted the outraged rogue.

Lissa nodded. "It is the price of calling upon Lathander."

"I didn't call him—or any other god," Pinch snarled, risking blasphemy within the Morninglord's very temple. "The damn thing just happened! I didn't ask for it."

"Nonetheless, it happened," she countered with the absolute resoluteness of one whose faith can only be unquestioned. "Therefore within your heart you must have called upon Lathander's might. How else could you have gotten his mark?"

Pinch stared at his numbed and blackened hand, fearing the scars before his eyes. If he could never use his hand again, that would destroy the only talent he knew. Without a good hand, how could he hope to pick a lock or nip a purse. A one-handed thief was a cripple to be pitied by his companions and mocked by his former prey. This then was the Morninglord's revenge. "Damn the pain!" the rogue bitterly hissed. "Can you make my hand work?"

Lissa hesitated, and that hesitation was not encouraging. "I—don't know. All I can do is try. It is a great honor, you know, to be marked by the Morninglord."

"Wonderful. I'm a prophet now."

"Not like that," Lissa shushed him as she prepared her healing work. "It means that Lathander sees in you something different, something greater than common men. Prophets, sages, bold captains—all of these have borne the mark."

"Greatness—hah! I'm no prophet or king." Pinch's

heart was filled with bitterness right now. His world was crumbling around him regardless of what the god saw in his future.

"Nonetheless, Janol, our lord sees something in your future. Perhaps you will be a brave hero someday."

"Why not? I'm no good for anything else right now—thanks to your god."

"Mind your tongue!" Lissa snapped, furious at his casual blasphemy. She grabbed his wrist and twisted his hand palm-up, then made the passes needed to cast the spell. The burn tingled and then the pain subsided. The blackened flesh peeled away to reveal pinkish fresh skin underneath. The brand gleamed pinkish-white like a fresh scar. The pain vanished.

Experimentally Pinch tried to make a fist, but it was to no avail. The best he could do was curl his fingers into a clawlike grip, but the palm was a thick pad that would hardly bend.

"Crap. Your god has ruined me," Pinch moaned, his voice filled with sorrow. He sat staring at his useless hand, bitter salt filling the corners of his eyes. Everything he was, everything he could do, was in his hands. What kind of cutpurse could he be, unable to hold a knife? Would he be a rooftop man unable to hold a rope? Maybe he could take up mugging and beat his victims senseless with this paw—that's all it was good for. He was only half, less than nothing in the eyes of his peers.

"I'm a blighted cripple," he whispered to no one.

Fatherhood

It was well past dawn by the time Pinch and Sprite
left the temple, found their friends, and retired to the
back tables of the ordinary. There, in the tawdry depths
of the common room, Pinch drank. He drank with a
bleak-hearted vigor, without joy or camaraderie. He
drank with the bitter determination of a man trying to
blot away the memories of his life. He gulped the sack
without tasting it and demanded more before his cup
was even empty. With his stiff hand he fumbled at the
jug, and the more he fumbled the more he cursed his
fate and drank again, until he would bitterly sweep the
mugs, the crock, the candle aside in a rage and glare at
his friends with his aching dry eyes.

His friends let him drink, since there was little they
could say to stop him anyway. Sprite patiently poured
the blackjacks and picked up the scattered mugs, while

Maeve did her best to soothe Pinch's raging temper. Therin sat back and said nothing, quietly considering the possibilities of this new future.

"It ain't all lost," Sprite said once more as he tipped the jug. "It's not the hand that makes you, Pinch. You're more than just a foin or a verser. Any rogue can do that. It's what you got in your brain pan what makes you special."

"He's right," Therin added softly. "You can retire from the trade, take it easy. Look at the set-up you've got here—staying in a palace, fine food, and servants. All you got to do is sit up there, spot the rich marks, and make plans for others to do."

"It's sound advice," Maeve added, stroking the wounded man's hair.

Pinch grunted and kept his attention fixed on the wine.

"Of course," Therin continued with smooth oiliness, "there'd have to be a new regulator . . ."

Pinch looked up from his mug. "Like as you?" he snarled.

The Gur let the facade drop. "Like as me than a cripple."

"Cripple! I should have let them hang you in Elturel, bastard! I'm still regulator here and you'll mind it or—"

"Or what?" Therin bellowed back. "Or you'll carve me? Well, have at." The Gur drew two daggers and tossed one onto the table. It clattered among the mugs and pots. The sound was echoed by the scrape of his chair as the younger man stood back from the table and waited, knife casually poised. Sprite and Maeve pulled back, their eyes darting from Pinch to Therin and back again. At the taps, the innkeeper took notice, setting his ash-handled mace close at hand.

"Go ahead. Regulate me."

Pinch clumsily tried to pick up the dagger with his ruined hand but, unable to close his hand around the hilt, the effort was futile. At last he gave up and collapsed back with a fierce glower.

Therin smiled heartlessly, the grown son looking

down on his enfeebled father. "You've done me good, Pinch. You've done us all good, but now things have changed. It's come time for a new regulator."

Pinch's lean frame dwindled, perhaps due to the drink or maybe in resignation to the younger man's words. Finally, he unfastened the bulky pouch at his side, shoved aside their drinks, and set it on the table. "I suppose you'll want to deliver this," he growled as he undid the strings and pulled open the bag enough to show the golden glint of their stolen treasures inside. "First task as the new regulator."

"Aye," Therin allowed warily.

"The broker's waiting at the mausoleum. Tell him you're my agent and he'll deal with you."

Therin didn't wait for more but scooped the bag from the table before his old master changed his mind. Maeve looked on in wide-eyed amazement that Pinch had surrendered so readily.

"Go to it. Let's see what kind of regulator you are," the older man sneered.

Sprite sidled close to Pinch's side. "It ain't proper. You can't let him do this to you so easy," he pleaded, but the rogue held up a hand to silence him.

"Go on, do it."

With an uncomfortable swallow, Therin nodded. The ease of his victory unnerved him. There was supposed to have been a battle. He expected Pinch to rise to his challenge, to fight with every trick the old man knew. He was ready for that. He wasn't prepared for this gutless surrender.

The Gur had won, though, and he couldn't show weakness now. He glared at the three, shouldered the bag, spun on his heels, and strode for the door.

When he was two steps from the table and one from a pillar, Therin's dagger, the one he'd left on the table, sang by his ear and drove, point in, to the scarred wood of the beam. The weak sunlight quivered off the blade as it hummed with the force of its throw.

"You'll need a better plan for dealing with a lich than you have with me," Pinch announced darkly as the younger man wheeled about in frightened surprise. The older man sat upright, not nearly as drunk as he was before, his off-hand poised where it had stopped at the end of the throw. Sprite and Maeve had swung around to his side of the table, letting it show where their loyalty—such as it was—lay.

"Lich—you didn't say nothing about no lich." Therin's voice was weakly brave. His face, flushed with temper moments before, was rapidly losing its color to an ashen pale. "What lich?"

"Lich?" Sprite gulped, looking to Pinch. "We been working for a lich?"

"Aye," the old man answered, never once looking away from Therin. With his good hand, he drew another dagger from the scabbard at his wrist. "We're dealing with a lich."

Therin slowly came back to the table and set the bag down. "Maybe I was being a bit hasty, Pinch. It wasn't like a challenge—just a chance for you to live a gentleman's life while we did your dark work for you." The Gur looked desperately to the other two. "It was like that, wasn't it?"

As if joined in a single malicious thought, Sprite and Maeve let him dangle for a bit before answering. A line of sweat trickled down the young man's temple.

"Sure, Pinch," Maeve finally drawled, "he was only thinking about you and your well-being. Can't you see?"

"S'right. I'm sure he's touched with concern," the halfling added with a malicious grin. "Indeed, he even told me yesterday how he was thinking of giving you his share of the swag from this job."

"That's right, Pinch. I think you've earned it." As costly as it was, Therin seized on the halfling's suggestion. The fact that he had almost blundered into trading with a lich had unnerved the man.

The now-undisputed regulator nodded his head. The Gur stifled a sigh of relief. The nod was all he would get, but it was a sign the peace was made—for now.

" 'Tis proper generous of you, Therin," Pinch purred, "but you're building the house before the foundation's set. For there to be shares, we got to collect our fee."

"He's not likely to pay?" Maeve asked.

" 'It'—and it'll want us dead. Me, in particular."

Sprite prodded the goods in the bag. "Just who we dealing with, Pinch? This Cleedis ain't no lich."

Pinch massaged the rough brand on his palm. The drink and facing down Therin made him feel expansive. "Cleedis is just a go-between. Manferic's our real employer."

"Manferic?"

"The late king."

"Wounds!" Sprite sputtered wine all down his chin.

"Is he that vile?" Maeve asked hopefully.

"He's a lich. What do you expect?" Therin pointed out.

"Moreso and worse. I should know; he was my guardian. When I was ten, the peasants on the nobles' estates drew up a list of grievances against their lords. It seemed they were taxed at twice the rate demanded by the crown, old men were executed when they could no longer farm, and young boys were driven by whip into the ranks of the militia. Five of their bravest presented the list to Manferic—"

"And he killed them?"

"Nothing so simple," Pinch corrected. "That would have been almost human. No, he listened to their complaints and promised them action. The next day, while he 'considered' their request, he sent Vargo and Throdus with a detachment of priests to the houses of these five men. They killed the wife in each household and animated the corpse. The next day, Manferic said he

would enact reforms—provided the men loved and honored their wives for the rest of their days. Should one of
them fail, he would exact his revenge on all the rebels.
It did not take long before he had the chance."

Sentimental Maeve let a tear well up in her eye
while the other two looked uncomfortably at the floor.
"Unnatural monster," muttered Therin. "The Gur know
about lords like him—always persecuting our kind,
blaming us for their crimes."

"So what's this Cup and Knife got to do with it?"
Maeve asked to change the subject. "You told us how
they use them to pick a king, but how's that going to
help him? He's dead already."

"Won't do him no good at all, since Iron-Biter inter-
fered. The real Cup and Knife are still in the tower.
Right, Pinch?"

"No." Pinch looked about the common room. It was
deserted at this time of the morning. Even the landlord,
seeing there was to be no fight, had gone into the back
to tend to the day's chores. As he spoke, the regulator
unwrapped the pouch in front of them all. "Like you
said, Sprite, Iron-Biter's a fool. Remember that I had
two copies of the regalia made?

"Well, when Iron-Biter made me pass over the
garbage, he never thought to check for forgeries. All I
did was give him the other fake—so he switched fake
for fake. Never occurred to him that I had the real ones
on me all that time." With that, Pinch finished opening
the pouch and drew out four golden, jewel-encrusted
pieces. To the trained eyes at the table, the craftsmanship of the goldwork and the deep luster of the stones
was readily apparent in the genuine pieces. A collective
sigh of greed escaped the three.

Sprite scritched at his curly hair. "Why give it to
him, Pinch? We could scamper out and sell this for a
good price in Amn or Waterdeep."

"Cleedis found me once. If he did it once, he can do it

again—and I don't think Manferic will be as forgiving the next time as he has been now."

"Well, I don't see it. What's he gain from the stuff?" Maeve asked again.

"I'm not sure, but I think he means to control the choosing. Everybody's been saying Cleedis is backing a dead horse—my idiot cousin, Bors. Just suppose, though, that the idiot becomes king. Then Cleedis doesn't look so dumb. It's as certain as Sprite here rolling a rigged bale of dice that if Bors is chosen, Cleedis will name himself regent before anyone can protest."

"Fine for Cleedis, but that doesn't do a thing for Manferic."

"Cleedis is weak. His only strength is his loyalty. Make him regent and he'll be Manferic's lapdog for sure. Until Manferic does him in and takes over directly.

Therin shrugged. "So what's it matter to us if a lich takes the throne here or not?"

"Ever hear tales of Thay?" Maeve warned. Ruled by undying sorcerer-kings, Thay's excesses and cruelties were legendary throughout the Realms and were a particularly sore point with wizards of nearly every stripe.

"We don't," Pinch interrupted. "We don't a care a pizzle for who rules here. All we want is to get out of here alive."

"And rich," Sprite added.

A gloom fell over the group, one of those sullen silences that seems to strangle conversations at regular intervals, this one probably infected by Maeve's sour scowl. Drunkard and scalawag she might be, but she was still a mage and didn't like the notion of liches playing with their unnatural magic.

"Show us how it works, Pinch, this ceremony you were telling us about," Sprite asked in an attempt to lift their dour moods. He hopped up onto his chair and set the genuine artifacts in front of his fellow rogue. "Maybe that'll give us some clue."

The question brought back memories of Pinch's

youth, when he was Janol playing with his royal cousins
Throdus and Vargo. The two princes used to insist he attend their 'coronations,' so they could make him bow
and scrape at appropriate times and lord over him for
being outside their blessed circle. They loved playacting
the rite, nicking themselves with knives to let a few
drops fall into a table goblet while they mouthed all
sorts of holy prayers. Of course, each prince would naturally be the chosen heir, and so these little charades
usually ended with the young princes rolling on the floor
trying to thump the 'impostor' senseless. Pinch had always enjoyed egging them into a fight.

Why not? he decided. There was an irony that appealed to him. Now he could playact with the real thing
while his dear cousins would go through the real ceremony with fakes.

The master rogue grinned and rolled up the sleeve
on one arm. "As you will, Sprite; I will show you.

"First, there's a whole lot of business that consumes
time and makes the whole affair important. Every candidate has to step forward, announce his lineage, something like, 'I am Janol, only son of Sir Gedstad of Alkar.' "

"Sir Gedstad?"

"My father, Maeve, or so I've been told."

"Go on, go on. What happens next?" Sprite eagerly
chattered. He propped his chin in his hands and watched
intently, always keen on a good story. Even Therin, still
hesitant about where he stood, leaned in a little closer.

"So then there's some business from the priests, pre-
senting the Cup and Knife to each candidate. A lot of
prayers and the like for blessing the whole thing." Pinch
actually managed to remember a few and mumbled them
out while making pompous passes over the regalia. Without realizing it, he was letting himself get caught up in
the business, letting it distract him from his own woes.

"When that's done, the two objects are passed down
the line." Setting the Cup in front of him, he took up the

Knife and very carefully sliced the tip of his thumb. The knife cut through his skin like soft cheese. It stung sharply for such a small cut and, given what he'd been through in the past two days, Pinch was surprised that he noticed it so much. Almost immediately blood began to form a ruby red bead. "The prince pricks himself and squeezes a little blood into the cup." He let a few drops fall into the golden goblet.

"The cup gets filled with wine"—Sprite hopped up and, cradling the jug, sloshed the goblet full—"and the prince drinks."

Pinch raised the heavy goblet, waved it in toast to his friends, and drained it in one long draught. He set the Cup down like a tankard and let out a hearty belch before continuing. "If the prince is the chosen heir, then he'll be surrounded by a—

"Glow!"

It was a breath of whispered astonishment, simultaneous from the three of them. Their gazes were fixed on him, wide eyed beyond all possibility. Sprite tried to step back and practically fell off his chair, while Therin had to lean forward and support himself on the table. Maeve's weak little chin trembled up and down as she tried to form her lips to say something.

"What is wrong with you three? What's going on?"

"You . . ."

". . . you're . . ."

". . . glowing."

"What? I'm what? You're all drunk."

They shook their heads.

Pinch snatched up the Knife and looked in the polished blade at his reflection. There it was, a golden nimbus around his head, like the sun setting behind a cloud. Looking around now, he noticed that the whole dark corner of the commons was awash in the sunset hue. In terror, he dropped the Knife and ran his hands over his body to make sure there wasn't some weird growth manifesting itself on him. There was nothing.

"Maeve!" he roared when he couldn't deny that he was indeed glowing. "If this one of your tricks—the lot of you put me up to this!"

"No, dearie—I wouldn't. Honest," Maeve squeaked. She was still staring at him wide eyed. "Sprite?"

"Not me, Pinch. Wouldn't know how," he gulped in terror.

The regulator just glared at Therin, and the man's mute astonishment was enough to set his innocence. Pinch sank limply into his seat. The reflection in the blade showed the glow was still there, slowly fading as he watched. At last it was gone, like the sun behind the horizon.

He felt drained. "It's impossible."

"It happened, Pinch. We all saw it."

"It can't. It only works on those with royal blood."

"What about your father?" Maeve questioned.

"He was a no-account knight who died in battle. Not him."

"Your mother?"

"A lady-in-waiting to the queen, I'm told."

"Are you sure?" Sprite asked.

"I don't remember my parents. All I know is what people told me about them."

"Maybe they lied to you," Therin suggested.

"Lied? Why?"

Therin looked thoughtful for a moment, fingering the Cup. "You say this thing works only for royal blood. So who's got that in Ankhapur? The princes and Manferic—anybody else? Dukes, earls, counts, brothers of the king, people like that?"

Pinch shook his head. "Manferic did in his brothers—and his uncles and sisters, the whole lot. Purged his family tree. He was determined that no one would challenge him."

Sprite goggled. "He murdered them all?"

"He was king—he had absolute power. If he wanted you dead, you were dead. The beauty of it was he didn't even have to do it himself. That's what lackeys like Cleedis were for."

"If they're all dead," Therin continued, "and, like you say, that thing works only on royal blood—then Pinch, there's only one place it could've come from."

The regulator swallowed a great gulp of wine. He needed it. "You're saying—"

"Maybe that knight's not your papa."

The four all stared at each other, nobody wanting to agree but unable to deny the conclusion.

"Crap." Pinch broke the silence. "Crap! Damn Manferic's cursed soul!" Years of pent-up fury surged out of him. He hurled his mug across the room, flung aside the table, and kicked away the chairs. Sprite went scrambling for the treasures as they skittered across the floor, while the landlord hurried in from the back room, brandishing his mace. He was confronted by a raging madman, swearing and cursing at demons he couldn't see. The sight of Pinch in this state was more than enough to keep the landlord at bay. Seeing as he had their belongings upstairs for security, the landlord wisely scuttled well out of the way.

The three let Pinch rage, not that they had any power to stop him. He fumed about the room, sullenly kicking at chairs and cursing Manferic with every oath he knew. When he'd run out of damnations and tortures to inflict on the lich and his kind, Pinch stopped and turned to the trio who waited at the table.

"That bastard robbed me of my birthright," the master said as his shoulders quivered with exhaustion and rage. "He let his precious sons drive me out fifteen years ago and didn't raise a hand to aid me. I was supposed to have been a prince, not some back-alley bravo."

He righted a chair and slid it over to join the others. Enthroned on it, he lapsed into a dark silence. The others held their tongues. Their master was in one of his scheming moods, not to be disturbed until he returned to the surface with some plot in his grasp, like the diver who swims through the blind murk in search of the pearl.

Pinch pondered for a long time. There were so many questions and so many pieces: Manferic, Cleedis, Iron-Biter, and—most of all—the woman in the tunnels. Was she his mother? A nursemaid? A madwoman? Or something yet he could not fathom? There were too many questions.

"Therin, Maeve, Sprite—gather in," he said when he at last raised his head and noticed them. With his arms beckoning he drew them close. "How would you like to be rich—and respectable?" he asked with a conspiratorial whisper.

"Us, Pinch?" Sprite snickered. "There ain't nothing respectable about us."

" 'Struth for you, you little weasel, but I've a mind to be a lady someday," Maeve sniffed. "I could stand for being respectable."

"Respectable's not worth a whit without money. How rich?"

"A treasury at your command, Therin. Is that loot enough for you?"

"Aye. If you've got a plan, I'll go along with being rich." Therin still looked dubious. "Does your plan intend taking on this lich?"

Pinch looked very solemn until the worst fears of the others confirmed themselves in their looks. Only then did he break into a grin. "That would be a fool's task—so we'll let fools do that for us."

"So what's our plan?" Sprite asked, signaling his support of the enterprise. The halfling never could resist an adventure, no matter how rash.

Pinch studied the others to make sure they were all in before he went on. Their eyes told it clear: a bright hunger for adventure, revenge on all who'd looked down on them, but, most of all, money.

"The best of all plans—quick wit and light step. I'm going to shake the family tree and we'll see what falls."

"It's a thin plan for hanging our lives on, Pinch." Therin sounded less than confident.

"It was as much of a plan as I had for getting you off the gallows in Elturel—and that worked, didn't it, or you wouldn't be here complaining, you over-learned ogre," Pinch countered.

The big Gur rubbed at the rope-scar under his scarf with self-conscious discomfort. To say he'd been rescued from the gallows wasn't quite honest, though he had to allow that Pinch had rescued him. It was that business of being hanged and then saved that left Therin with nightmares. "It's just I don't relish dying again, Pinch."

"Then be smart and you won't." There was little sympathy in Pinch's words, and seeing that the younger man remained sullen, the regulator poured drinks around. "Here's what—we'll not take this alone. I've got a mind we should have some allies, though they won't be knowing it. Maeve, I want to you visit the priestess Lissa. Inform her I've tracked down her thief and that she should stand ready to come at my word if she wants to catch him."

"Me, Pinch? I'm not particular cunning with words."

"Don't worry, the lass is gullible. You'll make a touching plea, I'm sure.

"Therin, I've got a job with profit for you. Mind, it's going to take a light touch. Go to Iron-Biter—"

"Who?"

"That ox-head of a dwarf who spins in Vargo's orbit. Here's the charm: Tell him he's been tricked, that the real regalia ain't in the tower, but you can lead him to it. Of course, you'll want money."

"Of course, but where am I supposed to lead this prize ass?"

"You'll have to wait for Sprite to show you."

"Me?"

"Aye, you." The regulator stopped to wrap a bit of cloth around his still-bleeding thumb. "It's upon you to give the signal. Now, get away with your business you two." With a sharp nod he urged Maeve and Therin toward the door.

Just as he was leaving, Therin turned back for one last question. "What if we don't show?"

"Then sure as there's gods in the heavens, there'll be not a whit of loot for any of us, the master rogue promised. "Don't fail if you want your cut."

Therin grunted in sour understanding and was on his way.

"What about me, Pinch?" Sprite asked after he was sure the door to the street was closed.

"Two jobs for you, old friend." The words were soft, as if invisible ears might try to overhear. "First, you must follow Cleedis when he takes me to my rendezvous. Learn the way so you can guide the others to me."

"What's the other?"

Pinch tapped his brow. "Keep a weather eye on our fine Gur. I don't trust him. He's like to sell us all—me in particular—if Iron-Biter makes the right price."

"So why in the hells did you send him to Iron-Biter?"

"Fishing takes the right bait and the right hook. I'm the bait. Therin's the hook. Iron-Biter's a fool, but he's not gullible. Who's going to convince him—Maeve, playing a part, or Therin, who just might get it into his head to sell us cheap?"

Sprite stared into the dregs of his cup. "I'd feel better if the dice were more to our favor. It's a risky game you're playing."

Pinch poured them both another round. "Don't be so glum. We either live or we die. What other kind of game is there?"

Meetings

Pinch swept through the palace halls, leaving a trail of whispers and arched brows in his wake. The regulator paid them no mind. It wasn't how he was dressed, which was a like a proper lord, or the way he passed by. No longer did he casually slouch through the chambers like a bemused man observing the ways of some alien class. No—now he strode through upright and boldly with every sense of possession. He was transformed and carried himself confidently, absolute in the knowledge that he had a place here in his own right and not by the *noblesse oblige* of others.

These things did not set tongues wagging, although they were noticed and added fuel to the speculation. No, that wasn't what Pinch's sharp ears picked up. It was his very presence at all that set the courtiers abuzz. Clearly, word had gotten around—no doubt from

Iron-Biter—that he was missing and not expected to return. It pleased the rogue no end that his entry made such a spectacular impression. Now was not the time to be subtle. He wanted everyone to know that he had returned; the consternation it would rouse in certain quarters was only to his advantage.

It was late in the afternoon, and the palace was teeming with lord, ladies, pages, and squires. Tomorrow was the Festival of Wealth, which alone would have been enough to fill the palace. Tomorrow was a day more than that, though. The Red Priests had declared that day auspicious for the Rite of Ascendancy. Pinch was certain Vargo had played the astrologer for this choice. With Iron-Biter's assurance that Pinch had been foiled, Vargo would want to act quickly before the stakes changed.

Consequently, anyone who hoped to be anything—which meant everyone—had descended on the palace. Counts, knights, poets, and merchants hovered in the halls or held court in the salons. Like gamblers at the track, the courtiers flitted from one faction to the next, trying to guess the outcome of the race. No man wanted to side with the losing party, but no one wanted to look indecisive either.

Friends were to be rewarded, enemies bought or crushed, and neutrals ignored. That was the way of these things.

It amused Pinch to read the faces of those around him, their plots so easily exposed in the astonishment of seeing him. Pinch's appearance upset the odds. Suddenly the Lord Chamberlain's faction wasn't so weak and hopeless as it had been moments before. Everyone knew Cleedis had brought Pinch back to Ankhapur, but no one could say for sure why. Only Iron-Biter had any clue, and even he did not know the whole of it.

Pinch threaded his way through the crowded salons, passing through the circles of courtiers. First there were the revelers, blissfully dumb of the greater stakes that tomorrow held. Dressed in their festival finery, these vain lackwits came to drink, to dance, and to be seen. Pinch perused them with the eye of a poultry buyer at market, making professional note of their plumage and purses. In his other life, these would have been the targets of his trade. Even now he looked at his stiff hand and yearned for a chance to put himself to the test.

Reluctantly he plunged into the next layer, where the ladies danced in stately lines while their lords hovered in knots of casually earnest discussion. This was the realm of hopefuls, those who conspired to advance by guessing the right horse. They eyed Pinch with suspicion and lust, eager to know what he portended, afraid to approach lest they be branded his ally. There was no comparison for them in Pinch's previous life; they had been as far from his reach as the moon and stars. Now he was as much above them and warranted them less concern than he had the revelers of moments before.

The third circle, the core of it all, was his goal. There, in those salons deepest from the city, swaddled in the layers of bodyguards, claimants, and sycophants, were the objects of all concern—the three princes. Cleedis was right where Pinch expected to find him, at the center of Bors's faction. Dwarfed by the soaring pillars of the Great Hall, the shunned coterie of the Lord Chamberlain drifted forlornly, waiting for a vitalizing spark. The princely idiot Bors clapped to the music that echoed from the dancing halls while Cleedis stood in serious conference with the few plump, waistcoated lords committed to his side. They were an unhappy-looking lot, men trapped by their titles, friendships, and favors to what looked for certain a losing cause. Few held any belief that the benevolent gods of Ankhapur would choose Bors as fit to rule the city. Cleedis alone held firm in that faith, futilely trying to rally supporters to his cause.

Pinch's arrival carried that wanted spark. The paunchy old knights, former captains of Manferic's army, drew aside for the younger man, younger at least by comparison.

"Lord Chamberlain," Pinch said as he came up behind old Cleedis, who to that point had been quietly haranguing a flagging member of his entourage, the Royal Steward of the Stables.

The old man stopped talking with a sort of choked gasp and turned about all in one go. It was a credit to his years of toadying that the Lord Chamberlain didn't blurt out his surprise. "Master Janol, how fare you? Rumor was spoken by certain mouths that we would not see you again."

"Sometimes rumor are just rumors. I'm well, Cleedis." Pinch let the pleasant smile drop from his mask. "A word, Cleedis. Now. Privately."

The old man arched one graying eyebrow. "Of course, cousin. Glindon, send word to Princes Vargo and Throdus that should they hear tales of their cousin's absence, they are not to worry. Tell them such talk is completely groundless and that he is well and with us here."

The page rolled his eyes, trying to remember the exact wording, and then hurried off to complete his task.

"Lords, excuse me." Taking Pinch by the arm, Cleedis hurried them both into a small side chamber, barely larger than a dressing closet. The old man shut the door, latched it, and turned on his agent, the bluish veins on his temple standing out.

"Where have you been? Vargo's had it out that you're dead or scuppered off someplace. There's been havoc to play with the ranks, positive mutiny. They think I've lost control." The chamberlain was hopping with indignation, furious but dependent on Pinch for answers.

"It was near enough to the truth, but I've made it."

"Do you have them—the items?"

Pinch found the old man's haste annoying. Brokering was a fine art that, properly done, should be approached casually. This eagerness was unseemly.

"They're where I can put my hands on them. Let's talk payment.

"We did. Fifty thousand bicentas."

Pinch regretfully shook his head. "That was then. Now I think the job's worth more."

Cleedis sucked at his teeth, clearly unwilling to name a figure. Finally he expansively offered, "Ten thousand more."

Pinch laughed a short, derisive snort. He held up his branded hand. "My price is another fifty thousand."

It was the chamberlain's turn to sputter. "Fifty more? Impossible!"

"I have the items; you don't."

"What of that? They're not necessary for the plan," the old man snapped.

Pinch pricked up his ears. It was the first Cleedis had let on that he knew the whole of Manferic's scheme. He answered with a heartless drawl. "It would be unfortunate if the genuine articles were discovered by Vargo or Throdus."

"I'll kill you myself first!"

"Harm me and it's guaranteed.

Cleedis glowered. "Thirty more," he finally said with a sullen mumble.

"Forty-five."

"Thirty."

"Forty, or Vargo learns everything."

The old campaigner broke into a hacking cough. "Forty then, damn you," he gasped as the fit subsided.

"Forty more it is, Cleedis." With triumphant cheer, Pinch clapped the other on the shoulder. "In gems—

mixed sizes and properly appraised. Don't try to cheat me on that. My friends have good eyes for stones. Agreed?"

"Agreed." There was hardly any cheer in Cleedis. "It will all be ready when you deliver the Cup to Manferic."

"Me deliver? No, I'll pass it to you."

"Our lord insists you bring it to him. The stones will be ready then." It was the chamberlain's turn to drive a hard bargain. "If you do not deliver, there will be no payment."

"When?"

"Tonight—after the banquet."

Pinch didn't like it but he could not refuse. There was still one more card in this game he needed to play. "Agreed, tonight."

Cleedis shuffled to the door. "After the banquet. Now, I must return before more bolt from my side."

Just as the old man started to open the door, Pinch played his last trump. "One other condition, Lord Cleedis. My mother—you will take me to my mother.

The hand stopped on the knob. "That's . . . impossible. She's dead."

"Don't lie to me, old fool. I know she's alive and that Ikrit guards her." Pinch was bluffing on a dead hand, but there was no need for Cleedis to see that.

"How much do you know?" the chamberlain whispered.

"Everything. Manferic, Mother, all of it."

They locked gazes, gamblers trying to read the bluff in the other's eyes. The stakes were new to Pinch, but the game he knew. Cleedis tried his statesman's best, but in the end the silent struggle went to the younger man.

"I can't," he whispered. "I didn't even know she'd survived all these year until you came. Ikrit was supposed to have killed her long ago."

Pinch smiled grimly. The bluff had succeeded; what

he'd guessed was true. "Why, Cleedis? Why did he deny me for all these years?"

The chamberlain shook his powder-white head. "That you'll have to ask Manferic when you see him—tonight." With that, the weary official slipped away before Pinch could impose any more conditions.

The questions asked, Pinch suddenly felt the weariness of his life settle over him. He'd been about for days now with barely a rest, twice beaten, twice healed, underfed, and overimbibed. He couldn't take another revelation, another wonder, without first the benefit of sleep. With a perfunctory bow to the lords assembled, he took his leave of Cleedis's clique and headed for the relative safety of his rooms.

As he passed a small salon, he was hailed by a voice that could not be ignored.

"Cousin."

Pinch stopped and gave a weary bow. "Greetings, Prince Vargo."

"Cousin Janol, stay awhile. I want a word with you." With a sharp signal, the dark-haired prince dismissed those clustered around the chaise where he'd been lounging. "Sit here and attend me." Vargo pulled aside the sweep of his dressing gowns to open a seat for his guest.

Pinch inwardly cursed himself for blindly straying too close to the prince's orbit, but now snared he could not escape. A quick scan of Vargo's hangers-on revealed Iron-Biter was not present, and that was a small relief. There was no saying how the dwarf might greet him and Pinch was not ready to find out. Stifling his resigned sigh and falsely filling himself with enthusiasm, Pinch took the seat offered.

"There was word you were unwell, cousin," Vargo said as he sipped at his morning tea. He oozed the charm of an unquestioned superior merely marking time to his ultimate victory. "Everyone was concerned."

Pinch accepted the tea a servant offered. "My lord, as you see, I am quite well. You should be wary of those who spread gossip. Perhaps they sought to embarrass you."

"I considered my source unimpeachable." The false concern was slipping away from his royal host.

"And yet I'm here and your source has been impeached."

Vargo set his cup aside. "What service have you done for old Cleedis? I know you, Pinch. You're a guttersnipe playing at nobility, like you always were and always will be. Well, guttersnipe, name your price. I can make you a wealthy man. That's what you want, isn't it?" The words hissed with soft anger between them.

Pinch ignored the cut. His pride could not be wounded by hollow words. There was only one thing untrue in what Vargo said—he wasn't just playing at nobility. He had the blood in his veins—all these years. Vargo's taunt was the finger that released the bolt, the magical words that triggered what was locked inside him. All the memories that he'd forgotten, set aside, and ignored roiled back to the surface—the slights at his parentage, the constant reminders that they were greater than he, the threats and promises that always began, "When I become king . . ." Vargo was right, he did have a price. So why not steal from them the only treasure they cared for? It would be the grandest theft of all and it warmed the cold side of his heart.

Draining the last of his tea, he stood and politely bowed to his enemy. "What I want, you won't pay me, Vargo."

"Name it. Gold? Magic? Women? Charter for a thieves' guild? Iron-Biter? Maybe you'd like the dwarf for your revenge? Take him, do what you want. He's yours if you want him."

Pinch just shook his head. "Your crown, the one you covet. For that I might even give you back your life."

The prince's face went red, then purple, and Pinch thought for certain he was about to explode in a gale of rage. All at once Vargo burst into a thunder of laughter. The servitors and courtiers craned their necks to see what was happening even while they pretended not to notice.

"Wit—even in the face of defeat!" the noble kin croaked out through gasps of air. A tear moistened his cheek. "It is one of your most pointlessly admirable traits, dear Janol.

"But know this, cousin," he added as his fit subsided, "you've made a bad choice of stars to set your fate by. Bors will never be king. Should it be Throdus or should it be I, we'll pluck you from our scalp like the flea you are. Now begone. You no longer amuse me."

At another wave, the courtiers closed back in again. The audience was over. Pinch snaked through the chambers, brushing away the insignificants who wanted to talk to him, and returned to his rooms. There the magnificently overstuffed featherbed welcomed him with outstretched pillows. Pinch collapsed into it like a sailor drowning in the arms of the sea.

"Sprite, you here?" he asked as he lay staring at the canopy.

"Aye, Pinch," came the halfling's nasal voice in answer.

"Any troubles?"

"Getting in? No—slipped in behind you and you didn't notice," Sprite bragged. "You're getting almost as bad as those guards, blind as posts. It was an easy walk."

Pinch smiled where he lay. It was true, the halfling had managed to evade him completely. "What about out?"

"I can crack the door and slip behind their backs without notice," the little sneak answered with great confidence. "Like I said, blind as posts."

Pinch closed his eyes and felt the abandonment of sleep flowing over him. "Excellent, my friend. Now, get out of here and see that the others are ready, then be back. The meeting's tonight. Be ready to follow me when we leave. Don't fail me on this one, Sprite. I've got the feeling that this one could be my neck. Do you sense it?"

"Aye, Pinch. The fur of my feet's quivering," drifted in the halfling's reply, and then there was darkness.

* * * * *

The scrape of stone on stone alerted Pinch and he sprang out of bed, still fully dressed, with the expectation of constables pouring through the door. There were no constables, no bed in a cheap stew, no laughter of harlots down the hall, only the warm night air that played over the thick tapestries. In the moment it took to establish his whereabouts, the secret door in the bedroom wall swung open and a sword waveringly emerged from the darkness. Satisfied that no one was lying in wait, Cleedis entered the room, brushing dust and cobwebs from his robes.

"Good," he noted, "you're ready. Let's go."

"Go through there?"

The chamberlain scowled. "Of course. Did you expect me to traipse you through the halls for everyone to see? People would wonder what we were about at such an hour."

If all was right, Sprite was waiting outside for just that signal. Going through the tunnels meant bypassing the halfling and that meant his entire plan was for naught.

"This seems like an ill idea to me. There's things down there, trying to kill me. I say we use the door—I can lose anyone who tries to follow us."

The old man was adamant. "The tunnels—Manferic

waits for us there."

"It's too dangerous."

"Nothing will harm us."

"How can you be so sure?" Pinch challenged in feigned anger, his voice rising in hopes that Sprite would hear it through the door. To increase the odds, he strode into the sitting room as if in a restless fury.

"Because I am the chamberlain of the Famisso household, right hand of Manferic the Great, and nothing down there will dare attack me or anyone carrying the privy seal of our lord," Cleedis blustered in exasperation. "Now, end this nonsense and let us go—unless all this is just to hide your own failure. You do have the regalia, don't you?"

The clear suspicion in the lord's voice warned Pinch not to press the issue any further. "Very well," he practically bellowed in his false temper, "we'll go by the tunnels!" Even as he did, he prayed to Mask and any other god who cared to grant Sprite particularly sharp ears.

Gathering up his goods—his well-used short sword, a fine black cloak, and the velvet sack that held his treasure—Pinch followed his guide.

"Close it," the chamberlain grunted as he set a taper to the lantern he'd brought with him. The rogue seized the handle and pulled the heavy wall shut. Just as it was about to close, he slipped the hem of his cloak into the gap so that it dangled like a pennon on the other side. Though it pained him to ruin such fine clothes, Pinch slashed the fabric away before Cleedis was done. He was barely able to manage it, forgetting until that moment that he had only one good hand.

When the sputtering lantern was finally lit, sparks rising from its wick, the old general led the way. The cobweb shadows quivered like veins against the crumbling stone walls. The lantern gave barely enough light to see the way by.

"You could have brought a wand or something

enchanted with daylight," Pinch sourly observed.

"Lord Manferic disapproves," was all the explanation he got.

"Of course, I forgot. He's dead."

They ventured farther into the tunnels and Pinch could not say if these were routes he'd traveled before. Unsure that Sprite could follow their dust-marred trail, Pinch set to slicing off more bits of his cloak, scraps of cloth for the halfling to follow, assuming he made it this far. He was barely able to grip the fabric in his crippled hand, and the task threatened to be noisy. To cover his actions, he became unusually talkative. "Why do you serve him, Cleedis? He's dead and it's better he was gone."

"Lord Manferic is a great man."

"He's not a man anymore, and he was more monster than man when he was alive."

"He did what he must to protect Ankhapur from its enemies. The city is strong because of him."

"What about me, Cleedis? What reason was there to hide my past from me?" Pinch shot back. "How did I threaten the city?"

"I'm sure he did what he thought he must," was the old official's icy reply.

"Is that what you'll say when he turns on you?" The rogue cut free another strip of cloth as they reached an intersection. He let it drop at the start of the branch they took.

"I have been loyal to Lord Manferic and he recognizes that. He will reward me for my effort."

"I see. Bors will be prince, you'll be the regent, and Manferic will dangle you both before the crowds as his puppets. Always the dog, never the one holding the leash, eh, Cleedis?"

The old man never broke his slow stride, though Pinch knew the words stung his warrior conscience. "There is no dishonor in loyalty, no shame in the rewards. I have done well by my life, far better than your mangy existence."

Another piece cut away. Pinch palmed it and continued his work. "I, at least, have my freedom. I choose what I want and I take it."

"Hah! That pathetic lie. Tell me, Janol, are you here now because you choose to be or because you've been trapped by your own greed and lust? You scramble for what I have, and not able to earn it by your own skills, you steal it from others. Or you used to—I've seen your hand though you try to hide it. Tell me, what becomes of a one-handed thief?"

Suddenly, Pinch lost his taste for conversation. He followed behind his guide, who was showing unusual vigor as they wound though arched passages, down stairs, and through vaults until they finally reached a large crypt just beyond a bridge that spanned an underground stream. Even before they entered the chamber, Pinch could feel the tingle of fear that had touched him in the necropolis. Manferic, cold and decaying, was near.

Cleedis stopped at the entrance to the room, sheltering the light from the door. "Lord Manferic, I've brought Janol," he announced to the darkness.

"Bring him in," resonated the chill voice of the dead.

Pinch paused at the door. If Sprite had followed him, he needed to stall for as much time as possible while the halfling scurried back for help. His plan, such as it was, depended on the others. He had few doubts what fate Manferic intended for him once the goods were passed over. He needed the distraction the others would provide if he wanted to escape alive.

Cleedis was in no mood to dawdle, perhaps motivated by fear of his dread lord. He impatiently drew Pinch through the door and into the center of the floor. The chamber had the pungent air of shriveled leather, the peculiar dry scent of decay.

The chamberlain fiddled with the lamp, lowering the
wick until the flame was little more than a spark. It ex-
aggerated the limestone walls even further until they
were black canvases upon which played a grotesque
shadow play of leaps and shimmers.

Something moved at the very outer layer of this
bleak hell. Pinch saw it only by a shadow that stretched
the thin limbs into an enormous insect scuttling across
the wall. The shadow moved with a chiseled rattle that
spoke of bones. It sounded like a skeleton the rogue had
once stumbled into while breaking into an alchemist's
garret, but it made him feel like a moth drawn too near
the deadly flame.

"Chamberlain, you kept me waiting. There is no time
for waiting," the shadow rasped like a bellows wheezing
stale air, whispery yet harshly echoing from the stone
walls.

"My apologies, Your Highness," Cleedis fawned.
Using his sword as cane, the old man stiffly got himself
down on one knee and bowed his head before the former king. "The path here confounds old men, my lord,
and makes them loose their way. I have brought you
Janol so that you can reward his service."

The shadow scraped closer, stepping into the edge of
the dim light. In the sheltering darkness of the catacombs, Manferic the lich stood uncloaked before them
both.

It wasn't as disgusting as Pinch expected, in fact it
was barely disgusting at all. The thing that had been
his guardian—Pinch could not change guardian to father so quickly—this thing almost looked alive. Certainly at midnight Manferic could have hurried through
the streets unremarked, at worst a poor consumptive in
search of good air. His face was drawn and stripped of
fat. The skin was pearly gray and translucent as if
someone had painted it over with wax. Pinch had expected the eyes to be deadest of all, but it was just the

opposite; they burned with a life more ferocious than any living man's. They were the furnaces of Manferic's will, the driving ambition that kept him alive.

In that gaunt face, Pinch barely recognized the likeness of his guardian, now father. Death had not changed him nearly as much as the fifteen years apart from each other. He was thinner and sharper of bone, and he stood half-hunched as if bowed by some great weight. But when he moved and when he spoke, even in that sibilant whisper, he was still Manferic, the imperial arrogance just as Pinch remembered.

As Manferic stepped farther into the light, the first impression was denied. A flicker of the lamp highlighted a white spot on the lich's cheek, a spot that suddenly wriggled and twisted. Pinch was suddenly aware of the pale grave worms that wriggled out of the smooth skin and dropped to the floor with every step. They crawled out of the ruin of the lich's ears and tangled themselves into the matted filth that remained of his hair. Manferic, when alive, would never had tolerated this. Dead, the decay that was corrupting his flesh was of no concern. The lich was sustained by the dark combination of magic and will; the body was only a husk to hold it all. This was no longer Manferic the king, but a thing that Pinch could never call else but "it."

"Give them to me," the thing coldly demanded. It turned its burning gaze full on Pinch. The fires of its desire riveted him and then proceeded to pour into his soul the cold terror of its existence.

Although the lich was appalling to behold, there was no logical basis for the intensity of his fear. Had it been his sword, his purse, even a friend that the lich demanded, Pinch very certainly would have succumbed, so oppressive was the fear on his heart. Fortunately, what the lich demanded cut to the soul of what mattered for Pinch—to surrender without profit.

The rogue clutched the bag. "Payment first."

The Manferic thing scowled, unaccustomed, as both lord and omniscient horror, to resistance from a mere mortal. "Indeed," it clicked through its lipless mouth. "And what is that?"

"Fifty thousand nobles," Pinch responded, the burden of fear lifting from him. Haggling with a broker, no matter how fearsome, was something he understood, and understanding broke the dread awe.

"Vile rogue! The price was set at forty," Cleedis interrupted.

Pinch assumed an air of great injury. "Liar? I spoke the truth, dread lord," he lied brazenly.

"Enough," rasped the undead thing. "I can well guess the truth of it, Pinch. You forget; I know who—and what—you are." Those fire-filled eyes blazed into the thief, boring pits through the bone. A dread discomfort crawled like lice over the regulator's brain, itching and poking at the very thoughts of his mind.

Pinch fought the feeling, tried to block it out. He knew what it meant. The lich was probing his mind, rummaging through the tangled mass of his thoughts and memories. Pinch knew the trick well enough; it was one of Maeve's old standbys.

"I see it clear. You hoped to cheat me of forty—"

Manferic cocked its head with the looseness of death. "Father," the lich whispered. Without breaking its transfixing gaze, the thing spoke to the chamberlain, who had prudently stepped aside. "Cleedis—he knows," the mealy lord hissed.

"Yes, my lord," the old man fawned, trembling at the darkness in his lord's voice. "He only just confronted me."

"So, Janol—you are fatherless no more."

Perhaps there was still a mote of sentimentality in the creature that Manferic had become, for the thought probes retreated. Pinch held back his sigh of relief. The lich's feelers had come too close. If Manferic learned he was bargaining for a fake, that would be the end of the whole plan, and Pinch's life, too. Of course, if Sprite didn't arrive soon with the cavalry, it would all be over. He needed to stall.

"It explains much," he answered, doing his best to sound detached from the emotion it raised in him. "And nothing. Why did you deny me?" the rogue asked as calmly as he could.

Manferic's eyes flared as if to say, "I do not answer to you, mortal," but then the light of hate died away. "You are a bastard. When Manferic was alive, it was not proper to acknowledge a misconceived son."

The lich spoke of its living existence as if that were the life of another being.

"So why did you keep me around?" Pinch demanded before Manferic could press him for the regalia. He needed the time talk bought.

The lich shuffled closer, rotted lips drawn back to show yellow-black teeth, a horrid grimace that might have been a smile. "Because—because Manferic liked you.

"Do you think it was an accident—or chance—that Cleedis brought you here? There are a hundred thieves in Ankhapur, but I sent Cleedis for you. It was no accident; it was planned. With your help, I will rule Ankhapur." The lich rattled to a pause, letting the offer register in Pinch's eyes.

"I need your eyes and ears, my son. You will be the master of my spies, you will find my enemies and reveal them to me." The ragged Manferic looked at his maggot-ridden hand with bemused interest. "You will introduce them to me and I will entertain them," he whispered more to himself than to Pinch. Just as abruptly, he once more fixed his fierce gaze on Pinch. "I'm offering you Ankhapur, my son, not just a handful of paltry coins. Who else will do you that well? Give me the regalia and let us share the glory."

"So you can kill me as soon as I do?"

"I could kill you now and take it," the lich rasped, "but I want you at my side. Manferic knew this day would come."

"You and your plots drove me out of Ankhapur."

"Strength in woe—that was tempering. You would not be who you are now if you had stayed. You would be a lackey of your legitimate brothers." Manferic pointed a skeletal finger at Pinch's chest. "Now you are strong and resourceful enough to take a place at my side."

"Lord Manferic . . ." Cleedis finally found the where-withal to speak. The old man had pulled from inside himself the fearless cavalryman of his youth. His stooped shoulders were pulled up, the lined face smoothed with determination, and all framed by the billows of his thin white mane. Gone were the trembles, the ague, and the arthritis that had bled his majesty. So firmly outraged, Pinch could see the Cleedis of years past, the fencing master and horseman Pinch had so long ago admired. His voice was filled with cautious indignation. "I have served you loyally, great king, in expectation of my due—"

"Lord Chamberlain, my faithful servant." The lich twisted around to look on the old officer. "There has always been the most honored of places for you in my plans. Indeed, your greatest service is about to come."

The chamberlain smiled and bowed with all the humility of a fox, but before he could look up a ray of light the color of an algae-choked pond lanced from Manferic's fleshless finger to strike the loyal noble in the center of his head. It was as if the old man had been struck by a hammer. With a scream, he reeled back but the beam played on him. It rippled over his head and across the side of his face. Everywhere it touched, the skin festered and burst into red-black sores of diseased corruption. Cleedis flailed his arms as if he could beat the light away, but all that did was crisscross his arms with the bloody sores.

The scream became a whimper and the whimper became a sloppy gurgle of pus and blood as the ray destroyed deeper and deeper flesh. Cleedis stumbled backward until he fell to the floor and then, mewling, he crawled away, smearing a track of red slime over the rough stone floor. Manferic kept the grotesque ray mercilessly playing over the chamberlain's body as the pathetic wreck tried to drag himself to safety.

As the whimpering became bubbling sobs, Pinch turned away. Even for Cleedis, with all his ambitions and lies, this was no deserved end—this ulcerated mass that was bleeding its life out on the floor. Pinch didn't look back until the crackle of the spell had faded. What was left of Cleedis was unrecognizable—a mass of blood-soaked clothes and bubbled flesh that spared not a single feature.

"You killed him," Pinch gulped. The grotesque execution stripped away the rogue's normally chill demeanor, leaving him only to gawk at the horror on the floor.

"It has all been planned for," Manferic croaked, teeth bared in a garish smile. The undead king turned to Pinch once more.

"Give me the regalia, Janol, my son. Join me against your half-brothers and we will be masters of Ankhapur."

"Or?

The lich ratcheted its head toward the oozing mass. "Or die," Manferic promised.

The cavalry had not come; the choice was no more. Reluctantly, Pinch opened the bag at his side and carefully set the Cup and the Knife on the floor.

"Ankhapur together it will be, Father."

18

Heart-to-Heart

"Attend me," Manferic wheezed in his throat-grinding way before withdrawing into the darkness. "Bring your light and come. There is time before I must act."

Why should I follow this dead thing, Pinch wondered? The instinct to flee rose in his mind. It was a good instinct, one that Pinch had learned to heed and treasure over the decades. He'd listened to it as a thief, and even before when he'd fled Ankhapur. It was urging him to flee now. It would be easy to outrun what Manferic had become, and he was willing to risk a spell in the back rather than enter this monster's lair.

Perhaps Manferic knew his bastard son too well, for with a single word he understood Pinch's mind and acted on it.

"Ikrit."

A stealthy rustle and a throaty animal growl demanded he look to see its source. Sure enough, behind him was the silver-white shadow of Manferic's pet quaggoth. A feeling of professional amazement incongruously struck Pinch as he marveled at the creature's skill in escaping notice. Of course Manferic would have resources here. Pinch should have known. The lich might be dead, but that didn't matter. It was the power of its mind that sustained it.

There was no choice. The choice had already been made, and there was no avoiding the consequence. Perhaps it would be no worse than remaining in a room with a still-festering mass of flesh. There was an odor beginning to rise from it, the scent of rotted fish. It was something more than that, the smell of an almshouse during plague, where the wretched diseased, too poor to donate to wealthy healers, suffered through their erupted pustules and fevers to live or die as the gods chose.

Carefully avoiding the puddles of putrescence, Pinch followed his newfound father into the dark void. A heavy tread confirmed that Ikrit was close behind. The flame that clung to the end of the lantern wick guttered and swayed as he walked, creating ghastly shadows that wrapped themselves like veils around the tattered cloak of his guide's corrupted flesh. Pinch didn't follow too closely, pushed back by the stench of decay. He hadn't noticed it before, his sense of smell sealed by fear.

As he followed the lich through the tunnels, Pinch's mental wheels sought to formulate a new plan. There was still a hope that Sprite would come and pick up the trail. Indeed, even he, no tracker or woodsman, could have followed the trail of rot and grave worms that dripped from beneath Manferic's cloak. Of course, it was more likely that all help was lost to him.

Alone, there was little hope. With his branded hand, he could hardly manage a sword, so there was no chance of cutting his way past the quaggoth, even if he were a trained swordsman—which he was not. Likewise, he had no magic the match of Manferic's skills, so escape by that means was unthinkable. He could try slipping into the darkness in hopes that they would lose him, but that was a fool's chance he wasn't yet so desperate to try.

The single choice that remained was to take advantage of what Manferic offered, as duplicitous and uncertain as that offer might be. Pinch had no faith in the truth of the lich's words. The creature wanted him for something, though for what he could not say.

At last they came to passages familiar to Pinch, passages beneath the palace. These they followed past branches the rogue ought to have known, if he'd had more time, until at last they reached a stairs he was positive he knew. The way rose up and curved, and ended in a blank wall. They had returned, back to Pinch's apartment by some roundabout way. The quaggoth dutifully pressed against the barrier, and the stone swung open with a grating groan. No fabric fluttered out of the jamb, Pinch quietly noted. Sprite and crew were somewhere underground.

"The lights, put them out," Manferic commanded, standing aside to let the rogue through. Pinch did so, all save one, as the quaggoth followed him about the chambers. When the job was finished, the beast herded him over to a hard stool by the bed, there to stand watch over the man.

Once the room was dim, Manferic ignored his prisoner to rummage through the drawers and chests of Pinch's belongings. At first, Pinch feared the lich had guessed his deception, but the search was far too calm for that. It was going through his clothes, tossing aside cloaks, doublets, garters, and robes, apparently selecting a wardrobe.

"Get dressed," the lich croaked, tossing the clothes to Pinch. "You don't want to miss the ceremony." The creature clicked its teeth in cold laughter.

Pinch did as he was bade, all the time watching for some chance to escape. There could be no good end for him in all this.

"You have questions, don't you?" Manferic teased while the rogue slowly dressed.

Pinch said nothing, suspicious that the lich's sudden garrulousness was some new trap.

"Of course you do—like why did Manferic raise you? Go ahead, ask," the lich urged with a rattling chuckle. "Ask and you will learn."

"Then why?"

The rotting face did its hideous smile. "You were Manferic's insurance," the lich explained, persistently talking about its own past as if it belonged to another. "Insurance against his sons."

"Insurance?" Wonders of all, Manferic apparently felt talkative, like the aging father passing his wisdom down to his son. The lich was sentimental in a cold and heartless way.

"If his sons rebelled and he was forced to kill them, he wanted you alive to continue the bloodline."

"So he fathered me and kept it secret—"

"So you would not turn against him as he feared his sons would."

The cold-blooded reasoning of it matched Manferic's mind perfectly. "Why did he force me to leave? I don't believe a word about making me stronger." Unconsciously, Pinch talked as if Manferic were someone else, too.

"Manferic realized he could create me. Why should he try to continue his dynasty through the blood of others when he could live forever? You became a danger to making me," the lich answered.

From the way the lich talked about itself, Pinch could only decide it was mad. The spells, the will, and the decay had destroyed something in Manferic's mind. The lich might have the memories, the evil and the cunning, but it was no more Manferic than Pinch was. It was a transformation of souls, as the old king descended into something even viler and more grotesque than it had been in life. Pinch had seen fatherly love in all its forms—fathers who trained their sons in the highway law, fathers who sold their daughters to wealthy men, even those who turned in their own to the authorities for coin—but even these could not compare to the scale of reptilian cruelty that Manferic aspired to. An involuntary shudder seized him at the thought of such cruel manipulation.

"So Manferic tried to kill me and get rid of the problem," Pinch said bitterly as he finished dressing. The heavy hand of the quaggoth forced him back into his seat. Meanwhile, the lich produced a gem from the folds of its robe and set it on the floor between them.

"No," the undead thing sighed, "it was not Manferic. It was your half-brother, Prince Vargo. Manferic simply withdrew his protection from you. He did not want you dead, only gone. A good scare to send you away. There was always a chance he might need your bloodline, that his plans might fail."

"Who was my mother?" Pinch was still stalling for time, but he truly wanted the answer to this.

"As you were told, the Lady Tulan, lady-in-waiting to the queen."

"What happened to her?"

"Manferic hid her in the catacombs until the baby was born," the lich answered with icy detachment. "Then he gave her to Ikrit."

Pinch looked over his shoulder at the huge, hairy man-thing. "You guard the lady?"

The creature bared a fang and grunted, no confirmation or denial. It was as much as the creature would say before its master.

The lich's burning gaze fixed on the dirty white creature. "Interesting . . ." it whispered.

Pinch sensed that he'd spoken more than he should. If it had been only Ikrit, he would have irked the two to conflict, but there was another at stake here he did not want to sacrifice—the lady in the tunnels. If she was his mother, Pinch wanted to protect her from harm. He needed her to prove his claim, he rationalized, forgetting that his chances of escape were slim. "So why drag me back?" he asked to quickly change the subject.

The lich's fiendish gaze shifted to Pinch. "Does this look like success?" It snarled as it brushed its wormy cheek with a skeletal hand. "All the books, all the scrolls never promised anything like this! I need a new body . . . and you will provide it. Ikrit, hold him!"

The quaggoth clamped its paws on Pinch's shoulders till the claws stabbed into the flesh. This was the last moment, he knew, so the rogue twisted and fought with all abandon. He kicked at Manferic, but the lich stayed well out of the way, and all his writhing only made the giant guardian press him down all the firmer. While he kicked and screamed, the lich coolly went about its preparations.

"Scream as you wish. No one will come." Pinch gave it up, knowing the monster was right. No doubt Cleedis had ordered the guards to leave them undisturbed when he first came in. "Hold him, but don't hurt him," the creature warned. "I want my new body undamaged." The lich seemed positively cheerful. "You see," it explained as it arranged the gem between them, "I don't intend to spend eternity looking like this. I want a strong body."

"You could have had anyone. Just steal one off the streets," Pinch protested between kicks.

"And walk through the halls wearing the husk of a street rat? The palace guards would never let me in." The lich positioned itself opposite Pinch. "I was going to use Cleedis, but he's so . . . old. The other princes are too well known. There was too much to learn to be one of them. Their friends would be suspicious. You are perfect. A place in the palace and no past to encumber me."

"I have friends."

"Ah, your three companions. I know about them. Cleedis informed me. He was quite thorough—right to the end." Preparations finished, the lich sat at the edge of the bed. "No one will mourn their deaths. Just sewer scum the city is best rid of."

Pinch winced at that. He had worked hard to protect himself and the others from that fate, and now his efforts would be to no avail.

"This will be interesting," the lich continued. "A new experience. You see, I will replace you in your own body, while you will be trapped in this jewel." It nodded to the stone between them. "And then, I will have Ikrit crush the jewel and your essence will vanish into the void. An interesting experience for you, though rather short-lived."

The lich drew itself up, ready to utter the words that would close the spell. Hands raised, it parted its teeth and—

"Your plan is flawed!" Pinch blurted, trying to sound more confident than he felt.

The lich sensed his desperation. "It will work perfectly," it sneered.

"Oh? What about Cleedis? How can you rule Ankhapur if your broker is dead? You needed him to be regent, and like a fool you killed him back there. No one in Ankhapur would tolerate me as their sovereign." Pinch tried to sit himself up straight in support of his bluff.

The lich shook its moldering head. "Is this my only spell? Why should I be one person when I can be three? It is a simple thing to change a face with a single spell. I will be Janol or Cleedis as I choose, but I will always be Manferic in my soul. When all the princes fail the test, they will be forced to name me regent.

"Enough of this—Ikrit, don't let him escape."

Pinch lashed out wildly as the lich began the rite. He tried every foul move he could, aiming his elbow for the creature's lower regions and stamping to break the beast's foot. None of it worked. The lich droned through its litany, brittle voice rising in triumph as it reached the last syllables.

At the final phrase, the lich's body collapsed like the dead body it truly was. The legs folded uselessly, the raised arms flopped, and the head lolled in meaningless directions as the carcass fell to the floor. A scattering of lice and worms spilled from the sack—the scattered pollen of death.

It didn't work, Pinch exulted. The lich's spell and his plan had failed. With burst of joyous strength that caught the baffled quaggoth off guard, Pinch broke from the beast's corded grasp and dashed for the door. He would throw it open, the guards would come, and—

An invisible, intangible spike hammered right through Pinch's brow. It was a heated nail of hateful ambition that cracked his skull and burrowed into the heart of his brain. It ripped at the lines of his self, the ties that anchored his being to his body. With swift cuts, Pinch's body vanished from his psyche. He went blind first as something seized his eyes. The sounds of his crashing across the room vanished next, leaving only the rush of pain as his connection to the world. Pinch tried to fight this waylaying of his body, to concentrate on who he was, but his effort was crushed by a ferocious onslaught of hateful will. In a brief glimpse, he saw the form of it, the raw essence that had kept his father alive—even beyond death.

And then there was nothing.

Blind, mute, and disconnected from his nerves, Pinch was stripped of the weight of his flesh and cast into a void. There was no color, no darkness, not even the sense of seeing. There was no pain or absence of it, no stale smells of prison-trapped air. There was no body to breathe. All that remained of Pinch were the lessons life had given him, the bitter memories, the ambitions, and the uncertain belief that he still existed.

But just what was he? With ample time to consider, for time too was lost to him, Pinch arrayed the options that memory presented him. Manferic said he'd be trapped in the jewel, but also that he was going to crush it. So was he alive . . . or dead? He compared all the ends he'd ever heard described, but his bland, existenceless state was hardly the vile doom predicted by the thundering prophets who'd railed against his sins. None of them had ever said, "You shall spend your eternity in a colorless void." Pinch rather wished they had; perhaps if he'd known he'd spend his eternity adrift in a blank, he would have amended his ways. The prospect of being trapped here—wherever *here* was—was not a promising prospect.

But what, it dawned on him, did he mean by the end of time? Cut loose from his moorings, what was now and what was then lost all meaning. He tried to guess the timed drops of a water clock or the sweep of a sundial's shadow, but without his body to set the rhythm, it was no use. His second could be an hour, a day, or an eon someplace else.

A panic roiled his thoughts—that alone was curious. His thoughts fled in all directions and refused to be marshaled, but he never felt the clutch of jolted nerves that would normally signal his desperation. It was fear on ice, intellectually there but unacknowledged by the primal signals that made it live.

What if there is no end to time? What if time ends, but I live on? If one can't feel its passing then how can it end—or start? Without time, is there a forever?

Pinch knew that whatever the answer was, he would go mad in this empty hell.

A glare of brilliant light brought the end of his speculations, followed by a rush of sensation that over-

whelmed his mind. Sight, scent, feeling, and sound—
the echoing crack of a shattering. Pinch's sight was all
skewed. He was too close to the floor and everything
was brighter than it should have been; even the darkest
corners the room were well lit. I must have passed out
and this is where I fell, he thought. How much time has
passed? was his second thought.

With great care he tried to look around, barely turning his head just in case Manferic and Ikrit were watching. He must have fallen harder than he thought and
banged his head, because his joints were stiffer than
they ought to be. He noticed that, except for his sight,
all his senses were curiously dulled. His mouth was
salt-dry, too.

From where he lay, Pinch caught sight of Ikrit just at
the unfocused rim of his vision. The big creature was
pulling on something. At first Pinch couldn't tell what,
but then the grate of stone made it clear. The quaggoth
was going through the secret door, leaving him alone.

The rogue didn't understand. According to Manferic,
he was supposed to be trapped in a gem or dead, his
spirit dissipated throughout the universe. He certainly
did feel like either, not that he regretted the lich's error.
Something must have gone wrong, ruined the spell, and
driven Manferic away. Maybe the cavalry had arrived
just in time. There had been more incredible strains of
luck in his time.

Half-expecting and hoping to see his friends waiting
behind him, Pinch started to rise. He set his bony, half-
rotted hand—

A squirming maggot plopped to the floor by his
thumb.

It couldn't be his thumb, not this gray-green, decaying thing. It was Manferic's hand, it was . . .

Slowly Pinch raised his gaze and looked about the
floor. There it was, the source of the cracking noise
that had greeted him when he woke: a scattering of

crystalline shards and razorlike powder. It was the remains of Manferic's stone. It had trapped him, and Ikrit had crushed it, just as the lich had promised.

But now he was in Manferic's rotting body and that wasn't supposed to happen.

The regulator stumbled to his feet, struggling in the unfamiliar body. Everything about it was the wrong length, with the wrong play of muscles. He lurched to the great mirror that hung over traveling chest. The light that was painfully bright to his eyes was a gloom in the glass and barely enough to reflect his features. After one look, Pinch was thankful for that.

Pinch calculated himself only mildly vain, but such an estimate was impossible when a man couldn't look truly outside of himself. Intentionally or no, Manferic had give the rogue that opportunity. The mirror reflected a horror—the wriggle and twitch of the things that lived under the skin, the peeling patches of the scalp, the black shredded ruins that were once lips; even the tongue was a swollen, oozing mass. A grave worm wriggled through a small gap in his teeth.

Pinch choked. He wanted to throw up, but his body wouldn't obey. There was nothing inside him, not even breath on which he could gasp. Liches didn't eat, didn't breath. They had no blood in their veins.

Now he knew the level of his vanity. If condemned to remain like this, he would rather die. His face and his hair, no amount of fine clothes would ever hide these. This was more than just a branding of his hand. He had railed against that, but when it was over he knew he would live—even keep his old trade. This compared not at all to that. He wasn't Pinch anymore; he wasn't even a man. Life as a monster was intolerable.

Perhaps Pinch had inherited more from his father than he ever knew, for when he finally pulled himself away from the horror that faced him, he did not give up. The choice came to him—to end it, though he was uncertain just how a lich might die—but he rejected that plan in favor of another. So long as Manferic walked, there was hope that he could force the creature to reverse what it had done. If he died trying, he could certainly be no worse than he was now.

Determination filled him, gave him a glint of the light that had filled Manferic's eyes. Holding back the disgust that it filled him with, the rogue tested his new body, rose to his feet, and resolved to repay the monster for what it had done.

It did not matter where it had gone wearing his own shell; there was only one place he could go in its. That was back underground. If Manferic was wandering the halls of the place, he could not follow. His last hope lay in Ikrit. If Tymora spun her wheel and it favored him, the rogue knew he just might be able to track Manferic's brute servant back to the dead king's lair.

Shuffling to the secret passage and shedding soft blobs of his borrowed body, Pinch forced the wall open and set off in search of his prey. As he descended the steps, his mind eagerly sought out the grandest punishment for vile Manferic it could devise.

Walking Dead

The first thing the regulator noticed as he eased
himself down the narrow staircase was the uncanny
brightness of the place. Then he realized he hadn't
brought candle or lantern with him. There was at least
one advantage to having the lich's body, though it
hardly compensated for the crime wrought upon him.

The next thing Pinch noticed was how much easier it
was to track. He understood now how the quaggoth
moved through the tunnels so easily. The dark passages
had the appearance of an overcast day.

The question was, where had the beast gone? The
creature had a considerable head start and could have
chosen any number of paths. The rogue's only resource,
the dust-laden floor, was a useless guide now. It was all
churned and muddied by comings and goings till it was
far beyond his ability to read anything in it.

In this the rogue's luck held, for the quaggoth was just in sight. The great white beast was ambling down the passage, not imagining it was being followed.

The second fortunate thing was that being dead had not robbed Pinch of all his skills. He still knew to creep and skulk about, though knowing was not the same as doing. It was one thing to know how to step lightly, but the rogue wasn't sure he could get the rotting hulk that was his prison to cooperate. There was only one way to know, and that was by trying. He set out as light-footed as he could, but in his desire for stealth every noise was agonizingly magnified. There was no time to gain a proper body sense of the lich, so every move was accompanied by a cluster of scrapes and bumps even the dullest novice could have avoided—and Pinch especially if he had been in his own flesh. His bone-bare feet went scritch-scritch over the hard stone. Little bits of his body splashed softly splashed into the puddles at the wet spots. They weren't loud noises, but they were loud enough to Pinch's ear and pride.

Nor did they pass unnoticed. Several times Ikrit stopped and eyed his back trail suspiciously, even at moments when Pinch swore he made no noise. The beast wrinkled his broad nose, and that's when Pinch realized he had another complication.

The corpse stank. It was "the corpse" and not himself—the rogue refused to accept Manferic's body as his new identity. He remembered that Manferic's body could foul the air of a perfumery. The body's nose was apparently immune to its own fetor, for he could not catch a whiff of it, but apparently the quaggoth was not immune. Now not only did he have to be stealthy, he apparently also had to remain upwind of his prey. If not, he'd be the first thief ever discovered by his stench. Not the epitaph he wanted on his grave, that was for certain!

The stalking game of cat and mouse continued, although it was never clear who was the cat and who the

rodent. Ikrit stopped far too frequently to suit Pinch yet
never seemed to tumble to the rogue's presence. It was almost as if the quaggoth were hearing something else that
eluded Pinch's dulled ears. The result was a maddeningly
slow pace for the thief. He was of the utter conviction that
time counted for everything, that his body had to be regained by the coronation. After that, reaching
Manferic/Janol/Cleedis—it was impossible to choose a
single name for the lich—would be well-nigh impossible.
The privileges of the palace would surround the creature,
and between the guards and the lich's spells it would be
impossible to get close to the dread lord. Pinch's mind had
already plotted that the best hope lay in the sheltering
confusion of the festival. The lich was most apt to be distracted now before its triumph was complete.

But what then? Assuming he found Manferic, how
was Pinch supposed to get his body back? The rogue
had no idea. Manferic certainly wasn't going to give it
up easily, not after all the trouble he'd gone to just to
collect it, and Pinch had no spells to force the issue.
Damnation, he wasn't even sure what had happened to
him! All he had was his faith in improvisation, the belief that if somehow he saw his way through, something
would give him a chance.

There was only one problem with his determined op-
timism. Ikrit wasn't cooperating. With his improved
eyesight and his past experience, Pinch knew enough to
say the ape-thing wasn't bound for Manferic. It was
avoiding all the tunnels Pinch remembered and plunging into areas the thief did not recognize. Admittedly,
there was only so much he could remember about darkened stone, but the haze of dust clearly meant that no
one had passed this way in recent time.

This was not good, but what could he do? Short of
marching through the halls of the palace, Ikrit was his
only lead. He had to follow where the beast led.

Thus he was trailing the creature, slipping into a

crack in the catacomb wall when it paused for the hundredth time, that Pinch was caught unawares. As he was peering carefully from his shallow hiding place, the angry buzz of a hornet sang loudly in his sense-clogged ears. A shadow hurtled past and skipped onto the stone between him and the quaggoth with a rattling clatter.

As the thief was held prisoner by amazement, trying to fathom what had just happened, the silence was rent by cries of war. Ahead of him, doing all things at once, the quaggoth bellowed with bloody rage, dropped into half-doubled crouch, and charged, talons bared, straight down the corridor for him.

Gods pluck a rose, Pinch panicked, he's seen me! With his instinct to run in full alarm, the regulator spun about as quick as the rickety body would let him—

And came nigh-on face-to-face with two hundred-plus pounds of charging dwarven hate. The barrel-chested, black-bearded little man had cast aside a crossbow and was in the act of whirling an iron-studded mace over his head for a furious blow. "Death to the king!" Iron-Biter roared.

Pinch flopped his decrepit body back into the niche in which he'd sheltered. He was barely fast enough. Just in front of him, all forces collided in the narrow passage. Iron-Biter's mace hit the wall scant inches from the rogue's forehead. Stone ripped in sharp splinters and ricocheted around his head. The shards tore into Ikrit's outstretched arms as the quaggoth slammed into the stocky dwarf like a brawling stevedore. The impact flung the dwarf backward, and it was only his warblood, which even a surplice couldn't change, that gave him the determination to hold his footing. Ikrit slashed with his broken claws, ripping ragged gashes through the dwarf's armor. Blood leaked over the rent chain mail.

Pinch squeezed into the scant hollow as deep as he could. The battle raged too damn close for him to be safe. Ikrit's back-cocked elbow slammed him in the chest, spraying rot over his tattered cloak. If he'd been Pinch and not this festering thing, the blow would have punched the wind out of him like a noisy sack. Fortunately, at this moment, he didn't breath.

"Clubs!" Maeve's familiar voice shrilled from down the passage. It was a warning to her friends to stand clear, a slang the mage used just before she was about to cut loose with a spell large and nasty.

"Maeve, for the gods' sakes—NO!" Pinch yelled with the realization that he was almost certainly standing at the blast center of whatever it was. The scream, though, was absurd: far too shrill, far too unbelievable to be heeded. Abandoning the wisdom of eyes to the foe, Pinch threw his cloak up and huddled against the wall.

Almost immediately, the clang and squeal of battle was complemented by a thunderous crack. The rogue had heard the sound oft before, and every time it reminded him of the bang of smoke powder rockets from Shou. The air exploded in a tingling concussion of heat and static, punctuated by first one metallic howl of pain and then a second, more bestial, squeal. Jagged ribbons of blue fire embraced the huddled thief, rippled the scant hair, and sparked in front of his eyeballs. The maggots and worms fell in roasted flakes from his corpse, but the electric agony Pinch awaited never materialized.

Staggered by amazement, Pinch rose from his huddle to confront the battle once more, except that there was no battle left. The passage in front of him was a bloody smear of white fur and broiled flesh. What was left of Ikrit had been flung a good rod down the passage. The body was there, but the quaggoth's flattened broad head was all but gone, transformed into a smoldering, blood-strewn blot. Ikrit was dead, without even a convulsive hint at life.

Even as he absorbed the sight, the battle began again all too fast. "Die, you thing of evil!" a shaky voice commanded. Iron-Biter was staggering to his feet even as he held forth the seal of his order. The dwarf was calling upon the majesty of his god to undo the evil that bound this undead thing to the world. The only problem was that, being undead only in the flesh, Pinch just didn't fit the mold. The words and the display had no effect on him.

Nonetheless, the dwarf gave it his best, screwing up his blood-splattered face in a grotesque mask of concentration. He was bleeding from gashes over his shoulders and chest, his leather and iron helmet was twisted black from the bolt, blood flowed from a loose flap in his scalp to soak his bearded cheek, and his whole frame shook with exertion, but the dwarf intoned his orison with a will. Behind him, well back and awaiting the outcome, were the rest of the ragtag band: Sprite, Maeve, Therin—and Lissa in their tow.

Pinch almost wanted to laugh at the futility of it, but there was no time. Realizing this monster was not to be turned, Iron-Biter threw aside the effort and changed his chant. The words and gestures were a spell. Pinch didn't know what, but it couldn't be good for him. The dwarf had death and murder in his eyes. Pinch had to stop him now or not at all.

Besides, there was the matter of old scores to settle.

Even as the dwarf raised his voice in the final binding of the spell's power, Pinch lunged forward. He had no weapons, little hope of besting the bear-sized dwarf in a hand-to-hand battle, and no particular courage for straight-up fighting, but it was a long sight better than standing still to be blasted to shreds.

His lunge startled the priest, who expected to fight with magic and not his hands. Pinch got one hand on Iron-Biter's arm, wrenching awry the intricate patterns he'd been weaving in midair. To the rogue's amazement, the skin beneath his corrupt fingers instantly turned an icy blue, the lines of his chilling touch tracing their way up the dwarf's veins toward his heart. Seizing on that opening, Pinch got his other hand closed around the throat, squeezing to a gurgle what would have been a scream if the rogue weren't crushing the little priest's windpipe. The frozen blue pallor spread underneath the dwarf's beard and emerged on his cheekbones.

Iron-Biter was far from defenseless, though. With his free arm he swung his holy symbol, a weighty replica of the Cup. It cracked against hollow ribs with enough force that Pinch knew it had caused harm. His mind told him that, but his nerves remained dead to the blow. No pain, he thought, a lich must feel no pain.

He squeezed tighter, and that's when he made his next discovery. Along with the icy touch, Pinch had inherited the lich's strength. His bloodless fingers squeezed down. Flesh tore and bones snapped within his grasp. Iron-Biter's eyes bugged as he corded his neck muscles to hold off the pressure. It was a losing battle and the dwarf knew it. He dropped the mace and scrabbled for something at his belt.

No mercy, Pinch knew. Iron-Biter would show him none, and he couldn't afford to give any. He squeezed harder, starting to hear the clicking grind of cartilage giving way.

Over the dwarf's shoulder, five motes of light hurtled from Maeve's fingertips to strike Pinch cleanly. With each he rocked a little, like the impact of an arrow, and like the mace he knew these were hurting him though he felt nothing. This had to be ended quickly or his friends would kill him, all the time believing him to be Manferic.

The dwarf pulled something from his belt—a short stubby stick of intricate workmanship. It was some kind of magical rod, Pinch knew, especially since the end glowed with magical fire.

The dwarf never got a chance to use it. Discovering his strength, the rogue heaved the massive dwarf easily from the floor and slammed him against one wall and then the other. It was exhilarating, hurling his tormentor about like a helpless rat. With each crash his grip on the dwarf's windpipe tightened until at last there was a loud crack as the vile priest's neck snapped. Triumphant against his own odds, Pinch hurled the body to the floor.

"Should have killed me in the tower, you bastard!" the rogue snarled in victory.

"Clubs!"

It was Maeve again. The target clear, she was readying another of her massive spells, one that Pinch knew in his heart he would not survive.

He did the only thing he could thing of. He dropped to his knees and threw up his hands in complete submission.

"Maeve—don't! It's me, Pinch!" His voice was a dry screech, ignoble but to the point.

The woman's hands raised—

And then dropped. It had worked. At least Maeve hadn't blasted him to shreds. He could see the four of them in hasty conference.

Finally Therin sidled to the front. "Move and she'll finish her spell. Understood?"

"Of course, Therin," Pinch croaked back, his heart in his mouth—if he still had a heart.

"Who are you?" Therin shouted, not coming any closer.

"I told you—Pinch. Manferic switched bodies with me."

There was another huddled conference at the far end of the passage.

"Impossible. That's bull-"

"It happened."

"Prove it.'

Prove it? How in the hells was Pinch supposed to do that? He thought for some secret that only he would know. "Sprite," he finally called out, "remember Elturel, in the Dwarf's Piss Pot last summer? What did you do with those emeralds you lifted off of Therin?"

There was a hushed silence at the other end. "Emeralds?" a voice, Sprite, finally squeaked. "What emeralds?"

"You remember, don't you Therin," Pinch rasped back, "those big ones that you lifted off that jeweler from Amn?"

"He stole them off me?"

"He's lying—I wouldn't nip you, Therin!" Sprite squeaked again.

"Well then how the hells did he know?"

"I'll bet that lich tortured it out of old Pinch," the halfling replied. It was hard to say how much of that was in good faith and how much was a lie to save his own hide from Therin's wrath.

Damnation, this wasn't working, Pinch thought. It was a bad choice of example. He needed something stronger.

"Maeve!" he bellowed as best this wretched husk allowed him. It was getting passing uncomfortable on his knees, even without the feeling of pain. He'd never been on his knees to anyone before and he didn't know as it was likely in the future. It was undignified and crass and that bothered him, but he was able to swallow it so long as it kept him alive. Pinch, master thief, was a practical man in no hurry to die. If saving his life meant being on his knees, then so be it. Dead men had a hard time getting revenge, some would say, although Pinch wasn't so sure in this case. Manferic had made a fine job of it.

"Maeve, probe my mind, if that's what it'll take to convince you."

A third quick conference took place. There was considerable debate on this one. Finally, Therin, clearly acting as the new regulator in his absence, shouted, "No trickery—we've got bows and we've got a priest!"

"No trickery."

Pinch closed his eyes, calmed his mind, and waited. Just because exposing his mind was his only hope of proving himself, it didn't mean he wanted her to know all his secrets. Without really knowing how, he tried to bar certain areas of his mind from her prying.

When she came, it was a tickle like what he'd felt under Manferic's gaze, although her scan did not carry with it the painful itch of the lich's hateful will. Pinch did his best to stay calm under the scan. He tried to think about the drinking bouts, the jobs they'd pulled, even Therin's hanging where she'd played an important part. Most of all he put it into his mind to increase her share of the take. Certainly a bribe wouldn't hurt in a time like this.

Like the devil in all things though, those thoughts that he'd never entertained more than once in a year of fortnights now all decided to make their appearance, or so it seemed. Things he'd never said and regretted, cheats he'd pulled on his own gang, even the squeals he'd made to get rid of his foes all chose to surface now. Maeve was reading a mindful, there was no doubt, and there was nothing he could do to stop it.

At last the tickling stopped. She withdrew her mind and let him rest. Not that his dead muscles felt strained. What rest did a lich need or ever take? If it slept, the fierce will that kept it alive might waver and fade. If that happened there would be far fewer liches in the world.

All he could do was wait nervously for Maeve's decision.

And she damn well took her time. He knew he was Pinch and he knew she'd read enough of him to know that, but she was lingering on her pronouncement. No doubt, he raged to himself, she was enjoying having him on the spit. If he ever got out of this, he'd have to make sure she gained no profit from the venture.

"It's Pinch all right," Maeve said with a touch of awe. "I ain't sure what happened, but I know his fashion. It's him."

"That . . . thing is him?" Therin drawled, clearly filled with disbelief.

"He knows garbage what only Pinch would know, like how we fetched your body after the hanging in Elturel. More than that, too, like jobs we've pulled where there ain't nobody who knows them and all. I tell you, it's Pinch."

Therin looked back at the kneeling lich-thing. "Pinch, that really you?"

" 'Swounds, it's me, you big hay-headed Gur! I should've left you as that fortune-teller's stooge for all the good you're doing me."

Sprite and Maeve both looked at Therin with keen interest. It had always been a question between them just where the old master had found the big Gur.

"Well met, then, I guess," Therin hailed, face reddened at his secret. "Come over—but slowly, old man."

Lissa looked at the lot with a highly jaundiced eye, more than suspicious of their easy familiarity with this creature called Pinch. They talked all too freely of jobs and hangings to be anything like honest folk. She'd always had suspicions, but every time they arose, she'd convinced herself or let others convince her otherwise. Now, she finally realized, she'd been blind to it all this time.

"You're all a lot of thieves!"

"What did you imagine we were—lousy prophets?" Therin snapped.

"You lied to me!"

"We lie to everyone, miss," Sprite explained with glee. "It's our stock and our trade. Don't feel bad for being taken. We'd be pretty poor rascals if we couldn't fool anyone."

"Sprite's right, dearie," Maeve added to the chorus. "Consider yourself honored into our company. Pinch called upon you in particular for aid, so he must think highly of you—and it's Pinch now we've got to see to."

"Aye," Sprite echoed. He looked at the moldering

form that shuffled closer. "What happened, Master Pinch?" There was still a hesitancy in his voice, lest this be some hideous creature approaching.

"Manferic," the corpse croaked. "He traded bodies with me—though I don't think that was his full intention."

"What happened?" Maeve demanded, magical business making her sharply attentive.

As quickly and clearly as he could, Pinch explained the course of his meeting with Manferic. He had no idea what clues were needed to restore his body and so, against his true nature, he spared nothing in the telling. When it was done, Pinch croaked, "Ladies, tell me. How do—"

"I'm not sure I should even help you, thief," Lissa cut in, still rankling at her discovery.

"Leave me and you leave Manferic. Would your conscience feel better by placing a lich on the throne, priestess? What would the Morninglord think of that?" Pinch snapped. He didn't have time for this. That he knew instinctively.

Lissa went white, then reddened, horrified at the prospect yet outraged as his tone. "Very well, in this . . . but in this only!"

With that settled, the two spellcasters looked thoughtful as they debated. Like plotters on the stage, they whispered dramatically to each other as they considered various possibilities.

"Pinch," Sprite asked while they waited, "if it can be done, what the plan?"

"Plan?

The halfling gave a wan smile. "Sure, a plan—you've always got a plan."

If he could have sighed in this musty body, he would have sighed. "You know, Sprite, all through this game I've had plans and schemes and thought I was in control. Now my life turns out to be one of Manferic's grand plans. Pinch the master planner—hah! Well, Sprite, this time I've got no plan. All my other plans have turned into traps as Manferic twisted my plots around. This time we're just going to improvise and let's see him plan for that."

"Great plan," Therin remarked gloomily.

The two spellcasters ended their conference and Maeve spoke for them both.

"About your body, Pinch. We don't know—"

"But there might a chance. If we can get you close enough to you—er, Manferic—I might be able to dispel the magic that holds you."

"And then?"

Lissa bit her lip. "I'm not really sure. You should switch bodies."

"Or?"

"Or both of you vanish into the void, like Manferic said."

"That's it? Just get this," Pinch gestured to the rot that was himself, "into the middle of a coronation and—"

"What was that?" Sprite hissed as he waved his hands for attention.

"What?"

"Quiet. Listen," the halfling commanded. He stood on his hairy tiptoes, his head cocked so that his pointed ears where tipped to catch the least chitter in the halls. "That—did you hear it?"

The others strained, hearing nothing.

"Ikri . . ."

There was a voice, faint and distant.

"Ikrit . . ."

From somewhere in the depths of the tunnels, a woman was calling.

"Ikrit!"

Pinch looked at the blasted white mass that choked the passage ahead. The quaggoth had been going somewhere, but not to Manferic. There was only one other choice. "The woman . . ."

"What? What woman, Pinch?" Sprite demanded.

"Lady Tulan, my mother," was the answer.

"By the Morninglord," Lissa gasped, "your mother's down here? I thought you were an orphan."

"It's a long tale to tell now." Pinch dismissed it with a wave of his rotted hand. His dead eyes suddenly glowed with cold light, a small spark of the willpower he'd inherited from his father. "We've got to find her. I know what revenge Manferic deserves."

"He's gone maundering. Wit's left him,' Maeve whispered to Therin.

"Comes from being dead." The Gur tensed his muscular frame, just sensing the need if Pinch got violent.

"I'm not mad," their corpse-bodied leader growled, surprising them with the insight of his senses. "Just help me get back my proper body and I'll nip what Manferic and Vargo prize most. The first thing is to find my mother."

"Think she'll take a ghoul as a son?" The halfling, who had raised the question, didn't figure the query needed an answer. He was just reminding his captain of the realities of the situation.

"Gods' pizzle," he swore, "she can't see me like this! She'll think I'm Manferic." Pinch flapped the rags that hung on his body, waving his frustration.

"Leave her and we'll be out of here," Therin suggested.

"Mask curse you!" the regulator swore with a clear vehemence that was undimmed by his lipless elocution. "She's my mother."

"Yesterday she could've been a common stew for all you cared then!" Therin snapped back.

"Therin, he's got a plan," Sprite interceded, laying a hand on the bigger's arm. The small face looked up with ridiculously large eyes: Sprite's playing his looks for the sympathy of the crowd. "If we don't help him, then there ain't none of us like to get out of Ankhapur alive.

It's you who should go find this Lady Whatever."

"Me?"

"You've a way with ladies. Besides, you think she'd heed me, only a halfling?"

"I'll go, too," Lissa volunteered, trying to do the noble thing.

"No—Maeve, go with Therin," Pinch ordered, treating the suggestion a done deal. "I'll need you, priestess, if we're going to be facing a lich."

"And what if I should say no?" Therin asked.

"Relish the rest of your life down here, do you?" Sprite added. When Therin frowned, the halfling added, "Then get going."

"How'm I supposed to find my way out?"

"She'll know the way," Pinch growled, flashing his yellow teeth through a cold smile of hunger. "Just be at the Rite of Choosing.

"He's right, Therin. Let's go." Maeve gathered up a lantern and waited for the Gur to come.

The regulator immediately dispensed with them and turned to Sprite-Heels and Lissa. "I'll need you two with me. Sprite, can you pace us out to someplace other than my rooms?"

The halfling nodded. "Couldn't get this lot back into your kip, so I had to find another way in. That's what kept us from . . ." Sprite let it trail off as he wasn't sure it was good business to raise his failures up right now, especially since Pinch hadn't fared too well.

"Then stop prattling and go. Late off the start's almost cost the race already."

There was a disconcerting way to Pinch's saying it that gave life to the blue-gray pallor of his skin. He was a cold thing with a hunger that was only going to be satiated with cold revenge.

Coronation Day

Sprite moved with uncanny confidence through the twisting passages, rejecting branches Pinch thought looked more likely. The rogue had no choice but to trust his lieutenant. The others stayed ahead of him, unwilling to look on his terrible visage any more than they had to.

At length they reached a dead-end. "Here," Sprite held the light to the polished stone. An iron ring was set in the wall. More to the point, with his newly sensitive sight the transmigrated rogue easily traced the outline of the jamb, where the cracks let the least glimmer of light in. Even Sprite, with his talent for finding things, probably couldn't see the outlines.

"Beyond's a side courtyard not far from your apartment—"

"The rite'll be held in the main feast hall."

Pinch seized the iron ring and pulled as hard as he

thought was right, forgetting his body's strength in the process. The door flew open with nary a sound. Whoever had engineered this entry was a master, for the heavy, veined marble slid with ease. Pinch practically tumbled backward from the lack of resistance.

The courtyard beyond was lit by the palest of moonlight that barely reached over the high buildings enclosing the artificial forest within. Verdant shrubs filled squat pots, and fine-leaved trees waved gently to the rhythm of the splashing fountain in the far wall. Moonflowers spread their ivory petals to absorb the night. Caged birds hung from the beam ends all around, and a few nightingales woke to sing their arrival. As the door gaped wider than was needed to spy, Sprite and Pinch both scrambled into the shadows, acting on years of larcenous instinct. Had an observer been in the small garden, he would have assumed that Lissa alone had managed the great door. Fortunately, there were no observers.

When there was no alarm, the two rogues moved quickly through the potted jungle, getting the lay of the land. Of the three other doors, one in each wall, two led to nothing, just rooms shuttered up for the night. The third was a gate of wrought iron that opened on the avenue linking the Great Hall to the world beyond the palace gates. The pair took care not to be noticed, for there was a steady stream of revelers all bound in the direction of the feast.

Pinch was just checking the oil on the gate hinges before opening it when Sprite touched his arm. The halfling had a cloth from his sleeve to cover his face. "Wisely good, but how you going to get around, Pinch? You ain't your inconspicuous self."

Lissa, who'd kept herself silent and distant to this point, added, "You've got the stench of death to you, too."

Pinch's smile was an awkward grimace. "Sprite, boy, do you know what day it is in Ankhapur?"

"Some sort of festival, Pinch."

"It's the Festival of Wealth, my halfling friend. For one day, the fine citizens of Ankhapur celebrate the gods of money with food, drink, and masked balls."

"So?"

Pinch looked to Lissa, mindful of her disapproval as he spoke his true mind. "We're thieves, boy—scoundrels. Out there the streets are filled with folks in costumery—gowns, cloaks, and . . . masks."

"Who just need a little persuading to help us out." A sly smile enriched the halfling's face. " 'Struth, Pinch. I'm sure some kindly generous souls truly want to help us."

"Ankhapur is noted for its generosity." The dead-bodied rogue nodded, flaking little hunks of his neck as he did. "All it takes is a little proper explaining."

"So how are we planning to get them in here? Nobody trusts a halfling—"

"And I'd scare them off."

The pair turned to look at Lissa.

"No. No—you're not suggesting I go out there and—"

"Our need is great," Pinch croaked.

"It's only once," Sprite added.

"It's a sin in the eyes of the Morninglord!" she resisted, shaking her head.

"Maybe he's not looking. Gods can get awfully busy, you know." The halfling at her side couldn't help being flip, and for it she gave him a wicked glare.

"I suppose Ankhapur will manage." Pinch tried for a sigh of resignation, but without breath it sounded more like a quack. "And I'll get used to living in the tombs, where I won't have to walk the streets and listen to the screams of the women and run from the swords of men. The tombs are quiet. I'll have lots of time to . . . sit."

Sprite sniffed.

"Enough!" Lissa threw up her hands. "I'll do it. I just want you to know, you're vile and evil and I hate you both!"

The two rogues, one dead, the other short and shiftless,

smiled and did their best to look angelic.

"That's not very fair," Sprite sniffed, his tears turning to wounded honor before they'd even welled up in his eyes. "We're only this way because there's no other—"

"You are a person to rely on," Pinch extolled. It was best to shut the halfling up before he changed her mind for her. With a hand on her arm he steered her toward the gate. "Be quick—three people, our size, with masks." Before she could have regrets, he gently pushed her into the street.

Fifteen minutes later, three revelers, two men and a woman, one short, two tall, hurried toward the Great Hall. The woman wore a delicate domino mask and a gown that didn't fit quite well, too tight at the bodice and too long in the leg. The tall man was resplendent as a great black raven with a golden-beaked mask and a coif of feathers that flowed down into a lustrous black cloak that served well to hide the grimy clothes underneath. The little man waddled along, trying to keep up with the others, his effort constantly hindered by the papier mâché head that was as big as him. His tabard jingled with every step as the bell-stitched hem dragged on the ground. The shiny, grinning jester's face lolled drunkenly, threatening to decapitate itself at any moment.

"Wonderful choice," the short one groused. The nasal voice had a dead echo like the inside of a barrel. "It's not like you could have found a worse disguise—"

"Sprite, stow that," snapped the raven in truly dead tones. "Be thankful to Lissa she found anything."

"Oh, I should be thankful that I'm going to die dressed like this." The halfling struggled to avoid tripping over his jingling hem, casting an envious eye at the ease with which the priestess handled her oversized gown. "You know, Pinch, I'm not so sure this fighting a lich thing is such a good idea. I mean, you could just stay like that. You'd get used to it after a while and it's got some positive advantages. Think about the insurance we could

run. There wouldn't be no sensible merchant who'd with-
hold a payment from anyone who looked like you. We
could run ourselves a nice system, me and Therin
fronting it and you taking the collection—"

"Sprite—stay your rattling trap!"

So much was the vehemence in that voice that the
halfling squeaked quiet.

"We do this to save Ankhapur," Lissa announced to
no one except perhaps herself. She spoke with the vir-
tuous certainty that comes upon the sinner determined
to redeem herself. "There will be no turning back or
backsliding now. Understand, little one?"

From inside the bloated plaster head came a sour
grumble that lapsed into silence, but the halfling kept
pace with the others.

The entrance to the Great Hall was thick with the
royal guard, loyal soldiers standing in rows like overdressed mannequins. Pinch's teeth ground like mill-
stones as they fell into the line of guests passing through
the doors. A guard captain briefly scanned each reveler
as he or she passed. With his keen scent for the law,
Pinch spotted others who were doing a miserable job of
being inconspicuous: several servants who lingered in
the foyer with too little to do, and a robed "guest" who
lounged in the hall. Probably hired warriors and a mage,
and probably loyal to Vargo, just in case he needed to
force his ascension. Pinch had not forgotten Iron-Biter's
suggestion to take the crown by force if necessary.

Still, the lot looked distinctly uncomfortable, no
doubt because their commander, Iron-Biter, hadn't
shown. That pleased Pinch, thinking of the consternation that must be going through Vargo's ranks because
their lord's right-hand man had failed to appear.

The captain, seeing only another group of celebrants,
waved them by with hardly a glance. Their ill-fitting out-
fits were beyond notice in the garish crowd that surrounded them. There were mock medusas, gold-festooned

dwarves, even a hulking lizard man clutching a goblet in its taloned hand. Pinch judged that, from the interest the lizard showed in the ladies, many of whom had dressed to reveal and not disguise, that this guest was an enterprising wizard with a polymorph spell and not a true emissary of that reptilian race.

Once past the guards, the three slipped easily through the packed crowd. Everyone was here and everyone was gay. The rogue figured he could make a year's profit from the jewelry that dripped from the arms, necks, ankles, and ears of those around him. With so much temptation at hand, Pinch kept a wary eye on his small friend, although the halfling's oversized plaster head seemed an effective restraint.

When they finally squeezed into the Great Hall, past the ballrooms where the dancers turned to stately pavanes, past the tables creaking with roasts and pastries, and past the choke in the hallway, every head was craned for a view of the four princes on their thrones. Raised up on a broad dais, the four looked through their masks upon the crowd with the unconcealed habits of their natures radiating in their very poses. Vargo, foremost of the lot, awaited the ceremony with keen expectation, confident that he would be supreme no matter what the outcome. Throdus and Marac sat in their places with distinct unease, well cautioned of their brother's plans and perfectly aware of their own weakness to oppose him. Bors always loved the festival. The bright colors, music, and food appealed to his childish spirit. He laughed and giggled in his seat, but the importance of the occasion was lost on him.

It wasn't hard to spot their quarry. Cleedis—or rather, not-Cleedis—stood behind Bors, playing the part of the faithful retainer. Manferic, inside Pinch's shell and cloaked as the old chamberlain, did a masterful job of masquerading as his former servant. The princes wore masks, but the thing posing as Cleedis disdained any. Against the parti-colors of the festival, he was a somber specter of the occasion.

Pinch tipped his beak to Lissa and hissed, "Close enough?" indicating the spell she needed to use.

She shook her head and pointed to one of the pillars about two-thirds toward the front. "There!" she shouted back.

The black raven nodded his understanding and waved a cloaked wing for his small assistant to follow. Plunging straight forward toward the center of the dais was impossible. The throng was too thick and there was no room to operate, although Pinch wasn't quite sure what they were going to do anyway. He knew Lissa would cast her spell, but after that everything was a spin on the wheel of fate, the cruel dictum of Lady Tymora.

As they shouldered their way to the thinner flanks of the crowd, a bell pealed over the roar of the throng, its resonance magically amplified to seize the attention of the onlookers. The roar faded to a babble as a column of Red Priests entered from the back of the hall, forcing the host apart before them. The acolytes at the head held forth the banners of their sect, followed by the bearers of incense and the cantors. After these was the object of all attention, a lone priest bearing the Cup and Knife, closely followed by the Hierarch Juricale, his thick beard oiled and curled. Temple warriors flanked him on all sides, not that there was much threat to his eminence. They were a display of his might to anyone who needed to know.

Seeing the false artifacts, Pinch rapped the halfling's encasement and asked, "Do you have them?" The oversized head bobbed affirmatively while the little hands pointed to the bag at his waist.

The holy entourage moved with stately ease through the hall; Pinch and company did not. By the time they reached the pillar Lissa had indicated, the procession had reached the dais. The hierarch held the relics aloft and invoked the blessing of the gods. Immediately, Vargo rose to announce his claim.

"I am Vargo, son of Manferic III, grandson . . ."

"Close enough?" Pinch asked the priestess again.

She nodded and as best as possible reached beneath her skirts to produce a tightly rolled scroll. "When Maeve told me of Manferic, I brought some help. It's a scroll to dispel his magic." She tapped the paper meaningfully.

"And if that doesn't work?"

"I've another one memorized, just in case. Should I try it now?"

Pinch shook his head, almost hitting the onlookers in front of him with the great beak. "Not yet. Wait for a distraction."

Within moments, Pinch almost gave the word to go. Juricale presented the relics to Throdus, but the prince refused to rise. A wave of amazement soared through the crowd.

"Pinch, what's happening?" Sprite demanded, unable to see the thrones.

"Throdus has declined the test," the rogue answered with keen interest. Apparently Vargo's threats were working.

"Can he do that? What if he were the chosen one?"

"I don't know. It's his right, but no one's ever done it."

Bewildered, Juricale continued on to Marac. He, too, remained firmly in his seat. By now the audience hummed with speculation.

"Vargo's spread his threats well," the regulator said in admiration.

Juricale was visibly relieved when Bors stood to make his claim. The power of his temple resided in the ceremony, so any precedent that ignored it threatened his job. Pinch was amazed that Bors managed to recite the words of lineage, although it could have been done with a little magical aid from Manferic himself.

Now there were two candidates. Expectations

mounted as the Hierarch returned to Vargo. Pinch held his hand lightly over Lissa's arm, ready to give the signal. If anything was to happen it must happen soon.

Vargo seized the knife, proclaimed the words, and boldly pricked his thumb. Carefully the underpriests came forward and caught the ruby drops in the golden cup. Another carefully poured a measure of wine. Swirling the two, the Hierarch returned the cup to Vargo's hand.

"Drink now, so that all may see if you are Ankhapur's true lord." The priest's voice boomed over the silent crowd.

Vargo raised the Cup high and then set it to his lips. A collective gasp seized the audience as everyone waited for the sign.

Nothing happened.

With one breath a sigh of mass tension blew like a wind across the hall. Carried on it were the faint grumbles of those whose hopes were lost and the smug pleasure of those who'd won. Bors, they knew, would be the rightful king. Others, wiser perhaps, looked to the doors, mindful that what Vargo could not have by right he would claim by sword.

Just as the Hierarch turned toward Bors, Vargo clutched at his throat, an expression of horror twisting his visage. His pallor changed to an icy blue. All at once he coughed up a gurgle of blood, his knees buckled, and he pitched to the floor.

"Poison! Manferic's cup is poisonous!" Pinch blurted, suddenly seeing the whole of the lich's plan. There was a stunned silence of panic, and that the rogue knew was the perfect diversion. "Now, Lissa, now!"

Jolted from her shock, the priestess unfurled the scroll and began to read. Pinch braced himself, though for what he didn't know. Sprite struggled out of his costume, the gargantuan head ill suited to action. If Lissa's spell worked, he'd be standing next to a confused and unhappy lich, not the safest place in the world.

Lissa read the final word and immediately leapt to the side, expecting the worst.

No waves of disorientation overwhelmed Pinch, no change of view came to his eyes. He was still trapped in Manferic's body beneath the layers of the raven garb.

"It didn't work!" he snarled.

A shriek from the audience broke his claim. "Look!" Lissa shouted, pointing toward the dais. There Pinch's body stood, where Cleedis had once been. "It's dropped his spell of disguise."

As if her words had been a sign, the Pinch on stage glared directly at them, pinpointed by the magic she'd used. "You!" he bellowed, seeing through their disguises. As the crowd erupted into a pandemonium of confusion and fear, the transformed lich raised his hands to work a spell. The energies began to form and swirl about him.

For Pinch there was no time to run, for Lissa no time for a counter-spell. They could only brace themselves to endure what must come.

Just as the lich reached the height of his casting, the energies dissipated, swirling away like wisps of smoke. The lich was left bare, uncloaked by his magic, staring in rage in the branded hand of the body it occupied.

"My hand—it's crippled. He can't cast his spells," Pinch shouted with glee. "Again, Lissa! Try again!"

Now it was the priestess's turn to conjure as the lich shrieked in frustrated rage. She wove the spell with rapid ease, and before Pinch was ready for the shock, she uttered the final prayer.

The world lurched, shut off its light, and then flared back on. Suddenly Pinch was standing over everyone, looking down on the crowd, looking down on the threesome at the lonely center of cleared space.

From the black-ravened one at the heart of that group rose a shriek of unholy rage. The mask flew off and the feathered cloak dropped aside to reveal the moldering fury that was Manferic.

"Janol, you bastard son—you will die!" the true lich roared. With a sweep, magical might blazed from his now-unfettered hands.

Pinch dove for the shield of a throne as a scorching burst of fire tore across the stage. Blinded by the orange-white heat, Pinch could hear the screams of the Hierarch and the princes caught in its blast.

Crap, what to do? How to fight a lich? Pinch hadn't a clue, and it was all he could do to stay alive. Trusting his survival instinct, the rogue darted from his thin shelter and sprinted for the main floor. The stage was too exposed for any chance of safety.

As he ran, others reacted. Vargo's swordsmen, to their credit, were charging for battle. The hall was a swirl of confusion—revelers stampeding for the doors, priests wailing on the dais for their fallen leader, and at the center of it all the single point of Manferic, a whirlwind of magical fury. In that confusion, Vargo's loyalists latched on to the only obvious conclusion, that the thing on the floor was their enemy.

If he had time, Pinch would have admired these warriors for their courage, as hopeless as their cause was. As the swordsmen broke through the crowd, Manferic struck them down almost as fast as they appeared. Magic flashed from his fingertips in a display of utter power. All Pinch had time for was a small amount of thankfulness that they occupied all of Manferic's attention.

It didn't last long. Once the first rush of the boldest fell, so fell the enthusiasm of those remaining. The lich was quicker than death, but he did not stop there. With a quick gesture, commanded chaos descended on the ranks that remained. Strong men dropped to their knees in confusion, and friends turned on friends in a bloodlust of killing. The company was caught up in itself, men slaughtering each other or wandering aimlessly, their weapons limp at their sides.

The next to try was Lissa. Just as Manferic broke the wave of swordsmen, she lunged forward and clapped her hands on his shoulders. Pinch couldn't hear the prayer she mouthed; it was drowned out by the screams and moans of those around him. Suddenly the lich stiffened with rage, its dead body insensitive to the pain, as Lissa's spell flowed through it. Its death mask contorted by rage, the lich whirled about and uttered a spell directly into her face. Between them materialized a titan's hand, as large as Lissa was tall. Its skin was puffy and smooth, and there were even rings on its fingers. The priestess gaped in astonishment and, in that stunned moment, the great digits closed about her and grasped her firm. Lissa twisted and squirmed but there was no escaping.

Manferic barely gave his prisoner notice, confident that she was trapped. "Janol!" he shouted, scanning the hall for Pinch. "Stand by me, my son. Together we can rule Ankhapur!"

Pinch, on the main floor, paused in his mad rush for the shelter of a pillar. Manferic's offer didn't stop him; he knew that was a lie. Now was the time to run, get to cover, and get away, but he wasn't moving. When the constables were coming, you didn't stay to gather more loot. You ran, and that's just what he knew he should do now.

He couldn't. Lissa was in trouble and he could not abandon her. It was against every pragmatic, self-serving precept of his being, but Pinch was determined to rescue her. In her own naive and honest way, she was as much a part of his gang as Sprite, Maeve, and Therin.

The chance of success was dismal. Juricale and a dozen of his priests were sprawled and broken on the dais, caught unprepared by Manferic's attack. The floor was slick with the blood of swordsmen. The doorways were choked with revelers pressing out while the royal guard helplessly struggled to get in. Even those able within the mass were rendered useless by the seething panic.

Without waiting for Pinch's answer, the lich conjured

up another spell. Waves of sickly green smoke billowed
from the monster's fingertips, swirling into a roiling cloud
bank. Even well away from the cloud, the air was filled
with an ammonia tang that bit and burned. Slowly the
cloud began to sweep forward, rolling toward the arched
doorway and the floundering mass of people. As the gases
passed over the wounded and the dazed, their screams
and babble changed to choking gurgles and then silence.
The bodies that emerged from the cloud were blistered
yellow and still, blood oozing from poison-scalded skin.

When the former revellers saw the cloud, a unified
scream rose from the hysterical mass. Decorum and nobility were lost as rich men trampled their consorts and
pushed back others as futile sacrifices to the uncaring
death that closed on them. The sides broke and fled back
into the hall before the toxic haze could envelop them, but
the blind press at the front was a locked mass. Steadily
the deadly vapors flowed through them. The nerve of the
leading guardsmen broke and they tried to flee, turning
their swords on any who stood in their way. This only
added to the confusion, the blood, and the death.

Over it all, Manferic laughed, a harsh, mocking laugh
that ridiculed the weakness of the living. It was a laugh
of calculated terror. Boldly the lich strode up the steps of
the dais and turned to face the hall. "Nobles of Ankhapur, acknowledge your king, Manferic the Undying!"

While Manferic presented himself to the guests who
huddled in fear along the walls, listening to the screams
of those dying at the doorway, Pinch ran to Lissa. The
massive hand still clutched her. He sliced the unreal
flesh with his dagger. A great gash opened that did not
bleed and the hand held firm.

"No time," gasped Lissa, straining against the con-
struct's might. "Take this—use it." She wriggled and
twisted a hand through the fingers. "Take it!" In her
hand she waved the amulet of the Dawnbreaker.

"You're mad! I'm not touching it. It ruined me!"

"Death will do worse—thief," Lissa spat back.

"I don't even know what to do with it!"

"Neither do I, but it's marked you. You have to use it." She jingled the chain.

"Janol—away from her!" Manferic rasped, finally spotting his bastard son.

Pinch dove to the side but not quite in time. An icy blast seized his leg and he skidded to the stone floor as his muscles went numb. Lissa shrieked as the blast struck her full. Frost coated his hose and the chill sliced to his bones. Pinch knew he couldn't survive another attack like the last.

"Use it!" Lissa gasped as she weakly flipped the amulet his way. It skidded across the floor and Pinch grabbed it up, knowing there was no choice. He expected it to burn with pain and flame, but it did nothing.

From the dais, the lich looked at his son with a contemptuous sneer. "I blame you for all their deaths, Janol," he said, sweeping a rotting arm toward the carnage that covered the floor. The hysterical screaming had stopped; the poisonous cloud had seen to that. The survivors huddled dazed near the walls. Those still able to fight in both strength and spirit stood wary, waiting for someone else to make the first move. At the lich's words, all attention turned toward the thief.

Pinch held the amulet aloft, like he had the last time. It did not flare in his grasp and he despaired. Then he saw a small shadow moving slowly behind the thrones. "The deaths are on your hands—Father," he shouted back, keeping the lich focused on him.

"I should never have fathered you," the thing sneered. The shadow lunged forward and Sprite appeared behind the lich with his short sword poised high.

Perhaps it was a footfall or a hopeful glance, but the lich wasn't surprised. It stepped to the side just as Sprite lunged forward. The halfling had thrown his weight into the blow, and now there was nothing to

trike. As he staggered forward, Manferic easily caught
him around the neck and lifted the little one before
him. "Fool!" Pointing his finger inches from Sprite's
face, the lich uttered a single phrase of spell. A deadly
barb of light flashed from the lich's fingertip and sliced
into the halfling's face. Sprite screamed but there was
no release. Another deadly flare flashed and then more
in a steady stream. Sprite's screams were unrelenting
as the magical darts sliced his face to ribbons.

"Damn you, do something!" Pinch swore as he held
the amulet high. It was inert. What did he need to do?
What was he missing? Pinch felt his utter helplessness
as Sprite writhed in the lich's grasp.

And then he knew, he understood what truly mattered to him. It wasn't wealth or wine, it wasn't even
the thrill of defying the law as he leapt from rooftop to
rooftop. It was Sprite, Maeve, and the others. Pinch
knew he wasn't brave or noble, but his gang was all he
had. If Manferic wanted Ankhapur, he could have it,
but not his friends. Pinch could not leave them to this
cruel lich. He was fighting for them.

Pinch focused everything in him—his hate, passion,
ambition, even his greed—toward the one goal of saving
his friends. In his heart, he was willing even to sacrifice
his last good hand.

As if hearing that, the amulet began to glow. At first
it was the golden gleam of dawn's aura, lighting up the
room. The shadows of the hall fled with the rising of
his false day.

Bathed in the glow, the lich's skin began to smolder.
The creature hurled aside the shattered ruin in its grasp
and turned its deadly finger on Pinch. The magical mis-
siles rocketed across the gap, each one striking him dead
on. These arrows of mystical force ripped jagged punc-
tures into his flesh and rocked his body back. The pain
staggered him, but Pinch did not relent. He didn't even
try to dodge or hide. All his faith was in the amulet.

The glow's intensity swelled in his grasp. Now it was the sun rising over the horizon. The flare bleached the colors from the hall, until it dazzled all eyes. Figures became silhouettes cloaked in a luminous haze.

On the dais, in the heart of the light, an inhuman shriek drowned out all other sound. Against the white brilliance, a single torch of gold-red fire competed as Manferic the Undying was consumed. The lich reeled as the flames scoured past its frail flesh and blazed with the colors of its uncaged will. Tongues of gold, red, and blue leapt heavenward as the death that was denied reclaimed its due.

And still the intensity grew. The world became light beyond light, a brilliance so great that eyes open or closed barely made a difference. Voices tinged with fear and wonder whimpered in the void.

At last the light faded, although it was minutes before Pinch or any of the others could see clearly again. He stood blinking against the painful darkness, trying to see what had happened. Manferic stood no more. Where he had been was a crumbled heap of white ash, still holding the tracery of bone. When Pinch staggered up the steps, it fell away like snow swept away by the wind.

After the rush and roar of battle, the still of the aftermath was haunting. It was as a soft symphony of sobs and moans, the pathetic cries for help mixed with the weeping for the dead. From what seemed like far away drifted the urgent shouts of rescuers.

As quick as he could, Pinch stumbled over the bodies of princes and priests to find his friend. He found the halfling propped against a throne, raggedly breathing through his ruined face.

"Sprite!"

"Pinch—that you?" the little thief whispered. A little foam of blood bubbled on his lips. "What happened?"

"Manferic's dead. We won, I think."

"That's good." The halfling weakly groped until his